JESSICA FELLOWES

THE MITF⊙RD SCANDAL

sphere

SPHERE

First published in Great Britain in 2019 by Sphere
This paperback edition published by Sphere in 2020

1 3 5 7 9 10 8 6 4 2

A CIP catalogue record for this book
is available from the British Library.

ISBN 978-0-7515-7392-3

Typeset in Electra by M Rules
Printed and bound in Great Britain by
Clays Ltd, Elcograf S.p.A.

Papers used by Sphere are from well-managed forests
and other responsible sources.

MIX
Paper from
responsible sources
FSC® C104740
www.fsc.org

Sphere
An imprint of
Little, Brown Book Group
Carmelite House
50 Victoria Embankment
London EC4Y 0DZ

An Hachette UK Company
www.hachette.co.uk

www.littlebrown.co.uk

Jessica Fellowes is an author, journalist and public speaker, best known for her work as author of five ...cial companion books to *Downton Abbey*, various ...vhich have hit the *New York Times* and *Sunday Times* bestseller lists. Former deputy editor of *Country Life* and columnist on the *Mail on Sunday*, she has written for publications including the *Daily Telegraph*, the *Guardian*, *The Sunday Times* and *The Lady*. Jessica has spoken at events across the UK and US, and has made numerous appearances on radio and television. She lives happily in London and Oxfordshire with her family, an energetic Labradoodle and two chickens.

@jesssicafellowes

Also by Jessica Fellowes

The Mitford Murders
The Mitford Affair

FOR MY SISTER, CORDELIA,
AND MY NIECE, ELODY

1928

CHAPTER ONE

T uesday night at the Guinness's dance at the height of the London season began in an entirely predictable manner. No one was to know it would end with a dead body.

Louisa Cannon was working as a maid in the kitchens of Grosvenor Place, a temporary state of affairs, as she frequently reminded herself. She knew there was honour in her labour but, truthfully, she had wanted to leave her career as a servant behind. Still, needs must and rent had to be paid. After a long winter, the blossom in Hyde Park had come out in full bloom and soon afterwards so had the debutantes, ready to twirl their way through the season as decoratively as any well-tended perennials. Their husband-hunting was of no interest to Louisa, but the accompanying social whirl created extra work for a few months, which suited her perfectly.

On this particular June evening, the hostess, Lady Evelyn, had decorated her house in a medieval style, with posies of summer wildflowers thrust into pewter pots and dotted throughout, instead of the tall stems of roses commonly seen in the dining rooms of Mayfair. Smoke-blackened beams had been nailed to the ceilings and the rooms were lit with low-watt yellow bulbs in sham dripping candles, while the fireplaces smouldered and smoked rather than blazed. The resulting glow threw a flattering light on even the most decrepit dowager's décolletage. Louisa had been sent up the stairs and through the green baize door to retrieve a footman whom the housekeeper had spotted mistakenly taking up a tray of devils-on-horseback too early; they were intended for the 'breakfast', which would be served at one o'clock in the morning. It was now a few minutes to midnight, and Louisa was trying, as unobtrusively as possible, to find the elusive footman. There were several large rooms around the central hall, each of which were crammed with people in the half-light. She was walking through the library when she saw someone that made her freeze: Nancy Mitford.

Nancy was standing with her younger sister, Diana. It had been a few years since Louisa had last seen them, and while Nancy was almost unchanged, Diana was not. Her beauty, which as a young girl had been lightly sketched on her face, had developed into an oil painting, with masterful strokes of pale pink and cream. They were talking to a man rather intently and didn't notice their former nursery maid hiding behind a pillar. Perhaps she should have said hello but they looked so magnificent and confident, Louisa didn't want them to see her in a maid's uniform. So far as they knew, she had gone to London to live as an independent, successful and modern woman. She knew her letters to Nancy had done little to betray this vision.

'If you were a biscuit,' Nancy said to the man, 'you would be a ginger nut.'

'How so?'

'You seem wholesome but every bite snaps and you have a fiery aftertaste.'

He smiled and took a sip of his gin cocktail. 'I can live with that. You would be a chocolate éclair. Every mouthful of you is delicious but terribly messy.'

'I'm not sure whether to be shocked or delighted.'

'The perfect response.'

Diana struck a pose, her long neck twisted, her back arched. 'What am I, Mr Meyer?'

Louisa watched him regard her before he spoke slowly. 'A Florentine. Beautiful, but brittle.'

Diana straightened out and stepped back. 'I'm not at all sure that I—'

'Sshh. Look. There's Bryan Guinness.' Nancy jerked her chin in the direction of a slight young man on the other side of the room, talking in an exaggerated fashion to a woman who was holding an ear trumpet.

Diana reached out to a passing footman and nabbed a champagne coupe. 'What of it?'

'Don't be obtuse, you've been dancing with him all summer. It's quite clear what your feelings are.' Nancy took the glass from Diana's hand. 'And no more of this. You're only seventeen, two glasses are quite enough.'

Diana bared her teeth in mock anger but gave it up easily enough. 'I'm eighteen in three days and he's a superb dancer, that's why he's on my card so often, but *fine*. I'll go and say hello.' She wandered off. Louisa retreated further into the shadows. She really should try to slip away but she felt a compulsion to listen.

Nancy scoffed at Diana's retreating figure then stopped abruptly.

'Are you pouting?' Mr Meyer asked, a shocked expression on

his face, though Louisa suspected he might be exaggerating for effect.

'Don't. It's shaming enough having a younger sister who has all of London gawking at her beauty without her getting married off to a man as rich as Croesus before I've so much as had a sniff of a proposal. Besides, Muv would never allow it.'

'Why ever not?'

'Too much money. It's ruinous.'

'Well, I know how I—'

'Yes, yes, we know. Grapes and chaise-longues. You're so provincial.'

There was an awkward pause before he tried another conversational tack. 'Isn't this a repulsive party? What are you going to say about it?'

'I don't know. It's all the usual gang. Oh, look, there's Evelyn Waugh.' Her face had brightened. 'A promising novelist. Only, I've written that before. The Mulloneys are supposed to be here, they might be good for a story.'

'Who are they?'

'Kate and Shaun Mulloney, very good-looking, very amusing.' She gave a sigh. 'Only, there's nothing more to say about them *already*. We've got weeks left of this yet.' Her mouth returned to its sulky droop.

Mr Meyer was of a good height and his slim figure and well-cut clothes might have picked him out for attention, but his face, though attractive when looked at directly, had evenly spaced, unmemorable features. Louisa wondered if she'd seen him before or if he just had a face that made one think that. She watched as he scanned the room and ran off the roll of names. 'Princess Mary, Lady Lascelles, the Duke and Duchess of Abercorn, the Duchess of Devonshire – beautifully dressed tonight, as I suppose she should be as she is—'

Nancy chimed in and they said together: 'The Mistress of the Robes to Queen Mary.'

He sniggered. 'Why the richest woman in England must have a job bemuses me. The Duchess of Portland, the Duchess of Rutland . . . ' He trailed off.

'It isn't a job. It's the most senior role for a woman in the Royal Household.' Louisa recognized Nancy's father in these comments. For all the rows they'd had, they were as one when it came to protocol.

'Thank you, ma'am,' said Mr Meyer, doffing an imaginary cap. 'If I were the richest woman in England I'd be on my proverbial chaise-longue having grapes fed into my mouth one by one by an obliging young Adonis in a toga, not sucking up to the royally dried-out prune.'

Nancy didn't respond to this. She had heard it before.

'I suppose I had better telephone some of this through,' she said instead. 'My editor will be champing. I don't know that either of us are going to stick this. And I'm going to go and talk to Bryan. See if I can't put a spanner in the works.'

She wandered off, presumably to find a telephone and call the society magazine that she had told Louisa had obligingly taken her on for a few diary pieces, though she had not yet earned enough money, she had admitted, to merit the tiresomeness of friends who mimed buttoning their lips every time she came near.

Abandoned, Mr Meyer stuck his hands in both his pockets and wandered through to the ballroom and Louisa, having spotted the errant footman at last, did not follow.

*

Below the ballroom floor, the servants' quarters were no less a hive of orchestrated movements. The workers could hear a faint echo of the jazz beats above but there was no time to stand and listen. A stream of footmen, many brought in specially for the evening, went up and came back down the stairs with silver salvers with which to hand around or collect glasses. In the kitchen, the assistant cook and the maids had prepared and cleared up the dinner that the family and a few friends had before the dance began but the night was not yet over for them. Now there was the breakfast to prepare. Trays of bacon lay ready for crisping in the lower ovens of the range and a maid stood by a huge mixing bowl into which she had been tasked with cracking a hundred and fifty eggs. On the high wooden table that dominated the room there sat slabs of butter which needed to be shaved off and rolled into pats, and loaves of bread to be sliced and toasted. A vat of saffron-yellow kedgeree was already warming, someone stirring it continuously to stop the rice from sticking to the bottom. The room was hot from the ovens and the steam, and there was a constant cacophony of clattering saucepans as the scullery maid washed up, with orders shouted over the top of it all.

With all this stage-managed chaos going on it perhaps wasn't surprising that only Louisa heard someone knocking at the back door. She looked around and as she could see neither the house-keeper nor the cook, she went to open it herself. A man stood there, his hands stuck in his coat pockets, a pork pie hat firmly jammed on his head, despite it being a warm night. He looked in need of a bath and he stared at her intently. Louisa wondered if she had sixpence to send him away with but he wasn't asking for bread or money. 'I'm a friend of Ronan's,' he mumbled.

Louisa was confused. 'Sorry?'

That seemed to throw him, too. 'Aincha Rose?'

Louisa was trying to think who Rose might be – she didn't know the names of everyone working there that night – when a girl pushed past her, flustered. 'Thanks, Miss,' she said, 'this is for me.' When Louisa didn't move, momentarily unsure what was happening, the girl looked at the man and said firmly, 'I'm Rose,' then repeated to Louisa, 'Thank you.' She was younger than Louisa, afraid to dismiss her but clearly wanting her to go away.

'Of course,' said Louisa and walked off but she turned around just in time to see the man hand a small package to Rose, which she quickly put in her apron pocket.

Shortly after this, two young maids were walking through the kitchen, their thin arms each carrying an overloaded tray of dirty glasses, when they were spotted by Mrs Norris, the housekeeper. She called out to them and they stood to attention. Dark circles bloomed deep below their eyes – Louisa knew they had to have been up since half past five that morning, working to ready the house for the party. Mrs Norris sighed at the sight of them. 'You had better get going to bed, girls. We'll need you up early in the morning to put everything straight.'

'Thank you, Mrs Norris,' they chirruped as they put the trays down by the sink. Before leaving the kitchen, the housekeeper gave a nod to Louisa, a companionable greeting that accorded her a small measure of respect. Louisa looked around at the people working, each one busy at their task, and gave a little inward smile. Yes, the money was needed but so, too, was the company.

Louisa caught sight of the two young maids winking at their fellow worker cracking the eggs, as one of them stole a few devils-on-horseback off the tray. It earned them a shout from the assistant cook – '*Oi, them's for young Mr Guinness!*' – before they raced off up the back stairs. She lost sight of them then, and felt a pang as they ran, giggling together. It had been a while since she'd enjoyed such easy friendship.

Despite their sore feet, the sound of the music and chatter as they moved through the back stairs of the house enlivened the two girls. At one point, they glimpsed the ladies in fine dresses with beads that shimmered as their bodies dipped and swayed. Dot nudged Elizabeth in the side. 'Imagine having a dress like that,' she whispered, her eyes on a gold and silver fringed number. Elizabeth grinned and stifled a giggle.

On the fourth floor, they found their friend, Nora, a scullery maid, also on her way to bed. The three of them stood together for a moment, their ears cocked as the music faintly reached them. Elizabeth began to regale them with their tale of the dancing. 'I think we saw the Prince of Wales,' she said at the end.

'You never,' said Nora, punching her in the arm, though her wide eyes betrayed a question. They might have, mightn't they? Their master and mistress were richer than they knew was possible and all kinds of toffs came through the front door that was polished daily.

'We can look at them,' said Elizabeth suddenly. She inclined her head toward the large skylight, set inside a square of railings on their landing. 'There's a little hole there, in the middle, look.'

The other girls leaned over the railing. 'We can't see from here,' said Nora, her bottom lip pushing out. She was tired and quite hungry, and on top of that she felt frustrated to have missed the show. As if she'd gone to the Regal Cinema in Marble Arch and been forced to stand outside the door and listen to everyone roaring with laughter at the moving pictures.

Dot was eighteen years old, older than the other maids, and inclined to feel that she was responsible for them. Some were as young as fourteen when they began work in the house and they missed their older sisters when they arrived – the ones who had usually brought them up, while the mothers were busy with the babies – and Dot liked to be the one who showed them both affection and discipline, to help them grow up quicker. She opened the gate.

Nora put her hand over her mouth and cried out, 'What are you doing?'

'It's fine,' said Dot. 'I'll hold on to the railing. We can just lean out a bit further and look through the hole. Don't you want to see the Prince of Wales?'

'He ain't there,' said Nora. She looked on the verge of tears. 'Supposing Mrs Norris comes up here.'

'She won't come up,' said Elizabeth. 'She's still working.'

Dot went through the gate, her hands holding on to the railing behind her, her feet on tiptoes at the edges. Heat had risen through her suddenly and sweat had broken out on her forehead, which she wiped with her arm. Beneath the sheen, her skin was paler than the ivory ribbon threaded through her cap. Elizabeth, screwed-up courage written on her face, went through the gate as well. Nora kept hoping one of them would cry off so she could too. Something made her turn to the side and she saw another maid coming up the stairs, one she didn't recognize as living in the house. She hoped she wouldn't tell on them.

Dot bent her knees and twisted her body slightly, one hand holding on to the railing behind her, the other pressing on the skylight. The shadows moved beneath the opaque glass, the lights blurred like fireflies in the night. She let out a small gasp as her hand on the railing slipped momentarily, but she said no more and held on, as resolute as she was when blacking a grate.

Elizabeth was beside her now, bent too, and with one hand about to lean upon the glass. The music reverberated in their ears as they leaned further forward, and there was a tantalising view of the men and women below, smoking and laughing louder than the hyenas in London Zoo.

At half past midnight, the message went out round the kitchen that breakfast was soon to be served and Louisa was sent back upstairs again by the assistant cook to let the footmen know they would be needed for the synchronised delivery of kedgeree and scrambled eggs.

In the central hall, into which the stairs from the servants' quarters emerged, a steady stream of people entered and exited, either coming from or moving on to another party in London. A night during the Season was like Snakes and Ladders, sliding from Knightsbridge to Mayfair and then back again on a roll of the dice. Standing by the stairs, Louisa was surprised to see the maid from earlier, Rose, talk briefly to someone she recognized: Clara Fischer, one of Nancy's friends from years before. She was a pretty actress in the Clara Bow mould and one of the few of the inner circle that had talked to Louisa and not barked orders at her. Idling for the moment, Louisa watched as Rose disappeared back into the crowd before Clara handed her drink for a man to hold while she rifled through her evening bag; he had slicked-back hair and sapphire-blue eyes that looked about him and never at Clara. Louisa decided now would not be the moment to say hello to Miss Fischer; she was American and would have forgiven a maid greeting her at a party but the man might not. As she stirred herself to find more footmen, Nancy approached the pair and Louisa heard her call out 'Shaun, darling', which made him almost drop the glasses he held in each hand. He must be the glamorous man Nancy had been talking about earlier.

Still not wishing to be seen by her former charge, Louisa left them to go from there and through the ballroom, tapping a footman or two, then on to a small hall where the women would sit out the next dance if their cards hadn't been filled. It was brighter here than the rest of the house thanks to its high cream walls and a ceiling with a large skylight set with opaque glass so that one couldn't see the floors above. A chandelier hung from the middle of it on a long chain, its glass drops seemingly suspended in the air.

Somehow, above the chatter and the music, Louisa was sure she heard a creak from above, followed sharply by a cry. She was puzzled to see shadows moving across the glass. There was more than one and they were too big to be the house's pet cats, surely. Were those *people* on the glass? It couldn't be nearly strong enough to hold anyone. Louisa looked frantically about her, not knowing what she was hoping to see – something to catch them? Should she shout? But she didn't want to cause a scene, it might be someone fixing something and it could be terribly embarrassing if—

Without realising, Louisa had been moving as she was look-ing up, and she felt someone grip her arm. It was Mr Meyer, though of course he did not know her name. 'Watch out,' he said. He looked up, following her eyeline, and gave a gasp. 'What's up there?'

'I don't know,' she said, her pulse racing.

Before either of them could warn the others there was a crash, then a fast-moving, horrible sound as shards scattered everywhere, hands flew to faces and men threw their arms around the bare shoulders of the women, before the most sickening and terrible sound of all – a body hitting the floor.

There lay a young maid, absolutely dead.

Up above them another girl clung to the chandelier, blood pouring down her china-white face, her eyes squeezed tightly shut, her mouth a silent black hole.

CHAPTER TWO

⟋⟋⟋⟍⟍⟍⟋

For a second, every person in the hall stood still, petrified by the sight of the inert maid lying in the broken glass, her body twisted like a vine, blood pouring out from beneath her skull. As if in jest, the music and the chatter continued loudly next door; then, as the guests close by the maid stirred to action, the noise lowered until it completely stopped. In the echoing silence, several people ran to the body, covering it with a coat and shouting for someone to call an ambulance, someone get upstairs, someone fetch the housekeeper, someone find Mr Guinness. Somehow, in all the commotion, further servants and guests ran up the stairs and the second maid was rescued; she had been wounded by the broken glass, and was clinging on to the chain, her fingers stiff with fright. Some women had burst into tears and were being comforted; one had been removed to another room in order to hide her hysterics. The hubbub from the ballroom started up again, louder than before, but the music remained quelled.

Bryan Guinness, a narrow figure in white tie, with dark eyes set in a face that had a high forehead but otherwise perfectly proportioned features, had been the first in his family to react to the waves of alarm coming from the hall. He ran straight there, handed his drink to a friend, and knelt beside the body, seemingly not caring that the broken glass might shred his trousers and cut his knees. 'What happened? What happened?' he asked, staring at the white faces of the men and women around him.

An older man gripped him firmly by the elbow and pulled him up. 'Seems the young girls must have been trying to look at the party through the skylight, and fallen through.'

'She's dead?'

The man nodded and Bryan grimaced. 'Poor girl.'

In the next few minutes, his parents rushed to the scene, leading Bryan away as quickly as they could, encouraging the rest to follow. Two footmen were recruited to shield the maid's body from the party until the ambulance arrived – thankfully soon – to take her away, along with the second maid, who was shaking uncontrollably in spite of the enormous blanket that was wrapped around her. Lady Evelyn and Walter Guinness stood by the door to see out their guests as they left, apologising over and again for the shock and upset.

Guy Sullivan stood on the black and white marble floor of the hall of Grosvenor Place and marvelled at the coolness of the atmosphere. Outside, he had been sweating in his suit, though at least he was spared the indignity of the year-round wool uniform his colleagues suffered. Up above him, the skylight still showed the signs of its brutal smash the night before, with a chain hanging uselessly through it, the chandelier no longer attached to the end. Below, around him, it was as if nothing had happened, let alone a fatality. The place was gleaming with cleanliness, there were flowers everywhere and sunlight shone through the windows. While his superior, Detective Inspector Stiles, interviewed Mr Guinness, Guy had been taken on a tour of the servants' quarters below stairs, on to the back stairs and up to the fourth-floor landing. A servant's life was nothing so much as a continuous journey up and down steps, he thought. A close examination of the railing around the skylight had yielded nothing suspicious – it was as secure as a prison gate. Now, he was holding in his hand a list of the guests who had been there that night and his eye had just fallen on that of the Hons. Nancy and Diana Mitford of 26 Rutland Gate.

He hadn't seen either of them for over two years, when he had been at their parents' house in Oxfordshire, investigating a murder. That is, he hadn't been there officially, but he had discovered the culprit and the successful result had ensured his quick referral to the CID. Diana had been a young girl of fifteen then but Nancy he'd known a little better, from earlier still, when she was a debutante, emerging from the nursery but chaperoned by her former nursery maid, Louisa Cannon.

Louisa. The thought of her had never lost the power to stop Guy in his tracks, even though she had disappeared from view. He couldn't understand it: they'd been friends for so long, even if he'd always hoped it would turn to more. They had met in inauspicious circumstances, when Louisa had jumped from a moving train, escaping her uncle, Stephen. She'd been in distress but in spite of her scuffed clothes and wrecked hat, the first thing Guy had noticed was how pretty she was; then he'd admired her fighting spirit. After that, they had become close, as circumstances conspired to bring them together again. Still, though she could be exasperating, never quite seeming to make up her mind what she thought about him, they had never lost touch altogether – until recently.

So far as Guy knew, Louisa had planned to leave her job with the Mitford girls' parents, Lord and Lady Redesdale, in order to return to London and find work; she had been ambitious to be more than a servant. Not knowing where she'd gone, he'd written to her at Asthall Manor, hoping that if Louisa was no longer there that his letters would be forwarded. But he'd never heard back and could only assume that she'd requested his letters not be passed to her. Or simply not replied. She'd probably met someone and got married and not wanted to tell him. He could understand that; he'd made his feelings about her clear, even when he was unsure that she felt the same.

A thump on his shoulder shook Guy from his reminiscences. 'Righto, back to the station. Better write this up, get it all ready for the inquest. Gather it's happening in the next couple of days or so.'

DI Stiles was, in spite of his heavy hand, tall and lean, always dressed in a pale grey suit with a pastel-coloured tie. Standing together, the contrast between him and Guy couldn't have been sharper. They shared the same height and narrow frame, but the similarities ended there, at Guy's thick, round glasses and amiable smile. Stiles's silver hair was slicked back till it shone and his moustache could have been painted on. It was rumoured that the man he lived with was not his brother. Guy liked him chiefly because he wasn't snooty, even if he looked it. In fact, Stiles was distinctly unimpressed by anything he deemed snobbish and had taken a shine to Guy. In the last few months they had formed what amounted to an unofficial partnership, though Guy couldn't entirely rule out the idea that this was largely down to the fact that he was more willing than Stiles to complete the necessary legwork of a case, particularly when Stiles had a drink on offer.

True to form, the next thing Stiles said was: 'Don't mind if I hand over my notes to you, do you, old boy? I've got a long-standing at the Dog and Duck in about half an hour.'

'No problem, sir,' said Guy, knowing this was his cue to leave Grosvenor Place and return to the station alone.

Next morning at Pavilion Road, the Knightsbridge station to which Guy had been attached when promoted to detective sergeant, he dutifully typed up the notes made by him and Stiles. It looked to be a straightforward, if tragic, case. Earlier, Guy had interviewed Elizabeth, the maid who had survived the accident. Though still visibly distressed, no blame could be laid at her feet. She had described how she and Dot had wanted to look at the women's fine dresses and had crept out on to the skylight, to peer through the gap in the glass. But for a slip of the fingers, they might have had their moment of fun and that would have been the end of it. Instead, it had led to death. A brief conversation with the third maid, Nora, had confirmed her statement. There was only one thing she had said that niggled at Guy: she had seen a fourth maid come up on the landing, someone she hadn't recognized. 'She wasn't one of the live-ins,' Nora had said, 'probably one of the maids borrowed for the party. But I don't know what she was doing up there. I didn't see her after the girls fell.' Whoever this maid was, she could be an important witness. He would have to check against the names of all the staff on the list that the housekeeper had given him, and that would take time:

there had been over sixty people working there that night, the vast majority of them drafted in only for that party. Then again, given that the inquest was likely to conclude an accidental death with no suspicious circumstances, he thought it unlikely he'd be given permission to do this.

Then something happened that Guy couldn't have called a stroke of luck exactly – that would have presumed a happy turn of events. DI Stiles came over and handed him a telephone number, for a pub in Yorkshire, the Queen Victoria. Guy was to call the number and leave a message for a Mr Albert Morgan with a time that Mr Morgan could call him back. 'It was given to me because I'm leading the inquiry into the maid's death but I've got to go out,' said Stiles with a wink. 'Do it for me, would you?'

Guy was intrigued: he did as he was asked and at noon they spoke. Mr Morgan had a distinctive accent, and he sounded distressed. He started talking about how he was a simple farmer and had no understanding of London folk until Guy had to press him to tell him what the phone call was about.

'It's my daughter, Rose. She's gone missing. Her mam and me, we've not heard from her and she's not shown up at work. Someone from the big house she works fer called us and asked us if she'd come home, but she in't here.'

Guy took down some details: Rose worked as a maid for a Lady Delaney at 11 Wilton Crescent, she'd been there a year. But she'd gone to work at a big party a few nights ago. 'The housekeeper told us there was a terrible accident at the party, a maid died. It weren't Rose, I know that, but she's not been seen since.' The father's voice threatened to crack but he recovered his stoic tone fast. 'It's not like her not to let us know where she is. She knows we worry about her being in the city. We just want to tell her she can come home, we won't be angry. She's only seventeen, not much more than a lass.'

Guy reassured him he'd do everything he could to find her. 'I'm sure she's safe and well, Mr Morgan, and I'll keep in touch. Can I call this number when I need to talk to you?'

'Aye, someone here will tek a message to me or the missus and one of us will call you back. We've no telephone at the farm. I don't hold with them usually but I'm glad for it now.'

Guy thanked him and repeated his assurances. Privately he wondered if he could be so sure that the young Rose was safe and well somewhere. He shook his head sadly as he put the phone down; his work as a policeman had taught him that life could be brutish and short. In spite of his grand age – nearing thirty – Guy was not yet married and still lived in the house in which he'd been born. It was hard to leave when he worried about how his mother was coping. His father was alive but losing his mind, and she spent her days worrying about him, unable to leave him for more than a minute for fear he'd let himself out of the front door and walk into the road, never to find his way home again. Guy, the last at home out of the four brothers, was the only one to give her some respite, allowing her a breather to get to the shops or pop out to see one of the neighbours.

Even so, his mother loved him and wanted the best for her son. Perhaps it was time he did something about the lack he felt in his life and moved towards the place he really wanted to be. It was time, he decided, to get married. And he knew exactly the woman to ask.

CHAPTER THREE

A week or so after the Guinness party, Louisa Cannon was standing on the pavement outside the Albert Hall, wishing she had worn a lighter coat. She'd have liked to cross the road, kick her shoes and stockings off, and walk on the grass. It had been a wet June but when July arrived, the heat had come with it. On the other hand, she was looking forward to seeing Nancy and Diana. She looked at her watch and smiled. Ten minutes late already.

Louisa had been their nursery maid for more than five years but had left over two years ago at the start of 1926 to pursue a career in London, a city that had changed in those years since the war, offering new and better jobs for her kind than had ever existed for her mother's generation. Louisa had moved into a room in Chelsea, close by where she had grown up, though Mrs Cannon had long left to live with Louisa's aunt in Suffolk. Her father had died years ago. There was hardly anybody from her old life around any more, only her friend Jennie, but they met rarely. Even less since Jennie had married and had a baby.

At first, Louisa had taken any odd job she could, not wanting to commit to any live-in servant work in the hopes of something more interesting coming her way. At the start, she had applied for training as a policewoman but had been turned down, peremptorily and quickly. There had been one or two minor charges of theft when she was younger and under the influence of her uncle Stephen, but Louisa had crossed her fingers, hoping either that they hadn't kept a record or that they would overlook them – considering the assistance she had given the police since then – but it seemed neither was the case. She had thought about arguing that it 'takes one to know one' when it comes to catching criminals but suspected that this wouldn't help. Ashamed, she had hidden herself even further from those she knew and finally found herself a job as a seamstress for a dress shop in Mayfair, working out of the back with two others, running up the alterations for customers. It wasn't bad work. She had her freedom, no longer having to ask permission from Nanny Blor or Lady Redesdale to leave the house. And London was exciting after those years in the Cotswold countryside. There were nightclubs, restaurants, galleries and museums, not to mention theatres and picture houses.

But she rarely went to any of them. They all cost money and, even if she had enough to spare, it would have been unseemly, if not downright lonely, to go by herself. She couldn't eat alone in a restaurant, she couldn't go to a nightclub without a pal. The less she saw of anyone, the worse it got. At twenty-six years old, Louisa felt she'd missed the best of what life had to offer.

When she went to see her mother, who was quite old now – she'd had Louisa long after she'd expected to have the luck of bearing a child of her own – she was bombarded with questions about when she would marry. 'I don't know, Ma,' Louisa would say, trying to keep her exasperation in check. 'I haven't met anyone I like.'

'What about that policeman you used to mention?'

Guy Sullivan. He was a good man, and Louisa had liked him very much. But she had been so mortified when she had been turned down for police training – she had planned to surprise him by knocking on his door, wearing the uniform – that she had fallen out of touch with him. He'd written to her a few times but she had never replied and presumably he'd given up on her now. Even if he tried again, he wouldn't know the Mitfords had moved from Asthall Manor to Swinbrook House. She missed him.

Louisa would try another tack. 'Besides, if I got married then I couldn't work.'

'You could work,' Ma would huff in reply. 'I worked all my life.'

To this, Louisa couldn't explain that she wanted more than a job, she wanted a career, something that took her beyond her station, whatever that was. Her mother had worked long years as a laundress, her father as a chimney sweep – Mr Black and Mrs White she and Jennie called them – and Louisa was proud of them. But she wanted better than that for herself; work had made her parents tired and resentful. What she had seen when she had been working for Lord and Lady Redesdale had shown her that life was full of so many other possibilities. And the years after the war had promised change for the likes of her: a break with the past; a chance to do things differently. And lots of things were different – she couldn't deny that. The streets were practically choked with traffic so's one couldn't help but worry for the policemen with their long, white sleeves directing four ways of cars, buses and vans. There was a telephone in every house and in red boxes on just about every street corner: you could talk to almost anyone, anywhere, even America. Plenty of women went out to work, too, not just as cleaners and shop girls. There were secretaries and telephonists working in big offices, there amongst lots of other women and men, too. Some women did even more amazing things. Just a few weeks ago, Amelia Earhart had been a passenger in a plane that had flown across the Atlantic. Louisa had seen the newsreel that had shown Miss Earhart waving off, looking thrillingly glamorous in her pilot's outfit with hat and goggles, and those funny trousers that seemed to have wings of their own. Apparently, she hadn't actually flown the plane but she'd been there, sitting behind the pilot, and she probably would be the pilot next time. How Louisa had longed to fly right through that cinema screen and join Miss Earhart on the Fokker F.VII. As it was, the furthest she had been was Dieppe in France, by ferry, and that had been with the Mitford girls.

All this meant that when Louisa had received a message from Nancy to say that Diana was doing the Season in London, and would she like to meet them while they were in town, Louisa decided that she had to say yes. Naturally, they were behind the clock. Their father, Lord Redesdale, was a stickler for punctuality – he would even time the vicar's sermon, signalling if he ran a second over ten minutes – so it was a form of rebellion that his daughters would ignore the time whenever he wasn't around. Just as Louisa was thinking this, a number nine bus drew up at the stop, and amongst the people disembarking she spotted Nancy.

The eldest of the six sisters looked the same as ever: not tall but slim, in an elegant pale pink dress with a duster coat a slightly darker shade over the top, both of which fell to just below her knees; her eyebrows were long and thin, and her large eyes still had the smallest droop at the edges, with a glint that kept them from looking soft. But it was Diana who took Louisa by surprise, able to observe her more closely now than she had at the dance. Her chin was round and her jaw almost square, yet this made her look strong – like a Viking – rather than thickset. The effect was show-stopping, Louisa supposed, because of her fashionably short bob, barely reaching past her earlobes. Her features were ideally proportioned and symmetrical, with ice-blue eyes and blonde hair adding to the general impression that she might be leaning out on the prow of a ship. There was a stillness to her, in spite of her lively movements. If Nancy was the ripples in a millpond, Diana was the smooth pebble that had been thrown into the water.

'Lou-Lou!' Nancy called out as they walked towards her, the sunshine blinding them slightly. 'Darling, are we late?'

By twenty-five minutes.

Louisa shook her head. 'Nothing to worry about. It's lovely to see you both. Miss Diana, you look—'

'Don't say "so grown up",' grimaced Diana. 'All I've had for weeks is people comparing my height to a grasshopper's knees.'

'All right then, I won't. But it's lovely to see you.'

'You too,' said Diana. 'It's funny, isn't it? Now you're no longer our maid, it's almost as if you're one of us.'

Louisa didn't know how to respond to this but fortunately, Nancy, rather more sensitive, diverted the conversation. 'Let's walk down to South Ken,' she said. 'There's a sweet little café there and we can have a cup of tea. I'm terribly afraid to say that we haven't been up for all that long.'

'Dancing,' said Diana, her face alight with the pleasure of

her memories. 'Until the small hours. Muv was quite exhausted when we got home.'

'Oh, she loves it,' said Nancy. 'It's not as if she has to do it. Now I'm practically an old maid of twenty-four I'm quite senior enough to be your chaperone.'

'I'm not sure she's convinced that you would stick to me in the way that she does.'

Louisa enjoyed hearing them volley their lines like a game of tennis. Nancy was always the sharper wit but Diana had learned how to whet the blade. They had turned to begin walking down Exhibition Road when they heard a 'Hi!' call out. A young man was leaning out of the back of a black Bentley which had pulled up alongside the bus stop.

'It's Bryan Guinness,' said Nancy. 'I'd better say hello.'

'I think it's me he wants to see,' said Diana, a little pink colouring her cheeks, and she marched off at a faster pace, reaching the car ahead of her older sister, who, Louisa could see, was doing her best not to look put out. Diana leaned in at the car window and talked to him only briefly before he – or rather, his driver – drove off.

'Well, I say,' said Nancy as Diana returned to them. 'He didn't say hello. You know it was me who invited him down to Swinbrook last year? You were still a child, not even at that party.'

Diana shrugged but she looked pleased. 'He asked me if I was going to Westminster's dance on Monday.' This rang a bell for Louisa, she would have to look at her diary but she thought it may have been somewhere the agency was sending her to work that night.

'Are you?' Nancy was imperious.

'I am now.'

*

Cars sped down Exhibition Road, tooting their horns in greeting or impatience at the pedestrians. The noise and the heat momentarily made Louisa feel tired but she was buoyed by the company of Nancy and Diana. She knew she was not as handsome as either of them, and her clothes were cheaper, but she was confident they were happy to see her too. 'Who is this man then?' she enquired, in a way that she knew would have been a cheek if she'd been still in the Redesdale employ but not today.

'Bryan Guinness,' said Nancy. 'Rich and good-looking but worse than that, he's terribly nice. One of the few proper chaps about.'

'He's only one of many,' said Diana with a smile that showed her white teeth. 'They've been dropping like flies.'

Louisa, temporarily back in nursery-maid mode, decided it was best not to encourage this line of talk. 'Is he something to do with the Guinnesses that had the dreadful accident at the party last month? Where the maids fell through a skylight?' She knew she was being disingenuous but she didn't want them to know she had been working there in the kitchens. Even so, it had been a distressing night: she felt the need to talk about it with others who had been there. Only they weren't so willing.

'Yes,' said Nancy blithely, 'it truly was ghastly. We were there, although neither of us saw it happen and we were all hurried out very quickly.'

'The poor girls,' said Louisa, 'they were only eighteen.'

Nancy and Diana acknowledged this with a nod and a murmur but she could see that they had put the incident behind them already. 'What other news, then?' she said brightly, looping her arm around Diana's. 'Tell me *everything*. How is the new house? How is Nanny Blor? Is she still reading her terrible murder mysteries?'

Diana laughed, and off they strode, as if they none of them had a care in the world and only bright futures to look forward to. The young don't look for the clouds over the horizon.

CHAPTER FOUR

A t nine o'clock the following Monday night, Louisa was back at another grand house in a maid's uniform. The kitchen was stiflingly hot and she had volunteered to take out one of the full rubbish bins, just to catch her breath. She stood on the pavement, drinking in the warm air, as various young men and women in their evening dress and feathered boas tripped up the stone steps of the Duke of Westminster's town house.

Louisa knew the Season was coming to an end and wondered if for all these young people there was the promise of a finale, when the couples that had been dancing around – and with – each other for weeks would decide if they were going to continue their Charleston into the sunset or not. Just then, she saw two figures coming out. A man and a woman. Bryan Guinness and Diana Mitford no less. This could be interesting. Louisa bent down to tie her bootlaces, as if she were not deliberately concealing even from herself that she wished to eavesdrop. The night was not completely dark; the clear blue skies of the day were still as cloudless now, with stars pushing through the navy streaks. The doorway of the house was lit well enough to be a stage, and Diana's pale shoulders glowed, her face hidden as she bowed her neck. Louisa sensed the nerves in Bryan as he took her by the hand and led her along the pavement, into the shadows. He was a smidgen shorter than her, which gave him no advantage, made worse by the beseeching looks he was throwing at his fair maiden. They hadn't walked far when Bryan pulled Diana around, his hands on her arms, and brought her closer. Louisa, watching their silhouettes as she remained crouched beside a tree on the other side of the street, saw their heads come together, long enough for a kiss. Then the profiles parted. There were urgent whispers, which grew louder.

'Can't you tell how mad I am about you?' Louisa heard. 'You're all I want, day after night, night before day.'

'Do you always talk in iambic pentameters?' teased Diana.

'Darling, I'm serious. Do you think you could marry me? Do you love me enough?'

Their figures stood apart now. The white bricks of the house showed between them.

'I'm very fond of you,' said Diana.

'But do you love me?' persisted Bryan. There was a pause and when no answer came forth, he said: 'You kissed me.'

'A kiss means nothing.' At this, Louisa's own heart sank for the wooer. 'I do it without thinking as I'm used to kissing my family.' Diana's tone was light, perhaps deliberately so.

'I'm not your brother,' said Bryan, admirably keeping any hurt out of his voice. He took Diana's hand. 'We'll go back in. But promise me you'll think about it?'

Diana nodded. 'Yes, I will. Promise. Now please let's go back in. Cecil's promised me a Black Bottom dance.' And the two of them ran back through the stage lights, their moment in the wings over.

31

1929

CHAPTER FIVE

⁓

For what had been frequently referred to in the newspapers as 'the society wedding of the year', despite it being still only January, the excitement amongst the waiting crowds that lined the way to St Margaret's, Westminster, was palpable. A union between an heir to a fortune and a great beauty was enough to feed the diary columns and over-the-fence gossip for months. Sashaying down the path to the church door were the young men and women, as well as the elderly statesmen and dowagers of the country's aristocratic families, dressed in their very best silks, furs and diamonds.

Amongst them, in a rather less expensive outfit but feeling relief that the anticipatory nerves appeared to be over, was Louisa Cannon. She had found the build-up to the event quite terrifying, partly because the wedding marked a significant change in her life too. But for the moment, she was content to find a place beside the comforting presence of Nanny Blor, in one of the furthest rows at the back. It wasn't long before Louisa was commiserating with her at the absence of the bridesmaids

Decca and Debo (the family names for Jessica and Deborah), Diana's two youngest sisters of twelve and nine years old, who had developed scarlet fever seemingly overnight. 'Least, that's what the doctor said,' sniffed Nanny Blor, 'but he's not our usual one, of course, being in London. I think it's whooping cough myself.'

'Whatever it is, they must have been so sorry not to be here,' whispered Louisa. 'I know Miss Diana was very unhappy not to have them with her.' She and Nanny Blor had arrived a good hour early ahead of the ceremony and happily discussed each of the Mitford children and the goings-on of Swinbrook village.

'Inconsolable, the poor loves,' nodded Nanny Blor. (Her real name was Laura Dicks but she had been 'Nanny Blor' since Nancy had christened her as such almost fifteen years before, and nobody in the family could think of her as someone who had a life outside the Mitfords, let alone another name.) There were three men in morning suits shuffling by the door and coughing. Louisa thought she'd got a second look from one of them, and touched her new hat when he did so. It had cost her almost half of last week's wages but she'd needed the pep it gave her. Besides, after today she had no more rent to pay, nor even meagre meals to buy.

As they had talked, the church filled up with the clotted cream of England's society, ready to witness Diana as she was walked down the aisle by her father, Lord Redesdale. They were followed by eleven bridesmaids, including Nancy. Louisa spotted Unity, the next sister along at four years younger than Diana, if her complete opposite in looks, with straight, straw-like hair that stuck out awkwardly. She was tugging at her dress and throwing black looks at anyone she thought might be staring at her.

Pamela, the sister who was between Nancy and Diana, was not one of the eleven in gold-tissue dresses; instead, she sat beside their brother Tom and their mother Lady Redesdale, in the front pew. Louisa hadn't been at all sure that she, herself, should be at the service but Nancy and Diana had kindly insisted, and then there had been the question of her new appointment.

Two weeks before Christmas, Louisa had received a note from Diana, asking her to come around to the house at Rutland Gate the following day for tea. It hadn't been easy to get let out of work at the shop early – she'd told a small fib about a sore tooth – but Louisa had the sense that the summons wasn't just for amusement. And there was the fact that in spite of having quit her job with the Mitfords a few years before, she could never quite resist a request from them of any sort.

'Darling Lou-Lou,' Diana had begun, once she had poured out the tea, surprising Louisa with her mature manner and use of Nancy's own nickname for her. 'Everyone has *at last* agreed that Bryan and I can marry, so we're going to do it as soon as possible and afterwards we're going to set up in a little house, a sort of dolls' house really, in Buckingham Street. We've agreed that we want to do things the way *we* like to, and so rather than start with awful new servants that we don't know at all, we're bringing our favourites.'

Louisa had listened to this with a very full cup of tea balancing on her knees, and she had had to force herself to concentrate on what Diana was saying, rather than on the light blue rug that she was threatening to ruin.

'Bryan, that is, Mr Guinness, is bringing a parlourmaid from his parents' house, and Farve has agreed I can have Turner, from Swinbrook.'

'Turner?'

'Oh, he must have started after you left. He's a dear thing. The chauffeur. But the point is, Louisa, I'd like you to come, too.'

'Me?' Must she be reduced to one-word questions? She felt quite stupid.

'Yes. As a sort of lady's maid. That is to say, I don't really need a lady's maid, the idea of one is, I agree with you, quite absurd.' Louisa hadn't said anything or even changed her face so far as she was aware – did she agree? Diana chattered on. 'Nonetheless, everyone is insisting I will need someone to help me because they all think I'm still a child. To pack my clothes, for one thing, because Bryan wants to go abroad rather a lot. So do I, of course. Then there are endless parties – Bryan has so many divine friends – and we go to the theatre every night. There never seems to be quite enough time to make sure the things I want have been ironed let alone mended . . .'

She trailed off, smiling benignly, yet with her blue eyes firmly trained on her former nursery maid. Louisa still didn't know how to respond. She wasn't yet sure how she felt about this offer.

'The point is' – the voice was firmer now – 'you'd be a friendly face in the house for me, and everyone is probably right. I've never run a house before and though it doesn't seem terribly complicated to me, there are things it would be useful to have some assistance with. We'd pay you generously. Bry— *Mr Guinness* is very good in that way. What do you say, Louisa?'

Louisa, unable to think straight and bewitched by the silvery beauty of this young woman, found herself accepting – almost – on the spot. 'What about Lady Redesdale? She may not approve. I was not exactly asked to leave her employ but . . .'

Diana's face changed slightly. 'Lady Redesdale is no longer at liberty to tell me what to do. I shall be a married woman soon, with my own house. If I decide I want to employ you then that's my lookout.' There was a trace of a child's petulance, but she was, after all, only eighteen.

Louisa believed it was her duty to throw as many rocks in the path as possible. 'I'll have to give notice at the dress shop. It might be weeks before I can start.'

'Then you can start on the first day of my marriage – on the thirty-first of January. It'll be a new beginning for all of us and absolutely heavenly.'

So that was that. Once more Louisa was unto the breach of the Mitfords, and she wondered what battle she would find she had been drafted in to fight this time.

CHAPTER SIX

ᴀ fter the church service was over, the wedding party had
either gone on foot or been driven to the Guinness house
at Grosvenor Place, some preferring not to chance their luck
with the gathering grey clouds. Louisa had stayed beside
Nanny Blor, enjoying the sedate pace and the chance to overhear the chatter of the guests. It wasn't often that she walked
unnoticed amongst such people; Nanny Blor was uncharacteristically quiet and Louisa thought she, too, might be tuning
in, as if it were one of her favourite radio programmes. Diana's
looks – her golden hair, her clear, creamy complexion – were
much commented on by both the men and the women,
though it was not the men who noticed the parchment satin
of the dress she had worn, nor the antique Brussels lace veil,
nor even the unusual bouquet of hot-house lilies. They tended
instead to making spiky remarks about the fact that Diana was
not marrying at her own family house – was it not big enough,
nor grand enough? The queries were arch. Lord Redesdale
would have been incensed to hear such 'sewers' dismiss his

ambitious build, though Louisa knew the family hated the new house after their beloved Asthall Manor had been sold. Nanny Blor had told her it was so cold in the bedrooms that her wash bowl often froze over in the night.

Walking around them, too, Louisa spotted some of the faces that she had seen at the Guinness party last summer, her memory reinforced by the times she had since identified them in the society pages of the newspapers: the biographer Lytton Strachey; the artist Dora Carrington; Evelyn Waugh, the 'promising novelist'; the glamorous Mr and Mrs Mulloney; Lady Lascelles and the woman who worked for the Queen, she couldn't quite think of her name. She ticked them off in her mind and then caught herself wondering if she was after Luke Meyer's job – she had spotted his byline in the papers too – which also led her to wonder if she'd see him today. She rather thought she'd like to. Now that she was part of Diana's household, she felt bolder about such possible friendships.

As they approached the house, Louisa saw the crowd of newspaper photographers on the pavement and felt Nanny Blor nudge her in the ribs.

'I told Miss Diana this morning that no one would be looking at her but I wonder now if perhaps I wasn't wrong, just this once?' Nanny's eyes widened in her soft face; she was loved by the girls as much – if not more – than their mother, and it wasn't hard to see why.

'I think, Nanny, *just this once*, you were.'

They stood to one side and watched as the girl they had known since she was a child smiled prettily before the flashbulbs even as the drizzle started, her arm firmly tucked inside her husband's, his countenance rather more solemn and reluctant in the face of this attention.

Once inside – Nanny Blor had to be persuaded to walk through the front door and not the side entrance – a crowd of over a hundred and fifty had already gathered in front of them, and the abundance of hats made it hard to see across the room: wide brims with flowers and lace for the women, though the men had thankfully removed their black silk chimneys. In spite of the complete change in atmosphere since Louisa had last been there – now it was daytime, winter and a wedding – she was still unnerved to see the mended skylight through which Dot had fallen to her death. Nanny had left her to go and find the girls, when Louisa suddenly felt someone bump against her, then a cry and a smash as two full glasses of champagne fell to the floor. Instinctively, she bent down to gather the shards as quickly as possible and when she stood up she saw the embarrassed face of Mr Meyer.

'Oh God, I'm so sorry,' he gabbled. 'Here, please ... let me.'

'It's fine,' she said, still not looking at him, 'I've got them all now.' She straightened up. 'Hold out your hands.' Mr Meyer obeyed, and the wet shards were placed on to his open palms. She warded off any protestations. 'I'm sorry, but after you crashed into me, it's the least you can do. Look at me. I'm soaked.'

'Of course,' he said. 'I'm so sorry, again. Please, tell me what your name is.'

'Louisa Cannon.'

'Luke Meyer. I'd shake your hand but ... ' He shrugged his shoulders and something in the air was punctured. He looked at her again. 'Forgive me, but have we met before?'

'Sort of. It was when . . . ' She glanced upwards.

'My goodness, so it was. That's what I was looking at when I crashed into you.' He dropped his voice and stage-whispered to her. 'It's quite odd somehow to be here, after that happened, isn't it?'

She nodded, not trusting herself to say any more. She didn't want to be disloyal to the family of the man who was her new employer.

The two of them walked into another room where they found a footman to take away the debris and fetch them their drinks. While they waited, they both naturally stood with their backs to the wall, looking at the other wedding guests. 'Are you bride or groom?' asked Luke, the familiar wedding question to denote which side of the aisle a guest would sit on.

'Bride,' said Louisa, 'but I'm not a friend. That is, I sort of am.' She shook her head as if to throw off the confusion. Luke gave her a sympathetic smile; was he an outsider here in the same sort of way she was? 'I work for the family. I used to look after the children, and Mrs Guinness has asked me to be her lady's maid.'

'Did you know her in the nursery, then? I mean, she's not long out of it.'

Louisa nodded. 'Yes, I did. Oh, here are our drinks. It was a pleasure to bump into you.' She smiled again and started to turn away but as she did so, Nancy came up to them, in her gold-tissue bridesmaid's dress.

'Hello, Lou-Lou.' She jabbed Luke in the chest. 'Cheer me up.'

Luke poked her back. 'Whatever for? It's your sister's wedding and, according to all the papers, the pinnacle of all society events of 1929 even though it's only January. Where are the rest of your sibling gang? Don't you usually attack them for fun?'

'Two of them are ill. Unity is too young and dull for any conversation. Pamela isn't rigged up in this dress and she can't sympathise.'

'Why wasn't Pamela bridesmaid too?'

'Because she's engaged to Togo.' Nancy corrected herself at Luke's bemused face: 'Oliver Watney, he was the boy next door. Literally.'

'Brewing family?'

'You're quick. Yes, there's money in beer. It's so unfair,' sighed Nancy. 'I'm engaged too but no one takes it seriously.'

'The lack of a proposal or engagement ring will do that,' said Luke drily. Nancy pretended to ignore this remark and Louisa felt rather sorry for her. After Diana's engagement had been announced, Nancy had been quick to announce she had her own fiancé, a Mr Hamish St Clair Erskine. The rumours had swirled thick and fast, even reaching Louisa's ears. She heard he had a reputation as an amusing and amiable chap but also one who batted for the other side. In short, Nancy's considerable charms were not likely appreciated by Hamish.

'It's more than you've got,' Nancy said waspishly but Luke did not rise to this.

'I know. I disappoint everyone, except myself.' He gave Louisa a sidelong look. 'Can you believe, my aunt thought I'd propose to Diana? There's more chance of pigs taking passengers on a flight to Paris. Speaking of which . . . ' He turned to Nancy. 'Where's your brother Tom?'

'Just back from Vienna, where he's been learning German. He's here somewhere, probably boring someone silly with his rhapsodies about the Rhineland.' But she said this with affection.

'Didn't he know your fiancé Hamish at school?'

Nancy bristled at this and Louisa sensed dangerous territory. 'Possibly, I don't ask him about all his childhood pashes. Are you still obsessing over yours? Poor thing.' She drained her glass. 'I'm going to find another. Goodbye, Louisa. Mr Meyer.'

Luke pulled a face at Louisa. 'I know one shouldn't but it's hard to resist.'

Louisa tried to give him a look of admonishment, and failed.

'I'd better go, too. I'm here with my aunt and she doesn't like it if she loses sight of me for too long, and it's only because of her that I've been invited in the first place.'

'Are you not a friend of Mrs Guinness?' Louisa knew it wasn't strictly her place to ask such a question but there was something about him that bridged the gap, somehow.

'Not really. I mean, I've seen her at parties and Nancy and I gather gossip for our editors. My aunt is Lady Boyd, she knows Lady Redesdale a little – I gather they go back as far as the days when Aunt was plain Rachel Meyer – and so she got me in. I owe my career, such as it is, to her.'

'What is your career?'

'Diarist, for my sins. I'd like to be a proper journalist, writing scoops, but I haven't managed it yet. My editor caught the whiff of my social connections so that was my work cut out for the Season but I'm always looking out for a big story.' He gave her a wink. 'Let me know if you hear of anything, won't you? Maids are frightfully useful for that sort of thing, eyes upstairs and down.'

Was he joking? He must have seen something on her face for he quickly changed tack. 'Of course, I mean, I've very much enjoyed meeting you. Not for that reason.' He looked as pink as when he'd dropped the glasses and she decided to let it go.

'Of course, Mr Meyer. I'll let you get back to your aunt. In fact, I should probably find out if Mrs Guinness needs me, it will time for her to leave soon. We're off to Paris for the honeymoon.' She couldn't help allowing her delight to show on her face, even letting him in on the secret of how she felt. 'I'm terribly excited.'

'Gay Paree!' he exclaimed. 'Have a wonderful time, Miss Cannon.' He gave her a small bow and walked away. She wondered if he was going to play a part in her life from now on; something told her he would.

CHAPTER SEVEN

A s Guy saw her coming down the road, his heart lifted as it always did at the sight of her neat figure, tightly belted in a brown wool coat, a cloche hat pulled low but not enough to hide her brilliantly blue eyes. He stretched one of his arms out open wide and she ran to him for the last few steps, nestling her head right into his chest as he hugged her close and bent down for a kiss. That made her cry out and she pushed him off gently. 'Give over! Not in the street.'

'We're engaged, aren't we?' Guy tried not to sound gruff.

Sinéad stood back up and wagged a finger at him. 'Even so. My mam would have a fit. There's no one doing that sort of thing in the streets of Killarney.'

Guy smiled. 'There's a lot of things they don't do in the streets of Killarney that I'd like to do with you.'

'Oh!' She smacked him on the arm but she could never keep up being cross with him for long. 'What are we doing now, then?'

Sinéad Barry, twenty-one years old and as Irish as soda

bread, was Guy's fiancée and always wanting to know what was happening next. For the moment, she was living in the house in Regent's Park where she worked as a tweeny, a maid of all work, but as soon as they were married they'd have a house in Hammersmith, he hoped, not too far from his parents. The fact that they had not settled on where to live was the reason they hadn't set a wedding date yet, though it had been five months since Guy had presented her with a gold Claddagh ring and telephoned her pappy to ask permission for her hand in marriage.

Guy looked at his watch. 'It's six o'clock. We could go to the pictures, I thought. I looked in the paper and there's a new Louise Brooks film on at the Regal in Marble Arch.'

'I love Louise Brooks.'

'I know you do.' He cupped her chin and tried again for a kiss. She didn't resist this time.

Monday morning and back at work, Guy reviewed the various open cases that were on his desk. Most were typical for a CID junior, perfect fodder for someone who needed to prove himself to his superiors. Someone like Guy. He frowned and read over the notes of the one on the top of the pile.

Reported missing 15 June 1928, Miss Rose Morgan, seventeen years old. Last seen by Elizabeth Tipping and Nora Taylor at 10 Grosvenor Place; she had been 'borrowed' to work at the party for the evening. Employed at 11 Wilton Crescent. Personal items, including bank book, were left behind in her shared room.

Description: Five foot five inches. Brown hair, blue eyes. Last seen wearing a plain maid's dress of black with a white apron; her straw cloche hat and a green duster coat had been taken from the peg. Black boots. No distinguishing marks.

She could be anybody.

Mother and father live in Osmotherly, Yorkshire. They initially reported her missing after her employer — Lady Delaney — said she had not returned from the party. They have not heard from her. They have persistently requested that a search be maintained.

There then followed a list of her eight brothers and sisters, of which only three had been successfully contacted by the police so far. Miss Rose Morgan was not quite the youngest, there being one more sister after her still living at home, but the rest were older and married, and all living in Yorkshire. The local police were supposed to be following them up and sending back reports but Guy suspected they were being slow. It was likely that none of them had telephone lines and had to be sent letters; just as likely that they were either illiterate or saw no need to go to the effort of writing to the police that there was nothing to say. When Guy had tried to talk about the case with Stiles he'd dismissed it. 'You'll probably find her in Gretna Green,' he'd said. 'She's got a chap, don't you worry about that. Find him and case closed.'

But there was no sign of a boyfriend and Guy had spoken to

all of the maids she'd worked with at Wilton Crescent, as well as the housekeeper, a stern old bird with eyes that looked like steel fishhooks, and none of them could recall her mentioning anyone. Nor had she ever spoken of any desire to leave her job and go elsewhere.

However, there had been one maid, a slip of a girl called Lucy, who had mentioned something that jarred. And it was this that made Guy inclined to stay on this case and not give it up as just another missing person, where the person was all too likely to show up in a Brighton hotel with a seedy older man she'd been in bed with for a fortnight.

'She'd been learning French,' Lucy had told him. 'She'd never say why. I asked her and there was no holiday she told me of or anything like that. You'd just hear her repeating these French words over and over, while she swept the floor or scrubbed the dishes. She had a little pocketbook she would look at from time to time, where I suppose the words were written down but I never got to have a look. She was embarrassed about it, I think.'

A girl of no particular consequence, a maid who had in all likelihood run off of her own accord precisely because she didn't want to be found, was not important enough for Guy to be able to have any checks made at the ports. He had tried to get passenger lists from the ferries but they were reluctant when he didn't know on which day she had travelled. The brisk clerk at the end of the telephone had pointed out that there would be thousands of names for them to search through and who was to say there wouldn't be several R. Morgans? Guy had pushed him nonetheless to check the lists but no answer had come.

Instead, he was going to have to look elsewhere to find the path that Miss Rose Morgan had travelled on and it crossed his mind that there was one person who might be able to help him. Someone who had been on the servant grapevine and knew something of the acts a desperate woman might take. Louisa Cannon. The only problem was, as far as Guy was concerned, Louisa was a missing person, too.

CHAPTER EIGHT

⁓⸾⸾⸾⸾⸾

At Victoria Station, Louisa walked thirty yards behind Mr and Mrs Guinness as they were led to their carriage on the Golden Arrow boat train. She felt rather shy of them now, even if Mr Guinness – she couldn't quite say 'Bryan', even in her own head – was very courteous to her, as he was to everyone. But they were newlyweds, the last thing they must have wanted was someone on their tail, even if Louisa had been expressly asked to come with them. In spite of these mixed feelings, Louisa was thoroughly enjoying the thought of the journey ahead of her. She would not be on the Golden Arrow, the all-first-class boat train that the Guinnesses would travel on. Louisa had instead a third-class ticket on a parallel service. There would be a train to Dover, then a ferry, before the final leg from Calais to Paris. It would be extraordinarily quick too: it was only five o'clock in the afternoon, and they would be in Paris for breakfast. Louisa's transport might not have had the luxuries her new mistress would be enjoying – the white tablecloths and waiters, the dressing for dinner and the bed made with real linen – but it was *travel* nonetheless. Merely the sight of a changing view, the knowledge that she would be crossing water and waking to a country that spoke another language gave Louisa a sensation as nerve-making and thrilling as the feeling of falling in love described in novels.

On the platform there were two short red carpets and gold rope hanging between two stands to mark the Guinness's carriage door, which made Diana squeak with pleasure. As she stepped up, she turned back to wave to Louisa and gave a broad smile: 'We'll see you in Gay Paree!'

Louisa gave a brief wave in return and once she had satisfied herself that every piece of their luggage had been counted in correctly, was shown to the carriage where her mistress would be sleeping. She unpacked the overnight case, setting out the contents in the narrow bathroom for their own private use and finally disembarked to walk to another platform for her own train. On board, she sat with her back to the engine and revelled in the comfort of time alone with nothing to do and nowhere else to be. Louisa pulled out her book of short stories by E. M. Forster and settled back to watch the scenery change. By the time they had arrived in Paris she had read not a single word.

Rather than staying in a hotel, the Guinnesses were spending their honeymoon in the family *appartement*, an understated name for the colony of rooms that centred around a courtyard, albeit hidden modestly from the view of rue de Poitiers. Louisa knew that Diana was ecstatic to return to Paris, a place in which she had spent three months alone the year before she married. She had boarded in a house run by two elderly sisters who were not so severe that she couldn't walk down the road by herself to visit the painter Helleu or go for violin lessons, a blissful freedom that had made her quite giddy. Diana had been sent by her mother to learn the language and culture. 'Learn seduction more like,' Nancy had teased. Diana had hit her on the arm for that but the truth was that Diana had been banned from returning to Paris after she had come home for Easter, when she left her diary open in the drawing room while she was out on a walk. When Lady Redesdale discovered the entry recounting her trip to the cinema alone with a young man, all hell had broken loose. The other sisters, naturally, had been furious. 'How could you be so idiotic as to leave a diary out?' they had cried, for Diana's punishment meant they would all be under suspicion.

To return as a married woman was quite a coup. Not only that, but she was rich. Louisa wasn't sure that Diana understood how rich she was. She'd hardly been poor, after all, living in the beauty of Asthall Manor in the Cotswolds. But while Lord Redesdale and his wife were thrifty rather than mean, Louisa knew the wages of the governesses were paid for out of eggs sold each week, and the girls' clothes were all home-made by their own dressmaker, who was a competent seamstress but hardly Coco Chanel. Louisa knew how rich Mr Guinness was because that was the stuff servants' gossip was made of. 'Mr Guinness's father is only the third son of the Earl of Iveagh,' a maid had whispered to her in the kitchens at Grosvenor Place, 'but he was the richest man in Ireland. Just think of all the black stuff they drink over there, and himself's earning a pretty penny each time!' Rumours abounded about castles in Ireland and how much money the couple had been endowed as a wedding present, let alone the small fortune their new house must have cost. Yet Louisa was sure that none of this was why Diana had married her husband. For while the Mitford girls had often complained about their parents' parsimony – Nancy, particularly, griped about her annual stipend and how she had to pay for dressmakers, birthday presents and taxis out of it – they none of them truly cared about money, certainly not enough to try and go out to earn it. And talk of husbands was always focused on falling in love with 'the one', whether he be a prince or a pauper; there was never an idea of marrying for money. She supposed they assumed whatever they needed would always be there in some fashion, with all the confidence their class gave them. Unlike Louisa, they had never experienced true poverty.

On the other hand, Louisa wasn't entirely convinced that Diana had married in order to be with her husband either.

Once they had settled in, Diana summoned Louisa to her in the pretty morning room. The house, though it had been decorated by Diana's mother-in-law, thankfully bore none of the hallmarks of Lady Evelyn's medieval mania. Instead, the interiors were light, with dove-grey satin curtains and pale yellow walls. Louisa came through the door and observed Diana adjusting her position as she sat at the *bureau*, smoothing out her skirt and pushing her shoulders back. She looked graceful and confident, as she always did, if also a touch self-conscious. But, then, she was only eighteen years old.

'Oh, there you are!' Diana said with relief, though Louisa had only been rung for minutes earlier. 'How was your journey?'

'Very pleasant, thank you, ma'am,' said Louisa. She may have been several years older but she was determined to do things absolutely by the book now that her mistress was married.

'Oh, you needn't—' Diana started, and then broke off, as if

reviewing this. She abandoned the sentence. 'I just thought I'd let you know that I'll be spending the day with Mr Guinness, and we're going out tonight. I'll wear the black and white skirt and jacket, if you could iron the pink shirt?'

'Of course.'

'Tomorrow I'm going to go shopping, and I'd like you to come with me. Mr Guinness will stay here.'

Louisa nodded. Abruptly, a formality between them had sprung up, as if something in the wedding vows had changed the terms of their relationship too, and she wasn't sure if she could, or should, dispel it. It was probably only down to nerves on either side but if they didn't get rid of it now they'd be stuck with it for ever. Louisa decided to take a risk.

'All this is rather breathtaking, isn't it?' she stage-whispered, with a wave at their surroundings and a smile. Lady Redesdale would never have stood for it, Nanny Blor would be shocked and Louisa's heart stopped briefly while she waited for Diana's response. There was silence while Diana looked at her without expression, and then she suddenly laughed and clapped her hands once. She was the cat who hadn't got the cream so much as the entire dairy.

'I know, Lou-Lou! Isn't it? It's all perfectly *divine*.'

Something Louisa hadn't quite accounted for was the respect she would be shown by other servants as Mrs Guinness's lady's maid. She was addressed by them as Mademoiselle Cannon, which she found she rather liked. Otherwise, it was a little lonely in the house, as Louisa spoke no French and the other servants seemed reluctant to speak to her beyond showing her where she could hand-wash her mistress's underclothes, and signalling that it was time for breakfast. Perhaps they spoke no English. In light of this and in spite of the rather bitter wind outside, after luncheon and having ironed the shirt, she decided to go for a walk. After all, she was in Paris! She must make the most of it.

Only a couple of streets away was the embankment of the River Seine and Louisa walked along there for a while admiring the chic of the French women with tiny shorn poodles at the end of long leads, the funny flat hats of the policemen and the cafés full of men smoking and arguing. In the sky, from practically any angle it seemed, was the Eiffel Tower, the tallest and most impressive structure Louisa had ever seen. She wasn't sure she'd dare to go to the very top – wouldn't it be very cold? Down on the ground, every little thing felt different, from the texture of the pavement to the air itself, an intoxicating blend of Gauloises cigarettes and freshly baked baguettes. Even the horns that blasted from the traffic seemed to play a different note. Being so far from anyone she knew emboldened Louisa, and she turned away from the river when she saw a sign for the rue des Beaux Arts, which Nancy had told her was the heart of the Left Bank. This, Nancy had added, was the preserve of the artists, musicians and jazz singers; the very thought of it excited Louisa. Even though it was the afternoon everything seemed shut, so there were no shops to browse in. Instead she watched the young men and women who walked by, bearing the look of bohemians; at least she supposed that was what they were. She hadn't seen so many of them grouped together in London, not even in Chelsea. The men wore jaunty hats and long silk scarves, the women were draped in velvet coats and had wide patterned headbands that knotted at the side, with dark made-up eyes. Louisa could never be one of them quite but she had always enjoyed the brief freedom that jazz gave her when she danced to a band in a nightclub, allowing her to throw off the inhibition that she carried too heavily elsewhere. This glimpse gave her, she felt, a certain understanding of who these people were. And she certainly felt closer to them than to the stuffy enclaves of the very rich and grand. Paris felt like a place where she might have an adventure.

She was right.

CHAPTER NINE

'Just telephone and ask them where she is.'

The voice was fractionally impatient but also, Guy knew, full of warmth towards him. He was sitting with his friend Mary Moon, now Mary Conlon and married to his best friend, Harry, but Guy could never think of Mary as anything other than by the name she'd had when they had first worked together three years ago. The two of them were in a café in Sloane Street, catching a cup of tea before they both went back on shift. Mary was still a constable, while Guy had been promoted to the CID. He sometimes felt a pang of guilt about that but she'd kindly told him she was grateful to hang on to her job at all. A new rule had just come in saying that policewomen must resign on marriage, but because she was already married she had narrowly escaped it. 'Thank goodness. We can't live on Harry's practically non-existent wages, I've got to work,' she'd laughed at the time.

'Where's Harry playing now?' asked Guy.

'At the Hundred Club most nights, he's with a decent band

there but they don't get enough bookings. He's just auditioned for Hutch though, so fingers crossed for that.' She gave him a cool look. 'Don't change the subject.'

'I haven't, but I'm not going to telephone. If Louisa wanted to see me, she'd have let me know by now.'

Mary thought about this for a bit. She'd known Louisa a little, when the three of them had become caught up in a case involving the gangleader Alice Diamond and her Forty Thieves. They'd been on edge around each other at first, vying for Guy's attention, but this had soon changed to mutual respect. 'She's proud, Guy,' said Mary. 'If she was in trouble, I have a feeling she wouldn't want you to know. The last thing a girl like Louisa wants is to be rescued.'

'No, no, of course not. The thing is, I was hoping that she could rescue me. For this missing maid case, that's all.'

'Why don't you tell me about it? Lord knows I'd like to think about something other than my usual cases.'

'Missing cats?'

'Sometimes yes, but it's been rather more grim than that lately. There's a new school of thought that women who have been assaulted should have a policewoman in the room, while they're questioned. I don't do more than hold their hands but you hear such awful things.' She gave a shudder. 'So, go on then. What's this one?'

Guy pulled out his notebook and read out the vital statistics, such as they were. 'Not much to go on,' he said. 'Average height and looks, no distinguishing marks. Aside from the fact that she was last seen on the night of the maid's death – which the inquest concluded was nothing more than an accident – then there was no apparent reason to leave, no apparent person to meet. Left her bank book behind. Hasn't been in touch with her family.'

'A kidnapping isn't likely.'

'Exactly,' said Guy. 'Everyone thinks she'll turn up in a hotel room, having run off for an affair. And maybe they're right. But there's something about it that makes me want to dig a bit deeper.'

'Can you say what that something is?'

'A policeman's hunch,' shrugged Guy. 'One maid who worked with her, Lucy, talked about her learning French in a very secretive way.'

'Perhaps she was on her way to meet a Frenchman in Paris. She's probably having a jolly old time with onions round her neck, cycling along the banks of the Seine.'

'Yes, perhaps. That's the trouble with missing persons. They don't always think of themselves as missing.' Guy gave a sigh and pushed his chair back. They'd finished their tea. 'I need to do something though. I want a case of my own.'

'Can I ask who interviewed Lucy?'

'I did,' said Guy.

'Was she young?'

'Yes, fifteen or sixteen years old I should think.'

Mary put her hands in her lap. 'I hope you don't mind me saying this but sometimes a young girl will find it difficult to talk to a grown-up man from the police. However nice they are,' she said hurriedly, as she saw Guy take offence. 'Why don't I talk to her? See if she says anything else. If the two of them worked together closely enough for Lucy to hear her muttering in French, I wouldn't be surprised if they had confided in each other.'

'I agree with you, as it happens.'

'So may I be your official uniform assistant for a CID case?'

Guy was amused by her eagerness. 'Yes, you may.'

'Good, now we've arranged that, ring Lord Whatsisname and find out where Louisa is. Whatever you say, I know that's what you want. I'm going now, got to get back to the beat.' Mary got up and touched him affectionately on the arm as she left, letting in a blast of wintry air when she pushed the door open.

CHAPTER TEN

Paris was less of a whirlwind than a typhoon. During the day, Diana had been encouraged by Bryan to shop for her new life as Mrs Guinness; Louisa realized that the shortcomings of her mistress's previously home-made clothes were made all too abundantly clear when set against the *haute couture* of Paris. And just as one can never paint one room in a house because it makes all the others look instantly shabby, one new dress led to new shoes, new bags, new evening coats, new scarves and then on to new day dresses, new nightclothes, new underclothes and ever further on into the depths of the wardrobe. Diana's much-admired slender figure was eagerly robed by even the haughtiest of *ateliers* and Louisa soon began to enjoy sitting beside her as the mannequins walked up and down before them, displaying every angle of the latest fashions. Diana also appreciated Louisa's inside knowledge on seams and darts from her work in the Mayfair shop, checking the quality of the lining or the firmness of a button-stitch.

On one particular day, Diana and Louisa went to see

someone Diana had been told about as being a very grand couturier, Louise Boulanger. She had a salon at 3 rue de Berri, just off the Champs-Elysées. Mme Boulanger had appraised Diana's figure with narrowed eyes, before she stalked off and returned with a single dress on a hanger. 'This one,' she said in a thick accent. 'A sample but it might fit you.'

Louisa and Diana went to the dressing room to try it on, with Diana giggling. 'Just one dress? Normally everyone tries to offload half their wares on to me.'

'I think that means this one dress might cost as much as half of all the wares of anywhere else,' said Louisa. The two of them had never mentioned money but the heavily perfumed atmosphere and the sheer weight of the expectation had overcome her.

In a moment, her mistress emerged, a pleased smile on her face. The dress was short, stopping at Diana's knees, closely fitted and made of a pure white, lightly ribbed taffeta. At the back an immense sky-blue bow hung down from the base of her spine to the ground. It would need to be fitted and ordered before it would be hers but there was no doubt: with this, Diana had discovered the power of clothes. It wasn't long before Diana had joined the elevated ranks of the best-dressed women of the French capital.

After this encounter, Diana had the confidence to buy from the very best, one of whom was an Englishman with a French name, Mr Molyneux. He was in demand, however, so Diana asked her friend Kate Mulloney to pull some strings and get her an appointment more quickly. The three of them met at the salon, though Louisa quickly saw her role was to stand at the side while Kate bossed Diana around, pointing out the dresses she ought to order. It might have been rude except that Mrs Mulloney clearly had a style that was both chic and daring, with her own short black bob that shone like sealskin and usually wearing mannish trousers in bright colours. While Louisa was standing by the dressing room, waiting for Kate and Diana, a young assistant came through. She started to say something but then seemed to see something in Louisa's face that startled her. Abruptly, she left the room and Louisa didn't see her again.

When the appointment was over, they went outside and saw a handsome man standing on the pavement, smoking a cigarette, a wry smile on his face. 'What are you looking at us like that for?' said Kate.

'Can't a man wait for his wife without showing a little impatience? You said you would be out twenty minutes ago.' But he didn't look displeased.

'I'm so sorry, Shaun,' apologized Diana, and Louisa remembered seeing him talking to Clara and Nancy at the party last summer. She hadn't thought about that night for some time and something else pulled at her mind but she couldn't quite think what it was. Then again, he looked very like the actor Gary Cooper from the film she'd seen a few weeks ago. Perhaps it was no more than that and she was almost cross with herself for even noticing.

As soon as the dress from Boulanger arrived, Diana wore it to a dinner and from the exclamations Louisa could hear as she walked into the drawing room, she knew it had electrified the small crowd that awaited her. Nor was it unusual for there to be an audience awaiting the star of the show to arrive. In the days since they had got to Paris, there had been little sign of the newlyweds spending time alone. Reams of people came to the house for cocktails at six o'clock, and they would leave in great gangs to go to dinner before taking in a show and then on to the clubs. Louisa was never quite certain of what time they came home – Diana had relieved her of the usual lady's maid's duty of undressing her and preparing her for bed – but her mistress did not like to be woken before noon, when Louisa would take her breakfast tray in bed. When Louisa did catch glimpses of her mistress and husband together, they were never less than affectionate – Mr Guinness, particularly, would look at his bride with love practically shining out of his eyes – but this was a honeymoon they appeared to be sharing with half of the city.

So perhaps, when Louisa saw him, she shouldn't have been as surprised as she was.

It was their fourth afternoon in Paris, and Louisa had dropped into the drawing room, the one that overlooked the courtyard with silvery velvet sofas and a vast antique mirror that ran the length of one wall reflecting the windows. She had only intended to be there for a minute, looking for a pair of Diana's evening gloves which had gone missing, when she happened to glance at the mirror and saw the image of Luke Meyer, standing very still by the window watching her, not looking at the view.

'Beg pardon, Mr Meyer, I didn't see you there,' said Louisa, feeling uncomfortable for reasons she couldn't quite discern.

Luke took his hands out of his pockets and laughed. 'That was funny, giving you a shock like that.'

Was he mocking her? 'Have a good evening, sir,' she said and made to leave the room.

'No, Louisa, don't.' He had grabbed her by the elbow and his hold was firm, a little too much so. She shook him off. She was finding all this very bewildering, he didn't seem the same as when they had met at the wedding.

He dropped her arm and flushed. 'I'm sorry. I wasn't laughing at you, it's just your face—' But he saw Louisa's hackles rise again and held his hands up in surrender. 'Please. Can we start again? And call me Luke. That is, if I may call you Louisa?'

Louisa dropped her defences. For the moment. 'Yes, you may call me Louisa.'

'Thank you. I say, do you know how to get a drink around here? It's six o'clock somewhere in the world, after all.'

Louisa went to the drinks cabinet and opened it – there were crystal decanters of every spirit, from the clear waters of gin and vodka to the varied ambers of malt whisky. Engraved silver labels hung on delicate chains around the necks of each one. 'Would you mind if you helped yourself? I'm afraid I don't know how to pour these.'

Luke carried on talking as he clinked the ice cubes into the shaker. 'What's the news, then?'

Louisa had half an ear out for noises beyond the drawing room door. As nice as Mr Guinness was, she didn't think she should be found chatting with one of their guests. 'Oh, nothing much. They *are* on honeymoon.' She felt she should emphasise this, even though the last time she had seen Luke had been at the wedding. It wasn't as if he wouldn't know.

'True, true. What about you, then? Have they let you out to see the sights of Paris?' Luke had poured himself a generous gin martini by the looks of it and was taking his first sip.

'I'm here to work,' Louisa said proudly then wondered why she was taking the moral high ground. She exhaled as she thought about the pleasures of the last few days. 'It's . . . well, it's wonderful,' she said. 'When did you get here?'

'This afternoon. But I'm not staying here, I'm in a hotel nearby. They're not expecting me.' The look on her face must have alarmed him. 'Don't worry – I've got a letter of introduction to keep it all quite proper, from my aunt.' Luke indicated to the low table in front of the fireplace, where a letter addressed to The Hon. Mrs Guinness lay on top of a black box, with a silk purple ribbon tied around it. 'I've come with some chocolates, too,' he said. 'A sort of bribe, I suppose.'

'I see,' said Louisa, though she didn't really. Diana would never eat the chocolates at any rate; she'd already learned that her mistress's narrow figure was carefully maintained. She might try to sample one herself at some point, Diana almost certainly wouldn't notice it. In any case, what was Luke bribing Diana for? Except – he worked for a newspaper, didn't he? Would Diana not mind a diary writer on her honeymoon?

There were footsteps coming along the hall. 'I'd better go,' said Louisa. 'Have a nice evening.'

'Perhaps I'll see you later?'

'Perhaps.'

The next day, when Louisa took Diana her tray at noon, she found her mistress in a chatty mood. Bryan always left the bedroom well before Louisa's arrival, to have his breakfast downstairs. Setting the tray on a table, she drew the curtains to reveal the bright winter sunshine, the sort that could fool you into thinking that spring was round the corner, though the snowdrops had barely begun to push through.

'Good morning, Lou-Lou,' said Diana. She was sitting up in

bed, her blonde hair pushed back off her face, as she reached for an emerald satin dressing gown that had been dropped by the side of the bed. She wrapped it around herself before adjusting her position, ready to take her breakfast. 'Oh, goody. Boiled egg. Though I'm never quite sure these French chefs can do it as well as Mrs Stobie at home. No soldiers, for a start.'

'What shall I get ready for you today, ma'am?' This had become their routine.

'I'm going to meet Mr Meyer this afternoon. He's promised to show me the most filthy pictures in the Louvre,' she said in a kidding tone, and Louisa was reminded again how young she was and how little of the world she had seen. 'So I think perhaps the yellow dress, with the matching coat.'

Louisa went to the wardrobe – or *armoire* as she had been told by Diana it was called in France – and started to pull out the newly acquired clothes, together with the stockings and biscuit-coloured shoes that Diana wore with nearly all her day outfits.

'Bryan's spending the day with his grandfather, the Pocket Adonis. Everyone calls him that because he's achingly good looking but *tiny*,' she carried on, her happy chatter and excitement at what lay ahead perhaps making her forget her usual form of only calling her husband 'Mr Guinness' in front of the servants. Or perhaps they had started to blur the lines of servitude and friendship again, reverting to their previous relationship as nursery maid and child. 'I think you should come with us, Lou-Lou. No one could be safer than Luke. But for appearance's sake, you know how these gossips are.'

'Of course, ma'am. I'd be happy to.' And she would. Louisa had not managed to see inside the Louvre yet and she had heard the *Mona Lisa* was hanging there. Would she be able to tell if the young woman in the painting was smiling or not? Still, she felt she had better check something.

'Mrs Guinness?'

'Oh, I *do* feel a thousand years old when you call me that. Yes, what is it?' Diana scooped up a mouthful of egg yolk with a silver spoon.

'It's not for me to say perhaps but you do know that Mr Meyer is a writer for the *Daily Sketch*?'

'Yes, but you don't need to worry about anything. His aunt is a friend of Muv's, he showed me a letter from her last night. He's perfectly safe, in every way. Besides, I'm not sure I mind too much if he does write anything, there's nothing terribly terrible to report.'

Louisa wasn't particularly assuaged by this but she nodded as if she was and went back to fidgeting with a loose thread on Diana's coat.

Diana gave a yelp. 'Look at the time! Run my bath, Lou-Lou, we should push on. I said I would meet him at two o'clock.' And so it was they hurried to meet Luke who would, it turned out, soon have something 'terribly terrible' to report.

CHAPTER ELEVEN

The Louvre was miles and miles of oil paintings and statues, and after they had seen the *Mona Lisa* – 'She's definitely wretched,' declared Diana, 'how could anyone doubt it?' – and Luke had taken them around the Renaissance galleries, they could only muster half-hearted giggles at the nudity on display. Louisa suspected that Diana was already too sophisticated for this kind of joke in any case. She had followed a few steps behind them, not joining in their conversation, though Luke was kind enough to throw some sympathetic glances her way and even pointed out one or two particularly well-known pieces of art. Louisa was grateful for the visit but she'd rather have been alone, sitting on a bench before the *Mona Lisa* and spending at least an hour or two trying to work out what the secret was that the Italian beauty was hiding from everyone who looked at her. When they turned a corner and saw another long avenue of partially robed statues with various missing arms and legs, Diana gave a sigh.

'This has all been simply divine, darling. But I think now I'd better go back to the house. Bryan will be wondering where I am and I haven't even found out yet what we're doing this evening.' She signalled to Louisa that they would be off. 'Thank you, Luke. It's been . . . *enlightening.*'

Luke looked crestfallen. 'Wait,' he said. 'There's a bar, not far from here. It's not the usual sort but I promise you'll love it.'

Diana hesitated.

'Just a minuscule cocktail?' he pleaded. 'Go on. We can always telephone up Bryan from there, see if he'd join us.'

'Just one drink, then.'

Luke was true to his word – the bar was very close, on a narrow street and hidden behind an innocuous-seeming door that displayed neither sign nor doorbell. Luke pushed it open and they found themselves in a narrow hallway, with a bored-looking girl behind a counter who took some money from him and offered to hang their coats.

'Do you think I should be here?' Louisa whispered to Diana.

'I think I absolutely need you to be here,' Diana whispered back. Her voice was low and urgent but her face remained as composed as ever. They followed Luke down a short flight of stairs and through a beaded curtain, out into a room that was no bigger than the library at Asthall, only with lower ceilings and black-painted walls. Though it was dusky outside, it was only four o'clock in the afternoon, so it was somewhat disconcerting to see a number of young women walking around in short evening dresses, their faces heavily made-up, sequinned headbands on brassy hair. There was a short bar along one wall and a few men leaned up against it, their backs to the barmaid. They were, thankfully, not old men but rather dapper young ones in wide-legged trousers and spats. 'Dandyish, aren't they?' said Diana to Louisa, preferring to whisper to her, rather than to Luke, it seemed. He had pushed ahead and found a table for them to sit at, with a lamp on it that had a red shade. A piano played a jazzy tune in the background but there was a strangely heavy atmosphere, as if everyone was waiting for something to happen. Nobody was talking much, and Louisa realized there were no couples in the room – that is, the few women there were, were walking about and the men either stood or sat, watching them with lazy eyes.

She and Diana exchanged a look, which clearly showed they both wished to get out but Louisa also knew Diana wouldn't want to lose face. If Luke was trying to shock her, or trip her up on her lack of worldliness, she wouldn't give him the satisfaction. Years of being goaded by Nancy had trained her to keep her mettle.

They ordered Old Fashioneds for Diana and Luke, and a coffee for Louisa (which came in the most miniature cup she'd ever seen outside of Debo's dolls' house and was thickly black). Plates of sandwiches were put down, which Luke and Diana didn't touch; Louisa ate two to be polite, but they were fish-paste and not very nice. They were only there, explained Luke, because alcohol could only be served at that hour with food, something to do with the Parisian licensing laws.

None of them said much else but just as the silence had turned awkward, there was a sudden change in the piano's tune, and a pair of red curtains were pulled back to reveal a round stage. A spotlight came on and there was a shuffle in the room as the men turned to face it, and the women sat down or melted away. To the piano's honky-tonk notes a woman came into the light, shimmering in a cheap beaded dress and see-sawing a pink feather boa across her shoulders, tapping out a few jazzy steps with her feet. The make-up she wore was caked on so that the skin's own texture couldn't be detected, the mouth was strangely unsoft beneath the red lipstick and the eyes were dull beneath the heavily kohled rims and drawn-on eyebrows. After a minute or two of this, Louisa started to feel very uncomfortable. There was no microphone, so the woman wasn't going to sing. What was she going to do? She caught Luke giving her and Diana sideways glances. He knew what was coming, she was sure of it, and she was pretty sure, too, that whatever it was, was designed to outrage them. Diana's face remained admirably blank, though her cool blue eyes were fixed on the dancer.

The feather boa was dropped to the floor and a muted cheer went up from the men. The spotlight had thrown them all into deeper shadows – the red light from the lamps did nothing to illuminate the scene around them. Louisa felt a heightened frisson shiver through the audience and then she saw the woman had turned around and was dropping the straps of her dress.

'Mrs Guinness,' Louisa whispered. 'I think we should go.'

'Shh,' said Diana.

Luke looked at them and smiled.

The dress had fallen to the floor now and the woman kicked it to the side. She was wearing stockings and a girdle that bound her tightly from chest to upper thighs. A man reached out and stroked one of her legs and she smacked him away playfully but when another man tried to do the same, a hulk in black tie came out of the shadows and pulled him away with force. It couldn't be possible but the lights seemed to go lower, and Louisa watched the tips of cigarettes glow in the dark, hardly able to see the hands that held them. The music got faster and the men cheered again. This time, the girdle was being rolled down inch by inch, the dancer deliberately tantalising her audience. Louisa thought she was going to be sick but whether it was the show, the cigarette smoke or the fishpaste sandwiches, she didn't know. Luke was excited now, leaning forward, grinning and clasping his hands as if to stop himself from jumping up and waving them in the air.

Further down the girdle rolled. Louisa looked – how could she help it? The chest was bare now, completely flat and pale, so thin the shadows of the ribs could be seen. Faster played the music, brighter glowed the tips and finally as the last of the girdle was rolled down the woman had her back to the audience, showing her naked white behind. Louisa looked at Diana, who gave nothing away but at least didn't look frightened. Finally, there was a roar from the crowd and demands of '*Montre nous!*'

Show them what?

As she turned around to cheers and the stamping of feet, Louisa and Diana finally understood. The woman was a man.

CHAPTER TWELVE

G uy tried to call Lord Redesdale at Swinbrook House, where according to the directory they now lived (they'd moved, then, since he'd last seen them all, and he was rather sorrowful for a second; Asthall Manor had been his idea of the perfect country house, all pale grey stones and rolling fields around). It was the housekeeper, Mrs Windsor, who answered. She recognized Guy, and hadn't hesitated when he asked if there was a forwarding address for Louisa. So perhaps his letters had been forwarded on and Louisa hadn't replied. He wasn't sure if that made him feel better or worse.

'She's in Paris, accompanying Mr and Mrs Guinness on their honeymoon,' said Mrs Windsor. 'They're expected to stay a few weeks. If you have a pencil, I can give you the address there?' Guy took it down – 12 rue de Poitiers – and before he could finish thanking her, she had rung off. Guy tucked the piece of paper in his pocket and told himself to forget about it.

*

A few days after Mary had urged Guy on, and having made the necessary arrangements, the two of them went to 11 Wilton Crescent to interview Lucy, the maid who had worked with Rose Morgan. It was only a short walk from the station and the street was typically grand, with a wide curve of cream-painted houses, each front door glossy black, with perfectly polished and buffed Bentleys and Rolls-Royces parked outside. 'I wouldn't leave if this was where I was living,' said Mary as they approached the front door.

'Depends on the promise of what you thought you might get instead, doesn't it?' countered Guy.

They knocked and the door was answered quickly by a butler, keen to shoo them inside. He muttered something about the reputation of the house with the police turning up and hurried them below stairs to his office, where they waited while he looked for Lucy. Guy and Mary took in their surroundings but there was nothing out of the ordinary; a sparsely furnished room that somehow did not invite them to sit down on the two available chairs and make themselves feel at home. Before the butler had returned, however, a young girl of about twelve, with long hair tied back in a ribbon and wearing a dress with a sailor's collar, came in unaccompanied. She greeted them with a handshake and a serious look on her face that made Guy feel rather sad for her somehow.

'Hello,' she said. 'I'm Muriel Delaney. I know I ought to wait to be introduced but Jones is looking for Lucy and I know you're looking for Rose. Have you found her? Have you good news?'

Mary stepped forward and shook her hand. 'Hello, Miss Delaney. I'm Constable Conlon but you may call me Mary. I'm very sorry to tell you that we have no news of Rose but we are still looking for her. That's why we're here to talk to Lucy, in case she might have remembered something that could be useful to us.'

Muriel nodded but her face dropped and tears welled in her eyes. She blinked them back. 'I don't understand why no one has talked to me,' she burst out passionately. 'Rose was my best friend.'

Mary and Guy exchanged a look. He took a step backwards.

'You may talk to me now. We'd be very interested to know any thoughts you may have.' Mary smiled at her warmly.

'Are your parents here?' Guy felt he ought to check that everything was in order; he had telephoned earlier to arrange the appointment with Lucy so the family should know the police were coming.

'We lost Father last year,' said Muriel. 'Mother is resting upstairs. She often rests at this time. It's quite all right, Jones will let her know you are here.'

She gave Guy a sidelong glance and edged closer to Mary. 'You're taking the female perspective, are you?'

Mary placed her hand on the girl's shoulder. 'Yes, you're quite right. That's exactly it.'

'My governess was a suffragette,' said Muriel. 'She's been teaching me all about it.'

'Shall we sit down?' said Mary, pulling a chair around from one side of the butler's desk, so that they could sit together.

Guy took this as his cue to move to the window, where he stood looking out of it with his hands in his pockets, trying as much as possible not to appear to be listening in. Of course, he heard every word.

Mary took out her pocketbook and a pencil, and the girl looked pleased at this. She was being taken seriously.

'When did you last see Rose?'

'Before she went to the party. She had been lent out by Mother. It gave Rose a bit of extra money, you see, and that was good for our . . .' She stopped.

'For your what?' Mary spoke softly.

Muriel was silent.

'Miss Muriel, did she tell you where she was going?' There was a silence. Guy did not dare to turn around.

Mary tried again. 'Rose has been missing for a long time now, and nobody has heard from her. We're worried, as you can imagine. But that doesn't mean we don't think we can find her and help her, if she needs it. Is there anything at all she said to you that might have indicated where she was going?'

Muriel spoke in a small voice. 'She was going to catch the train to Dover.'

'Dover. That's where the ferries go to France. Was she planning on a trip to France?'

'I don't know why she didn't take me with her,' Muriel burst out. 'We were going to set up our own dance show together, in Paris. Rose and Lily Leaf, we were going to be called. We'd been practising our steps for ages. But then she left me behind. And now I'm here. On my own.'

Mary comforted Muriel. Guy was impressed. She'd been right, he couldn't have interviewed the child in the same way. 'Was there any particular reason for going to Paris?' she asked. 'Do you know if Rose was going to meet anybody there? A boyfriend perhaps?'

There was a loud sniff. 'No, it was just going to be us. My aunt married a dressmaker over there, he's got a shop. I thought we could go and see her. I knew we could count on her to keep our secret. She's an adventuress, you see.' Guy could hear a hint of pride in the girl's voice.

'Can you remember his name, Muriel?'

Her big eyes blinked. 'No, I can't. It was something beginning with M, I think. Rose wrote it down.' She looked as if she might burst into sobs.

'That's very helpful, thank you,' said Mary, quick to reassure her.

'I was teaching Rose how to read and write, as well as a bit of French,' volunteered the girl. 'She didn't get much schooling when she was growing up, she said. She mostly had to help out on the farm.'

'Ah, I see. I can tell you're a very clever girl, Muriel.' Guy didn't look but he knew the girl would be basking in Mary's praise. Muriel didn't have the air of a child who was told very often how clever she was.

'There's something I want to ask you and I would like you to think very carefully for me, because I think this could help us to understand better what has happened. Do you know of any reason why Rose would leave without telling anyone where she was going, or letting her family know that she was safe?'

Muriel said nothing.

Mary's voice got a little lower, a little warmer. 'I think the two of you were great friends. And I promise she won't be cross with you for telling us anything that was said secretly between you before, because we need to be sure she's absolutely well and safe, you see.'

Muriel shook her head. 'No, there was a man used to come here that she said she didn't like ... But I don't understand why she didn't come back here to see me, before she left. She never said goodbye. She went to work at the other place and that was the last time I saw her.' Tears came down her cheeks and she wiped them away furiously with the flat of her hand.

'Thank you, Muriel, you've been invaluable. When we find Rose, I know she's going to be very grateful to you.'

'Do you think she'll come back to me?' The loneliness caught in the girl's throat as she spoke.

'I'm sure that she will if she can,' said Mary encouragingly. 'We'll certainly let her know that you would like to see her. She's probably been worried that you might be cross with her, for leaving you behind.'

'If you see her, tell her I'm not cross. Tell her I want her to come back,' said Muriel.

Guy turned around then and walked back. 'We'll be off now,' he said and shook hands solemnly with the young girl again. 'Thank you, miss. Most sincerely.'

After the girl had left the room, Lucy had been brought in but even with Mary's gentle questioning she had had nothing further to add, other than to confirm that Rose had been apparently learning French, and that her sudden departure had been surprising. Now they knew this tallied with Muriel's account of her plan with the maid, it seemed that Paris was the place to go if Rose was to be found.

Guy remembered the piece of paper in his pocket with the scribbled address of where Louisa was staying in Paris. Was that what his mother would call 'a sign'? He wondered if he would – or should – try to look her up when he was there. The thought of Sinéad caused a thickness in his throat. But deeper inside him he could feel the pull on his heart from a thread that only Louisa held.

CHAPTER THIRTEEN

Louisa, Luke and Diana returned to the Guinness apartment in an atmosphere that was hard to pin down. Louisa felt as if she had drunk a bottle of champagne then witnessed a car crash. There was a sharpness, a sense of danger in the air, and yet it was blurred by the strangeness of Paris and of the bar they had been in, both having so quickly followed the beauty of the paintings at the Louvre. She felt very far from home.

Luke was quieter than before but he kept giggling. Nerves, probably. Diana hadn't made it clear yet exactly what she thought of what she had seen but as they approached the front door, she said, without looking at either of them: 'I don't think we'll speak of this to Bryan.'

'It can be our secret,' said Luke, and Diana shot a look at him then of intense loathing.

'Don't ask me to keep secrets from my husband,' she said, sounding very much like her mother. 'It will come to no good. But I see no reason to make him dislike you so I suggest we do not talk about it again.'

Luke had flushed at this and said no more, not even to excuse himself as he might have done. Diana then turned to Louisa: 'I think you had better go in by the servants' entrance, don't you?'

Louisa's breath was stopped at this. 'Yes, of course,' she managed to say. She had known she wouldn't go through the front door with the two of them, she just hadn't expected to be so forcefully reminded. She left them without saying goodbye and walked fast around the corner to the back entrance, where three quick knocks were responded to by a surly maid who let her in without so much as a '*bonjour*'. It was the final straw: Louisa ran upstairs to her room and lay on her bed, not crying but feeling an ache behind her eyes that was almost as exhausting.

Louisa didn't lie there for long. After only twenty minutes, the maid who had let her in was knocking on the bedroom door, telling her that 'Madame Guinness rings 'er bell' and Louisa had to go and see what her mistress wanted. The events of the afternoon seemed to be long ago already, though the after-effects of the fishpaste sandwiches were disturbingly present. Louisa made her way through the back stairs and up to Diana's bedroom, a haven of cool colours and a four-poster bed. Diana was sitting at her dressing table, applying face powder.

'I need to change for the evening,' she said, as if nothing had happened between them. Perhaps she didn't think it had. 'I was thinking perhaps the Boulanger. I know I've worn it twice already but we have the Mulloneys joining us this evening, and they haven't seen it yet. Might you be able to do my hair differently? That will change the effect for Bryan at least.'

Louisa tried to speak but the words stuck in her throat, so she nodded and went to fetch the white dress. Fortunately, Diana had worn it indoors only, so the long bow that fell to the ground was still clean. She selected a white fur stole for Diana to wear with it if they left the house, and a silver clutch bag. In silence, Diana undressed and handed her the clothes she had worn that day, then stepped into her gown and stood still, waiting for Louisa to fasten the hooks-and-eyes at the back. Then Diana resumed her seat at the dressing table and handed Louisa two hair clips studded with diamanté, which Louisa slid into the spun-gold hair. They had sharp pins and she pricked her finger without realizing. There was no pain, and it was so swift that it was only as she put her finger to her mouth that Louisa realized she had spilled a drop of blood on her mistress's head. She decided not to mention it. The flashes she had seen of Diana's temper did not tempt her.

When Diana had applied her lipstick, she put it into the bag and then turned around to face Louisa. She started to say something and then stopped, as if changing her mind. Had she been about to apologize? It looked like it. But it wasn't what she said.

'We're only going to dine out tonight, there's no show. I don't think we'll be back too late. Wait up for me.'

'Of course, ma'am,' said Louisa.

After Diana had gone downstairs to the drawing room, Louisa made her way to the kitchen. Supper for the servants would only be served once Mr and Mrs Guinness and their guests had left for the evening but her stomach would not be stilled and she was hoping to find some bread and butter she could snatch from under the watchful eye of the chef. He wasn't too keen on anything other than the strictly allocated foods making their way into the servants' stomachs – unless it was his own, judging by the large protuberance that drooped over his tied apron string. But when Louisa came in, the chef was happily busy fussing over dough that was presumably meant for the breakfast next morning. With his back to the rest of the kitchen, she could steal into the pantry for the bread. Only she was caught off-guard when she saw that Luke was in the kitchen, too.

'What are you doing here?' she asked, before she could stop herself.

'I was hoping to find you.'

She felt flattered for a moment but quashed the feeling. 'Why?'

'I felt bad about earlier. I shouldn't have taken you both there. I just thought it would be funny. Something different.'

'She's younger than you think,' said Louisa, keeping her voice low in case any of the other servants were listening in. 'Not as worldly as she seems.'

'I know, I know.' Luke ran his fingers through his hair, which had grown longer; thick chestnut curls were beginning to form. 'My aunt would be furious.'

'Does she need to find out?'

Luke laughed at this. 'No, you're quite right. You're not the sort who minds keeping a secret then?'

She wondered what he was really asking here but the tightness in her chest had begun to unfurl. 'No, I'm very good at secrets.'

'That sounds promising. In that case, meet me here later? I'll tell you all about the evening.'

'I have to wait up for Diana as it happens. I'll come down here afterwards.'

'I knew it. No servant can resist gossip from upstairs.'

'Careful, Mr Meyer.' Louisa gave him a stern look she didn't really mean, but he took her hand and kissed it, then ran out through the green baize door and upstairs, where she could not follow him.

CHAPTER FOURTEEN

G uy disembarked from the train at the Gare du Nord feeling slightly dazed. It was not the sights and smells of Paris that made him feel at odds with himself – although that was a part of it – it was the result of twenty-four hours in close proximity with his good friends Harry and Mary Conlon. When Mary had found out about Guy's plan to go to Paris, she press-ganged him into taking them along with him. 'Harry needs to meet the bands that are over there, to get more work as most of them come over to London. And you could do with my help on this case, go on, do admit.'

Guy knew he was powerless.

'What's more, I know you're not allowed to look for this girl officially over there, you've got no international warrant.' This was true, Guy had to allow. The permissions required would take too long to obtain and the longer Rose was missing, the harder it would be to find her.

Mary pressed on. 'If you've got me and Harry with you, it'll look like a holiday.'

'All right!' Guy was laughing now. 'Stop! You're preaching

to the converted. You can come, too. You'll have pay your own way, mind.'

'I know, that's fine. I've got some cash saved. Oh, I could kiss you. Harry will be *so* pleased.'

In truth, Guy was more than happy to have them with him. The thought of going to Paris by himself was a little desolate. Sinéad would never come with him – an unmarried couple in a hotel being another thing nobody would do in Killarney – and he was also a trifle nervous. He couldn't speak the language and it was a huge city: was he up to the task of finding Rose? There wasn't much to indicate that she would be in Paris after all this time – beyond the fact that she'd been learning French and that the girl, Muriel, had said they had talked about her aunt, married to a dressmaker with a shop in Paris. That might have been a starting point but they had no name, only the initial 'M', and if Rose had become a dancer, she could be in any number of clubs. Who was he kidding? It was like looking for a four-leaf clover in an acre of grass.

Guy and Harry had been friends since they had both been rejected for conscription in the war – thanks to Guy's short-sightedness and Harry's asthma – and had both gone on to work for the railway police, in a bid to do something courageous for their country. Guy had remained in the police service but Harry had left and become quite a successful jazz musician. Diminutive in height, comedic alongside Guy's tall frame, he was good-looking enough to be mistaken for a Hollywood actor in shadowy clubs. An asset he had happily traded on until he met Guy's colleague Mary Moon; their romance had flared quickly and the flame still burned bright, two years since their wedding.

Dropping down on to the platform behind him, Mr and

Mrs Conlon looked irritatingly free of any sign of their raucous behaviour, having started their holiday early with a late night on the train. Harry was as neatly dressed as always, like a brand-new pocketbook, and Mary wore a new cloche hat and a beaver-trimmed coat wrapped tightly around her waist. They each carried brown leather cases, containing just enough for two nights. No hotel had been booked but Harry had been told by his fellow band members that they should head to the Montmartre district, where the best jazz clubs were, as well as plenty of rooms cheaply available for the many out-of-town musicians, singers and dancers that flocked there. It might also be the sort of place that Rose Morgan had ended up if she, too, was trying to live off only a few francs.

'Shall we get the Metro to Montmartre?' asked Mary.

'Get the what to the what?' Guy was flummoxed.

'I've been reading up on what to do. The Metro is their underground train system. Montmartre's where we're headed, remember?'

Guy pushed his glasses back up his nose. 'Fine, I'll follow you.'

Harry gave a wry smile. 'A wise decision where my wife is concerned, I've learned.'

Emerging on to the pavement in Montmartre, Guy was assaulted anew by the sounds and smells of Paris. This was, it was clear, the seedier part of the city. There were more cafés and bars than shops, and signs advertising '*les girls*' and '*cabaret*'. Harry took them down a side street and knocked on the door of the first they saw that advertised '*chambres simples et doubles*', and within ten minutes of arriving they had booked two rooms, dumped their cases and headed back out to look for a bar.

'What's a windmill doing in the street?' said Guy, squinting at the peculiar building, apparently sitting on a flat roof. There was no doubting it: a squat wooden structure with four enormous windmills turning.

'That's the Moulin Rouge,' smirked Harry. 'Paris's best cabaret show. Famous place. Old King Edward VII had a jolly old time there, I've heard.'

'*We* won't be going there,' said Mary primly but she winked at her husband as she said it and the two of them tittered. Marriage suited her, thought Guy, she was more at ease with herself somehow, quicker to find things funny. He hoped it would have the same effect on Sinéad.

'No,' said Harry. 'First off I'd like us to go to Le Cirque.' He took a piece of folded paper out of his jacket pocket and opened it. 'It's close to the Moulin, I've got the directions here. After that, we'll try Chez Moutarde.'

'It's pronounced "shay" not "shezz",' said Mary.

'As long as they can pronounce "gin",' said Harry, 'the Frenchies can say "shay" to their heart's content.'

Six bars later, the stars had come out in the black sky and the neon lights of Montmartre were flashing their flamboyant colours. Harry was walking rather slowly, concentrating hard on trying to keep to a straight line, while Mary nudged him in the right direction with her arm hooked through his. Guy had stopped ordering anything other than water after the third bar, so was clear-headed, if tired. He had shown the photograph of Rose Morgan at each place to the staff who worked there but nobody had recognized her.

'She probably doesn't even look like that any more,' said Mary.

'She'll have dyed her hair if she's got any sense. Oof, Harry, do try to stay on the pavement.' She pulled on her husband with an impatient sigh.

'Whaddya mean?' said Harry. 'I'm as straight as a lie. I mean a die. Do I? That rhymes! A die, do I ...' He trailed off, singing nonsense.

'I'd better take him home,' said Mary with a shrug. She didn't look cross.

'I'm going to try one more place,' said Guy. 'We'll meet at breakfast?'

'I will. I expect Harry will be in bed nursing a headache.'

They parted and Guy dived into a bar that was practically opposite the Moulin Rouge, crammed with men and women and with a saxophone playing loudly enough to blot out any thought in his head and yet not quite loud enough to obliterate the buzz of chatter. As with the other bars, a heavy pall of cigarette smoke hung above their heads and there was a strong smell of wine and *pastis*, the strong aniseed alcohol that Guy suspected had led to Harry's sharp demise in sobriety. As usual, Guy's glasses had steamed up almost as soon as he had walked in so he took them off and polished them with his tie for the nth time of the evening. With them back on he took a closer look at his surroundings. It was another small room with posters stuck haphazardly on the painted red walls, advertising various Paris shows. At the back there was an archway that seemed to lead through to a bigger space, equally crowded. Guy pushed through and saw there was a stage at the back here, where a man was singing, a six-piece band behind him. On the front of a large drum was painted 'Lee Palmers and the Dixie Players'. The singer, he guessed, was Lee Palmers, presumably American.

He was black, as were several of the customers at the bar. In fact, this had been the case at every bar – Paris was different to London on that front, thought Guy. In Soho, in the clubs where Harry played, there had been several black singers but he had hardly ever seen a black person enjoying the show as a member of the audience.

Suddenly tired but also a tad relieved not to be with Mary and Harry for a moment, Guy decided to sit down at one of the tables this time and order a proper drink. He looked around to find a waitress he could summon and when a young woman walked over to him he only made out her slim shape and the tray she carried before her. When she bent down to take his order, he noticed with alarm that she was wearing a very low-cut top that revealed more than he had ever seen even on his Sinéad. Flustered, Guy asked her for a carafe of red wine – he'd learned just enough since arriving to order this in French though his accent must have left quite a lot to be desired – and then something made him touch her arm and stop her from leaving. Motioning for her to wait, he pulled the photograph from his pocket and showed it to her. 'Do you know this woman?' he said, in slow English. To his surprise, the woman answered in an accent that was straight out of Manchester.

'That's Rose,' she said with surprise. Then she snapped her mouth closed and looked at him with fear and suspicion. 'I ain't saying no more. I shouldn't have said that.'

'Please,' said Guy, 'I mean her no harm. I'm just looking for her. Her family are worried.'

'She's not here any more,' said the waitress. 'She left.'

'Do you know where she went?'

But the woman shook her head and retreated out of his sight.

CHAPTER FIFTEEN

⟨⟩

Diana had predicted accurately and returned from the dinner at around midnight without plans, for once, to carry on at a show or club. Louisa was summoned to Diana's room minutes after they had arrived home. 'Bryan is carrying on with the others but I'm too tired tonight to go on,' she explained as Louisa helped her to undress, hanging her frock up and putting wooden trees into the shoes. Diana was not someone who drank beyond her limit as a general rule but her words were sliding tonight, making Louisa think of hospital corners on a bed being tugged loose. She always read before turning her light out, and Louisa had retrieved her book from the drawing room earlier, but it looked as if she would drop off as soon as her head touched the pillow. The newlyweds were sharing the same bed, though Louisa had yet to see the two of them in it at the same time. It wasn't that it would matter, and Bryan would certainly be at ease, having grown up in households where servants came in and out of the rooms all the time, but Louisa was less used to it, having done the greater part of her work as a servant in the nursery. The rule that a lady's maid, or indeed a valet, did not knock on a bedroom door before entering made sense, she knew; a maid had to be able to do her work efficiently, without having to wait for the command to 'come in'. Nevertheless, Louisa couldn't help but hesitate each time her hand took the doorknob and she made sure that she was never in the bathroom when Diana took off her dressing gown.

Her duty done and Diana already snoring gently by the time Louisa had left the room, she went downstairs to the kitchen. The light was on and she was concerned that the bad-tempered cook might still be there but thankfully, having had no supper to prepare, he had taken advantage and gone for an early night to bed. In fact, no one was in there but Luke, sitting on the well-scrubbed wooden table in the middle, his legs swinging.

'Good evening, Miss Cannon,' he said in a jolly voice. 'I was beginning to wonder if you had forgotten our assignation.'

'Sorry, have you been waiting long?' Louisa caught herself admiring his velvet jacket and handsome face and almost as quickly stopped herself. She had been disappointed before, when she had believed that a friend of Nancy's was a friend of hers; they were from different worlds and it did no good to forget it. Besides, she had to keep reminding herself that he worked for the newspapers – he might only be after a story he could sell.

'No. I saw Mrs Guinness depart for bed, gave it enough time for her to get undressed and so on, then came down. I've only been here a minute or two. I'm guessing she needed your help this evening?'

'A lady's maid never tells,' said Louisa.

'Ha, no. But your mistress was rather free with the martinis this evening. It was charming, actually. I enjoyed seeing her let herself a little loose for once. Now, speaking of which – where are the glasses? I smuggled this down.' He opened his jacket with a flourish to reveal a silver hip flask nestling in the inside pocket. 'Don't look like that, a drop will do you no harm. Do you good, I should think. You need to live a little.'

'My stomach still feels a bit funny from earlier. Those sandwiches in the club you took us to . . .' She pulled a queasy face.

'Aunt recommends dry biscuits for nausea,' said Luke.

'Yes, that's a good idea.' Louisa found a few in one of the cupboards, as well as two tumblers, and Luke poured out a generous slug of clear liquid in each one.

'Finest gin,' he said. 'Here's to us.'

They drank. The gin burned in Louisa's throat but it wasn't unpleasant. She rarely drank alcohol and for a giddy moment, the sensation of light-headedness was pure pleasure. 'Go on, then,' she said, 'what happened this evening?'

'Ah! Curiosity got the cat after all. I knew it would.' Luke put his glass down. He was still on the table, Louisa leaning against the cast-iron cooker, facing him. The lights were too bright but the room was warm, and there was the pleasant sensation of a party going on elsewhere in the house.

'First of all, Diana kept her promise and did not tell her husband about what happened this afternoon.' Luke opened his eyes wider, in mock surprise.

Louisa knew she should tell Luke to refer to her mistress as 'Mrs Guinness' in front of her, if she was to stick to protocol, but she was enjoying this intimacy.

'You're lucky,' she said instead.

Luke waved his hand and took another mouthful of his drink. 'Maybe so. But if you ask me, she didn't mind keeping a secret from him all that much. I suspect she quite enjoyed it. Every now and then she would look at me from across the table and give me what my aunt would call an "old-fashioned look".'

'Who else was there?' This sort of prying was shocking, really.

'The usual crowd, from what I could gather.' Luke reeled off a few names that Louisa recognized, from Diana's conversation rather than from the newspapers. 'Also Shaun and Kate Mulloney. They were at the wedding.'

'I've seen them briefly,' said Louisa.

'You'd only need to see him once. Very dashing. Irish, though no accent. Shame, I rather like a Dublin lilt on a pretty boy.'

Louisa briefly questioned that last remark. Another time perhaps she'd ask about it. 'Where did you go?'

'Somewhere unpronounceable and artistic, and Bryan picked up the entire bill, which was frightfully generous. Particularly as Mr Mulloney had a fondness for cocktails and kept ordering round after round. I couldn't keep up.'

Louisa nodded at their drinks. 'You're managing now.'

'Only because I paused earlier. He's one of those toffs that drinks four bottles of champagne while he's dressing for dinner. I wasn't brought up that way.'

Louisa spotted her opportunity. 'Weren't you?'

Luke looked at her and put his drink down. He seemed to think for half a minute. 'In short, no. We weren't poor but my father left my mother on his return from the war, remarried and moved to Scotland. He has a new family now and apart from a letter or two a year, I have no more to do with him. Mother and I got by, largely thanks to my aunt, my father's sister. She paid my school fees and would have seen me through Cambridge if I hadn't dropped out. I know my way around the cutlery, put it that way.'

That made Louisa smile but it also confirmed for her the

feeling she'd had that there was an outsider element to Luke. It was probably why he was as happy to sit in the kitchen with her as he was to dine out with the Guinnesses.

'Go on,' she said.

'Oh, I don't know if there is all that much more to tell. I stared a lot at the glamorous Irish couple. She is . . . not beautiful exactly, not in the way that Diana is, but she is arresting. You can't help but look at her. And he is louche but witty.'

Louisa's stomach suddenly turned. 'I'm sorry, Luke,' she said. 'I'm not sure the biscuits helped. You're going to have to excuse me.'

'We've finished the gin anyway,' he said. 'I'd better go back upstairs, see what they're all up to. Last I looked they were practically scrabbling at the back of the drinks cupboard hoping to unearth an exotic liqueur.'

Louisa shook her head. 'Didn't you excuse yourself earlier? Won't they wonder where you went to?'

'I doubt they're in much of a fit state to notice. Besides, I'm not the centre of a crowd like that. I find I often slip easily in and out of a room.' He tapped the side of his nose, gave her a comedy wink and left. Louisa watched him go, her hands on her middle, then turned and ran to the nearest loo.

The next morning, Louisa woke early, the light a thin line in a dark grey sky. She could hardly call it waking when she had barely slept a wink. All night she had vomited violently, her stomach churning as if a rotary blade was twisting her guts. At last, with nothing left inside, she had passed out on the top of her bedclothes, exhausted. Finally, she got up and staggered to the bathroom to splash cold water on her grey face and as she was walking back to her room, one of the maids came to her to tell her that Diana was ringing her bell rather insistently. Louisa quickly changed her dress. Her bedside clock showed that it was not yet eight o'clock in the morning. It was almost unfeasibly early for her mistress to be awake, but then she had had an earlier night than usual.

Louisa soon discovered that the reason for Diana's rousing was not the dawn chorus of the birds in the trees by her window. She entered the bedroom to find her mistress up and out of bed, the curtains hastily pulled aside, and Bryan sitting in the armchair in the corner, still in his clothes from the night before. He was pale, completely still and quiet. Diana was pacing, her trembling hands pushing her hair back.

'Close the door,' said Bryan, uncharacteristically abrupt. Louisa pushed it shut gently and almost tiptoed across the room. The air was heavy with tension and Louisa prayed nothing had happened to either the Guinness or Mitford families. It would be a terrible portent for the start of their marriage.

'Louisa,' said Diana, her voice hushed but suffused with relief at the sight of her maid. 'You must help us, we don't know what to do.'

Even Bryan looked young and vulnerable. 'My parents aren't going to bear the scandal,' he started before seeming to realize he was confiding in his wife's lady's maid. He turned to the window and looked out, his eyes glassy.

'What's happened ma'am?'

'It's Shaun Mulloney, who had dinner with us last night, and came back here. His wife, Kate, has just telephoned. He's dead.'

CHAPTER SIXTEEN

*

G uy had stayed in the bar for another half an hour but
another waitress had brought his wine and he had been
unable to find the one who knew Rose again. He worried that
for whatever reason she had decided it was too dangerous to
talk to him, it meant that she was losing money by cutting short
her shift, so he decided to leave. He had left his name and the
telephone number of the *pension* where he was staying with the
barman, though he was not hopeful it would get passed along.
He hadn't even caught the waitress's name and thanks to his bad
eyesight and the dim lighting, was not even completely certain
that he knew what she looked like beyond the disturbingly low-
cut top. Disheartened, Guy had returned to his room and gone
to bed. There had been no sign of Mary, who was presumably
beside her husband, sleeping off his earlier enthusiasm for the
French grape.

The following morning, the sky was brighter and so was their
mood. Harry's long sleep meant he bore no ill effects and Mary
was full of the joys of Paris. The three of them decided to go for

a walk, to find a typical Parisian brasserie and order croissants. It was then that Guy told them something he'd decided on as he'd tossed and turned on his thin mattress. 'I'm going to go and find Louisa this morning,' he said as the waiter set down the pretty rolled pats of butter and a pot of blackberry jam.

Harry looked shocked. 'What? Not that old chestnut, Sully.'

'That's not a very nice way to talk about a lady,' said Guy.

'Ha ha. No, but I thought you'd never heard from her again? Do you mean to say you know she's in Paris?'

Guy had withheld this from Harry and Mary. Quite possibly, he'd withheld it from himself, too. For all his flirtatious teasing, Harry was straight up and down when it came to marriage. He would no more look at another woman now he had Mary than he would smash his saxophone on the pavement. 'And if I did look at another woman, that's exactly what Mary would do to my saxophone,' he had laughed, when he and Guy had had this discussion before, prompted by yet another pretty young girl offering to buy Harry a drink at the end of a set.

'Yes, she's in Paris. She works for one of the Mitford sisters, Diana. She's here on her honeymoon and Louisa's her maid.'

'Coo,' whistled Harry. 'I thought she'd left them after . . . well, all that business at the party. With the murder.' He rolled his eyes comically but Guy remembered; it had been a serious and disturbing time.

'I think she did leave them for a bit but it seems Diana Mitford, or Mrs Guinness as she is now, has taken her back.'

'Louisa will be a familiar face for her in her new world,' said Mary. 'I understand it. Harry darling, these croissants are delicious. *Do* have one.'

'The point is, what about Sinéad? You're engaged.'

'I know I'm engaged, Harry. I'm not proposing to change anything on that score,' he said, as firmly as he could. 'I thought she might help with Rose. The servant grapevine and all that.' He was aware of Harry eyeballing him but he carried on. 'A few days ago I telephoned to find out where she was and the housekeeper said she was here. It's too much of a coincidence not to follow up, don't you think?'

'What if she doesn't want to see you? I mean, old chap, you've not seen her for some time.'

'I know. I'll admit a part of me wants to know why, though I've no right to ask. But I don't feel the same about her any more. There's no danger.' As Guy said it, he knew he was denying a truth. He was desperate to know what she had been doing for the last few years and why she hadn't replied to his letters. He knew that was wrong, with Sinéad, but there it was.

'I see,' said Harry. 'You knew Louisa was here. Anyone else you're keeping up your sleeve for me? Queen of Sheba here and all, is she?'

'Don't be so silly.' Mary blew Harry a kiss across the table. 'Now, eat.'

The scene over, Guy decided there was no time like the present and arranged to meet Mary and Harry for lunch at a brasserie they had spotted close by. Thanks to a friendly waiter he was able to look up Louisa's address on a Paris map and, with the directions written out, set off.

Having decided the Metro was too complicated to undertake alone, Guy had decided to walk to the Guinness house, which was likely to take an hour but the weather was dry and clear and he was happy to have the chance to take in the Paris streets. As he walked southwards the view changed dramatically, with the streets growing broader and the buildings wider and grander. In the final furlong, Guy walked across the bridge from Place de la Concorde to the other side of the river, and he felt as if a big band was playing tunes on his heart. Was it the glory of the Champs-Elysées, where the image of Marie Antoinette and her bewigged friends on sleighs came easily to mind, or was it the thought that he was getting closer to Louisa?

When at last Guy arrived at 12 rue de Poitiers he wasn't at all sure where to ring the bell. There was a rather imposing gate in an archway of the house that seemed to lead to an inner court-yard, but that seemed rather too stately for his own requirements. As it was, Louisa might not be pleased to see him, and especially not if his arrival meant she was reprimanded by Mr Guinness for the impertinence. So he walked along the side of the building until he found a more modest door and knocked. After a long minute, as Guy was thinking perhaps the whole thing was a mistake, the door was opened.

'*Qu'est-ce que c'est?*' said the young maid who opened the door. She looked pale and harried, as if she had been expecting someone else and was frustrated by the appearance of this stranger.

'Hello, miss,' said Guy. 'Sorry, I don't speak French. Is Miss Louisa Cannon there?'

'*Comment?*' But she blinked and then said. 'Ah, *oui*, Mademoiselle Cannon. *Entrez.*' She walked off and left the door open, so he assumed he was to follow. Inside, the house was remarkably stylish, with its muted colours and thickly tufted rugs laid on polished wooden floors, even though he was surely in the servants' quarters. He walked behind the maid along a narrow hallway until they reached what must have been the housekeeper's siting room. '*Attendez ici, s'il vous plaît.*'

'Er, yes,' said Guy, unsure exactly to what he was agreeing. He stood nervously in the small room, turning his hat round in his hands as he looked at the rather uncomfortable chair in front of the desk, the neatly ordered papers and sharpened pencils in a glass pot. He couldn't hear anything – those thick rugs masking the footsteps of anyone approaching, he supposed – and was, therefore, completely startled when all at once Louisa was standing before him.

'Guy? What on *earth* are you doing here?'

CHAPTER SEVENTEEN

'Louisa, I'm sorry to have surprised you like this.' Guy knew he was stammering. His idea of coming to see her might not have been so ingenious as it had seemed back in London, but he couldn't contain the feelings of deep pleasure rising up in him at seeing her again. She looked as pretty as she always had done to him; he even liked that she looked a little older, a touch of tiredness about the mouth. Her figure was as slim, her eyes still dark brown with flecks of light hazel. She was staring at him, as if she couldn't comprehend that he was standing there. That was probably fair. He was the last person she would have expected to turn up in Paris.

'No need to be sorry,' she said. 'But – are you here because of what happened last night? Are you here on police business?'

Now it was Guy's turn to be alarmed. 'What? No, I'm not. Well, not quite, there was something I wanted to ask you, but – what do you mean? What happened last night?'

'Someone died.'

'Someone *died*?'

'Yes, a friend of Mr Guinness's. That's why I somehow thought they might have called the British police, though of course not. Even if they had, you couldn't possibly have come this quickly.'

'No, but why don't you tell me what happened, what you know anyway. I'll take notes, in case it's of use to the police later. Are the French police here?'

'The *gendarmes*. Yes, they have been here but they don't think anything suspicious is going on. It was just a very unfortunate event. His wife says he was allergic to sesame, and he must have unknowingly eaten something with sesame in it.'

Guy wanted to take her in his arms. He couldn't, he knew. Even if he tried to pretend to himself that it would only be to comfort Louisa, it had been too long since he had seen her – and then there was Sinéad.

'A horrible shock for everyone, nonetheless,' he said, as warmly as he could.

Louisa nodded. 'Yes, horrible.'

There was a chill in the room, the fire hadn't been laid, given the upset to the household. 'Come into the kitchen,' said Louisa. 'The cook is a bit stern but I'm sure I could get you a cup of tea. Even if Nanny Blor was right after all, it's not the same over here as it is at home. I can't tell if it's the water or the milk, or what.'

Guy was so relieved she had dispelled the tension in this way he almost laughed but stopped himself in time. The two of them walked down the corridor to the kitchen, practically following the smell of garlic. Did the French eat it for breakfast?

Louisa boiled some water and after a search found the milk. Guy couldn't help but think of when he had once followed her down to Asthall Manor years before and she had made him tea then, too. He watched her as she moved around the kitchen, finding the cups and teaspoons, none of the French staff helping her. She seemed suddenly very alone and the old yearning he had always had to take her home almost clutched him by the throat. Guy coughed and Louisa looked at him. 'One minute, almost there.'

When they were both sitting down at a corner of the long table, out of the way of the maids who were peeling vegetables and feverishly whispering to each other, they began to talk. For all his questions, he felt he had better stick to the more immediate matter in hand.

'What happened last night?'

Louisa pulled in closer to him, and when she spoke her voice was low. 'I think it's being kept secret from the other servants, so we'd better talk quietly.'

Guy nodded.

'I think they – that is, Mr and Mrs Guinness – are trying to avoid any rumours and distancing themselves from this as much as they can.'

'Understandable,' said Guy.

'Yes. From what's been said so far, they all went out to dinner and drank rather a lot. Most of them came back here, Mrs Guinness went to bed—'

'You can't call her Miss Diana any more?' asked Guy, slightly incredulous.

'I know, it's funny after I looked after her for all those years in the nursery but I have to call her Mrs Guinness now or "ma'am"—'

'You call her "mum"?' Guy's voice was in danger of reaching a shrill pitch.

Louisa got the giggles. 'That's just how you pronounce it,

it's M-A-apostrophe-A-M. Then she has to call me "Cannon" if anyone else is in the room but she calls me Louisa when it's just us.' She took a sip of tea. 'Anyway, she went to bed and I came down to the kitchen and Luke Meyer had come down to meet me here—'

Guy had to interrupt again. A sharp stab had pierced his chest. 'Luke Meyer? The gossip columnist?' Guy had seen his byline in the papers when reading up about the party at which the maid had died and Rose had gone missing.

'He's a sort of friend of Di— I mean Mrs Guinness's. And mine, too, in a manner of speaking.' She took a breath and carried on. 'He told me that there had been a lot of cocktails drunk and the party was still going on. He noticed particularly that Shaun Mulloney had ordered a lot of drinks.'

'Sorry, who is Shaun Mulloney?'

'That's the man who died. He's married to someone called Kate, she's the one who telephoned this morning to tell Mrs Guinness what had happened. Oh, please excuse me.' Louisa turned pale and put the back of her hand to her mouth. There was a gentle hiccup. 'I was sick all night. I don't know what it was. I thought I was feeling better but I haven't had much sleep.'

'Can I get you some water?'

'No, I'm fine.' Louisa managed a small smile.

'When did Mrs Mulloney find him? Does she know what happened?' Guy took a sip of tea but he'd left it too long and it had gone cold.

'They went to bed when they got in last night, about three o'clock in the morning. She says he was very sick when they got in but she assumed it was all the alcohol he'd drunk, and then she passed out herself. When she woke a few hours later, to get herself a glass of water, she found him dead on the bathroom floor. It looks as if he choked on his vomit. Sorry, I know it sounds horrible.'

'Natural causes, then.' No gun, no knife. Guy was almost disappointed, wrong as he knew it was to feel this way.

'Yes. I just feel a bit frightened because . . . ' Louisa looked at him and his heart lurched. 'No, you'll think me silly.'

'What is it? I'm sure I won't.'

'It's just that I was sick and in pain all night, too. It's an odd coincidence, yet I can't account for it. I had my supper here and they were all at a restaurant.'

'Could be the water. Did you drink from the tap yesterday?'

Louisa thought back. 'Yes, but I have done every day. So do all the servants here.'

'But they might be used to it, the French water, I mean. Not to mention there have been reports of tuberculosis in the system. My mother told me not to drink anything from the tap unless it had been boiled first. You can't trust the foreign water, she said.'

'Just like Nanny Blor. Perhaps there's something in those old wives' tales.'

'Good old-fashioned bad luck for Mr Mulloney and you, then,' said Guy.

'Yes, it seems so.' Louisa gave him a smile and his heart lurched. It made him despair – after all this time, he hadn't been able to change how he felt.

CHAPTER EIGHTEEN

Louisa did not linger long in the kitchen with Guy because she knew that Diana would need her upstairs, for the comfort of her familiar presence on this unfamiliar morning, if nothing else. She sent him off but not before he had extracted from her a promise to meet him later and given her the telephone number of the *pension* where he was staying. She had asked him why he was in Paris and he'd said that he was on a short holiday with Harry and Mary – Louisa thought it would be nice to see them, too – and some sort of police business that he hoped she could help him with but he didn't go into it, only said he'd tell her more later. A bribe, perhaps, to make sure she'd get in touch. He knew her own curiosity for a mystery.

It had been quite wonderful to see him. When she had been feeling lonely during those long barren months in London, embarrassed by her failure to join the police or make something of herself, she hadn't written back to him, believing he would think less of her if he knew what had happened. Seeing him again, she finally understood he was a more generous person than that, in fact he probably would have helped her, if she would only allow herself to be helped. Guy hadn't asked her about where she had been or why he'd never had a reply – they had been too concerned with Mr Mulloney – but she knew it would have been on his mind. She hoped so, anyway; she couldn't bear to think that he hadn't missed her at all, even if his few letters had dried up quite quickly. Louisa knew she would have to explain herself to him eventually, but for the moment she hoped they could simply enjoy each other's company, away from London. When the drama was over, she hoped she might continue to enjoy the freedom of this novel city, uninhibited by the usual expectations of behaviour. She knew it was silly to feel that way; everything was changing, in London as well as Paris. Everywhere she looked there were well-dressed women striding around with purpose. In the newspapers there were constant stories of women who had earned impressive degrees at university, who were making great scientific discoveries, exploring new territories and flying aeroplanes. They beamed out from the pages, with broad, confident smiles and short haircuts, wearing wide-legged trousers. 'Look at us,' they seemed to say, 'we can do anything any man can do!' It should have inspired her but instead it made her feel weaker: all this opportunity before her and what had she done? Worked as if she lived in the Victorian age, as a servant and seamstress. She could have swapped lives with her grandmother and no one would know the difference.

Being in Paris made her feel more hopeful that she might yet achieve something special. Especially now that Guy was here. For the moment, just feeling that was enough – she wasn't willing to investigate exactly why quite yet.

*

Back upstairs, Diana and Bryan were in the drawing room, along with six or seven of their friends who had gathered from their various hotels and apartments in Paris to discuss the news. Louisa peeped through the gap in the doorway, looking for Luke, who glanced up and happened to catch her eye. She moved to the side in the hall, out of the line of vision, and soon he came out to talk to her.

'You've heard what happened?' Luke looked as if he hadn't slept. His clothes had been changed from the night before but he looked rumpled, where he usually looked sleek. His eyes were bloodshot and his breath smelled stale.

'Yes,' said Louisa. 'I was summoned to her bedroom this morning, not long after they'd had the telephone call.' She looked behind her, though she didn't know what she was checking for other than she felt it wasn't her place to discuss this. 'What are they saying?'

Luke ran his fingers through his hair. 'Not much. The police took a statement from Kate, which she found very upsetting. I don't think French *gendarmes* are particularly gentle. They've asked those of us who were at the dinner last night to leave our names and addresses, in case there are further questions to be asked. There's the question of an autopsy.'

'An autopsy?'

Luke exhaled shakily. 'Yes, it's not entirely clear why he died.'

'What do you think?' It was dark in the hallway, with no lights turned on in spite of the grey clouds outside. Louisa couldn't see Luke's face clearly as he answered.

'The doctor says it was something he ate that caused the extreme vomiting.'

'But was it deliberate?'

'I say, old girl, where does your mind go? He was allergic to sesame. I say it was nothing more than bad luck. Most likely something he ate at La Coupole. We were in Montparnasse, it's a rackety part of town.'

Everyone thought it was bad luck, then. Except for Louisa, who had something in the pit of her stomach that was quite different from whatever had made her feel sick all night.

'You'd better go back in.'

'Yes, I will. Are *you* feeling all right?' Luke sounded concerned.

'I wasn't but I'm better now.'

'Good. Do you know where the nearest telephone is, by the way?'

'There's a study just off the entrance hall,' said Louisa. Then, because she could not help herself: 'Who do you need to ring?'

'Just my aunt, to let her know I'm well. And possibly my editor.'

But before Louisa could respond to this – *he wanted to ring the newspaper?* – another voice interrupted.

'What are you two whispering about out here?' Diana had come out of the drawing room without either of them noticing.

Luke jumped. 'Nothing, Diana. I thought we might ask for some coffee.'

'That's not Louisa's to fetch. I'll ring the bell if you really want some.'

'Yes, thank you,' said Luke and he escaped back into the party.

Louisa was about to turn away when Diana stopped her. 'Mrs Mulloney is coming here shortly. Understandably, she doesn't want to stay in their flat alone. Could you prepare the small blue bedroom for her? I don't trust the French maid to make it cosy, as we would.'

'Yes, of course. I'll do that straight away.'

'Thank you. I'm not sure what happens after today. Truthfully, I don't much feel like staying in Paris.'

Louisa didn't know what to say to this; if she could, she would have protested that she wanted to stay, very much. Instead she nodded and left to plump the pillows and put a fresh vase of flowers in the blue bedroom.

CHAPTER NINETEEN

A n hour or so later, Kate Mulloney's arrival blew through the apartment like a *mistral*. Louisa was in Diana's bedroom, rehanging her mistress's frocks and smoothing out any creases by hand – more in the absence of knowing what else to do with herself than because it needed to be done – when the two women came in. They seemed not to notice her at first, or it could have been that she was at least partly hidden by the wardrobe doors. The first thing that Louisa remembered as she saw her, as surely everyone did, was that Kate was quite the most strikingly attractive woman that she had ever come across. Diana was beautiful, of course, but it was a classical beauty and her youthful naivety kept a certain kind of attention at bay; whereas Kate was all sophisticated charisma: white skin, dark hair and a mouth that was perfectly red. More predator than prey. Her figure was not fashionable, with her full bosom and round hips, yet even Chanel could not have dressed her better, nor could any woman help but covet her form. More than that, there was an air about Kate that drew people to her; even Louisa had to resist an impulse to sit at her feet and watch her. No wonder Luke had been so captivated the evening before. There was a sexual power, yes, but that wasn't the full extent of her charm. All this even in her state of grief.

Grief? Louisa supposed so. There were no tears but this was hardly something to remark on. People cried alone, she knew that much about the world. Diana and Kate had both sat down on the end of the bed, and were holding each other's hands. Louisa thought she had better make her presence felt.

'Beg pardon, Mrs Mulloney. Mrs Guinness.'

Kate looked at her but said nothing.

'Sorry, Kate, I didn't realize Cannon was in here.' Louisa thought her mistress looked uncomfortable but whether it was because she was in the room, or because Mrs Mulloney was tightly holding both her hands, she couldn't say.

'We've met,' said Kate, her plucked eyebrow arched.

Diana coloured slightly. 'Yes.'

'A lady's maid on honeymoon. You're even grander than I thought.' Louisa started to walk towards the door as they talked, not particularly enjoying the sensation of their discussing her as if she wasn't there. But Kate had other plans. 'Wait, don't go.'

'Yes, Mrs Mulloney?' Louisa turned to face her, holding her gaze, though it took nerve. She was beginning to find the held hands rather disconcerting.

'Could you be a darling and fetch my vanity case from my room? There's something I'd like to give Diana.' Kate looked at Diana as she said this.

When Louisa returned a few minutes later with the navy-blue leather vanity case, stamped with Kate's initials – K. G. M. – the two women were apart, with Kate sitting back up on the bed, her legs up, leaning against the pillows and Diana standing by the window. Taking the case from Louisa, Kate snapped open the fastenings. Inside, amongst the diamond earrings and smaller jewellery boxes, lay a revolver with pearls inlaid on the handle. It was almost pretty, if one could call such a violent object pretty. Had Kate realized that Louisa had seen it? She wasn't particularly trying to hide the weapon, it seemed, but, still, Louisa was standing close to the bed. She had the strong sensation that she shouldn't leave Diana alone, and besides, she hadn't been told to go. Kate rummaged around the case and then drew out a red box. 'Here, darling. This is for you.'

Diana's face revealed little. 'Kate, please. Now is not the time to give things away, you might regret it later.'

Kate held out the box on an open palm and made a face of dramatic pleading. 'Shaun gave these to me but I hardly ever wear them. I want you to have them. You have been so kind to me today.' She broke off into a gulped-down sob.

Diana took the box from Kate and opened it. There were a pair of ruby studs, set in a circle of tiny diamonds. 'They're beautiful but—'

'I won't be argued with.' Kate was firm, and the case was snapped shut. This seemed to disturb them in some way and they both turned simultaneously to look at Louisa who had been standing there as still and colourless as a statue in the Louvre.

'I don't know what I'm going to do without him,' said Kate suddenly, still looking at her.

Louisa thought: is she telling *me* this?

'No, ma'am,' she said.

'Cannon, you may leave now.' Diana had taken charge again.

*

Louisa spent the rest of the day on various errands for Diana and Kate, who maintained a lucid stream of plans for her husband's funeral while consuming an equally steady stream of vodka martinis and cigarettes. Other people came in and out of the house throughout the day, offering condolences or, more frequently it seemed to Louisa, barely concealing their desire to hear grisly details. Bryan, who was a quiet man at the best of times, said little to anyone but sat in the drawing room by the fire, staring at the flames, an open notebook and pencil by his side. Now and then he would scribble a line down before continuing his morose observation of the burning coals. It was Luke who had taken over the duties of host and he was soon in his element, mixing and pouring the drinks, offering to ring the bell for sandwiches and whispering the latest news on Mrs Mulloney's grief to anyone who asked. Instead of finding this wearying, he looked better and better as the hours passed, the creases falling out of his suit, his eyes sparkling with the thrill of it all.

Which was not to say he was callous, thought Louisa, only that he seemed to come alive in company. Or perhaps in the fantasy of being a host in a grand drawing room in Paris. Louisa couldn't swear that she wouldn't be the same. Nor could she mind too much because Luke never sidelined her: every time she came into the room with a message from Diana for her husband, or to fetch something for her mistress (Louisa was, in all honesty, finding excuses), Luke would sidle up to her and tell her something about the latest guest who had arrived, or update her on the gossip that was even now setting fire to telephone wires between Paris and London.

The circulating guests were, it had to be admitted, alluring. Bryan had cultivated friendships with writers, artists, musicians and even the occasional actor, and there were plenty of them in Paris. Several of them were admitted to Kate's blue bedroom, and Louisa couldn't help but notice Diana's delight at some of these exotic and original people coming through the house. Diana's childhood at Asthall Manor had been charming in so many ways, set in the glory of the prettiest English countryside, with her and her sisters taught at home and given plenty of time to lie on a sofa reading in the library or out riding to hounds. But it had also meant long, dull weeks stretching out with few people other than cousins or uncles and aunts visiting the house. Diana particularly had always enjoyed meeting new people and hearing about another way of life than her own. Unlike Pamela and Unity, her older and younger sisters, she had an inner confidence – perhaps borne by her looks but also by her voracious reading – and there was no topic or person that she considered off-limits. The more outrageous, in fact, the more she wanted to hear about it. In this, Diana and Nancy were more closely aligned and Louisa knew they had become better friends as Diana had grown older; perhaps Nancy would hasten to Paris in the light of this news. While the death of Shaun Mulloney had been sudden and shocking, it also brought a heightened excitement that Louisa knew a young woman such as Diana could not help but be stimulated by, particularly when it was conducted in the company of such brilliant minds as Bryan's friends.

That first night after Shaun's death, several friends gathered in Kate's room. Kate held court even as she lay in the bed, wearing no more than a bed-jacket over her nightdress but with her hair perfectly brushed and diamonds in her ears, her lipstick in place as much as her grief. Louisa had come in with a silk scarf of Diana's that she had asked for, though when she entered the room, Diana was sitting on the end of Kate's bed next to a man Louisa didn't recognize and Diana waved her away. She broke off from her conversation and gave Louisa a dismissive look: 'I've changed my mind. Top up our glasses, would you. The bottle is over there.' This wasn't Louisa's job and Diana knew that; the butler would be furious but it was better to do as she was asked. The man was leaning towards Diana – whatever he was talking about he was doing so with an urgent intensity; while she looked as if mere listening was not enough and she wished to absorb his words through her skin. Louisa had to look away, it was almost too intimate to witness. Yet when she overheard what he was saying it was, to her ears, disturbing. 'Mussolini has sinister plans, mark my words,' said the man. 'He's ordered every woman to bear double the number of children she's willing to bear because he wants to increase the size of Italy's population. You know, so they can withstand a major war. It's all going to happen again if we're not careful.'

Louisa hoped he was misinformed. She moved to Kate's bedside table to check her glass as she talked to Bryan, who was leaning across the corner of the bed, his eyes all the while fixed on his wife and the man she was in conversation with. His face was impassive as he muttered soothing responses to Kate.

'I simply don't see the need for an autopsy,' she was saying, her hand fiddling with the pearls around her neck. 'No one will agree whether it should happen here, England or Ireland, and I think the easiest thing is not to have one altogether. It's quite clear what happened, and this will only delay the funeral.' She had been talking almost to herself but now she turned to Bryan and asked sharply: 'Don't you agree?'

He started and took his eyes off his wife. 'Yes, yes, of course, quite right. I'm sure you know best.'

Kate looked momentarily placated and took a large swallow of the wine Louisa had just poured. 'Yes,' she said. 'It will be far better that way.'

Her duties completed and with no further instruction from Diana, Louisa left the room with relief.

CHAPTER TWENTY

⟞⟞⟞

Finally, at seven o'clock that evening, Louisa stepped out into rue de Poitiers. The cold air felt a relief after the stifled tension of inside. With the fire continually stoked and the drinks pouring like waterfalls from the shakers, the atmosphere had become rather close. Fortunately, Diana had realized that Louisa had not had any time off since their arrival in Paris and suggested that, since she and Bryan would not be going out to dinner that evening, Louisa could have a few hours to herself. Louisa had immediately telephoned Guy's *pension* and left a message to say that she could meet him at La Coupole in Montparnasse. She reasoned that if he didn't get the message, she could at least buy herself something to eat and drink, while taking a look at the surroundings. There was something about Shaun's death that bothered her; she didn't know if simply going to the place where he had last eaten would give her any answers, but she had no better ideas.

Happily, she had only been there for twenty minutes, admiring the Art Deco ceiling and the painted pillars, trying to spot the one Picasso had done, when Guy, Harry and Mary walked in. On sight, they waved to her and came rushing to the table, and there were a few gay minutes of jostling and budging up tables and fetching a chair so that the four of them could sit together. In the bubble of their own foreignness they were able to brush off the French waiter's clear annoyance. A bottle of wine was ordered, with some bread and onion soup for all.

'So this is the famous La Coupole,' said Harry. 'I've been wanting to come here.'

'Is it famous?' asked Mary. 'What for?'

'All the artists come here, lots of Americans. Quite a few of the jazz players, I bet.'

'I've heard a lot of American voices in Paris,' said Louisa. 'I suppose they're here to get a drink, what with Prohibition over there.'

'That and the jazz,' said Harry. 'It all starts here – Hutch, Josephine Baker. That Gershwin fellow wrote *An American in Paris* here last year. That's why I'm here. It's gonna make me a star, baby.' He winked and leaned across the table to kiss Mary. Louisa enjoyed seeing the two of them together; she was fond of Harry, having known him exactly as long as she had known Guy, ever since they had both rescued her from the train tracks. And though she had harboured a natural suspicion of Mary when she had first worked with Guy – she was very pretty, with her sharp bob and pert nose – Louisa was past that now, and could see her for the alert, quick friend she was. She was, all in all, very glad to have the three of them back in her life again.

'But what are you doing here?' said Harry. 'Have you taken up the trumpet or paintbrush?'

Louisa wished she could say that. 'No, I'm back working for

the Mitfords. Diana has married, and she's here on her honeymoon. I'm accompanying her as her lady's maid.'

'Yes, Guy told us. I meant, why did you choose this restaurant? It's quite *avant-garde* of you.'

'Who's to say I can't be *avant-garde*?' said Louisa, in mock indignation. 'Diana and her friends dined here last night, so I thought I'd like to see it. Don't think it ghoulish of me, but they came here and one of them died in the early hours of this morning. Everyone thinks it was bad luck, just something he ate or drank, but I don't know . . . '

'You thought you might see something here?' asked Mary.

Louisa twisted her mouth. 'I know it's silly. He was allergic to sesame and I thought I might see if it was in any of the dishes on the menu but of course it's all in French.' She felt foolish. Everything else in the restaurant looked completely normal, she couldn't think what she'd hoped to see. An evil-looking waiter? She had better watch out or she was going to become the type of person that created trouble where none existed.

'Well, I won't order any seafood or drink the tap water,' said Mary. 'And besides, you've got me and Guy here, we can be on the lookout too. We've already got our policemen's hats on, as it were.'

Now it was Louisa's turn to be interested. 'Have you? I did wonder what you were doing in Paris.'

Guy gave a small cough. He was sitting opposite Louisa but hadn't said much so far. 'There's a missing girl, Rose Morgan, and it's possible she's in Paris.'

'Is this one of your cases?'

'In a manner of speaking. Not officially, though she has been reported. My boss isn't interested but her parents are still worried. I had the idea of talking to you about her.'

The waiter came and put down their onion soups. 'Why?' said Louisa.

Guy shifted slightly in his seat. 'It's just that she was a maid and I thought you might have heard something.'

'Servants' hall gossip, you mean.' She couldn't blame him; he didn't know she'd tried to do better than that, and here she was, a lady's maid. An upper servant but a servant nonetheless. She mentally admonished herself and told herself to concentrate instead on the fact that he'd asked for her help in a case. Wasn't that what she wanted?

'You'd better tell me everything you know about Rose Morgan.'

Guy covered the details as he knew them and then took out the photograph. Louisa peered at it. 'There is something about her that . . . ' She broke off and picked it up, holding it in a better light. 'I think she's changed her hair colour since that picture but yes, I think she's been working at one of the shops that Mrs Guinness has been at. I can't remember which one exactly but either Louise Boulanger, or maybe Molyneux. Actually, definitely Molyneux.'

That was a real breakthrough. Guy looked at Louisa. 'Thank you, you're a genius.' She thought for a moment he might kiss her. But of course, he didn't.

CHAPTER TWENTY-ONE

'I take it you haven't told Louisa about Sinéad, then?'

Louisa and Mary had excused themselves to go to the powder room, while Guy and Harry asked for the bill.

'I haven't not told her deliberately,' said Guy, trying to keep the defensiveness out of his voice. 'There's a lot we haven't talked about yet.' Much of supper had been taken up with the discussion about Rose and other desperate maids they had heard about and what they had done. When Louisa had asked how he knew where she was in Paris, he had been forced to admit that he had called up Mrs Windsor at Swinbrook to find out where Louisa was, though he hadn't liked to acknowledge he had needed to do so because they had lost touch so completely. In short, Guy did not want to know why Louisa hadn't wanted to talk to him, for fear of ruining the pleasure he was now experiencing at their meeting again.

Harry made no response but Guy was clear on what he thought nonetheless. Harry's old-fashioned loyalty was one of the reasons they were such firm friends.

Even so, he had to ask himself what he was doing, haring all the way to Paris on nothing but a hunch and a few words from a little girl.

Merely thinking this made Guy feel very nervous. He gulped down the last of the wine and had to thud himself on the chest to stop himself from coughing it back up. Harry watched him with amused detachment. 'Looks to me as if you'd better start talking, and soon,' was all he said.

Louisa and Mary returned to the table, Louisa now wearing some lipstick that Mary had obviously encouraged her to put on. Guy also noticed for the first time that Louisa was wearing a pretty blue dress, quite short, almost above her knees, even when she was standing up. She had good legs.

'I had probably better get back quite soon,' Louisa said as they sat down.

'What do you mean?' said Harry. 'It's not even half past nine. Come along to a club with us. You can't be in Paris and not hear some jazz. There's one or two places I still want to check out.'

'Yes, go on, Lou,' said Mary. 'Come with us. Spare me being the only woman out with these two.'

'Fine, just one bar, then I'll have to go. Half past ten is my absolute limit.'

Only a few streets away was a club that Harry had heard about, and it wasn't long before they were settled around a table with four cocktails, a few rows back from a dance floor in front of a band. Guy had been to a few places like this in London to watch Harry, though it wasn't generally his first choice for an evening out. He preferred to go to the pictures with Sinéad, or even just to sit by the fire with his mother, reading a good book. But sitting here, amongst the chic Parisians with the smooth notes of jazz in the background, and in the company of his friends, he felt himself relax. Louisa was sitting beside him, and he could feel the warmth of her body radiating from her. It was all he could do not to wrap his arm around her shoulders and pull her close. A new song started and Harry and Mary got up to dance. 'What are you waiting for?' said Mary. 'Let's dance!'

Guy looked at Louisa and there was no doubt about it: she wanted to get up. 'Come on, then,' he said to her a little huskily. Dancing was something he did even more rarely than drinking cocktails and he could never quite shake off the feeling that a man was judged on more than his footwork when he stepped out with a girl. Luckily, the song had a beat he recognized and with a surge of confidence, he took Louisa by the hand and led her up. Pressed together, his arm around her back and their hands held up high, they stepped in symmetry and moved around the floor in tight proximity with the other couples. The lights were low, the music soft and Louisa's mouth was daringly close. For the first few minutes, they danced without speaking, hardly even daring to meet each other's eyes. For all the years they had known each other, for all that he had felt, they had never been so near to each other's bodies. It threw Guy momentarily into confusion: he had spent so many years wanting this moment, now that it was here, he wasn't sure how he felt. When he dared to steal a look at Louisa, he thought she might be thinking the same; though she was serene in expression, there was a flicker in her eyelids that made him think an electricity might be running through her. Thinking this made him spring apart from Louisa, startling her.

'Oh God, I'm sorry,' he said. 'I thought I saw Rose.'

'What? Where?'

'No, it wasn't her.' He had lied but he hadn't known what else to say.

She looked at him apprehensively. 'I had no sleep last night, I think I'd better get back. I'm sorry, Guy. I was so enjoying the dance.' She stopped and looked at him properly then, and his mouth went dry. 'I really was. But I think I'd better go back.'

'I'll walk you back,' said Guy.

'There's no need. I don't want to spoil your evening.'

'You couldn't possibly. And I don't want you walking alone around here.' Guy was firm, and after they had said goodbye to Harry and Mary, they fetched their coats and were outside in the cold night air together. The streets were slick – there had been a short downpour in the time they had been in the club – and the yellow street lamps reflected blearily on the pavement. Along the road there were knots of women in twos and threes, heavily made-up and wearing short dresses with seamed stockings. The occasional car pulled up well out of the way of the lights and a woman would lean in through the window before getting in on the other side. Guy knew Louisa was worldly but he still felt uncomfortable at what was going on. With her arm looped through his, they walked quickly through the streets. Once out of Montparnasse and on to the wide avenue of boulevard Raspail – Louisa said they weren't too far now – he slowed them down a little and they started to talk.

'How long are you in Paris for?' he asked.

'I don't know. They were supposed to be here for a few weeks before going on to Sicily, though I was never joining them on that part of their honeymoon. But what with Mr Mulloney . . .' She tailed off. 'It might change things. What about you?'

'I have to go back tomorrow,' he said. 'Back to work. But when you get back to London, can we meet again?' He stopped walking then. Louisa was bathed in the light of a shop window, with two narrow mannequins in some sort of fashionable confection. He wasn't looking at them. He was looking at her. 'I've missed you.'

Louisa put her face up towards his. 'I've missed you too, Guy. I'm sorry I didn't write back to you.'

She had received his letters after all.

'The truth is, I didn't know what to say. I went to London and it all went wrong. I thought I'd failed. I couldn't bear to tell you. It seemed better somehow to get on with it by myself.'

'Only you would think that,' he smiled. 'You could never fail in my eyes. I think you're—'

But she had interrupted him and put her lips on his. For one moment he leant into her, his hands on her back, feeling nothing more than the softness and warmth of her lips, the feel of her body yielding to him.

He broke away. When he spoke he felt as if his mouth was filled with cotton wool: 'I can't.'

She said nothing but looked bewildered.

'I'm engaged to a girl,' said Guy. 'I'm so sorry.'

Louisa retreated into herself immediately, he could see that. She pulled the collar of her coat around her, almost obscuring her mouth. 'Why didn't you tell me before?'

'I know I should have but I didn't want to presume you wanted more than for us to be friends. I didn't know how you felt. I've never known.'

'That can remain a mystery then. You can forget about me, Guy. We shan't be meeting in London. And you can leave me here. I know where I am, the house is only a few minutes' walk.'

'But, please. Louisa.'

'No. I can look after myself.'

She left him, walking down the street, never once looking back.

CHAPTER TWENTY-TWO

The following day, Guy and Mary dropped in on the Molyneux salon to enquire about Rose Morgan. As he approached the address, he half wondered if he had the right place. Although he worked in Knightsbridge in London, where some of the smartest shops in London were, Guy had never had cause to go in them and he'd certainly never minded. They had looked like haughty places with shop assistants who'd sooner scrape Guy off the bottom of their shoe than serve him. These salons looked more like houses, with discreet doorbells, but there was no friendly housewife behind the front door. When Guy pressed the one for Molyneux, he was greeted by a woman who gave him and Mary the once-over with her perfectly made-up eyes and left him in no doubt that they were not welcome. He apologized for speaking English and asked if he might see Monsieur Molyneux.

'Have you an appointment?'

Guy had to admit that he did not.

'Then you will have to come back. Monsieur does not see

anyone' – there was an emphasis on *anyone*, as if to include Louis XIV himself – 'without an appointment.'

Guy knew his next move was not strictly legitimate but he was damned if he was going to be sent away like a stray dog. 'We're from the British police, madame. We're inquiring after a missing girl, and believe she may be working here.'

It took another half an hour of waiting before the designer came to see them, impatient and distracted. 'I've got a member of European royalty on the other side of that door waiting for me to fit her gown,' he said, taking Guy by surprise with his British accent. Guy knew he intended to awe them with his words. It worked. Mary appeared to forget their reasons for being there and Guy could see her trying to work out who it could be. If he wasn't careful, she'd slip through that door to have a look.

'We have reason to believe that a young woman who has gone missing, Rose Morgan, might have headed here.' Guy showed him the photograph, Molyneux looked at it briefly and shook his head.

'It's hard to be absolutely certain,' he said. 'We have plenty of girls coming through here wanting work. But I don't think she would have been quite the right look for us. Perhaps in the backroom?'

Guy tried once more. 'We interviewed the daughter of her former employer, Miss Muriel Delaney. We believe the child's aunt is your wife?'

Molyneux snapped his fingers. 'Muriel! That little girl, she was rather sweet. Is she still?'

'Yes,' said Mary. 'Have you seen her recently?'

'Not for years. She came to my wedding in 1923. But her aunt and I divorced in 1924. I have not seen her since, nor heard any more of the family, and certainly not their maid. Now, please forgive me but I am very busy here. *Bon*.' He snapped his fingers again and beckoned to the assistant, who came running over. 'Find me the yellow silk, please.'

The interview was over.

Standing in the hall by the front door, waiting for someone to fetch Mary's hat and coat, Guy felt despondent. He had been so hopeful of a result after what Louisa had said. Another assistant came in with Mary's things but she wore a worried rather than haughty expression on her face and when she spoke it was with an English accent. 'I heard you were looking for someone?' she asked.

'Yes,' said Mary, and motioned for Guy to give her the photograph. 'Do you recognize this girl?'

The assistant nodded. 'She's Rebecca. Monsieur wouldn't know who she was because she worked in the backrooms, and she's blonde now.'

'Worked?'

'She left yesterday.' She looked as if she was plucking up all her courage. 'It was very abrupt. Might she have heard you were looking for her?'

Guy thought about the waitress at the bar – she could have tipped Rose off. Damn.

'Her family want to know she's safe and well.' Guy felt vexed with Rose Morgan – why was she needlessly putting them through this worry?

'Perhaps you could tell them that she is?' the young woman said.

'Do you have an address for her?' asked Mary.

The assistant shook her head. 'She kept to herself. I didn't know her very well but I thought you should know. I'm sorry. That's all I can tell you.'

1930

CHAPTER TWENTY-THREE

To celebrate their first wedding anniversary, Diana and Bryan had accepted an invitation from Kate Mulloney, who had taken a floor at the Hotel Excelsior on the Lido at Venice. Louisa couldn't say for certain what Mrs Mulloney's situation had been before, but as a widow she was extremely well-off. Her husband's death had been written up in the papers as a tragedy, a fatal allergic reaction; the fact of Kate having been so drunk she had passed out and failed to call an ambulance had been successfully kept out of the reports, and she remained as central to London society as ever before. A year with the Guinnesses had given Louisa a new understanding of what it meant to be rich, as rich people saw it. She grasped now why the Mitford girls had complained of their poverty. From where she had been standing then – having grown up as the daughter of a washerwoman and chimney sweep – they had seemed to be practically rolling in money. But now, having worked for Diana for a year, she knew what that actually looked like.

It meant, for a start, having the latest fashions in one's

wardrobe instead of one's dresses being made by the local seam-stress. Let loose with a chequebook, Diana had evolved a style of her own fairly fast, one that showed off her carefully maintained figure at its best. Unfussy in silhouette, though she was fond of flounces on shirt fronts and cuffs, she tended towards rich tex-tures of cashmere, wool, linen or silk in sharply contrasting dark and light shades; a white velvet cape over a long black coat was a favourite. Bryan was no dandy but he enjoyed complementing his wife with his own modern look. His beautiful suits were traditionally made in Savile Row, but he had certain touches – such as ties with narrow knots and jackets worn unbuttoned and loose, or off altogether, with shirtsleeves rolled up: tiny hints of his appreciation of the more artistic types.

Louisa liked her mistress's husband; he was unassuming in many ways, modest and kind, not entirely at ease – she felt – with his position as a privileged young man. Indeed, he had tried to work: having passed his law exams soon after marriage he had joined a chambers as a barrister but soon discovered that he was given no cases, the clerk having determined that the others needed the money more than he did. So the young couple were generally footloose and fancy-free, both day and night, which meant trips to Ireland – where Bryan's father lent them a vast house in Knockmaroon – or Paris. They had returned there at the end of the previous year with Nancy, who was now writing her first proper novel. She was a frequent visitor to their house, usually with a writer of some acclaim in tow, not least Evelyn Waugh, who seemed to think that Nancy's career as an author was as promising as his. Mr Waugh had only just published a new book, *Vile Bodies*, and dedicated it to Diana and Bryan; Louisa thought Nancy might rather have minded.

Most weekends were spent staying with friends in the country, hunting or shooting in the winter months. When in London, residing at their house in Buckingham Street (rather larger than a dolls' house as it had turned out), Diana and Bryan went to the theatre almost every night, or Diana went to concerts with her brother Tom, as well as to dinners, clubs or dances, or gave their own elaborate parties. For Diana's nineteenth birthday in the summer of 1929, they had held a party themed '1860', with a few hundred guests and the women required to wear enormous crinoline skirts with hoops. Only a month later they held an equally extravagant 'tropical' party on board the Guinness family yacht, the *Friendship*. Every outing was followed up by a newspaper report the next day, usually with a photograph of 'the ravishing the Hon. Mrs Guinness'. Often, but not always, the accompanying item was written by Luke Meyer.

Luke had remained a friend of both Diana's and Louisa's. In the wake of Guy's shocking revelation that he was engaged, Louisa had needed that friendship more than ever. Not, she strongly suspected, that Luke would ever be a romantic attachment, but she didn't mind that. She had sworn off that altogether. It wasn't as if she could be married and be a lady's maid, in any case. For while she knew she remained nothing more than a servant, there was much about the work that she had begun to enjoy. To begin with, it was not arduous. She couldn't even complain about lack of sleep as other lady's maids did, for although Diana often returned home late, when Louisa needed to be ready to help her undress and prepare for bed, she slept late, too. There was some work to be done in washing and ironing Diana's dresses and keeping her shoes, gloves, hats and bags spotless, but mostly it was a very 'upstairs' sort of life, with the two of them frequently going to the shops together, whether to prepare for the various parties or travel. Naturally, when Diana travelled, Louisa travelled with her and was accorded her own respect at the servants' halls of the houses they visited, often seated on the right of the butler at the staff meals; it never failed to amuse her that the servants were more self-consciously hierarchical than the people they worked for. Upstairs, Diana would sometimes tell her late at night, the young men and women enjoyed breaking the rules of their parents, eschewing the ancient rules of seating according to title – and once, Diana had snickered, a woman had refused to leave with the rest of her sex after dinner but remained with the men to drink the port.

Sometimes the younger sisters – Unity, Decca and Debo – would come to London and Louisa would take them out, which they would all enjoy. Diana adored her younger sisters and they were completely enthralled by her glamour; as a gang, Louisa enjoyed the sensation of being one of them, deep in the centre of their teasing and jokes. As for the rest of Diana's life, Louisa knew she was not one of the players but she somehow felt in the thick of the high life, often hearing the society gossip some time before it made it to the papers. Once or twice, slightly guiltily, she had even given Luke a story but never anything about Diana or Bryan. She might not have been curing disease or running for parliament like the fearless women featured in the newspapers but compared to where she had started in life, Louisa felt she had begun to achieve something, even if it was travelling more and meeting a wider circle of fascinating people than she was sure any of her ancestors would have done.

There was just one fly in the cold cream.

Louisa didn't like Diana.

She couldn't put her finger on why, exactly, or even when the rot had started to set in. Diana was perfectly nice to her, never high-handed or too exacting in her requirements. The excellent cook at Buckingham Street, Mrs Mackintosh (always called 'Mrs Mack'), was almost slavishly devoted to her mistress, as was May, the parlourmaid who had formerly worked for Bryan's parents. Nor was her employer dull or stupid: Diana was well-read, as up-to-date with the latest artists and writers as with politics, and never short of an opinion. She was very beautiful, of course – even more so now than when she had married, having lost something of her babyish plumpness around the chin and cheek-bones, even now that she was in the later stages of pregnancy. She could be stubborn, wilfully sticking to her point even when her argument had been clearly lost, but this could be said of Nancy, and Louisa remained as fond of her. It was more a certain coldness that Louisa detected, a frigidity that remained even in the face of the warmth of another's kindness. It was possible that at the root of it, Louisa felt sorry for Bryan, who was madly besotted with his wife, to a degree that she had to admit could not be easily matched in return. More than once, Louisa had found Diana asleep on the bed in the afternoon, with rose petals strewn on the pillow by Bryan as she slept, a newly written poem left beside her. This could be loving or oppressive, depending on your point of view, but was surely kindly meant and Louisa found herself reacting crossly to Diana's complacency about her husband's adoration.

With Diana pregnant now and the baby due in early March, Louisa felt an obligation to remain in her employ. And truthfully, in spite of this difficulty, she was reluctant to consider seriously giving up her work: she had a comfortable room in the centre of London, a roof over her head, the opportunities of travel, easy work … When she thought back to the squalor of the shared lodgings she had had to take in the time she'd spent away from the Mitfords, let alone the long hours working at the dress shop and the wandering hands of its owner, she wanted to retch. No, she had to stay with Diana and follow her, if not quite to the ends of the earth, then at least to Venice.

CHAPTER TWENTY-FOUR

⁓

When Louisa had first gone to work for the Mitfords in their pretty Cotswolds house, the beauty of the English countryside had struck her, even in the depths of a frozen winter. This picturesque memory faded as quickly as ice in the sun when she arrived in Venice.

The journey had been a long one, longer even for Louisa and Turner, the chauffeur and nominal valet for Bryan (who didn't like to say he had a valet, though he appreciated a man who polished his shoes and laid out the correct attire for a ball). The two of them had left a day earlier than Diana and Bryan, taking the train to Dover, then the ferry, and another train from Calais to Paris. Once there, they had crossed Paris – not as difficult as it might have been; Louisa was carrying the small case that contained Diana's jewellery, so Bryan had given them the francs to pay for a taxi – and, helpfully armed with *Cook's Continental Timetable*, caught another train to Venice, with one change in Milan.

Turner was not a man given much to conversation beyond the

mechanics of a car or philately (he carried a red leather book of his collection with all the *laissez-faire* of a man in possession of the Crown Jewels), but once they had won the minor battles over which train to catch and from which platform, Louisa was content to read her book and enjoy the peacefulness of the journey. France's landscape in January was not particularly adventurous, with large flat fields of brown earth broken only by the occasional line of tall trees. Of Milan she saw nothing but the railway station, though even the posters with Italian words were enough to give her a frisson of delight. When they arrived in Venice, Louisa was disappointed not to see any water but cars driving around as plentifully as in London; those paintings she had seen must have been exaggerations or perhaps it had all been paved over?

Only after she and Turner had met Diana and Bryan off the Orient Express and hauled their considerable luggage into a second taxi which drove for a surprisingly short amount of time, stopping at the waterfront, did Louisa understand that they had not yet reached their final destination. 'The train was heavenly,' said Diana, her hand resting lightly on her curved stomach as they stood by the water, 'but I am exhausted. It was a non-stop party the entire way. I expect your journey was less tiring.' She would have continued chatting but Bryan came up and put his arm around her: 'My love, let me show you this marvellous city in the best way possible.' Quietly, he steered her away for them to stand together while they waited for the two motorboats to arrive.

Diana and Bryan went in one water taxi, Louisa, Turner and the luggage in the second, following close behind. Though the boats were low in the water and about the same size as a long car, they were carried at a sedate pace, first through a channel marked out by tall poles before they were suddenly motoring along a wide watery avenue, high Venetian palaces on either side. The buildings were enchantingly old, with faded, coloured plaster and thick, leaded windows behind open shutters; through wide iron gates, gardens could be seen, dormant in the unforgiving winter. When Louisa recognized the Rialto Bridge from paintings she had seen by Canaletto at the National Gallery, she realized they were on the Grand Canal itself. The water was as grey as metal, the sky no less impervious, and yet Louisa felt herself as exalted by her surroundings as she was on a high summer's day. When they passed what she knew must be St Mark's Square, she caught a glimpse of the Doge's Palace, with its fantastical tiling and stern statues, the elegant height of the Campanile tower and even the dome of Saint Mark's Basilica. Italians in tightly belted dark coats and hats pulled low walked along narrow pavements lining the canal and it seemed almost impossible that they should be going about usual daily business, hardly aware of the extraordinary, rare beauty they were in. Louisa and Turner were sitting in the cold open air, and Diana turned around to wave at them both, a smile on her face, mouthing: 'Isn't it glorious?' Louisa could do no more than smile back and nod happily.

As they were not staying on the main island of Venice itself but on the Lido, the boats carried on beyond the neck of the Grand Canal, past other small archipelagos and drew up at a pier destined solely for guests of the Hotel Excelsior. There they were met by porters in burgundy and blue livery, their bags carried with much exclamation and fuss to the enormous lobby. Louisa and Turner stood to the side while Mr and Mrs Guinness checked in at a reception desk that seemed to be as imposing as the altar at Canterbury Cathedral. Louisa was slowly realising that the vast structure they had seen from the outside, resembling a sprawling Venetian palace, was in fact nothing but the hotel. The lobby's ceilings were too high to be able even to discern its colour clearly, the staircases that criss-crossed from several floors down were sweeping enough for an empress in full regalia to descend and their fellow guests had all stepped straight out of the latest issue of *Vogue*. As admiring as she was, it was with relief that Louisa spotted Luke across the lobby, even if he did seem to be in the company of a rather eccentric-looking older woman. Luke waved at her, went across to say hello to Diana and Bryan, then came over to Louisa.

'Miss Cannon, may I introduce you to my aunt, Lady Boyd? Aunt, Miss Cannon is Mrs Guinness's lady's maid.'

'Indeed?' said Lady Boyd. She was plainly dressed and plain to look at, with watery eyes and a firm chin. Her clothes were practically Edwardian, with a hat that was a far cry from the close-fitting cloches that Diana and her friends favoured; Lady Boyd's was high, with an upturned brim and a large yellow silk chrysanthemum tucked inside. Frizzy wisps of grey hair had escaped her hat erratically. Something about her looked familiar but Louisa wasn't sure if that was because she looked like a certain type of old-fashioned widow one often saw. She looked Louisa up and down and then gave her a small smile that showed no teeth. 'How do you do. Will you forgive me? I must speak to the concierge about our arrangements for the visit to the Rialto Bridge tomorrow.'

Luke watched her cross the lobby – she might as well have traversed an aeroplane hangar – and then turned back to Louisa. 'It's nice to see you,' he said. 'We got here three days ago, and none of the others arrived until last night. I think if I have to play one more round of gin rummy I might throw myself off the top of the Campanile.'

'I didn't know you were bringing her with you.'

'She's brought me, in a manner of speaking. The newspaper wouldn't pay, though I'm sure they'll love any stories I wire them, and I couldn't have afforded it otherwise. Thus I suggested to dear old auntie that she deserved a small holiday after all her work over Christmas, and that we could enjoy the delights of the Venetian churches together.'

Louisa was interested by this. 'What work?' She didn't know many titled women who went out to earn money.

'She gets brought in when a hostess wants an impressive menu for a party, though she doesn't do any of the cooking as such. Oh, Diana's beckoning, you'll have to go. I think everyone is having dinner here tonight, in Kate's rooms. She only arrived yesterday.'

'Not me,' said Louisa, though only to state the fact.

'No. But I'll try to find you later.'

'I expect you'll be able to ring up to a room in my name,' said Louisa. 'I don't know exactly where I'm staying.'

'Almost certainly near our rooms. We've taken the cheapest ones possible,' said Luke with a wink and, waving briefly at the approaching Guinnesses, strode off to fetch his aunt.

Louisa went to Diana, who was certainly anxious to talk to her. 'There was a message for us,' she said, her cheeks unusually flushed. 'Nancy is here, too. She has broken up with Hamish and needs consolation.'

'Is she alone?'

'No, she's brought Tom, thank heaven, and another friend with her, Clara Fischer. She sounds Jewish.'

'She's American,' said Louisa. 'An actress. She was at Pamela's party a few years ago when . . .' She looked at Diana, willing her to understand.

'When what?'

'When Nancy's friend was killed,' she whispered.

'Oh Lord,' said Diana, pulling a face. 'I do hope she's not a bad omen.'

'I'm sure she's not,' said Louisa.

But she was wrong.

CHAPTER TWENTY-FIVE

D iana and Bryan had three rooms and a bathroom that overlooked the sea with what was, to Louisa's eye, quite the most magnificent view she had ever seen. There were huge arched windows with a balcony, although it was too cold to sit outside. 'It's a very odd time of year for us to come here, isn't it?' Louisa heard Diana remark to Bryan.

'Kate gets bored and dreams wild plans,' he replied. 'Besides, I believe our anniversary was the excuse, was it not, my darling wife?' He went to kiss her but Diana motioned that they were not alone and he stopped. 'I'm going to go down and see where some of the others are. We'll find some luncheon I expect.'

'I'm going to ring up Nancy, then we'll join you,' said Diana. But as Bryan left, Nancy and Tom came piling in, with Clara in tow. Tom was a delight to see; just turned twenty-one years old, he had the fine profile and good hair of his father. As the only boy with six sisters he was remarkably even-tempered, less inclined to drama than his siblings. As she'd mentioned to

Diana, Louisa remembered Clara well; she had last met her at the end of 1925, when there had been a bad business – a young man, Adrian Curtis, had been pushed from the bell tower of the church close to the Mitford's country house during Pamela Mitford's eighteenth birthday party. It had been an uncomfortable few months as several of the guests had come under suspicion, but it had also been a revelatory time for Louisa, who had discovered the uninhibited pleasure of dancing for the first time, when she first accompanied Pamela to the infamous 43 nightclub. It had been there, in the semi-darkness, that the differences between Louisa and those that surrounded her had fallen away; but of course, it had not lasted. Clara, one of the group of friends, was an American actress and as strikingly pretty as any film star, if rather too timid for anyone to imagine her able to take centre stage.

The cold light of January was harsh but Louisa thought Clara looked less glamorously attractive than she used to. She had always been fashionably thin but now looked gaunt, with ashen shadows beneath her cheekbones.

There were flurries of kisses between them and Diana, and they each said hello to Louisa, though Nancy couldn't help herself in remarking to her sister, 'Has anyone else brought a lady's maid?'

'Only me, in my current state, you know.' Diana sounded apologetic but Louisa knew she had grown quite used to having her around, pregnant or not. Nevertheless, she felt it would be better to excuse herself with the unpacking.

Louisa went to the adjoining room with the various cases, removing the numerous dresses and shirts, each of which had been carefully ironed and wrapped in tissue paper, but as the door was left open she found she could hear their conversation quite easily.

'Aren't you simply *enormous?*' she overheard Nancy say in a stagey voice that Louisa recognized as her teasing tone, one that no one was allowed to take offence from but often did.

'The doctor says things are progressing nicely. I'm so sorry to hear about you and Hamish,' Diana replied, the sting in the tail.

There was a pause, and Louisa could picture Nancy drawing herself up with dignity. The very last thing Nancy would want from her younger (married, rich) sister was pity. 'There's nothing to be sorry about. We're going along in our usual jolly way.'

'Then what did you mean in your note? You said you had broken up with him.'

'Oh, I was in a fit. I suddenly minded about having a diamond ring but I've come to my senses now.'

'Naunce, is it *really* going to happen? I mean, he won't be able to make you happy in a way that a man should . . .' Diana's voice had tapered off uncertainly. Louisa knew she had more confidence in the face of Nancy than she had had in her younger years but the status quo was ultimately unchanged.

'You mean his pashes at school? Oh, I never pay any attention to that. All boys have their phase, don't they?'

'I think it's rather more than a phase in Hamish's case.' This was Tom, sounding like the young man he was now. In spite of his tall, handsome figure, his deep voice startled her nonetheless. She'd only ever thought of him as a boy, one she hadn't seen so much of, since he had, unlike his sisters, been sent away to school. When Louisa later recounted this conversation to Luke, he had interrupted with glee: 'There are rumours that Tom and Hamish . . . *you know*, at Eton.' Louisa had refused to believe it at first but Luke had been adamant, and she'd been forced to concede that he was more likely to know than she was. She knew by now that he preferred men to women but far from finding this disappointing, she revelled in the freedom it gave their friendship.

Louisa was inserting the wooden shoe trees into Diana's various shoes when she heard the murmur of conversation change to a more excitable tone. Luke had entered the room and it sounded as if Nancy were happy to see him, there were exclamations of greeting and Luke was introduced to Clara and Tom. Louisa was sure Luke had told her that he had met Tom before but they seemed to be saying hello to each other as if this were the first introduction.

'Lou-Lou?' Diana rarely called her that. She was showing off in front of Nancy, who had come up with the pet name years ago.

'Yes, Mrs Guinness?' Louisa came back into the room.

'We're going on an outing to St Mark's Square. Come along with us. If I get tired and need to sit out for a bit, I'd appreciate your company.'

'Of course, I'll fetch your things.'

Coming out of her room half an hour later, having fetched her own coat and hat, Louisa bumped into Luke and Lady Boyd. They were, as he had predicted, close by, having not quite the Guinness or Mulloney funds to spend on their own accommodation.

'Hi,' said Luke, 'walk down with us.'

Louisa detected Lady Boyd give a fleeting look of disapproval at this suggestion but she said nothing to object.

'Have you been to Venice before?' asked Louisa. She was agog at the thought of the trip to St Mark's Square.

'Never,' said Luke. 'But Lady Boyd has, haven't you, Aunt?'

'Before the war,' she confirmed in a tone that was wrapped in nostalgia for the good old days. 'Sir William Boyd and I stayed at the Gritti Palace, in a suite that overlooked the Grand Canal.'

'It's all been rather a downhill slope since then,' whispered Luke to Louisa, pulling a face. She started to titter but stopped when Lady Boyd looked at her sharply.

'Luke, dear,' said Lady Boyd. 'I'm not at all sure that you will be warm enough. Shouldn't you be wearing that nice muffler I bought you?'

'I'll be perfectly fine, no need to fuss,' said Luke patiently, rolling his eyes at Louisa as his aunt walked ahead.

In the lobby were gathered Diana, Bryan, Nancy, Tom, Clara – still looking wan – and Kate Mulloncy, together with three or four others that Louisa did not recognize but who had presumably been rounded up in the last half-hour for the excursion. There were stilted introductions between the young people and Lady Boyd – Louisa stood to the side for this – and then they were all led by Kate out to the Excelsior pier, where a liveried boat was waiting to take them across to St Mark's Square. The weather was fortunately dry, if bitterly cold, and the members of the party were almost all wrapped up in a variety of fur stoles, capes, hats and, in Kate's case, a full-length mink that made her look more like a Hollywood film star than Clara could ever manage. The image of Kate's small revolver in her vanity case flashed through Louisa's mind but she decided to dismiss it; there must have been some reason she felt she needed the protection at the time. There was lively chatter between everyone and Luke in particular seemed boyishly happy to be amongst them. Louisa turned her face to the view of the passing islands and the approaching mouth of the Grand Canal, quietly lost in her own thoughts until their arrival at the pier by the Campanile, when all her senses were at once overwhelmed by the sights and sounds before them.

CHAPTER TWENTY-SIX

B ack in London, Guy was at his desk, tidying his papers at the end of what had been a long but successful day. With DI Stiles, the two of them had concluded a case that had seen the accused, a burglar who had been operating in the area for several months, sentenced to ten years with hard labour. Guy's telephone rang and he picked it up with a smile, already anticipating another congratulatory message from one of his superiors. When he heard the operator ask if he would take a call from a Mr Albert Morgan he said yes and only a split-second later did he realize this was another sort of call altogether.

'DS Sullivan speaking,' said Guy.

'It's Mr Albert Morgan here,' said the voice, distinctively Yorkshire and speaking quite slowly, as if uncertain as to whether the telephone could really pass the sound along so many miles.

'Hello, Mr Morgan, it's good to hear from you.' Guy hoped it was. He hadn't forgotten Rose, the missing maid. There had been no reason to suppose that she hadn't gone on to find an amusing and interesting way of earning a living in Paris, that she had even been escaping from her family and had deliberately made sure that she wasn't found. Yet he had never felt entirely settled, worrying that he had not done his duty by her worried parents.

There was a rather long pause, and the line crackled. 'Sorry, Mr Sullivan, I'm sure you're a very busy man. But Rose's mam and me, we wondered if you'd heard owt about our Rose. It's been a year since you went to Paris and we know you said she'd been working there, and we know you said she's a grown lass that'd let us know if she wanted to, that she were all right . . .' He tailed off and Guy, knowing he had nothing of comfort to say, stayed quiet. There was a cough. 'It's breaking her mam's heart, that's all. I thought there might be something to tell her.'

'I'm very sorry, Mr Morgan. I've not heard anything. I take it she's not been in touch with you or any of her brothers and sisters, then?'

'No. Well, I suppose no news is good news.'

Guy felt sorry for the poor man. 'I know that's a phrase we all use but it is true. There've been no police reports about Rose, nothing untoward. We have to assume she is alive and well but, I'm sad to say, choosing not to get in touch.'

'Aye, well. She always was a one for doing things in her own way. All her brothers and sisters have stayed up here in Osmotherly, but Rose took off for London when she were but sixteen.'

'She knows how to look after herself, then.' Guy tried to sound as encouraging as possible. 'I'll put the word out again,' he found himself saying. 'You never know, someone might have seen something or remembered something in the meantime.' He shouldn't go promising anything but he couldn't help himself.

Mr Morgan's voice sounded brighter. 'Aye, good lad. That'll

cheer up her mam no end. I'll tell her police are still on t'case. Thanks, lad. Have you still got the number? The Queen Victoria pub?'

'Yes, I've still got it. I'll call you the minute I hear anything. Goodbye, Mr Morgan.'

'Goodbye, Mr Sullivan.' He rang off sounding as if he'd heard good news, when of course nothing had changed at all. Optimism springs eternal when a parent longs for a child to return, thought Guy. Or perhaps it was simply the only way to survive.

Remembering Rose put Guy in a contemplative mood and took him back to the low moment when he had left Paris the year before. He had returned to London determined to try harder with Sinéad. She was a good and kind girl, and proud of him. Hadn't she told all her family – which seemed to be a fairly extensive list, judging by the number of cousins that wrote and even turned up in London requiring a bed and a job – that she was to marry a British police officer? He couldn't deny it, her pride puffed him up. There were things they both did want, after all – a family of their own, a house and garden – and Guy's mother had been so pleased to know that he was going to settle at last. The worry she had over Guy's father had got no easier: there were increasingly days when he didn't seem to recognize his wife. Mrs Sullivan and Sinéad had whiled away many pleasant hours discussing the merits of baking Irish soda bread and the myriad ways one could cook a potato. Guy's mother had hinted more than once that she would appreciate the help of a daughter-in-law who understood the importance of family. Yet, they still hadn't married and he wondered if it was time he confronted the truth about why. Perhaps it wasn't only Rose he needed to find.

CHAPTER TWENTY-SEVEN

The gaggle of Britishers and the American were met off their boat by a guide that the hotel's concierge had arranged for them. 'So tiresome,' Louisa heard Nancy say to Clara, 'one just wants to go around at one's own pace.' But he turned out to be a delightfully informative Italian who looked rather like a professor, with white hair that stuck up in tufts when he removed his hat. Louisa, careful to stand at the back of the group, hung on to his every word as he took them around what they were taught to refer to as *la Piazza*; first to admire the astonishing views from the top of the Campanile, then the art in the Museo Correr to see 'only one or two jewels in *la collezione*, we cannot possibly see all the diamonds in the crown without walking all the way around and then you will be wrung out like the cloth that washes the dishes'. Finally, they went into the Basilica, with its wondrous gold dome and the professor – as they could not help but call him – had timed their arrival perfectly with the lighting of the candles, hundreds of them it seemed, so that each tiny gold mosaic reflected the soft light in undulating waves and shadows. Here they were left to walk around or sit and pray as they wished, arranging to meet at a café in the square at four o'clock. Louisa stayed close to Diana, who was walking around with Tom and did not seem in the least fatigued. They were talking to each other in an amiable way, having become closer in the last year than Diana was to any of her sisters. 'What are you going to do after this?' Diana asked him, as they stood before a frankly enormous nearly naked Christ bleeding on the cross.

'I'll get the train back to Berlin,' said Tom. 'Term starts soon.'

'How is it? It still seems frightfully strange, your reading law over there and not at Oxford. Even Manchester University would seem less odd.'

'I suppose it must but Germany is a wonderful country. Outside the city, one's not seen views like it, bigger than anything you could imagine and so ordered somehow, neat lines of hedges.'

'Hmm, Bryan would like that. I'd like to see the underground nightclubs of Berlin. Are they very bizarre? When we came to see you last year, we heard extraordinary things about tigers and half-naked dancers.'

Tom chortled at that. 'Yes, they are probably. But most of the students around me are less concerned with the nightclubs than with the politics. There are the most terrific brawls all the time – they're more of a draw than any cabaret.'

'What are the fights about?' Louisa could hear that Diana was genuinely interested, which wasn't so surprising. Although Diana had not been old enough to vote in the general election last year, she had pressed upon Louisa that she was to abstain, as it was simply not possible to vote for the Conservatives and 'that ghastly Stanley Baldwin'. 'Those poor, poor miners,' she had implored at the time, referring to the strike, 'you must think of them.'

'Fascism versus Communism mostly,' said Tom. 'The country is broke and they need a solution.'

'Do you take sides?' asked Diana.

'Oh no, it's their own affair. But if I were a German, I suppose I would be a Nazi.'

'Nazi?'

'That's the Fascist party,' said Tom. 'Shall we go and meet the others now?'

So that was the first time that Louisa – and Diana – heard the term Nazi. It would not, of course, be the last.

At the café in *la Piazza*, everyone chose to sit outside; in spite of the fading sun and cold, they were nonetheless intoxicated by their surroundings. There were three or four of the Guinness's friends that Louisa recognized and by now knew the names and gossip attached to them – there was the *Vogue* photographer Cecil Beaton for one, and the artist Dora Carrington, looking even more wraithlike than usual. It was hard to square her with the rumour that she lived as part of a *ménage à trois*. But just as they were settling into their chairs and squinting at the menu, wondering what an *espresso* was or a *pizza marinara*, there was a scream from Clara. Louisa, sitting at the far end of the three tables that they had occupied, saw that Clara had stood up and was frantically looking about herself. 'My bag!' she said, before repeating herself several times.

'I take it your bag has gone missing,' Kate remarked drily.

Nancy was sitting opposite Clara and had not removed either her hat or gloves, but she looked very at ease, as if she were a woman not easily stirred to drama. Something which Louisa knew to be quite untrue. She regarded Clara not coldly exactly but with a laconic eye.

'Is your passport in your bag?' she asked.

Clara sat down in her seat and put her hands in her lap. She looked completely defeated, thought Louisa, as if she had lost a war not a bag.

'No. I left that in the room.'

'All your money?'

'Some, but no, not all.'

Nancy crossed her legs and picked up the menu again. She might have been a detective inspector interrogating a thief that had been caught red-handed and already knew the answers.

'Then what could possibly have been in your bag that is making you so hysterical?' She barely lowered the menu as she asked the question.

Clara started to speak but stuttered and stopped. 'It had a favourite lipstick of mine, which I can't easily replace,' she said at last but not with any conviction.

Nancy raised an eyebrow at this but said nothing more.

'I suppose you had better report it to the local police,' Tom suggested. 'We can ask the waiter here where the local station is.'

'No!' Clara had shouted and all heads turned in her direction. 'I don't want to report it.' She felt the eyes upon her and continued, 'There really wasn't anything in there of importance. I wouldn't want to waste their time.' But she looked increasingly agitated as the various drinks were ordered – someone had inevitably suggested a bottle of champagne – and as the glasses were brought over she stood up and said, 'I'm sorry, I'll join you all later. I've simply got to go and look for it.'

Diana leaned over to Louisa. 'Why don't you go with her? So she's not alone. Looks as if we'll be here for an hour, and I'm perfectly fine. We're sitting down, and I've got Nancy and Tom here.'

Louisa nodded her assent and walked quickly to join Clara, who was already halfway across the square.

'Clara.' Louisa touched her lightly on the arm but she jumped as if she'd been hit.

'What is it?' Her American accent seemed to have strengthened in her distress.

'Mrs Guinness suggested I accompany you on your search,' said Louisa as soothingly as she could. 'To keep you company.'

'Fine,' she said but quickly thought better of it. 'I mean, thank you.'

They walked beside each other in silence, turning into a side street on the west flank of the Basilica. It was getting dark now, and the streets were fairly empty of people. Nor were there any shops along here, only high walls overlooked by blocks of apartments, indicated by the strings of washing that hung outside some of them. Louisa wondered why on earth Clara had chosen to come this way earlier, when the rest of the party was admiring the religious icons inside. At last they stopped when they reached a dead end. There was nothing there but the detritus of others who had obviously loitered in the spot – cigarette butts and the leavings of a cat. At this wall Clara began to cry.

'Miss Fischer,' Louisa started, not knowing how to comfort her because this was all rather mysterious. 'What has happened? What was in that bag?' She had remembered that around the time of the murder of Adrian Curtis – or rather, in the weeks after it – Clara had shown Louisa and Miss Pamela a small knife in her bag. To defend herself, she had said, though against what exactly she had not elaborated. Guy had suggested that, as Clara was an actress, she was more dramatic about things than might have been strictly necessary. Louisa had to admit there was something in that. But Clara's distress here seemed very real.

'I might as well tell you,' she said at last. 'We know each other a little, after all. But please don't tell anyone else. Nancy suspects, of course, and they're none of them the saints they make themselves out to be.' This last was practically spat out with bitterness. 'But it had my opium supply in there. I came out earlier to have a discreet smoke, someone must have seen me and decided to steal it from me. I was . . .' She paused and looked embarrassed. 'I was a little unaware for a moment or two. It wouldn't have been hard for a bastard to do it. Sorry.'

Louisa tried to take the shock off her face. She couldn't yet quite think what to say.

Clara started breathing too fast, shallow breaths, and crying again. 'If I don't get some more, I don't know what will happen to me. I never wanted to come here in the first place but Nancy said it would do me good. And now! Louisa. It will make me ill, desperately ill if I can't find any more.'

'Miss Fischer, I'm so sorry. I don't know how we can possibly find any more. And we had better get back to the others or we'll miss the boat back.'

'I don't give a damn about the boat.'

'Well, I do.' Louisa decided she needed to take a firm hand here. 'And you're no better off wandering around here in the dark. It's clear you're not going to find your bag or the . . . the stuff. At least at the hotel you can rest and think more clearly.'

Clara looked at her. Louisa realized that her prettiness had been lost to the drugs and that seemed terribly sad. She felt sorry for her. It wasn't Clara's fault, it was the demon of addiction that held her in its clutches. Slowly, they walked back to the café again, reaching it just as the bill had been paid. Louisa gave silent thanks for the dusk that meant no one could see the light that had gone out of Clara's eyes.

CHAPTER TWENTY-EIGHT

O n returning to the hotel, Diana said she would rest and asked Louisa to come later to dress her for the evening. This meant Louisa could take Clara back to her own room, where she could keep an eye on her. On the boat trip back it had become plain that Clara needed company, even nursing. Louisa only had a single bed but there was an armchair and she thought that, if necessary, she would sleep on that. Clara's distress had taken a physical turn for the worse very quickly; it was most likely as much the knowledge that she had no more opium to hand as it was the withdrawal itself. Weak and practically leaning on Louisa like an old woman by the time they had reached the staircase that led to her room, Clara ran to the bathroom and sounds of her retching could be heard. Louisa felt both sorry and exasperated. What a ridiculous situation for this woman to be in! She was beautiful and ambitious – why did she have to go and ruin herself like this?

As Louisa was standing in her room at a loss as to what to do next, there was a soft knock at her bedroom door. Luke.

'What's going on? I noticed you walk up here with Clara.'

Louisa put her finger on her lips and whispered. 'Yes, she's in the bathroom now.' Casting a glance at the bathroom door, still firmly shut, she heard Clara heave again. She decided to step outside the room, and pulled the door behind her. 'She told me not to say anything,' she said to Luke. 'But I don't know what to do.'

'What is it?' There was a gleam in his eye. That gleam always worried Louisa – was it genuine concern or the hope of a good story?

'She's an opium addict.'

'Ah. The drug was in her bag, that's why she was so upset at its being stolen.'

'Yes.'

'And why she won't report it to the police.'

'Yes,' said Louisa. 'She's sick, Luke. She's only going to get sicker. She can stay in my room but I've got to attend to Diana, and I don't know if she'll see a doctor. What happens? Can an addict die if they don't get their drugs?'

Luke didn't reply immediately but looked along the corridor that led to his room. There was a thick red carpet even here in the cheaper wing that softened any approaching footfall. 'My aunt was a nurse in the war,' he said at last. 'She might know what to do. I'll ask her to check in on Clara. Maybe get her some tea, that cures everything.'

Louisa nodded and went back inside.

Throughout the evening, while the party had dinner in the hotel restaurant and then moved into the drawing room, where further cocktails were drunk and Tom played the piano,

Louisa tended to Clara. She slept fitfully and had been sick again, several times, until there was nothing left in her stomach but water. More disturbing were her shouts of delirium, most of which were difficult to make out though she spent a lot of time crying out for someone. Louisa couldn't quite catch the name.

At around midnight, Clara was in a deep sleep so Louisa left her and went downstairs to the hotel reception. Fortunately, the man on the front desk spoke good English and he told her that the party of English people had finished their supper and were now in the large drawing room that overlooked the beach. 'Thank you,' said Louisa. 'There is a guest in my room, Miss Fischer. She's not well.'

'Ah, we have no doctor here . . . ' He looked alarmed.

'That's quite all right. She doesn't need a doctor, I don't think. She's asleep now but if she happens to call down, will you ring for me in Mrs Guinness's room? When I return to my room I'll telephone and let you know I'm back with her. Perhaps someone could take up some tea, with a bowl of sugar? No milk.'

'Absolutely, I'll see to that right away.'

Louisa thanked him and went to the drawing room and scanned the various guests for Diana but couldn't see her. They appeared to be in their usual various states of inebriation and enjoyment. She felt suddenly tired and exasperated that no matter what was going on in the world or even upstairs, they were always able to enjoy themselves. Luke saw her and raised his hand in a gesture of acknowledgement but she could do no more than smile lightly back. Nancy came over to her. 'Are you looking for Mrs Guinness? She's just gone upstairs, I thought she would call for you.'

'She might have tried,' said Louisa. 'I came down here a few minutes ago.'

'What's wrong?' said Nancy. 'You look positively grey about the gills.'

'I'm fine. It's Miss Fischer, she's not well. I took her to my room so that I could keep an eye on her—'

Nancy interrupted her with a tut of impatience. 'Don't tell me what it is, I have a feeling I already know. Stupid girl. She promised me she wouldn't do that here. I'll go up and see her with Mrs Mulloney. She knows what to do in these situations. Thank you, Lou-Lou. It's kind of you to look after her but I'm sure she'll be absolutely fine. She's an actress, you know, prone to being rather theatrical about things.'

Louisa thought that if this was a performance, it was probably one of the best Clara had ever given. But she had better go and see to Diana quickly if she wanted to hold on to her job: the last thing she needed tonight was one of Diana's hot-tempered outbursts. She thanked Nancy and went up to Diana's room, crossing her fingers as she walked.

An hour later, when she returned, to Louisa's relief Clara seemed unchanged. The tea had been delivered and it looked as if it had been drunk. Perhaps Luke's idea had worked.

She felt responsible for Clara, as a friend of the Mitfords, and as the only one the American had confided in. Most of all, she felt a pang for the loss of that beautiful girl with the head full of golden curls and dreams of leading roles. Louisa changed into her nightclothes and as Clara seemed still to be sleeping quite well, with only the occasional movement when a limb would jerk, she decided to try and catch some rest. She made herself as comfortable as she could on the armchair with a cushion and a blanket, and though she intended to read she soon fell into a deep sleep. Some five hours later, Louisa woke with a start as if there had been a sudden loud noise but nothing had changed. It was dark in the room with only a soft light from a lamp in the corner, not strong enough to illuminate Clara in the bed. Louisa folded back the blanket and stood a little stiffly from her awkward position in the chair. As she walked across to the young girl she tried to see if she was sleeping or awake but on touching her cold arm she brutally realized she was neither.

Clara Fischer was dead.

CHAPTER TWENTY-NINE

S tanding there, in the dark, alone with the lifeless Clara, Louisa's veins turned to ice. Her mind raced: was it her fault? Had she not heard something she should have, a shout or cry that would have alerted her to help? Quickly, she turned the bedside lamp on and looked at Clara. Her skin was whiter than the sheets, her lips blue. There was no obvious sign of any last-minute struggle with death, other than that she had thrown the covers off. Louisa drew the sheet over Clara then dressed and went downstairs to the reception desk, where she told a young man there what had happened. There was some confusion owing to Louisa's lack of Italian and the man's lack of English but eventually she made herself understood and interpreted his gestures that a doctor would be called. She did not wish to return to her room with Clara's stiff body, and sat on a sofa in the lobby until the dawn.

Although she did not feel particularly hungry, Louisa breakfasted and finally at nine o'clock she asked the desk to call up to Mr and Mrs Guinness's rooms.

'Louisa?' Bryan had taken the call. 'What's this about?'

'I'm so sorry to disturb you, Mr Guinness, but there has been—' There was a catch in her throat and Louisa had to compose herself before going on. 'There has been a terrible tragedy.'

'Come up at once.' The telephone rang off.

When Louisa entered their room, having knocked, Bryan was up and wearing a quilted-satin dressing gown with co-ordinating slippers of navy and green piping, while Diana sat up in bed, rather bleary-eyed, pulling on her bed-jacket. 'What is this, Louisa?' said Diana. As she was pregnant, she was not having such late nights as before but she had nonetheless not gone to bed until one o'clock.

'It's Miss Fischer,' Louisa burst out. 'She's dead.'

'Dead?' said Bryan. 'What do you mean? What happened?'

'Oh God,' said Diana, and immediately reached for the telephone. 'I'm ringing Naunce.'

Louisa knew that none of this looked good for her but she had to tell the truth. 'Miss Fischer admitted to me yesterday, when her bag was stolen, that she was an opium addict, and the bag had contained her supply. Without it she was quite desperate and quickly very sick, so I kept her in my room.'

'You told us none of this!' Her employer was angry.

'No, sir, I'm so sorry.' Louisa was trying very hard not to cry. 'I told Mr Meyer, sir. Miss Nancy knew of it, and she said she would talk to Mrs Mulloney too.'

'Why didn't they say anything to us?' Bryan asked.

Diana had hung up the telephone. 'She'll be here as soon as she can.'

'I don't know, sir,' said Louisa. 'Miss Fischer didn't want anyone to know.'

'Has a doctor seen her?'

'Not yet, the hotel has telephoned for a doctor and he will be here shortly to see ...' She couldn't bring herself to say 'the body'.

There was a brief knock at the door before it flew open and Nancy rushed in, hair askew, a silk dressing gown tied around her slim figure. 'Louisa, darling,' she said and much to Louisa's surprise, Nancy put an arm around her, which made the tears come fast.

Bryan lit a cigarette and turned to face the view outside, another steel-grey day.

'Go and wash your face,' Nancy instructed Louisa, 'then come back out.'

She did as she was asked and when she re-entered the room, Nancy was sitting on Diana's bed and Bryan was no longer there. He had probably gone to the adjoining smaller room to get dressed.

Louisa stood at the end of the bed and the two sisters turned to look at her. 'What do you think happened?'

'I don't know exactly,' said Louisa. 'It seems she died in her sleep. It must have been the withdrawal, though it seems very quick.'

'I had no idea you could actually die from *not* having drugs,' said Diana.

'I went to see her last night,' said Nancy. 'She was in a very bad way. Kate and I stayed with her for about half an hour, when Louisa had to leave her to bring your hot milk.'

Diana ignored this jibe.

'Does anybody know Clara's family? Someone will have to be told.'

'She lives, that is – she lived – in London for the last few years. I don't know where she came from to begin with. Oh, dear. What a ghastly thing. I knew she was an inveterate drug-taker and I was simply furious with her for that, but she didn't deserve *this*.' Nancy shivered. 'I'm going to go back to my room and get dressed. I will go and tell Kate.' She stood up and seemed to think of something. 'You know, it's funny. I'm not sure Kate was terribly fond of Clara. She made an odd comment while we were there.'

'What comment?'

Louisa's ears pricked up at this.

'She said something about Clara being a husband-stealer, and getting her just deserts. I thought she was being bitchy, you know how she can be. But what if there had been something between Clara and Shaun? I have to say, I wouldn't put it past Clara. Remember her and Ted?'

'It's almost exactly a year since Shaun died,' said Diana. 'What a horrible coincidence, if Clara was doing something like that.'

'Unless,' said Louisa, 'it wasn't a coincidence at all.'

'What are you saying?' Diana had pulled herself up to a better sitting position. Her pregnant stomach was not yet so large that it was making her uncomfortable but she had complained once or twice of looking like a snake that had swallowed a football.

'Sorry, Mrs Guinness. I said that without thinking. It was just what Miss Nancy said about Mr Mulloney. You see, once or twice, last night, when Miss Fischer was in a very bad way, she was calling out for a name but I couldn't quite make out what it was.'

'Could it have been Shaun?' Diana's blue eyes were wide with what looked dangerously like glee.

'I don't know, I couldn't be certain. It sounded more like "Rhodes" or "Rose".' Without warning, Louisa thought of Guy and remembered he had been looking for the missing maid, Rose Morgan. Could it have been the same person?

'Careful, Bodley,' said Nancy. 'We mustn't say anything to Kate unless she says something first.'

'Of course I won't,' replied her sister imperiously. 'Speaking of which, we mustn't let Luke know either.'

Diana turned to Nancy when she said this and there must have been a look on her face because Diana said, 'I like Luke, he's great fun. But I don't trust him not to telephone his editor if he hears something juicy like this.' She pointed her finger at her sister. 'I don't want you telephoning your editor either.'

'Don't be absurd. *The Lady* wants tips on the right sort of hat for a shooting weekend, not amorous tittle-tattle.' But she had a look in her eye, one that Louisa had seen before: it never boded well. 'I'm going now. Let's meet downstairs in an hour, perhaps by then the doctor will have given a more definite answer.'

Diana bore a weary look on her face that made her seem much older than her nineteen years. 'Now that she's dead, perhaps Kate will say something of her suspicions about her husband.'

'I thought I was supposed to be the novelist in this family,' said Nancy. 'You're looking for intrigue where there is none. Just a very sad, rather predictable tale.'

CHAPTER THIRTY

When Diana and Louisa went downstairs, they found the rest of the party gathered in the hotel's large drawing room that overlooked the beach. People were talking quietly to each other yet there was a charge in the atmosphere, a sense of drama that had rather added spice to the proceedings. Although it was not yet eleven o'clock in the morning, some of the party had already started on the cocktails. Lady Boyd sat a little away from the group, the only one with a silver teapot and china cup beside her. Tom and Bryan were standing by the mantelpiece, smoking, engaged in what looked to be serious conversation. Kate Mulloney, in a vivid blue shirt and wide black trousers, sat at one end of a sofa, with Nancy beside her and Luke perched on the arm. She looked calm – her Eton crop glossy black, her lips red – but Louisa could see the tremble of the cigarette she held. 'We mustn't allow an autopsy,' she was saying, as Nancy listened.

'Why ever not?' Diana's voice, clear and authoritative. 'Her family will want to know what's happened.'

'They won't when they discover it's opium,' Kate shot back,

though she kept her tone low. 'I had to do the same for Shaun. His family would have been destroyed by the scandal. We need to make sure the police allow her body to be sent straight back to America. She was suddenly, dreadfully ill. That's all they need to know.'

'What do you mean?' asked Nancy. 'Clara had no opium, that's why she was so ill. You've got nothing to worry about. Forget about this and let the police get on with their job.'

But Kate's fingers still trembled.

Louisa could not stay there; she turned to go back to her mistress's room, to see which clothes needed laundering or ironing. It was important that she keep herself busy. But just as she had stepped out, she felt someone close behind her and heard a cough. It was the man who had been on reception the night before. 'I was very sorry to hear about your friend,' he said.

Louisa was about to say that Clara hadn't been her friend and then realized that would be splitting hairs needlessly. She had been concerned for her, hadn't she? In those last hours, Louisa was as close as any friend could be, and certainly as wretched at her death. No one else had thought to ask Louisa how she was, having woken to find the body, and the kindness of this stranger's remark almost brought her to tears.

'There is a small concern . . . ' He looked around him but no one else was there, other than the usual traffic of a large hotel. 'I sent one of the maids up to your room with the tea and she is terribly afraid that she may be blamed for something.'

'Oh no, she mustn't worry,' said Louisa, rushing to assuage the poor girl's fear. 'She couldn't possibly have, you see it was—' She stopped. No one would want the hotel to know that one

174

of the guests had died in a drug-related incident. 'It was something she had been suffering from for some time. Please let the maid know.'

He shrugged. 'I will try. These things, they happen in hotels all the time but they frighten the new girls. I hope she does not disappear!' He didn't seem quite as sympathetic as he had done at first. 'Goodbye.' He gave a small bow. 'Enjoy the rest of your stay.'

Up in Diana's room, Louisa mechanically set about her tasks, but as soon as she had run out of things to do, she realized she was completely worn out – from both the lack of sleep the night before and the terrible tension before the tragedy itself had struck. She wanted nothing more than to lie down in a darkened room but Clara's body had not yet been moved. It didn't seem to have occurred to anybody to find Louisa another room to sleep in. In the end, she decided to take a small risk by sitting on a low but comfortable chair in Diana's dressing room and closing her eyes for a few minutes or until her mistress returned.

But sleep would not come. Her mind raced around, seeing only the sallow face of Clara the day before and her death mask in the early hours of the morning. She wondered if any of her family had been told yet, she remembered how fun and pretty she had been when Louisa had first known her, and she thought about Clara calling out for someone and wondered who that person was. Could it have been Shaun? Nancy had mentioned Kate's comment that Clara was a 'husband-stealer'. The name had sounded more like Rose. The same name as that maid Guy had been looking for, though that could only be a coincidence. The young American had been so dreadfully unhappy in all sorts of ways, she now realized. It was the notion that Clara had died from *not* having opium which didn't sit right with her. Louisa didn't know very much about drugs but, from anything she had read in the papers, people died of something they had taken rather than not taken, didn't they? What's more, why was Kate so eager to shut down a second autopsy?

It was at that thought Louisa opened her eyes and sat bolt upright. Nancy and Kate had gone to see Clara last night, hadn't they? And they had been left alone with her. What if Nancy had left Kate alone with Clara for a few minutes? Kate could have asked Nancy to fetch her something, or Nancy might simply have gone to the bathroom. That would have been time enough for Kate to slip something in Clara's mouth. In her state, she wouldn't have noticed, and even if she had, she'd have had no strength to protest. Any cry she made could have been easily brushed off as just one of another of her agonised noises. She had to find out what Kate knew, and if she had been alone with Clara.

A further thought shook her. If Kate was capable of slipping something to Clara, might she not have done the same to her husband? She knew he was allergic to sesame: it wouldn't have been hard to put some in his food, would it?

As bone-tired as she had been a moment ago, there was a surge of energy running through her now. She could not wait and ran down the stairs back to the drawing room. It had been an hour since she had left but nobody appeared to have changed position, although the drinks had been refreshed. She hovered at the door, wondering whether to make herself known, when

Luke happened to look up and caught her eye. He tugged at Nancy and the two of them came over.

'Louisa,' said Luke, 'you must be feeling ghastly. What a horrible shock you had this morning.'

A wave of misery flooded over her when she heard these sympathetic words, as if they had opened the dam. She couldn't do more than nod in agreement.

Nancy moved the three of them to the side of the doorway, so that they couldn't be observed by anyone in the drawing room.

'What is it, Louisa?'

'Has the doctor has signed off Miss Fischer's death as natural causes?' Louisa asked, aware that she had no concrete reason to contradict this finding yet needing to know the answer.

'Yes,' said Luke. 'I believe he's said it was a heart attack. Apart from anything else, it means her body can be flown back to America quickly. Nancy telephoned the mother and she's understandably anxious to have her daughter back as soon as possible. Jewish, you see.'

Louisa looked at Nancy. 'You had to telephone . . . ?'

Nancy nodded. 'It was awful.'

'The thing is,' said Louisa. 'I wonder if it was natural causes.'

'Not this again,' said Nancy.

'What do you mean?' asked Luke, his ears practically flapping.

'I just don't see how she could have died that quickly from opium withdrawal. People do recover from addiction. She had been very sick, it's true, but not enough to cause death.'

'But what else could it have been?' Luke had the bone, Nancy looked angry.

'I don't know exactly but someone could have slipped her something, poison or another type of drug.'

Luke was about to respond to this but Nancy flew at Louisa. 'Must it always be murder with you? You and I have had this conversation already and I tell you, it's not that. It was horrible, it was sad, it was *bad luck*.'

'But what about Clara calling out—?'

Before Louisa could say a name, Nancy had held out her hands, palms out, as if shielding herself from hearing any more. 'I am not going to have this thrown in. The whole thing has been distressing enough. Just stop it, Louisa. Perhaps you should give up being a lady's maid and become a policewoman. That's the proper place for this sort of nonsense.'

She turned on her heels and stalked back into the room. Luke looked at Louisa. 'What name did Clara call out?'

'I can't tell you, if Miss Nancy doesn't want it said.'

'I think I know,' said Luke. He glanced over his shoulder. 'I'd better go back in there.'

Two mornings later, the English newspapers were delivered. In all of them was the news of 'the hopeful starlet Clara Fischer's sudden death in Venice, while on holiday with high-society luminaries'. No connection was made between the presence of Mrs Shaun Mulloney and the fact that her husband had died equally suddenly, almost exactly a year before, in Paris. But in the *Daily Sketch*, there was a gossip item about 'wagging tongues in the group suggesting that the flapper Miss Fischer had been, shall we say, swimming in the Irish seas with a husband that was not hers'.

Everybody read it. Everybody knew that Luke wrote for the *Daily Sketch*. It wasn't entirely wrong but it broke the code of discretion.

Louisa was summoned to Diana's room not long after the papers had been sent up and was told that Mrs Mulloney had decided that she would be leaving that day. 'So are we, too. It's not as if any of us can have any fun after all that business with Clara. You'd better get started on the packing, Lou-Lou. We're going home.'

CHAPTER THIRTY-ONE

Louisa's mind on the journey back to London from Venice was full of murderous thoughts. Whether it was the detective novels she had been reading, the thwarting of her police career, Nancy's off-handed remark about her giving up being a lady's maid, or genuine suspicion, she would not allow herself to fully determine. But she could not shake the feeling that there was a connection between Shaun's death in Paris and Clara's in Venice. On the face of it, they were both unfortunate but natural: Shaun's an allergic reaction to sesame, most probably in something he ate at the restaurant; Clara's opium withdrawal.

Yet there was a possible connection and, if right, it was a simple one: Clara and Shaun had been having an affair. That would both mean the search for a motive did not have to go far and would immediately unlock the possible murderer: Kate Mulloney.

How would she have done it? Knowing of her husband's sesame allergy, the first task would have been a simple one – and given that they were alone in an apartment in Paris, it would have been easy for her to claim that she had been too drunk to notice what had happened to him. Clara's was more complicated, but perhaps it was simply that she saw the opportunity and took it. When Clara was taken suddenly so ill, all Kate had to do was make sure that she was left alone with her long enough to slip her something that would cause her death.

That left two questions. Did Kate definitely know that Clara was having an affair with Shaun? And if so, why would Kate have waited a year between the two murders? The answer must be that a distance of several months would seem less suspicious. She may also have been biding her time, waiting for the moment when she could do it easily. Nevertheless, it seemed very cold-hearted, which did not fit with Kate's easy humour and largesse, both of which indicated a woman of real feeling; and her grief after Shaun's death had seemed genuine, if a touch too contained.

Perhaps Nancy was right. Louisa was intent on creating drama where there was none. She might be better off confronting the fact that she was bored, and that she should not be settling for this life of servitude, however much she enjoyed some aspects of it.

By the time Louisa had arrived at 10 Buckingham Street, she had determined that she must find another course of action for herself. In spite of having finished her schooling at the age of fourteen – her mother had needed her to assist her in her laundry work and to bring in extra wages to the household – she felt that she did have a brain. Under Lady Redesdale's kind instruction, she had been guided to various history books in the Mitford library that had been used to tutor the girls. Art books, too, had offered her windows into the souls of painters and sculptors; something she still felt to be a privilege, as no one before had ever suggested that Louisa might know of them, let alone understand their works. Nancy, who had been a wide and enthusiastic reader from a young age, recommended to her novels of worlds past and foreign, teaching her of Victorian slums, Indian maharajahs and African deserts. Besides all that, Louisa had been disciplined in reading the newspaper daily and catching as much as she could on the radio. For her work with Diana, she had made studies of *Vogue* and *Harper's* magazines when Diana had finished with them, making sure she was up-to-date on the latest fashions and styles, so that she could be a proper advisor as lady's maid. (Though, truthfully, she found the insistence on 'must-have' hats of a certain shape or the distinctions between two apparently identical beaded dresses rather silly.) All in all, she had a mind of her own. Why did she not use it to greater satisfaction?

But Louisa's initial impulse to look for other work was quickly submerged in the sombre atmosphere that greeted them in London. Diana's generally sunny outlook as she awaited the birth of her first child in the spring was overshadowed by the grim conversations everywhere – between Bryan and his friends, in the newspapers and on the radio – about what 'Black Thursday' in America's Wall Street would mean for Britain. There was talk of economic collapse, rising unemployment and social unrest spreading across the Atlantic to Europe. Not, Louisa noted, that it yet affected the evenings of the feted Mr and Mrs Guinness. The near-constant weekly cycle of theatre, concerts, dinners and dances remained as predictable as a commuter train timetable.

It wasn't long before Kate Mulloney was one of the many

to arrive at the house for a dinner party. Friends of Nancy's or Bryan's had only to telephone for Diana to ask them over. Louisa could see she was eager to cultivate the friendships for herself, and was always careful to be especially pretty and charming as a hostess. She certainly knew what not to do, thanks to her father's infamous outbursts at Asthall Manor; one guest had been sent packing from a weekend for leaving her handkerchief on a hedge. Being young and fashionable, the hosting was little effort for Diana – although Louisa thought that, when set alongside Nancy, it was clear that she lacked her sister's sharp wit, even if she was quick to laugh at another's jokes. Her quiet confidence, too, could have grown into something rather steely and unforgiving had she not been softened by the warmth and generosity of Bryan, who was never less than kind or concerned about any other person in trouble. That did not mean there was complete harmony in the matrimonial state. The most common argument Louisa would overhear took place as Diana readied herself for an evening out. Bryan would come into the bedroom, see Louisa fetching a long dress or Diana putting her diamond earrings on and say: 'Darling, we're not going out tonight, are we?'

Immediately Diana would reply: 'I am. You don't have to, of course.'

'But then, who will you be with?'

Diana would tease – whether as part of a long-standing Mitford habit or deliberately to infuriate her husband, Louisa did not know – 'I shall telephone and find a suitor. I'm sure either Evelyn or Cecil would oblige. Luke is always a stalwart, too.'

Luke had, in spite of being caught with his hands in the till, as it were, when he sent through the story about Clara to the *Daily Sketch*, continued his friendship with Diana. He was good-looking, amusing, a tame pet almost, and always available to her request for a chaperone. Bryan knew he was S.I.T. ('Safe In Taxis'), so could not object on jealous grounds. All the same, he chafed.

'Darling,' he would begin again, in placatory tones. 'I only want to enjoy my wife for myself. A play, a dinner and then back home to listen to a gramophone record or we could read our books by the fire.'

Diana would put down her hairbrush or lipstick, whatever she happened to be holding, and turn to her husband with a calm but unmoved look. 'We can do that *any* night, and tonight is the Red Cross Ball/the Astor dinner/the Prince of Wales's cocktail party . . . ' And that would be that.

A compromise was to have the dinners at home with guests, which thanks to Diana's excellent cook, Mrs Mack, never failed to please. Mrs Mulloney came for dinner only three weeks after the fated Venice trip. Nancy and Luke were also in attendance, as well as Evelyn Waugh – who practically trailed Diana's every step these days, sitting on her bed as she read her morning letters and accompanying her to the shops – not to mention some other luminaries that Diana refused to call 'Bright Young Things'. Though that, Louisa knew, was very much what they were.

Louisa did not serve at these dinners – that job fell to the elderly parlourmaid May, with Turner occasionally helping out if they needed the extra hands – but she would find as unobtrusive a spot in the kitchen as she could and get on with some mending, so that she could enjoy the bustle and noise. It made her evenings less lonely. On the night that Kate was there for dinner, Louisa was not entirely surprised to see Luke come down to the kitchen looking for her, around the time the women upstairs must have left the dining table to retire to the drawing room with coffee.

Louisa and Luke did not meet as friends alone, as such, but whenever Luke came to the house to see Diana, he made a point of seeking her out. She appreciated the effort, and though she was wary now not to give him anything that she thought would end up in his social column, they still shared a certain gossipy appreciation of the life he was living. 'Our generation has freedom,' he was fond of saying. 'I can do things my father would never have done, or would belt me for doing. I've got to make the most of it!' Louisa enjoyed hearing him say these things, so full of celebration and verve, but it also made her feel remorseful. Was she 'making the most of it'? She suspected not.

Luke came up to Louisa, snatching two small chocolates off a plate that was waiting to be taken upstairs as he did so, and knelt beside her chair. 'You won't believe what's happened,' he said as he handed her one of the sweets.

'What?' Louisa put her mending down and smiled. Had one of the women come out without realising they had a rip in their stockings? Or had there been talk at the table of an MP's latest indiscretions with his private secretary?

'Kate was left alone with Clara the night she died.'

Louisa stopped chewing. 'Tell me.'

'I was sitting on Nancy's right, Kate was opposite us and I don't think they thought I was listening to them because I was supposedly listening to the woman on my other side. But she was a terrible bore and my ears were twitching for something more enticing.'

'Go on.' Luke had a writer's habit of building up every story when she just wanted to get to the facts.

'Apparently there's been a letter to Nancy from Clara's parents. They want to know everything about what happened in her final hours. They're not, understandably, entirely at ease with the idea that their daughter would die so suddenly for no apparent reason.'

'Have they reported anything to the police?'

'I don't think so. I think they have written to Nancy as a friend of Clara's, to ask her what happened. The point is, Nancy said to Kate, "Should I tell them you and I went to see her, or should I keep quiet?"'

'Why would she say that?'

'I don't know but then Kate said: "Don't tell them I was left alone with her when you went to the bathroom. They'll only make something of it if they find out about Shaun and Clara."'

Louisa didn't reply to this but she felt afraid. What had Nancy got herself caught up in?

'I'd better go back upstairs,' said Luke. 'Got to join the men for the port. Not that they want me there. They want to talk about Wall Street and I want to talk about Bond Street.' He grinned at her but Louisa was still too shocked to return the gesture.

After he had left, she sat there for some minutes, not moving. The conclusion she'd reached earlier had only been reinforced: she would have to investigate further. Could it be that Kate was guilty of Clara's death, possibly even Shaun's too? If she was, then Louisa would reel her in.

CHAPTER THIRTY-TWO

❧

A week later, Louisa had put Diana's breakfast tray down with the morning post and was running her bath when she heard her mistress call out for her. She quickly turned the taps off – she'd once left it too long and it had flooded the floor, causing a dreadful row – and went to see what it was. Diana was waving a letter around. 'It's from Naunce, apparently Clara's family did have an autopsy after all and now they say it was an opium overdose. So much for claiming they wanted a quick burial.' Louisa didn't know how to react to this.

'Idiot girl. I'm sorry, Louisa, but she fooled you. She hadn't had it stolen at all. Her kind are sly, you know.'

The ugliness of this remark took Louisa aback for a moment. Besides, she knew different. She'd been with Clara, she'd seen her distress. There was absolutely no possibility that she had opium hidden on her, and Louisa certainly didn't have any in her bedroom, where Clara had spent her final hours. She wondered what to do with these suspicious – at this stage, they could be no more than that – and decided that she had to say something. She was due to leave London for a few days to stay with her mother and aunt in Suffolk. Before she left, she sent a note to Guy at the station, saying nothing save the detail of the autopsy result and her own knowledge of that evening, together with the conclusion she had drawn. If there was anything to take further, then he could deal with it.

While Louisa was away, Bryan and Diana had planned to drive out to the country to look for a house. Most weekends they borrowed a Guinness place in Sussex but now it was deemed necessary for them to have one of their own. Louisa reserved judgement on this but she could see that, with her baby due in a few weeks, Diana was at last embracing Bryan's notion of happy families in the wilds of the English countryside she had once been so desperate to escape.

Louisa's time in Suffolk, in the pretty village of Hadleigh, with her mother and aunt fussing over her and cooking her favourite dishes, helped her find perspective again. She knew she was obscurely influenced in London by the people she worked for, and the people they spent time with, not to mention her friendship with Luke, which was both enjoyable and unsettling. Without a close friend or Guy to confide in, she found it harder to hold on to those parts of her she knew to be true. Though she had grown up in London and would always love the solace of the crowded pavements and familiar bus routes, she found a peace in the country walks and the beauty of winter there, which had bewitched her since her first morning with the Mitfords. Her mother was also happy to remind Louisa of her good fortune with her work: 'I had backbreaking, thankless years as a washerwoman. You've gone up in the world and I'm glad of it, my girl.' After three nights of family gossip, helping her mother mend the chicken's coop – a side of the fencing had fallen and looked dangerously vulnerable to a fox's attack – and long, dreamless sleeps from the fresh air, she was ready to return to her work.

She also had had time to think about the deaths of Shaun Mulloney and Clara Fischer. She was afraid for Nancy, who had so decisively warned Louisa off investigating Clara's death, together with her concealing the fact that Kate had been alone with Clara for a certain amount of time before her death. Had she become caught up in something dangerous? Nancy was a difficult person to confront. Years of sparring with their hot-tempered father and barbing her younger sisters had made Nancy a formidable verbal opponent. Louisa needed to ask her directly what had happened that night but was certain that she would be dismissed before she could finish asking the first question. Nancy and Diana had grown closer in the last year; it wasn't inconceivable that Nancy could convince Diana to sack Louisa for impertinence. Even if Louisa knew she wanted to find another line of work, she wanted to get to the bottom of this first. And she would not be helped by being dismissed without a reference.

Still chewing this over in her mind, Louisa was walking from the Underground station on her way home when she turned the corner into Buckingham Street and ran smack into Guy. Too stunned at first to say anything she stepped back and couldn't think, momentarily, what it was she felt or wanted to do. It had been over a year since she had kissed him and it had taken all her strength to forget about him. Yet, she had sent that note. She had tried to deny to herself that she wanted to see him but of course, she did. Without saying anything she gripped her case a little tighter and carried on walking.

'Louisa!' Guy shouted. 'Please.'

Louisa stopped but didn't turn around.

Guy walked round to the front of her, forcing her to look at him.

'Louisa, I know what happened last time we met. I'm so sorry. I've never stopped being sorry.'

Still, Louisa could not bring herself to speak. She didn't know what she would say. She couldn't remember if she was angry or sad or what. The feelings wouldn't rise in any recognisable order, there was only a jumbled tangle stuck in her chest.

People were walking past them, some tutting in an irritated way at the two of them blocking the pavement.

'I've been waiting here for hours, hoping to see you. I thought you would come out to run an errand before long.'

'I've been away,' she said, her voice husky as if she hadn't spoken for weeks.

'I can see. Your case.' He made an attempt at a chuckle. 'That's how good a policeman I am.'

Louisa was desperate suddenly to stop being angry or neutral or whatever it was, and share his bad joke with him. But this thought immediately entered the boxing ring with the memory of Guy telling her that he was engaged to someone. It had been a year, he was probably married now. She tried not to look at his hand, to see if he was wearing a wedding ring.

'Why are you here, Guy?'

'Because of your note. I wanted to make sure ... well, I had to find out if you were all right. And to thank you.'

'What do you mean?'

'The American actress.'

'I see,' she said, though she didn't really.

Guy looked at her with equal puzzlement. 'The CID have been brought in to investigate her death. Thanks to your note. I thought you knew.'

'Obviously not. I've been away, remember?'

A fat drop of rain fell on to Louisa's head. Then another. Six drops and she'd have to get inside or she'd be soaked.

'The thing is, Louisa …' Guy looked at her with tears in his eyes.

'Yes?' The rain started but Louisa couldn't move.

'Nancy Mitford has been arrested.'

CHAPTER THIRTY-THREE

Louisa said nothing but ran the last few yards to the house, with Guy following her. At the side entrance she stopped and turned. 'I don't think you should come in.'

Guy's face fell. 'I want to help.'

'Is Nancy going to be questioned by the CID?'

'Yes,' said Guy.

'Then surely you and I cannot talk? I was there that night, too. I was alone with Miss Fischer when she died.'

The rain was pouring now, trickling off the back of Guy's hat and soaking his coat. 'It's not just you,' said Guy. 'We're anxious to talk to any others who went to her room that night.'

'Then why haven't I been brought in for questioning, too?' Louisa's chest felt tight.

'That's partly why I'm here. You will be. I wanted to warn you.' There were tears in Guy's eyes but Louisa felt nothing but hot anger.

'Just go, Guy. I will deal with this by myself.'

She went inside and closed the door firmly behind her.

Having quickly taken her case to her room and removed her damp coat, Louisa went in search of Diana and found her in the morning room with Lady Redesdale.

'Good morning, Lady Redesdale, Mrs Guinness.' Louisa always had to stop herself from curtseying to her former employer. She wasn't the queen but she looked as if she could be.

'Hello, Cannon,' said Lady Redesdale. She had lost none of her composure, sitting erect on the sofa beside her daughter, dressed plainly, her hair still dark though she was almost fifty years old. There's an old wives' tale that if a woman loses her looks while pregnant, she is going to have a girl; it seemed as if Lady Redesdale had borne the cost of her own six good-looking daughters.

'Thank goodness you're here,' said Diana. She, too, had learned a lesson from her mother in emotional repression but Louisa could see genuine gladness in Diana's eyes that she had returned. In the hall, as Louisa had tried to find her mistress, May the parlourmaid had whispered that Mr Guinness had gone to his Railway Dining Club, which took place on the train to Birmingham. This explained why Lady Redesdale had been summoned to the house in the wake of the news about Nancy.

Louisa thought it would be best if she didn't reveal that Guy had already told her what had happened. It might look as if she had an inside track to either the crime or the police that would put her out of favour.

'Is everything not as it should be, ma'am?'

Lady Redesdale sat up even straighter, though her spine was barely discernible from an iron poker. 'Nancy has been arrested and taken in for questioning at Knightsbridge station. Lord Redesdale is there with her now.'

Louisa allowed herself to look surprised but didn't over-egg it. Neither would have appreciated histrionics and they would have plenty of that to deal with from others. 'May I ask what she has been arrested for?'

'For the murder of Clara Fischer,' said Lady Redesdale but there was a catch in her voice.

'It's absolutely absurd,' said Diana.

'I don't understand,' said Louisa, her detached manner harder to maintain. 'How could she possibly have done it? I was there most of the time. I don't think Miss Nancy was even alone with Miss Fischer at any point.'

'She visited Clara with Kate Mulloney during the evening,' said Diana.

'Yes, at around midnight, when I was with you.'

'It seems Mrs Mulloney alleges that Nancy was left alone with Clara and that she had the opportunity then, to slip her something.'

Now Louisa *was* surprised, and she must have shown it. 'Mrs Mulloney says that Nancy did it?' she repeated, agog.

Diana nodded. 'The worst of it is, it's her word against Nancy's.'

'No, it's not,' said Louisa. 'And Mr Meyer can prove it.'

'Are you sure, Cannon?' Lady Redesdale was looking at Louisa with an ice-cold stare. 'You have brought murder to our door before and this is not reassuring me.'

'Lady Redesdale, I know how it must look. But please believe me, I don't invite these elements into my life. It's simply that they happen and I cannot help but look into the solution.'

Lady Redesdale merely raised an eyebrow.

'I think we had better telephone Luke and ask him to meet us at the police station.' Diana stood and went into the hall, where she could be heard asking the operator to connect her to a Belgravia telephone number. Louisa, uncertain what to do with herself, said she had better go and fetch Mrs Guinness's coat and hat.

Less than ten minutes later, Louisa was sitting in the front passenger seat of the Bentley next to Turner, with Lady Redesdale and Mrs Guinness beside each other in the back, on their way to the Knightsbridge police station. The wipers thwacked back and forth, and Louisa was grateful for the sound of the rain pelting on the roof, drowning out the heavy silence inside the car. Diana had spoken briefly to Luke and asked him to meet them there, which, she told Louisa, he had agreed to do. Louisa had already explained that Luke had overheard a conversation between Mrs Mulloney and Miss Nancy at the dinner that would confirm Miss Nancy's version of events. At the station, Turner pulled up outside and opened the door for Lady Redesdale, who hurried in quickly, her head bowed – managing both to avoid the rain or anyone in the street recognising her. Diana and Louisa followed close behind. In the waiting area sat both Lord Redesdale and Luke Meyer, neither of whom knew each other, hence both were surprised to find that the trio of women who came in greeted the other man.

'Sydney, what are you doing here?' Lord Redesdale, tall and elegant, if somehow always a fish out of water, or rather a countryman out of the country, when in London, looked pale and defeated. 'I told you not to come.'

'Things changed,' said his wife, briskly.

Their group caused something of a commotion in the station and it was only a minute before Guy stepped into the waiting area from the office behind. He couldn't have been back there long – there were traces of dampness on his collar from the rain – but he held a sheaf of papers in his hand. He greeted Lord and Lady Redesdale, who needed no prompting on who he was: he had solved the murder at their house five years before. As Guy was talking to them, Louisa walked over to Luke, who was standing outside the group. She was surprised to see he was shaking from head to foot.

'Louisa, why has Diana asked me to come here?' He lit a cigarette on the third match.

Louisa felt alarmed by this. 'I can explain.' She watched him inhale deeply. 'There's nothing for you to worry about. Why are you shaking?'

'I don't know,' he muttered. 'I don't like police stations. Please, just tell me what's going on.'

'There was an autopsy on Clara's body back in America and it appears she died of an opium overdose. Of course she didn't have any, so someone must have given it to her.'

Luke turned the colour of paper. 'I thought they were Jewish.'

'What? What's that got to do with it?'

'The Jewish bury their dead quickly. I thought the parents wouldn't want an autopsy.'

Louisa couldn't make sense of this. 'I shouldn't think anybody wants an autopsy, but they weren't satisfied with the doctor's certificate stating natural causes. And they were right.'

Luke looked around for an ashtray, found one and stubbed out his Player's. 'What's Nancy got to do with it? They surely don't think she gave opium to Clara?'

'Mrs Mulloney has told the police that Nancy was left alone with Clara, and that she had the opportunity to do it.'

'What would the motive be?'

Louisa remembered Nancy's angry reaction when she had first suggested that Clara might have been murdered. Had she been hiding something then? 'I don't know. But Luke, you need to tell the police what you overheard at the dinner that night.'

Before he could respond to this, Diana came over to them. 'I've told Mr Sullivan that he needs to talk to you,' she began, then cried out in pain. Clutching her extended stomach, she bent down quickly, one hand holding on to Louisa's arm.

Lady Redesdale rushed over and helped Diana stand up straight. 'I'm taking you home. We should never have come here. This is no good for the baby.' Giving the assembled company dark looks, Lady Redesdale escorted her daughter outside where Turner and the car would still be waiting. Lord Redesdale sat down heavily on a wooden bench. 'I'll stay here for Nancy,' he said, as tired as a balloon with all the air gone out of it.

'I'll ask someone to fetch you some tea,' said Guy kindly but Lord Redesdale could do no more than raise his hand in a gesture of thanks. 'Come with me, please,' Guy added to Louisa and Luke, and the two of them followed him out of the waiting room to a long corridor, where they walked past several closed doors. What sounded like someone shouting and banging on metal could be heard in the not-too-far distance. It gave Louisa the shivers. At last Guy turned a handle and they were let into a small room with only one high window. There was a wooden table and four chairs. Guy gestured for them to sit. 'I'll be back soon, I need you to wait here.' He left the room and closed the door.

'What's happening, Louisa?' said Luke.

'I don't know,' she admitted.

'I don't like it in here. It's filthy, and cold.'

'I don't think it's designed to be warm and inviting.'

'Ha bloody ha.' Luke stood up and stuck his hands in his pocket, fishing for his cigarettes and matches again but before he could light them, another man came into the room, with Guy behind him. This man was dressed in a brown suit that looked too big, as if he had recently lost a great deal of weight and not yet managed to buy new clothes to fit. He had a rather feeble moustache under his nose and two bushy eyebrows, as if they had come out of a costume kit and been stuck on in the wrong places.

'Right, Mr Meyer. I'm Detective Sergeant Stroud. You're staying here with me and we're going to have a chat. I understand you've got something important to tell me?'

Guy hovered in the doorway. 'Miss Cannon, can you come with me, please?'

Louisa turned back to see Luke looking as if he had been asked to sit in the executioner's chair.

CHAPTER THIRTY-FOUR

G uy led Louisa into another room, with two chairs on either side of an identical table to the one they had just left Luke sitting by. 'For obvious reasons, I cannot interview you,' said Guy. 'Someone else will be along in a moment.'

'Fine,' said Louisa. She so desperately wanted to talk to him about everything that was happening, to ask him if he had married, if he had thought of her at all in the last year. But she would not.

They sat awkwardly in silence with Guy shuffling through the papers he had in his hand and Louisa fiddling with a button on her coat until a man in a beautifully tailored pin-striped suit with a lemon-coloured tie came in. 'Ah,' he said, 'you must be Miss Cannon.'

'Thank you, sir,' said Guy. He left the room but not before he'd cast a backward glance at Louisa. She did not return it, but not because she was still trying to punish Guy: she was afraid. She knew, of course, that she was blameless, at least of Clara's murder. However, she also knew that her sort were often suspects. She had to assume she'd be treated as guilty until proven innocent.

'I'm Detective Inspector Stiles and I'll be conducting this interview.' He sat down and pulled out a notebook and fountain pen, and as he did so he flashed Louisa a brief smile as if to say she had nothing to worry about. But would this be true?

'Can you please confirm for me your name and place of residence.'

'Louisa Cannon, 10 Buckingham Street, London.'

'Occupation?'

'Lady's maid to Mrs Guinness.'

'Hmm.' Stiles scratched these details down, as well as making a note of the date and time of the interview. 'Can you confirm for me where you were at five o'clock in the morning on the twenty-seventh of January this year.'

'Yes, I was in my room, number 236, at the Hotel Excelsior on the Lido, Venice.'

'Were you alone?'

'No, sir.' Louisa's head started to swim. She hadn't eaten anything since her mother had given her bread and butter and sweet tea that morning shortly before her train journey back to London. 'I was with the late Miss Clara Fischer.'

'Why was Miss Fischer in the room with you?'

Louisa knew there was nothing she must hide. 'The day before, she'd had her bag stolen while near St Mark's Square. Mrs Guinness suggested that I go with her when she left the group to try and find it. As we walked together, she admitted to me that her bag had contained opium.' Louisa paused as Stiles wrote quickly in his notepad. 'She said she had left the Basilica earlier, which the group had been visiting, in order to go and have a smoke. She thought that while she was, well, *unaware*, sir, that someone must have taken the bag from her. She was desperate to find it, or get some more opium. I persuaded her to return to the hotel and said she could rest in my room.'

'Did you tell anyone else?'

'Yes, I told Luke Meyer. Mr Meyer asked me what had happened and although Miss Fischer had asked me not to tell anyone I was very worried about her. Quite soon after we had arrived back at the hotel, she seemed to suffer badly from opium withdrawal.'

'That seems very quick.' Stiles was watching Louisa's face carefully but not, she thought, unsympathetically.

'Yes, sir. I thought perhaps there was a psychological effect, as well as a physical one. Knowing that she was somewhere she could not get hold of any more opium.'

'Hmmm. You looked after Miss Fischer, you say. How did you do this?'

'She was quite delirious and very sick. I tried to help her drink water, although that mostly made her vomit again. I kept pressing a cool cloth on her forehead, and I tried to say soothing things to her.'

Stiles smiled at that. 'Was anyone else left alone with Miss Fischer at any point?'

'At around midnight I had to go and attend to Mrs Guinness, to prepare her for bed. I was away for an hour or so. I understood that Miss Nancy Mitford was going to visit her at that point, too.'

'How did you understand that?'

'I had seen Miss Nancy when I left Miss Fischer to attend to Mrs Guinness. I told her something of what had happened and she was concerned for her friend. She said she would look in on her while I was away.' She paused and thought about the man in reception and what he had asked of her. 'There was one other person, sir.'

'Who was that?'

'A maid at the hotel delivered a pot of tea at my request. I think Clara drank some of it.'

Stiles put his pen down and pushed his chair back from the table. He crossed his arms and looked at Louisa. At once, she saw his demeanour had changed completely.

'You have a history of law-breaking, Miss Cannon.'

She felt as if he had slapped her across the cheek. She tried to regulate her breathing and not be made to feel scared. Yes, she had a history of law-breaking but this had nothing to do with the crime that had happened. 'It was a long time ago, sir. I was a child.'

'Nevertheless. It makes your character somewhat questionable, shall we say?'

Louisa said nothing to this.

'Was this the first time you had met Miss Fischer?'

'No, sir. I met her some years ago, when I was working for Lady Redesdale, as chaperone for her daughter Miss Pamela Mitford. Miss Fischer was in the group of friends that my charge knew.'

'Did you become friendly with Miss Fischer?'

'No, sir. That is, we were not unfriendly, but I was a servant, sir.'

'Yes, yes. I do see that. But I'm intrigued, why should she have confided in you when her bag was stolen?'

'I think she was desperate.'

'Did you steal her bag?'

'What, sir? No, I did not!'

Stiles stood up and started to pace around the room. 'I think you saw the perfect opportunity. You have the means, you know how to steal. We know that from your past. You saw her smoke opium, you knew that she would be desperate – that she would do anything to get it back.'

'No!' Where was Guy? Louisa felt panic rise in her chest. Would no one else witness this? Would no one else vouch for her character?

'When she realized it was you, you had to kill her. And you had once more, the perfect opportunity. She was alone in your room, delirious. Desperate. Offered a smoke, she'd have taken it greedily.'

'No, no, no. It wasn't me. Where is Mr Sullivan?'

'Detective Sergeant Sullivan to you. He can't help you.'

'He can, he – he can vouch for my good character.'

'What good character? You have broken the law before, you'll do it again. I know your type well enough.'

Rage now overcame the panic. Her *type*?

'DI Stiles. I did not commit this crime.' Her voice was amazingly calm.

'Perhaps you didn't steal the bag.' Louisa's heart rate slowed down but then he started again. 'In which case, tell me where you bought the opium. Was it in England, or was it in Venice? It's not hard to buy, after all.'

'I have never bought opium.'

'You'd know how to though, wouldn't you?' Stiles sat back down in his chair, pulled it in and leaned forward so his face, now hard and set, was only inches from her own. 'I think it's something you keep in your bag. Just in case. We could have a look in your bag now, or in your room. Would we find some there?'

Louisa said nothing; she tried to remove herself somehow and concentrated on breathing as regularly as she could.

'I think we would. You supply some to the people you work for? What could be a better cover than you? No one would notice, no one would know. And your job is safe.'

'No,' she said simply. 'None of that is true.'

Stiles sat back and looked at her. He smiled.

'No,' he said. 'None of that is true.'

If there had been a signal, Louisa didn't see it but at that moment Guy came in without knocking. Stiles stood up.

'She didn't do it,' he said and left the room.

CHAPTER THIRTY-FIVE

❧

O utside the room, Louisa stopped Guy. 'Tell me what's going on.'

But Guy said nothing. He carried on walking a few more doors down and opened another. Inside was a uniformed policeman standing in the corner, and Nancy. She flew to Louisa. 'Lou-Lou, thank God you're here. It's been hell.' She was wearing an elegant navy coat and skirt but the curls in her hair had gone awry and she looked as if she hadn't slept for a week. All her make-up had rubbed off and there was just a faint outline of dark red on her lips.

'When did this happen?' asked Louisa. She felt, strangely, as if she were in a position of power in this room, though she knew it not to be true. But having been accused then exonerated while Nancy had been arrested and held, meant that Louisa, for once, held the cards.

'This morning. Oh, it's been simply ghastly. Awful. The only good thing about it is I can probably use it in my next book. How is Farve? He's been such a darling, waiting for me. No sign of Muv, of course. Mr Sullivan, have you got a cigarette?'

Guy took one out of his pocket and gave it to her. Louisa looked at him in surprise. 'Useful for favours,' he said quietly.

'Lady Redesdale did come, just now,' said Louisa. 'With Mrs Guinness, but they've had to go back home. They're worried it's not good for the baby.'

'But fine for me?'

Louisa decided to take the Nanny Blor line of not dignifying this sort of remark with a response. Even now it was as if Nancy had never left the nursery.

'Mr Sullivan.' Louisa turned to Guy with the formality that always arose between them when a third person was in the room. She was grateful for it today. 'Can you please explain what's happened?'

'Yes. Please, take a seat.' Nancy and Louisa sat down on one side of the table in the room – it was another identical space in the police station – and Guy dismissed the uniform before taking a chair opposite. 'I'm sorry, Miss Cannon. I had to wait until your interview was over to clarify.'

Louisa nodded, and Nancy looked mystified but now wasn't the time to explain it. She did understand, sort of, though she felt as if she were in shock from the interrogation she had just had. For the moment it was a relief to sit and listen.

Guy continued. 'I'm late to all this myself as much of it happened at the weekend and I wasn't on shift. But Stiles and Thorne filled me in when they discovered I was a friend of the family.' He paused there and Louisa knew it was because he was worried he'd overstepped the mark by describing himself as a friend but Nancy was either too distracted, or actually agreed, to say anything. 'As you know, Miss Fischer's parents paid privately for an autopsy. The report came back that she had died from an opium overdose. As her parents were unaware of their daughter's addiction, they contacted the police in Venice to say they suspected foul play. But the Italian police said that as Miss Fischer and all of the group had been living in England, that side of the investigation was best handled by the British police, so it was sent to us in CID. The Italians are questioning the staff at the hotel, as I understand it. Our priority, of course, was to talk to those who had been with her in those final hours. Initially, we assumed that Miss Fischer must have taken the drug herself, and this was confirmed by other witness statements from Miss Nancy Mitford and Mrs Mulloney over the weekend. But Louisa's note changed our inquiry.'

'What do you mean?' asked Nancy. 'Clara had no more opium. It wasn't possible that she had taken it herself. I saw her: she was extremely sick without it.'

Louisa thought she had better explain. 'Exactly. Someone else had to have given it to her deliberately. And there were only a few people in that room.'

'One of whom was me,' sighed Nancy.

'Yes,' agreed Louisa apologetically. 'I'm sorry. I had no idea you would be treated as a suspect.'

Nancy took up the story at this point. 'Yes, well. From my side, I was called into the police station on Saturday morning, which I can assure you I was *not* thrilled about but I was assured that everything was perfectly routine. I gave them the names of everybody at the party that weekend, told them that you had taken Clara to your room, and that Mrs Mulloney and I had been to visit her, too.'

'Did you tell the police about what happened to Clara and her bag?'

'Yes, and what was in it. That was it and I was dismissed. The next I knew, this morning they were at Rutland Gate to arrest me. Darling Farve, I thought he was going to die of a heart attack.'

Louisa turned to Guy. 'Why was Miss Nancy arrested?'

'In her interview on Sunday, Mrs Mulloney told Stiles that when she and Miss Mitford visited Miss Fischer, Miss Mitford was left alone with the victim for several minutes. Miss Mitford, in short, had the means and the motive.'

'What motive?' Nancy and Louisa cried this out in unison.

'Embarrassment. Miss Fischer was a drug addict, she was suffering withdrawal and the assumption was that Miss Mitford would not want to be exposed as her ally. She claimed that Miss Mitford was also an opium addict.'

'Talk about clutching at straws,' said Nancy. She waved the cigarette in her fingers though she had not yet lit it.

'I agree with you, Miss Mitford,' said Guy. 'I doubt that this will be taken any further, particularly now that Mr Meyer's statement has been taken.'

'What?' This was news to Nancy, of course.

Louisa turned to explain: 'Mr Meyer told me that he'd over-heard your conversation with Mrs Mulloney at the dinner table last week.'

A shadow crossed Nancy's face. 'Were you and Mr Meyer discussing me?'

'Mr Meyer was concerned for you.'

Nancy looked away. 'Have you got a light?' she said to Guy. 'This isn't much use without one.' He reached into his pocket and pulled out a matchbox, striking a flame at once. Nancy exhaled. 'Well, come on then. Tell me what he said.'

Guy decided to take this up. 'Mr Meyer has given a statement to the effect that he heard the two of you discuss the fact that Mrs Mulloney had been left alone with Miss Fischer and that she wanted this to be concealed.'

Nancy continued to smoke her cigarette but her eyes flickered uncertainly.

'Miss Mitford, I need to ask you: why did Mrs Mulloney want this concealed? It looks suspicious now, the fact that she tried to push the blame on to you. I know this is a difficult situation. She's a friend and—'

'*Was* a friend,' said Nancy.

'Was a friend, then. And it's her word against yours, albeit we now have Mr Meyer's statement, but if you know something, you have to tell us.'

'Mr Sullivan, I'm not fond of Mrs Mulloney. She's always been a difficult woman, if well-connected and good-looking. But I don't think she's a murderer. I think she's worried that it *looks* as if she has a motive.'

'What is that motive, Miss Mitford?' Guy was asking the question but Louisa found herself holding her breath waiting for the answer.

Nancy looked off to the side and spoke nonchalantly, though it sounded false. 'Shaun was indiscreet. He wasn't, one might say, known for keeping his loyalty to his wife. There were rumours about him and Clara. Obviously not rumours I knew before I took Clara to Venice, and she never confessed to me. I only heard them after she died.' She turned to face Guy again and this time, she spoke more seriously. 'But you have to listen to me, Mr Sullivan. This kind of thing goes on amongst people like us. There were plenty of rumours. Even if it's true, it's awful and upsetting for Kate but not a motive for murder.'

Louisa looked at Guy. Was he thinking what she had already decided? If evidence could be found of the affair, Kate Mulloney could be arrested for the murders of both her husband and Clara.

CHAPTER THIRTY-SIX

W hen Louisa, Nancy and Guy returned to the waiting area
at the front of the station, Lord Redesdale was pacing up
and down. Luke was sitting on a hard chair, his legs crossed,
his foot twitching. He leapt up when the three of them entered
the room. 'Nancy,' he said, 'thank goodness. I wasn't sure if—'

Nancy cut him off. 'Thank you for what you did, Luke. I
think.' Then she turned to her father, who had stopped pacing
and was watching the group, stupefied. 'Dear old human, could
you take me home now, please?'

Lord Redesdale took his daughter's arm, then gave Guy a
stern look. 'This nasty business had better all be over now.'

'It is for Miss Mitford, my lord,' said Guy.

'Humpf, what?' But Lord Redesdale thought better of enquir-
ing further. He wanted the hell out of there. The two of them
left without saying goodbye.

Louisa, Guy and Luke were left staring at each other. She
knew that she should return to work, but she also knew that
Diana wouldn't necessarily be aware that she had been released

as yet. And she needed a grown-up drink, even if it was only the afternoon. Luke looked as if he felt the same.

'Mr Meyer,' said Louisa and he looked at her with confusion.

'Why aren't you calling me Luke?'

Louisa flicked her eyes towards Guy, who shuffled uncomfortably. Good.

'I think the two of us should go out for dinner,' she continued, with a confidence she did not feel, and Luke exhaled a large sigh of relief.

'Yes, and a huge brandy.'

Guy started to say something then stopped, but just as they had said their goodbyes and Luke was walking out of the door, he touched Louisa lightly on the arm. 'Can I see you again?'

Louisa looked into his kind face. His eyes blue and large behind their thick glasses, his fine nose, his mouth so full of sincerity with its nervous smile. She wanted, so much, to see him again.

'I don't think it does either of us any good, do you?' she said and left. But this time, she turned around when she got to the pavement and Guy was still watching her.

'I think this deserves the Ritz,' said Luke as they walked along the street. He had perked up tremendously. His face somehow rearranged back into its usual harmonious good looks, the curls of his hair adding to the general buoyancy. Only his crumpled shirt and lack of a tie revealed the earlier harried state in which he had had to leave his aunt's house.

'No, Luke. There's nothing to celebrate. Can we just dive into the nearest pub and hide for a while?' She was regretting not saying that she would go back to Diana immediately, where she might have been able to lie down on her bed and try to think through everything that had happened. She felt the hurt she had inflicted on Guy as if she had stabbed her own heart.

It didn't take them long to find a pub, the Rose and Thorn, hidden away in a mews and once the drinking hole of coachmen after they had put away their horses for the night. It was perfect for her mood: dark, low-ceilinged, a surly barmaid. They tucked themselves into a booth with a brandy each. It would knock her out but that might bring blessed relief. The first sip burned her throat and brought a numbness that was the panacea she sought.

Luke gave a deep sigh. 'That's better. I'm not sure which was worse today, the police interview or telling Aunt that I had been called in. She was much more upset than I was.'

'Did you tell her why?'

'No, I hardly knew myself. I had a summons from Diana to meet her at the police station. I was feeling pretty desperate as it was. I had been up until the small hours drinking whisky with disreputable types in Soho.' He barked a short laugh.

Louisa studied Luke for a second or two. His dark brown eyes were hard to read. Was the hangover the reason for his trembling hands earlier? She always had the sensation that he was hiding something but could say with no certainty what that was. That he was a homosexual was understood by all the group, and though the likes of Nancy and Diana would make reference to this in passing with coded phrases – 'he wears lavender' – it would nonetheless be something he had to conceal from most of the world, most of the time, she knew that. Hiding a part of yourself was exhausting. Louisa knew that, too. But there was another danger: it could make deception a habit, something that came as easily as tying your shoelaces.

'Are you going to ring the newspaper?'

'About what?' Luke swallowed this question with another mouthful of brandy.

'You know what. Clara. Nancy.'

Luke shook his head. 'But I can't deny that I wouldn't like to eventually. If it became a proper story, I mean. I don't want to live in the gutter of the diary, I promise you that. I'd like to be a real journalist.'

'Hmm.' Louisa drank the last of her brandy. It cleared her head. 'Why are you sitting here with me now, Luke?' It gave her a small thrill to call him by his first name. Almost everyone in her daily life had to be addressed formally, apart from May the parlourmaid. But the kitchen maids had to call her 'Miss Cannon'. She'd liked it initially but it created a distance that soon became too wide to cross.

'We're friends, aren't we?'

'Yes, but you're also friends with Mrs Guinness. The woman for whom I am a lady's maid. It is unusual.'

Luke's response was warm. '*I* am unusual, and I have a feeling you are too. Perhaps more accurately, we're both outsiders. I know I am a friend of Diana's, but only up to a point. I am not one of them – I don't have their money, their background, their confidence. They accept me as an amusing pet. Some might say it was pathetic of me but because it lets me in, I put up with it.'

'What do you want to be? Where are you going to go in this life?'

'Goodness,' said Luke. 'You are in a philosophical mood. I think we need another drink.' He signalled to the barmaid for more of the same. Her response was to throw a dishcloth over her shoulder but then she pulled out two more glasses. Luke took a

214

minute to think, giving the question proper consideration and as he did, Louisa tried to think what her own answer might be. 'I keep hoping we're living in a new and different world,' he said at last. 'Different to our parents' world, that is. Since the war, so many things have changed. All the cars, the telephones, the radio. Women are voting.'

Louisa raised her glass. 'Hurrah to that.'

Luke clinked his and then winced. 'Sorry,' he said. 'Nancy told me once not to do that.'

'Carry on, I'm enjoying this.'

'I feel as if there's a chance for anyone to do anything, in a way that wasn't possible before. I'm lucky, I've had a good enough education and I have my aunt supporting me. But she and I are not the same. She fiercely disapproves of modern life and would like the world to go back to the way it was.'

'Where people knew their place?'

'Exactly.'

'Where you and I would not be sitting together, having a drink in a pub.'

Luke burst out again, and this time Louisa joined in. The brandy on an empty stomach had relaxed every muscle from her shoulders to her scalp and she was enjoying the pleasurable sensation of almost melting into her seat. She never wanted to leave the safety of the booth.

'Clara was having an affair with Kate Mulloney's husband,' she said, rather abruptly. Her mind had skittered back there inevitably, like a bagatelle ball on a slope.

Luke put his drink down on the table. 'I know.'

'I guessed that from your diary piece.' Louisa gave him an arch look. 'But how did you know?'

'There were rumours.' He gave her a wide-eyed look. 'You don't think Kate . . . ?'

'It's possible,' said Louisa. She knew she was saying things she wouldn't have said if she wasn't two brandies down but she couldn't quite stop herself either.

'Can it be proved?'

Louisa shrugged. 'I don't know. We don't know if Mrs Mulloney knew for certain that Clara was, well . . .'

'What if there was proof for that?'

'Proof Mrs Mulloney knew what her husband and Clara were doing behind her back?'

'Yes,' said Luke.

'I'd say it wouldn't help her case, but it would help the police's.'

'Then I think you'd better come back with me to my aunt's house.' Luke stood and paid the bill and inside of five minutes, they were in a taxi to Wilton Crescent.

CHAPTER THIRTY-SEVEN

A t the end of a wedding cake line-up of painted houses
was 31 Wilton Crescent, standing slightly oddly next to
the Anglican church, St Paul's of Knightsbridge. Briefly, the
thought occurred to Louisa that the street name rang a bell but
she couldn't think why – was it something to do with Guy? But
she didn't want to think of him and she pushed it to the back
of her mind.

Luke fished out a key attached to his belt loop on a thin silver
chain. 'My aunt doesn't trust me not to lose it,' he said with a
grin and let them both in. 'We don't have a servant.'

'None at all?'

Luke shrugged. 'Apparently no one is to be trusted. Not quite
what you'd call Christian forgiveness for someone who goes to
church twice on Sundays. It makes it rather dusty, I suppose, but
I've got used to it now.'

They walked along a short, dark hall off which there was
a small study and a dining room behind. 'Wait here,' Luke
instructed. Then he called out, 'Hello?' but there was no reply.

'Good,' he said, 'she's still out. She wouldn't like it if she found us here. A man and a woman alone. Old-fashioned, you know.' There was a faintly musty smell and the decoration looked to have been done some time in the previous century: there were wallpapers with faded fussy prints and Persian rugs on smutty wooden floors. Few pictures were hung and they were all of nondescript landscapes, featureless pale green fields with lonely trees.

As Luke had been talking he had led Louisa up the stairs and taken them into a drawing room that was on the first floor, its two tall sash windows overlooking the street. One wall was entirely taken up with a vast oil painting of a man in what he clearly considered to be his prime, with a grey beard and moustache and a stomach that Louisa guessed had been diplomatically painted to be less large than it actually was. At his feet stood a proud boxer dog with a thick red collar.

'Sir William Boyd,' said Luke. 'Aunt's husband. She was nineteen and he was fifty-three when they married. My mother told me that everyone assumed he was rich – he had the title and this house, after all. But it turned out he wasn't, and when he died in 1918, Aunt was left with nothing but, well, the title and the house.'

'Why didn't she sell the house?'

'Pride,' said Luke. 'She would never admit she needed the money. And she likes the fact that it's next to the church. Wait here a moment, sit anywhere you like.'

Louisa sat down on a green velvet sofa, antimacassars draped on the back, while Luke went out of the room for a few minutes. It was quite dark but for the two lamps that Luke had switched on – Lady Boyd's displeasure with the modern world did not, it seemed, extend to electricity – and Louisa had to wait for her eyes to adjust. Soon, Luke placed a slim diary in her lap, with '1929' embossed in gold on the front. He looked at her with glee in his dark eyes.

'What is that?' asked Louisa.

'Kate Mulloney's diary.'

Louisa recoiled. 'It can't be. Where did you get it from?'

'I can't tell you that.'

'I assume Mrs Mulloney does not know it is in your possession.'

'No comment,' said Luke. Then he gave the book an impatient tap. 'But come on! Don't tell me you don't want to know what's inside it.'

Merely having the diary on her lap made her feel complicit in a terrible crime. 'I don't know that I do, Luke. Shouldn't we hand it over to the police?'

'Maybe, maybe.' Luke was dismissive, leaning over her, flicking through the diary. 'Most of it is pretty standard stuff. Doctor's appointments – quite a lot of those – dress fittings, luncheon with Lady Snooks and that sort of thing. But then, look at this.' Luke held out an open page and Louisa lacked the willpower not to look, though she did resist taking hold of the diary itself. If she didn't touch it, she might be able to pretend that she had had nothing to do with it. The two pages were obviously intended to cover a week's entries, in January. But instead of sparse details there was a dense, continuous flow of narrow handwriting in black ink that sometimes splotched from the force with which the writer had pressed on the page. The words were too small for Louisa to be able to make them out.

'What does it say?' She hadn't wanted to ask. But also, she had.

'She has seen Clara and Shaun kissing. At the end of the

night, after a New Year's Eve party in their house in Ireland. It seems they didn't see her. She writes ... hang on.' Luke moved the page nearer to the light and started to read out loud. *'That little bitch has had her claws in S for months, I knew it. He told me I was going mad, imagining things that weren't there and all the time those two bastards were going at it like frenzied animals.'*

'That's enough,' said Louisa.

'No, wait a bit. Listen to this. *I'm not going to give them the satisfaction of telling them that I know. If that cow wants my husband, she'll get him over my dead body. Or his.'* Luke raised his eyebrows as he read the final two words with dramatic exaggeration. 'What do you think of that, eh?'

'It doesn't prove anything,' said Louisa. 'She was angry. Of course she felt like that, anyone would.'

'Her husband was dead a few weeks later, Louisa. Then a year later, Clara too.'

'Fine. Then we have to give Kate the diary back but we'll call Guy—'

'Guy?'

'DS Sullivan, I mean.'

'I didn't realize you were on such a friendly footing. This whole thing gets more and more interesting.'

'We're not,' said Louisa, too quickly. 'I mean, we were. That's beside the point here. We can tell him there are reasonable grounds to bring Mrs Mulloney back for a further interview.'

'They must have done that already, surely? Given my statement.'

'Yes, that's true. We'll telephone the station anyway, and take the diary back to her. It seems only fair that she should have it in her possession. This is, whatever you may say, a piece of stolen property.'

'How will we explain how we came to have it?'

'How will *you* explain it, you mean. I had nothing to do with it.'

Luke narrowed his eyes at Louisa. 'If I'm in this, so are you. I don't see why we should hand it back.'

'We have to. Either you have to admit to the police that you stole it, and it could look as if you are framing her. Or you have to confess to Kate that you had it but you are returning it, and give her a fair chance to explain herself.'

'What if we just say nothing at all? We owe nothing to Kate, or the police.'

That stopped Louisa. If the diary was, as she suspected, simply the raging words of a jealous, betrayed wife, then what did anyone have to gain by treating it as proof of her motive to kill? On the other hand, there was a very strong likelihood that Kate was guilty. And the diary would provide some kind of evidence, if not all, in bringing her to book.

'Louisa, why are you so determined to do this?' Luke was watching her. But she couldn't bring herself to admit the truth. She wanted Guy's admiration. She wanted him and the rest of his department to know that she had helped them to catch a murderess. She wanted to prove there was more to her than someone who fetched and carried for a rich, spoilt woman who was nearly ten years younger than she was.

'It's the right thing to do, that's why,' she replied. 'Show me where the telephone is, please.'

CHAPTER THIRTY-EIGHT

ouisa put down the telephone to Guy. Luke had been standing in the hallway, listening to her side of the conversation,
his foot tapping.

'What do you think?' he asked.

'I think we had better get to Mrs Mulloney's house before the
police do, and give her the diary.'

'What? They're going to go and fetch her this evening?'

'I think there's every chance.'

Luke balled his hands up into fists. 'Didn't they interview her
for the second time this afternoon?'

'Yes, it's not long since they sent her home. That was as much
as Guy could tell me.'

'There's been no confession then.'

'We don't actually know that there's anything for her to confess, Luke.'

'Perhaps we should make sure of it.' A muscle was twitching
in Luke's jaw.

A grandfather clock struck eight o'clock and the sound of

the echoing bell, together with the tension between them, the gloominess of the hallway and the seriousness of what they were saying made Louisa jump out of her shoes. 'I didn't realize how late it was. Diana will be wondering where I am.'

'Let her wonder,' said Luke. 'This is much more important.'

'You don't want to do this by yourself is what you really mean.' Why had she been dragged into this? Guy had been confused by her telephone call, quite naturally, particularly as she wouldn't explain on what grounds she knew, only that if the police went to Mrs Mulloney's house shortly, they would find proof that she had known that her late husband and the late Miss Fischer had been having an affair and she had been distraught and angry. 'Enough to kill?' Guy had asked but Louisa had demurred. She knew nothing for certain but she wanted him to think she knew something that was worth his while. The rest of the conversation had been stilted and awkward. She had made her rather melo-dramatic farewell earlier – as it seemed now – only to telephone him a few hours later.

'Will the police telephone Kate, to let her know they are returning?' asked Luke. He was holding the diary now as if it were burning hot.

'I don't know,' said Louisa. 'How should I know what the procedure is?' She was almost shouting.

'But what if we see the police there?' Luke cried out. 'We should have made an anonymous telephone call. You've made a terrible mistake.'

Louisa felt cold, she wanted to rub her hands for warmth but they were too clammy. She didn't know what Luke was so afraid of but she needed to bring him down. She deliberately slowed her breathing, talking slowly and quietly. 'Keep calm. The worst you are going to be accused of is stealing the diary. The police are concentrating on solving a murder.'

Luke was agitated. 'I need another drink but there's never any in the house.'

Louisa needed to get out of there; she put her hat on, but when she turned to Luke he was standing still in the shadows, looking straight at her. Her mind scrambled, confused by the different signals from Luke, the oppressive tension, the need to get out. But just as she decided she was going to leave, whether or not Luke came with her, she heard a key turning in the lock.

Louisa saw Luke frantically put the diary in his jacket pocket as the front door opened.

Lady Boyd came in as they were both standing there, in the near dark; her entrance rooting them to the spot. Louisa's knees almost buckled with the relief.

'You're here?' Luke's aunt looked as if she had seen a ghost.

'Yes,' said Luke uncertainly.

She stepped into the hall and Louisa could see she was trying hard to recover herself. 'There were no lights on. I thought you must still be at the police station. I was terribly frightened that—' Lady Boyd abruptly stopped herself.

Luke attempted a jovial laugh that didn't quite come off. 'What?' he joshed. 'Did you think I'd been arrested for Clara's murder?'

His aunt looked at him, her eyes not quite focused. 'Well, I . . . I don't know what I thought.' She took a breath and smiled at him. 'Of course not. You're here and you're fine.' Then she happened to look over his shoulder and saw Louisa.

'Miss Cannon,' she said, the displeasure in her voice leaving no room for doubt. She returned her gaze to Luke's. 'Is there something I should know?'

'We came in for five minutes. I'd forgotten something. My cigarettes. Sorry, Aunt. I know you don't like me smoking.'

'I loathe it,' said his aunt with feeling. 'Filthy habit.'

Luke pretended to look bashful. 'I know. I promise I will give it up.' He tried to change the tone though Louisa could hear the tremor in his voice. 'Anyhow, we had better get a push on. We're late.'

'Late for what? I wasn't aware you had plans for this evening.'

'I have to attend to Mrs Guinness,' said Louisa. She felt it might be better not to remain silent.

'Yes, Miss Cannon is returning to work and I am out for dinner. It's rather last minute. With Mrs Mulloney, and others.' Luke obviously believed that a half-truth made the better lie.

Lady Boyd clicked the front door shut, which had been open and sending a cold wind through the hall. She slowly started to take the pins out of her hat and removed it, gently patting her hair back into shape. 'Is that wise, dear? It's been a shocking business the last few days. I don't know that I would like you to spend any more time with those people.' She looked at Louisa again, still hovering uncertainly behind Luke. 'Not, of course, your Mrs Guinness,' she said with a thin smile.

'Sorry, Aunt, we really must leave now.'

Lady Boyd had removed her coat and as she stepped closer to Luke, under the light that was hanging in the hall, she said, 'Luke, please won't you stay with me for dinner? I should so much like to talk to you about today.' Louisa saw there was no getting out of it for him.

'Yes, Aunt,' Luke said, his shoulders dropping. 'I'll just walk Miss Cannon out while you change.'

'Good boy,' said Lady Boyd approvingly. 'Goodbye, Miss Cannon.' That was her final word. She went past them and up the stairs.

Luke took the diary out of his pocket and gave it to Louisa. 'I'm so sorry. You're going to have to do this alone.'

'Guy will be there. Perhaps it's better you're not there anyway – seeing as it was you who stole this.' She watched his response carefully but he was hard to read.

'I didn't . . .' He gave up. 'Thank you.'

CHAPTER THIRTY-NINE

~~~~~

Luke had given Louisa the address for Mrs Mulloney's house, as well as the fare for a taxi, and fifteen minutes later she pulled up outside a narrow house in Knightsbridge with a sky-blue door. All the windows were dark but for a single upstairs room. Standing on the top step, Louisa had just summoned the necessary courage to ring the doorbell when a police car drew up and parked close by. A young uniformed policeman and Guy got out of the car and walked towards her.

'Miss Cannon.' Guy sounded grim. He did not look pleased to see her. In fact, her appearance seemed to be a disappointment.

'DS Sullivan.'

'Have you got this evidence with you?'

'Yes, I have.'

It was dark on the step with the nearest street light at least thirty yards away. Louisa took the diary out of her pocket and handed it to Guy. 'It's the entry on the second of January that we thought might interest you.'

'We?'

'Luke Meyer and I.'

'And how did either you or Luke Meyer come to obtain this diary?'

Louisa saw the uniform go back down two steps and cast his eye along the street. No one was there. It was still early evening but this was a quiet road.

'I don't know.'

Guy put the diary in his pocket and rang the doorbell. Louisa turned and started to walk away but Guy stopped her. 'Stay here, please.' The softness had returned to his eyes, though he remained unsmiling.

Nobody answered the door. Guy pressed the bell again. A car drove slowly down the street. There was no movement to be heard inside the house.

'Did you telephone Mrs Mulloney to let her know you were on your way?'

'No,' said Guy. 'We thought, given what you had said, that the element of surprise was needed.'

'Perhaps she's out.'

'But why would that one light be on?' Guy looked up at the window though it revealed nothing but the cream-coloured lining of the curtains. 'And it seems strange that there are no servants here.'

'I believe this is only somewhere she comes to stay occasionally,' said Louisa. 'Her main house is in Ireland. She might not have anyone living in.'

'I hope she hasn't left the country,' said Guy. 'It will mean an international warrant if we want to question her. Which we do.'

The uniform gave a cough. 'Excuse me, sir. But I wonder if it might be worth looking under the mat for a key?'

'That would mean entering a residence without permission or a warrant, Constable,' said Guy severely.

'Absolutely, sir. Sorry, sir. Just a suggestion.' He resumed his position of scanning the pavement.

Guy and Louisa exchanged a glance. 'It couldn't hurt just to check though, could it?'

They looked under the mat and there was no key. But then Louisa looked at the stone urns that were placed on either side of the doorway and sure enough, there was a key under the one on the left.

For the third time, Guy rang the doorbell and for the third time there was no answer. He took the key from Louisa and opened the door.

Inside was dark. Guy took a torch from his pocket, as did the uniform behind him. Louisa came in last. They moved swiftly up the stairs and on the second floor was a closed door with light coming through the gap at the bottom. Guy knocked. 'Mrs Mulloney? It's the police, we're coming in.'

There was no reply. The silence rang in Louisa's ears.

Guy turned the handle and pushed the door open, almost jumping into the room. As soon as he did he put his arm out to the side as if to stop Louisa from seeing what was inside. But it was too late.

Lying on her bed was Kate Mulloney. Beside her was a note with a few short lines written in navy ink, in her right hand was the pearl-inlaid revolver Louisa had seen before in her vanity case. Staining her cream satin dressing gown, a trickle of congealed blood trailed from her heart.

THE DAILY SKETCH

14 APRIL 1930

SOCIETY WOMAN'S SUICIDE

NOTE CONFESSES TO DOUBLE MURDER

BY DIARY CORRESPONDENT LUKE MEYER

The deputy coroner for Westminster (Dr Hinchley) held an inquest on Friday, on the death of Mrs Katherine Niamh Mulloney (27), 19 Basil Street, Knightsbridge, who was found shot through the heart on Monday evening.

Mrs Mulloney, whose main residence is in Castleknock, Dublin, was widowed a little over a year ago when her husband, Shaun Mulloney, died in Paris, apparently from a fatal allergic reaction to sesame. They leave no children.

The inquest was held at Paddington Coroner's Court and the Deputy Coroner sat without a jury.

DS Sullivan of Knightsbridge station found the deceased in her own home at approximately 8.30 p.m.; she was alone in the house. The detective sergeant entered the premises in the company of a witness, Miss Louisa Cannon, who was known to Mrs Mulloney.

The coroner: Can you tell the court for what reason you entered the premises?

DS Sullivan: There were a number of ongoing inquiries for a separate case and the witness believed that Mrs

Mulloney would be able to assist further. I hoped to approach her for further questioning.

The coroner summed up the findings made by DS Sullivan and the witness: Mrs Mulloney was on her bed, dressed in her nightclothes and a dressing gown, still holding a revolver, with a shot through her heart. She was already deceased on their arrival.

A LETTER

Further inquiries by the police found that a maid, a Miss Gloria Holmes (29), worked regularly for Mrs Mulloney when she was in residence in London. Miss Holmes stated that she had arrived on the Monday morning at seven o'clock as usual and taken up a breakfast tray at half past nine; Mrs Mulloney had left the house for a luncheon appointment at midday and returned in the late afternoon. The coroner asked Miss Holmes what state of mind Mrs Mulloney had been in, to which Miss Holmes replied she had noticed nothing unusual. She had been asked by her employer to prepare a simple supper tray and lay the fires in the bedroom and drawing room before departing at six o'clock.

Dr Stuart Burton of St George's Hospital said there was a gunshot wound through the heart, which had caused instant death. The revolver was found nearby and it was clear the deceased had shot with her own hand.

DS Sullivan was then returned to the stand. He was asked if he had been able to corroborate Miss Holmes's version of events, to which he replied that Mrs Mulloney's appointment book had been discovered, which recorded a luncheon with 'R' at Chez Franco's at one o'clock but nothing else for the day. It appeared from the same appointment book that she had delayed a return to Ireland, following the earlier questioning by the police at the weekend, and was due to travel on the Tuesday. He had corroborated a change to her ferry tickets.

The coroner: She left a letter addressed 'to whom it may concern', in which she confessed to the killing of her husband and a Miss Clara Fischer. She also wrote that this explained her desire 'to go to God'. Is that correct?

DS Sullivan: Yes. It was the inquiry into Miss Fischer's death with which we had hoped Mrs Mulloney would assist us.

The coroner, who did not disclose the exact contents of the note, said that from its contents there was every indication that Mrs Mulloney had taken her life during a fit of temporary insanity. There was no evidence of foul play and the coroner delivered a verdict of suicide.

1932

CHAPTER FORTY

❦

At one o'clock in the morning, Diana returned home to the house in Buckingham Street. Louisa was waiting up in the kitchen, drinking warm milk and talking to the parlourmaid, May. The household had grown a little now that there was Jonathan, almost two years old and adorable with it, plus Desmond, a perfectly plump six-month-old baby. Bryan had brought in his own Nanny Higgs to look after the boys. She was old and old-fashioned, approving of Diana's preference to clothe the boys in dresses ('so much prettier,' said Diana) and marching them around Kensington Gardens on strictly timed outings in a vast Silver Cross perambulator. However, she did not allow Diana to spend much time with the babies – 'she seems to think they should be admired from a distance,' Diana said plaintively. Nanny Higgs and Louisa did not see eye to eye, and Louisa had learned that any suggestions about what the boys might want or need had to be done with tact. Being not overly fond of the nanny either, Diana liked Louisa to be her spy, and so Louisa had taken on some of her former nursery maid duties again.

But even without a cosy companionship with Nanny Higgs, Louisa had the company of May, and they both enjoyed their late-night talks, having become friendly, particularly when the family were at Diana and Bryan's country house, Biddesden in Wiltshire, bought the year before. There, Louisa had immersed herself happily in the landscape, in the quiet beyond the city where the evenings consisted of little more than helping Nanny put the boys to bed then reading by the nursery fire. Even the days frequently left plenty of time to contemplate the miracles of the garden, where Louisa could pretend she no longer cared about the hustle of London. She was encouraged in this by her renewed friendship with Pamela Mitford, too. After Pam's engagement to Oliver Watney had been broken off, not long after Kate Mulloney's suicide, Pamela had been invited by Bryan to come and live at Biddesden and run the dairy farm for them, overseeing the herd of four hundred and fifty Jerseys. Louisa had never seen the young woman as happy as she was when she chatted to the cows in the daisy fields or when she oversaw the skimming of the milk for the yellow cream and the churning of the butter that would both later make their way to the Guinness dining table. All these things had made Louisa's dislike of Diana a little more bearable.

Her equilibrium was only disturbed by the arrival of Diana and Bryan's regular house parties. These groups were noisy, extravagant and, to Louisa's mind, stiff with unbearable show-offs. That some of them were genuine talents could not be denied. Louisa had read Evelyn Waugh's *Vile Bodies* almost undercover, so darkly true was it of the life that her mistress led. She told herself she should not be so damning. Diana was still only twenty-one years old, with two small children, and naturally had a youthful desire to indulge in the things good fortune had sent her way: money, fashion, the attention of the newspaper diarists and grand society hostesses. Bryan seemed to see it differently. He had all these things at his disposal too, but was most content when he dined alone with his wife or went on long walks with his dogs and a gun. Though he was infinitely more gentle, and possessed no temper, Louisa did wonder at the irony that in her bid to escape her parents, Diana appeared to have married her father.

The shadow that fell across their green and pleasant lands was the Depression that had bloomed in America and spread over Europe like mould. Louisa had had letters from her mother detailing the ever-increasingly poor fortunes of some of their relatives. (Another good reason Louisa did not dare to quit her job.) On the radio, she heard news programmes about the long lines of starving men and women queuing for bread from Chicago to Seville. But although there were many long nights in the dining room at Biddesden, when the port was drunk dry by the men arguing about what the solution might be – Bryan and Tom had visited Austria together the year before and there was general agreement that the Nazi party had transformed the country's economy for the better, though no one could see them attaining any real power ('a murderous gang of pests,' Lord Redesdale called them) – there was little change to be detected in the general behaviour of the rich and their friends.

On this particular night, Diana had gone to Barbara St John Hutchinson's twenty-first birthday party. Louisa knew that whatever was happening in the world that day – *The Times* had run another story on the rising unemployment figures across Europe – Diana would have been served champagne and oysters, fine steak and chocolate cake. (Luke had told Louisa this was the fashionable menu and that even he had become 'heartily sick of oysters'.) Louisa and Luke had remained friends, bonded even more closely after Kate's body had been discovered with the note confessing to the murders of Shaun and Clara. It had been a relatively neat ending to a messy time, and she had been grateful that at least there were no children left behind by the tragic Mulloneys. The three dead – Clara, Shaun and Kate – had been young and indulgent when alive, seen now as relics of the Bright Young Things that had since become outmoded: the mood of the newspapers had been that they had more or less deserved what had happened to them, Luke's voice amongst them. He had graduated at last to writing full-length articles, though they were mainly about the interior designs of the rich and infamous. His frustrations were still apparent, but it nonetheless niggled Louisa now and then that Luke had done so well out of others' misery.

Louisa got up to wash her cup and as she did so the bell rang indicating that Diana was home and back in her room. 'Good night, May,' said Louisa and went up the stairs in a reasonably peaceful mood. Diana was sitting at her dressing table, already wiping off her make-up with cold cream and cotton wool. Louisa came up behind her and pulled out the hair pins before she started to brush her mistress's short golden hair. 'How were the boys tonight?' asked Diana.

'Good little things as always,' said Louisa. She really did love them.

'Desmond doesn't sleep as well as Jonathan did at that age.'

'Maybe not but Nanny gave him his milk and he seemed to go off without much fuss. Nanny let me read Jonathan a story at bedtime. You know how he loves Winnie-the-Pooh.'

'I am glad,' said Diana. She was alone tonight, Bryan having opted to stay at Biddesden; Louisa believed he was attempting to write another novel, though he never attained anything like the success of his friends.

Her hair brushed, Diana stood and as Louisa was unbuttoning her dress at the back – a slightly complicated concoction of a column of tiny pearl buttons that ran from nape to waist – she asked if there had been anybody interesting there that night. It was their usual conversation. 'Not especially,' said Diana. 'I spent most of the evening talking to Victor Rothschild. On my other side, Barbara put me next to a man you might have read about in the newspapers, Sir Oswald Mosley.'

'The politician?'

'Yes, he used to be quite high up in the Labour Party, practically PM-in-waiting, then he resigned and left to form his own – the New Party. Now he sits behind the Tories. I told him I was a Lloyd George Liberal and I don't think he was terribly impressed. One's heard all sorts of scandalous rumours about him.'

Louisa was careful not to press on this. She had learned that a servant was better protected not stirring up gossip with their masters; although, it almost went without saying, there was an underground grapevine that rivalled anything Luke's former column could have ever dug up. Occasionally, when they stayed in other houses, Louisa would pick up stories from the other lady's maids she was seated beside in the servants' hall for their supper. She'd heard of this Oswald Mosley, too, and not from the newspapers, but wasn't going to say anything now.

'He's married to a very sweet little mouse, Cimmie Curzon. She was there tonight, too. Everyone says he's a lady-killer who has torrid affairs with just about any woman who crosses his path.'

'Better be careful then, ma'am.'

Diana dismissed this. 'No danger there, I promise you. He is rather dark and good-looking, I suppose, but his magic didn't work on me. He told me that he'd spotted me in Venice and at a ball last summer but he could easily have made that up.'

'It's possible.' Louisa took Diana's clothes and went to the dressing room next door to hang them up, while Diana took her underclothes off and slipped her nightdress on. 'Would you like some milk tonight?'

'No, thank you, Lou-Lou. I'm going to go right off to sleep now. You know, Sir Oswald said he had some very certain ideas about how to fix things. He says he knows how to cure unemployment.'

'I see. Good night, ma'am.'

Louisa closed the door with the feeling that something was scratching at her below the skin, a niggling discomfort that something had got in that would not now leave them alone. A portent that the settled routine of the household was soon to be fatally disrupted. She was right.

CHAPTER FORTY-ONE

G uy and Sinéad sat opposite each other in the Lyons' Corner House on the Strand. It had become something of a ritual every Tuesday evening. In fact, they had done this now for so long that they had forgotten the routine had begun as a treat. Sinéad was fond of the café, a place which she felt was smart enough to impress but not so much as to be overwhelming. Guy had once tried to take her to the restaurant at Fortnum & Mason and she had been so nervous that she had spilt milk all over her lap, which had made her embarrassed and cross. In her temper, she had stood up to leave and then knocked her full cup of tea all over the table. It had taken her about a week to forgive Guy for that.

On this particular Tuesday, the waitress brought over their regular order – one pot of tea, two cups, lamb stew with mashed potatoes for Guy and cold ham pie for Sinéad – and they sat silently as she clinked the china and set out the cutlery. Sinéad's neat brown bob was tucked behind her ears. Guy had always admired her clean, fresh look; she never had a loose button or stray thread, her stockings were diligently mended, her shoes carefully polished. She was proud and capable, and she would make any man a wonderful wife. But his? Guy was no longer as certain as he had been.

Guy poured the milk into Sinéad's cup and his, then picked up the teapot as she was digging around in her leather handbag. Guy knew she polished it with care every Sunday night. 'I got a letter this morning,' said Sinéad.

'Oh?' said Guy. Sinéad received letters, several of them, most days. How she found the time to write back he never knew but there seemed to be about nine different ongoing, constant conversations that she was having with her family back and forth over the water.

'It's from Mam. She's not well.'

Guy finished pouring the tea and set the pot down. 'I'm sorry to hear that. Does she say what the matter is?'

'No, she never would. She says it isn't much but I know her, she won't complain. She says it's just a funny thing with her heart, it skips a beat now and then. Makes her out of puff and she can't walk from the house to the end of the road without wanting to sit down for a rest and—' Sinéad burst into tears.

Guy put his hand out across the table, trying to reach for hers, but she waved him off and dug in her handbag again until she had retrieved a white handkerchief. Perfectly ironed, of course, with a shamrock embroidered in the corner.

'I'm sorry,' she sniffled. 'It's just that I know Mam. She's saying it's nothing but that's only because she won't want me to worry. But she's all on her own and I can't help but worry.'

Guy was puzzled by this. 'I thought your four sisters were still back home.'

'Oh, Mary's busy with the church, every day up there and

cleaning it and arranging the flowers. Clodagh is pregnant with her third, Bridget is working in the shop and Susan is useless. She does nothing of any help. I'm the only one that Mam can rely on and I'm all the way over here.' She looked at Guy pitifully.

'Why don't you go back home for a bit, then. Aren't you due some holiday from work?'

'Yes, but ...' Sinéad had dried her eyes now and blown her nose. Her cheeks were flushed red but she had recovered. 'Guy,' she said and his heart lurched. He knew what was coming. 'I miss home. It's not just my mam. I can't settle into London, like. I don't like all the traffic, all the fast girls and everyone rushing about all the time. I miss the country, I miss the sea, I miss going to the pub and knowing everyone there. I thought I wanted the bright lights but it turns out ... I don't.'

Guy felt deep sadness at these words, because Sinéad was a good woman and she did not deserve to have less than happiness. At the same time, he felt something like a pang of hope and excitement at the change that was about to happen.

'You want to go home for good, you mean.'

Sinéad nodded sadly. 'I know you can't come with me. I know you're in love with someone else.'

This blindsided Guy. They had talked before about how he could not leave England because of his career and he had expected her to say that. He didn't want to acknowledge what she had just said – he wasn't even sure how true it was, he couldn't think of it now.

'I so wanted to marry you, Guy. I did. You're such a nice man and, oh. Sorry.' She had been about to start crying again but bit her lip and stopped.

'So did I.'

243

Sinéad looked at the untouched pie. 'I haven't had a bite but I don't think I could manage it.'

'No,' said Guy. 'It doesn't matter. Let's get you off home. Will one of the girls be there when you get back? I don't want you being alone.'

'Yes, Maeve's in tonight. Thank you, Guy. I feel awful about us but – I'm so sorry, I'm just so happy at the thought of getting back home again. Real home, I mean.'

Guy really did smile then. 'I know. It'll be grand.'

'Oh, you did learn something off me then, the Irish lingo.'

'I learned a lot. Come on, Sinéad.' He helped her out from the table and they walked out into the cool evening air and boarded the bus together for the last time.

With the emptiness of his love life, Guy threw himself into his work, keener than ever to prove that his career was something worthwhile. Even if he did still live at home.

Alongside DI Stiles, he had been investigating a sad case involving a man shot by his wife when she had suspected him of having an affair with his secretary. The inquest was coming up shortly and Guy decided to have a preliminary chat with the pathologist on the case, a Mr Stilligoe, who worked out of St George's Hospital, only a short walk away.

Mr Stilligoe was tall and wide with a parting in his hair that looked to have been made with a ruler and a comb. He was also, for a man who dealt daily with corpses, very jolly.

'Ah, Sullivan, my good man. What can I do for you today?' He leaned back in his enormous leather chair, flipping his tie as he did so. Guy explained that he had come to discuss the Jenkins case and Stilligoe started to take him through his findings, all of which aligned with Guy's previous investigations.

'There is one thing I find rather puzzling, however,' said Stilligoe. 'There was very little blood spatter from the shot.'

'What does that mean?' asked Guy.

'Well, he was a relatively healthy man. Forty-six years old, probably drank too much but who doesn't, eh?' He gave a loud guffaw. 'You'd expect, forgive the expression, blood on the walls. It was as if his blood had started to congeal before he was shot.'

'Sorry, sir. Could you spell it out for me?'

'I mean to say, it looks as if he was dead *before* he was shot.'

Stiles and Guy discussed this intriguing theory at some length when Guy returned to the station but it was on his walk home that he suddenly realized that there was another relevant case, too. The case of Kate Mulloney.

It had been two years since she had been discovered by him and Louisa, and a brief inquest had wrapped it up: Mrs Mulloney had left a note confessing to the killings of Shaun and Clara, and had committed suicide. Together with the diary, it seemed that the case of Clara was sewn up and so, too, was Shaun's, though the knowledge that he had been deliberately killed had been very upsetting for his parents. Her funeral had been held rapidly in Ireland and Kate's father, patriarch of a powerful Dublin family, had ensured that the stories in the newspapers had been minimal. Guy had tried once or twice to contact them to see if he might not pursue the case of Shaun Mulloney and Kate's part in it, but the avenues had been closed down, and the father had intimated that if Guy tried to take it further he would find his career as a policeman at an end. They did not want the scandal, having had enough to endure already, and perhaps that was understandable.

Guy remembered that there had been very little blood spatter around Kate Mulloney's body. Could Stilligoe's theory mean that she, too, had been dead before she had been shot? Was there a possibility that she had not died by her own hand but someone else's?

The spanner in the works was that Kate had tried to throw Nancy into the fire, claiming that Nancy was the one who had been left alone with Clara. Why would she do that, if not to throw suspicion off her?

There was another spanner, too: who would want Kate dead? He needed to find out more about who her friends and enemies were. The case was officially closed, he had no permission to open up this particular can of worms – if indeed he was right – but it seemed like his best opportunity for recognition from his seniors, given that he had some access to the people involved. The first step, of course, would be to contact Louisa. A coincidence? Guy decided not to answer that question, even to himself.

Once Guy had retrieved the records from the court inquest, he could review who the prime witnesses and suspects in the case might be. Taken from this new angle – viewing Kate's death as murder rather than suicide – the facts appeared rather differently. Kate's movements that day had been given by the maid, Gloria Holmes, who worked as a daily when Mrs Mulloney was in London. It was presumably rather an undemanding job, being paid on a retainer, as she had only to be available as and when they were in town. So far as they knew, Gloria was the last person to see Mrs Mulloney alive.

Guy needed to find Gloria Holmes. And Louisa. Of course, Louisa.

CHAPTER FORTY-TWO

꧁

The following day, Diana, Nanny Higgs, Louisa and the boys decamped back to Biddesden, a good three-hour drive out through the flats of Berkshire before the land turned soft, undulating and rural. Driving through the wrought-iron gates and seeing the house with its vines all over the front, Louisa breathed in the sensation of having returned home. It was a very pretty house, the inside made even more so by what nobody could deny were Diana's skills with interior design. Being so young and new when she had first moved into the house on Buckingham Street, she had not had so much to do with the furnishings there, leaving it mostly up to Bryan and whatever they had been given as wedding presents. But at Biddesden, comfortable now with spending money, Diana had freely ordered heavy cream curtains for the five windows of her bedroom, together with a four-poster bed and eighteenth-century chairs covered in white and oyster damask. A gazebo was designed by an architect friend, portraits painted by further acquaintances were hung on the walls, and all those who came to stay remarked on the pretty cobalt-blue painted gates and doors of the farm buildings.

There was only one painting Diana did not dare either to change or move: a vast oil portrait of General Webb on his cavalry charger, the man who had built the house in 1711. It was said that if the painting was moved he would haunt the house by riding his horse up and down the stairs. Pam had stayed in the house for three months while her cottage on the farm was being readied for her, and after one entirely sleepless night spent with an unseen malevolent presence at the head of the bed, at Bryan's suggestion she moved to another room, where she was left undisturbed.

Though she was down at the farm for the most part, Pam had come up to the house to welcome the party back. Louisa and Nanny Higgs took the boys off to the nursery but at teatime were summoned down to the library with them, where Louisa was happy to see that Nancy had arrived, with her fiancé, Hamish. Unity was also there, now seventeen years old and having lost her awkward manner, another beauty in the Mitford line-up. Nancy, Unity and Pam greeted Louisa with friendly enthusiasm, though Louisa felt keenly the distance between her and Nancy. (With Pam it was less so, with her working on the farm they were somehow almost equals.) As Louisa sat with Jonathan doing a jigsaw puzzle, Diana distractedly joining them, she heard Nancy talking with delight about the success of her novel, *Highland Fling*.

'It's selling thirty copies a day,' she was telling her sisters, 'which is apparently a very respectable number for a debut novel.'

'Are you going to become a fearful success?' Diana sounded mocking.

'I hope so,' said Nancy, for once not rising to the bait. 'I simply can't take any more buses to get about. I'm practically an old woman.'

'You're not yet thirty,' Hamish said.

'You only say that to feel better about the fact that we've not had our wedding yet.' Nancy said this lightly but Louisa noticed that she turned away quickly as she said it, as if to avoid Hamish's reaction. They had now been formally engaged – a ring from Cartier had even been produced – for four years, but no date had ever been set, and in the meantime, Hamish had been sent down from Oxford for 'dissolute behaviour'. It wasn't looking too hopeful. Predictably, Nancy turned on Pam, a fellow old maid. Her engagement had been broken off, but though she had seemed upset by it at the time, there didn't appear to be any urgency on Pam's part to take up with anyone else.

'What's this I hear about you and the pauper poet?' asked Nancy.

Pam, as usual, took her sister's teasing mildly. 'You mean John Betjeman? Dear thing, he's just asked me again to marry him. I've asked for a month to think it over.'

Nancy's green eyes darkened. 'What? He's proposed *twice*?'

'He keeps coming back to stay in spite of the ghost,' said Diana. 'John told Bryan if it wasn't for Pam he'd have refused all future invitations here.'

'I like it when he brings his kite down. We take it to fly on the hills,' Pam said in reply, but it was with finality. This was not a subject she was going to discuss, and she put down her plate, having eaten a slice of fruitcake in three mouthfuls.

There followed a short silence in which Diana concentrated hard on finding the right place for her jigsaw piece. 'I met someone rather interesting last night,' she announced, having clicked it in. Jonathan chortled with delight and Diana kissed him. It crossed Louisa's mind that she saw Diana do that rather less with baby Desmond, who was in Nanny's arms being shown the sights of the garden through the window.

Nancy and Pam looked at Diana; Hamish looked bored.

'Yes, Sir Oswald Mosley. I was put next to him at Barbara's dinner.'

'Isn't he meant to be a frightful cad?' said Nancy at the same time as Unity exclaimed, 'I've read he's a marvellous speaker.'

'Probably both of those things,' said Diana. 'Though it didn't work on me. I expect some might say he was good-looking ...'

Just at that moment, Bryan came into the room. 'Sorry I'm late down. I was keen to finish my thousand words for the day.' He kissed Diana, who did not return it. 'Nancy, darling, how lovely to see you. And you, Unity. How was your journey down? Not too troublesome, I hope.' After this, Diana did not mention more of Mosley, nor did her sisters ask any further questions. Instead, they talked in a general way about Tom and his studies in Berlin. 'He writes such fearfully straight letters,' said Nancy. 'One wonders what's actually going on in that clever head of his.'

'It's not looking any better in Germany,' said Bryan. He looked in Hamish's direction as if hoping to spark off some conversation but failed to make him bite. 'Still, I suppose his money stretches quite far there. The deutschmark is worth about two-thirds what it was in 1929.'

'You liked Austria when you went there with Tom, didn't you?' asked Diana.

'Terribly, yes, it's a beautiful country. Marvellous hunting and everyone so well organised. But I'm not cut out for all that *sturm und drang*.'

'I should love to go,' said Unity. 'But I expect Farve would rather I went to France or Italy. Only Tom was given permission to learn German.'

The telephone rang in the hall and they heard a footman answer it. He came in and whispered to Bryan who went and took the call. 'Who was that?' asked Diana, as he came back into the room, before she had quite noticed that his face was ashen. 'It was Ralph,' he said. 'Lytton has died.'

Tears immediately sprang to Diana's blue eyes. Bryan stepped towards her but she took hold of Jonathan and hugged him close. 'Poor darling Lytton,' she murmured, rather to the boy's confusion, who was not in need of comforting. The sudden change in the atmosphere sent his bottom lip quivering and Louisa stood, ready to take him back to the nursery.

'Lytton Strachey?' said Nancy. 'That is sad.'

'We knew it was coming but even so, Dora will be in pieces,' said Diana.

Dora Carrington, the artist, thought Louisa, remembering her slight figure with the blunt, blonde bob sitting on the sofa in Venice.

'Is that his wife?' asked Unity innocently. Diana and Nancy exchanged a glance.

'No,' said Nancy in a rather worldly tone. 'She was very much in love with him. She's married to Ralph Partridge but everyone knew – even Ralph – how much Dora loved Lytton.' She turned to Diana. 'Everyone thought she'd poisoned you that first weekend you went to stay at Ham Spray House because Lytton was so taken by you.'

'With her famous rabbit pie,' agreed Diana. 'She shoots the rabbits herself. I was terribly sick and so horribly embarrassed. I'm sure she was nothing to do with it because she was so sweet to me the whole time. Poor Dora.' Diana held Jonathan out to Louisa. 'I think the boys had better go back up.'

'Yes, ma'am,' said Louisa, reaching out to take his soft, pudgy hand.

Poison and shot rabbits. Sometimes she thought she would never understand the inner lives of the people she worked for.

CHAPTER FORTY-THREE

Mary Moon jumped at the chance to help Guy with his inquiries. A policewoman, Lilian Wyles, had recently been promoted to chief inspector, though not in Guy's office. 'It makes me think that perhaps it's not completely hopeless,' said Mary to Guy. 'I hear she's only doing cases with women victims but it's surely a signal that they're willing to take us more seriously? I have to show them what I can do.'

'Yes, let's hope this can help,' said Guy, knowing what he'd heard the men say about Wyles's appointment; it hadn't been complimentary to either her skills or her looks, and there was a general agreement that it had been a way of paying lip service to the 'difficult and demanding' Lady Astor, MP. But he was pleased to have Mary to help him. First of all, they needed to interview Gloria Holmes.

Gloria had given her address to the inquest, a shabby street in the East End and easy enough to find. Guy took Mary with him on the basis that a strange man turning up on a woman's doorstep in the evening – he had to do it outside his working hours, seeing as there wasn't officially a case to be investigated – would be better done with a woman at his side. As luck would have it, Gloria was in when they knocked on the door. As was her entire family, all gathered in the front room, each one as rotund as the last: mother, father, two brothers, a younger sister and a baby. Guy was unclear on whose baby it was, as it was passed gurgling happily from arm to arm. Eventually, Guy managed to persuade them to leave and allow him and Mary to interview Gloria alone, which, with a great deal of grumbling, they did. The sound of them all squeezing into the kitchen was hilariously audible and there was no doubt they were listening in: every question Guy asked was answered with a brief hubbub of murmurs from behind the door.

Gloria confirmed the facts as she had stated them at the inquest, without any deviation. 'How was her mood when Mrs Mulloney returned in the afternoon?' asked Guy.

'I don't know,' answered Gloria. 'She went straight up to her bedroom and I didn't see her again.'

'You stated that you prepared her a light supper. Could you tell us what it was, please?'

'Some cold chicken with mayonnaise and a slice of buttered bread, sir.'

'Did you leave her a drink?'

'She asked me to uncork a bottle of red wine and leave it in the drawing room with two glasses and her tray.'

Guy wrote this down. 'And did you see her when you left at six o'clock?'

'No, sir. She was upstairs in her bedroom. I called out that I was going and that I'd be back next morning.'

'Had she been affected by her husband's death the year before?'

Gloria's plump cheeks were sucked in. 'I don't know, sir. I never heard her cry or nothing.'

Guy looked down at his notes and Mary jumped in. 'Were you surprised by that, Gloria?'

'No, miss.'

'Can you tell us why?' urged Mary. 'You worked for them for seven years. You must have got to know them pretty well.'

Gloria squirmed in her chair and the murmurs were even louder than before. 'Mr and Mrs Mulloney weren't like any married couple I know. They went out together every night but they rowed something awful at home. You never heard the likes of it. Most mornings I was clearing up broken glass. Even in the day, there'd be terrible shouting. Made me want to hide, it did. I tried to leave but Mr Mulloney . . . well, he always managed to talk me round.'

'Meaning?' Mary thought she saw something in Gloria's face that demanded further questioning.

Gloria lowered her voice. 'He could sweet talk me, could Mr Mulloney.'

'Did he make a pass at you?'

But this was too much for Gloria, with her entire family's set of ears pressed to the door. She shook her head and wouldn't say any more.

Guy and Mary tried to press her further but the interview had come to an end, and they politely thanked her and excused themselves.

Out on the street, Mary and Guy walked back to the underground station. 'Do you think she was having an affair with Mr Mulloney?'

'I couldn't be certain,' said Guy. 'She can't be ruled out as a suspect because she prepared Mrs Mulloney's supper and opened the wine. There was a chance for her there to poison the drink easily enough but she lacks the motivation. I don't think she was very fond of Mrs Mulloney but I can't see her as a murderer. There was one clue there though.'

'What was that?'

'She said Mrs Mulloney asked her to leave a tray with two glasses. Either she had someone in the bedroom with her, unbeknownst to Gloria, or she was expecting someone to arrive that evening. We need to find out who that someone was.'

Mary pulled her hat down a little further against the chafing wind. 'There's nothing in the inquest that says anyone arrived that evening?'

'No, apart from Louisa and me, when we discovered the body.'

'Did she see anyone else that day?'

'Yes, I found her appointment book which said that she was due to meet "R" at Chez Franco's at one o'clock.'

'But you don't know who this "R" is. Did anyone check through her address book?'

'No,' said Guy. 'You have to remember, this wasn't a murder inquiry. It was merely confirmation of her suicide. After all, she was discovered with a note and an apparently self-inflicted shot to the heart. There was no need to spend police time on it.'

'But there is now,' said Mary as they walked into the station, each to take their own trains home.

CHAPTER FORTY-FOUR

The following morning, Guy plucked up the courage to telephone 10 Buckingham Street. An old maid answered and though she sounded surprised at the request, said she would fetch Miss Cannon.

Guy heard the click as the telephone was picked up again and his mouth went dry.

'Mr Sullivan?'

'Louisa,' said Guy, using her first name as if he could jolt her back into intimacy. 'I'm sorry to disturb you at work.'

'It's fine,' she said. There was a silence. 'What can I do to help you?'

'Could we possibly meet? I'm investigating something and I think you could help.'

Louisa sighed. 'I don't know . . . I probably can't.'

'Please, Louisa. I'll come anywhere, any time.'

The hesitation was brief enough to give him hope. 'Come to Jimmy's Café this afternoon at half past five. It's in Lexington Street, close to here. I should be able to get away then.'

'Thank you. I do appreciate it.'

'I'm sure you do.' The line went dead.

At five o'clock, Louisa walked into Jimmy's Café. She had had a few rather upsetting days. Diana and Bryan had come to London for Lytton Strachey's funeral, and this had meant a lot of people dressed in black coming through the house at various hours, all of them – it seemed to Louisa – competing with each other as to who was the most affected by his death. There were histrionic tears, long speeches, and no drink could be drunk unless it was downed in one gulp. One woman had lain on the sofa for three hours refusing to move in her 'stupor of grief', though she had miraculously recovered when there was a proposal for everyone to go and have dinner at the Ritz, 'because Lytton would have wanted it'. Louisa tried not to pass judgement on how other people felt things but she found herself losing patience with the false emotions of the Guinness's sillier friends. Diana's grief was genuine, she knew that, and her quiet tears in the bath had made Louisa feel much more pity than anything else. In this rather exasperated and worn out mood, she went to meet Guy.

He was sitting there already, waiting for her. Of course he was. Guy was nothing if not unfailingly polite and punctual. She had braced herself before seeing him but was pleasantly surprised that her chief feeling was one of comfort. The sight of Guy was like looking at a familiar and much-loved painting on the wall. It couldn't be anything other than restful and pleasing, no matter what one's mood had been in the moments previously.

Guy stood as she approached the table and waited until she had sat down before he did so himself. She removed her gloves and put her bag beside her. It had been two years since they had seen each other. She was sure she must look older, though he looked only the better for the seriousness the lines around his eyes gave him.

'How are you, Guy?' she said and she knew he was relieved to hear her address him by his first name.

'Very well, thank you,' he said. 'How are you?'

'Fine. There was a funeral yesterday, of one of Mrs Guinness's good friends, so things have been quite tense in the house. It's good to get out.'

A waitress came up and they ordered a pot of tea.

'I'm sorry to hear that. Whose funeral was it?'

'Lytton Strachey. He was quite a famous writer.'

'You move in elevated circles,' smiled Guy.

'Not me,' Louisa reminded him, 'the people I work for.'

She was ridiculously embarrassed that there was neither engagement nor wedding ring on her finger. Nor on his, but men often didn't wear one.

'I may as well come straight to the point,' said Guy. 'I wanted to see you because I'm investigating the death of Kate Mulloney. You were with me when her body was found, I wanted to know if there was anything about that time you remembered. Perhaps it didn't seem significant at the time but it might now.'

This was a shock to hear. 'I don't understand. Didn't the inquest conclude it was a suicide? It was pretty clear to us that that's what it was.' The sight of that lifeless body was not one Louisa had forgotten.

'I know, but too many things about it aren't right. I can't get it out of my head.'

She wondered, briefly, hopefully, if he couldn't get her out of his head either. Might that be the real reason he had contacted her?

Louisa leaned forward just as the waitress set down their tea things. 'What things?'

By the time Guy had finished outlining his suspicions, as well as the interview with Gloria, it was as if he and Louisa hadn't spent more than a day apart in the last two years. He had also confessed that this was not an official case, only something he was doing in his own time. She had teased him then: 'You have a habit of that. Perhaps you ought to leave the force and set up a detective agency.'

He gave her a look that indicated he might have thought of that once himself, and they had both smiled at each other then in a way that forced Louisa to turn aside. Both their shared understanding and the long time they had known each other ran deep. If she swam in those waters alone she would drown.

'In short, there are several things you need to know,' she summed up, bringing herself back to the surface. 'You need to find out who the "R" was that Mrs Mulloney met for luncheon that day, in case that person saw something in her mood or perhaps even was the one returning to her that night.'

'Yes,' said Guy. 'In police parlance, we need to eliminate that person from our inquiries.'

'Right. Then you need to find out who she was expecting to see that evening, and if anyone turned up. Did the inquest have any statement from the police about whether both those glasses of wine had been drunk?'

'No, but I could probably find out which officer wrote down all the details and find out. Hopefully they would remember.'

'If Mrs Mulloney didn't commit suicide, but was murdered,

that would mean the note confessing to the deaths of Shaun and Clara was faked. Have you checked her handwriting from the appointment book against the note?'

Louisa was quick off the mark here, he said. Yes, the handwriting matched, or was close enough to his eye. But the note was short and it wouldn't have been too difficult to imitate the penmanship.

'I still don't see why a murderer would bother to go to that trouble.'

'Well,' said Guy, 'we know that Clara Fischer was murdered because of the opium – that she didn't have – found in her body. Given the affair she had with Mrs Mulloney's husband, that leads us to the possibility that Mr Mulloney was targeted too. If the suicide and the note were faked, then we have someone deliberately trying to throw us off their scent.'

'And that person could be "R",' said Louisa. She had drunk all her tea and had to get back to the house as Diana would be dressing for dinner soon. But she didn't want to drop this. She was enjoying being in Guy's company, enjoying using her brain. 'I think we need to retrace Shaun Mulloney's steps in Paris first. It's entirely possible that his death was down to the sesame allergy and nothing more sinister than that.'

'Without exhuming the body, we won't know for certain. It just seems somewhat unlikely that he would have ordered any food at the restaurant that contained sesame.'

'Unless it was something that didn't usually contain that ingredient. A French recipe and he hadn't realized.'

'Don't you think that if you had such a serious allergy you would be careful?' asked Guy.

'Yes,' said Louisa, 'but I've seen those people. They drink too much and they're careless. They're rich and young and they believe themselves to be invincible.'

'You're probably right about that. Can you remember anything else about that evening? About what happened when they returned from the restaurant? Were you there?'

'I saw Diana and assisted her as she prepared for bed. They had returned at midnight and I remember thinking she had drunk rather more than she usually did. Mr Guinness, Mr and Mrs Mulloney went to the drawing room and I believe they carried on drinking there; I didn't see them, though I heard them a little. They played some records on the gramophone player.'

'You didn't talk to anyone that night, didn't see anything unusual?'

'Luke Meyer was with them. He came down to see me in the kitchen, after Diana had gone to bed. We'd arranged to meet.'

'Why?'

Louisa couldn't help but be pleased at detecting a tiny note of jealousy. 'We'd had a rather strange afternoon. Luke had taken me and Diana to a bar where—' She broke off and smiled apologetically. 'It's shaming to say but there was a woman who danced to music, she took off her clothes and she turned out to be a man.'

Guy blinked. 'I see.' It was clear that he didn't fully comprehend.

'I think Luke felt badly. Diana didn't react well, and I think coming down to see me was a way of apologising almost. Though I did wonder . . .'

'What?'

'He was writing a column at the time, a diary for the *Daily Sketch*. I was wary, in case he was trying to get information out of

263

me for it. We had a drink – he had brought some gin down to the kitchen. But we didn't talk for very long as he wanted to get back to the others. I went to bed and I was horribly sick that night.'

'I remember. We thought it was the water.'

'In the bar that Luke had taken us to, I'd eaten fishpaste sandwiches. They'd tasted horrible so I assumed it was those. Neither Luke nor Diana had had any.'

'You definitely didn't eat anything that Shaun Mulloney could have eaten?' Guy was leaning on the table now, their voices had lowered so that only they could hear each other and their whole bodies were angling towards each other.

'No, I don't think so.'

'Then we have to talk to Mr and Mrs Guinness.'

Louisa's heart sank. 'Yes,' she said. 'I suppose so.'

Louisa and Guy parted having arranged that she would break it to Diana and Bryan that Guy would like to interview them about what had happened in Paris. Meanwhile, Guy was going to look up the reports on the death of Shaun Mulloney; he suspected he would have to ask for help from the French police, which was not going to be very easy.

CHAPTER FORTY-FIVE

When Guy returned, he found a message on his desk: 'Miss Rose Morgan came to the station asking after you. She says you'll know what it's about. You can find her in the Regency on the King's Road until her shift ends at six.'

Rose Morgan? Guy had to think twice. There was only one Rose Morgan he knew, the maid who had been missing since 1928. He'd stopped looking for her when it seemed that she was alive but didn't want to be found. Now she was back in London and working, it seemed. He hoped she'd told her parents; he'd liked what he knew of Albert Morgan and had felt pity for his bewildered grief. Without even unbuttoning his coat, Guy hastened back out of the station and walked to the Regency restaurant, an establishment he knew of for its reputation of good but inexpensive food, popular with the artists who lived in Chelsea. When he arrived, he took a table and asked the waitress to let Miss Morgan know that he was there. She came so quickly, Guy was still reading the menu when she spoke.

'DS Sullivan?'

Guy looked up and saw the girl from the photo he had kept in his desk for all this time. She was a little older, of course, and her hair was now blonde and short but her smile was as shy and pretty as he remembered.

'That's me. And I take it you're Rose Morgan, no longer a missing person,' said Guy.

Rose looked apologetic. 'I'm sorry for all the trouble I caused.'

'Don't be. I'm glad you're here. It's good news for your family.' He regarded her carefully. 'You have let them know, haven't you?'

'Yes, I have.' She glanced over her shoulder. 'Would you mind if it looked as if I was taking an order? The boss might have a word otherwise.'

Guy propped up the menu in front of him and pretended to study it carefully, while Rose pulled out a notebook and pencil from her apron.

'Can you let me know where you've been for all these years?'

Still looking at the menu, there was silence and Guy wondered if she'd heard him but then she started to reply.

'I was in Paris for a long time. I had to leave London, I got caught up in bad things.'

'Bad things or bad people?'

'Both. I was working for the Delaneys, and they were nice, I liked the daughter but they didn't pay much. I wanted to send money back home, prove that I had done well moving up to London. Mam hadn't wanted me to leave, you see.'

'I understand.'

'I started doing a bit of extra maid work on my nights off, at other houses. Lady Delaney knew someone who worked at grand parties and she would hire me. The money really helped,

I had enough to send some home and even keep a bit back for myself. Then I met this man, he stopped me one night going into a house, and said I could make a lot more, if I just helped him out a bit.'

Guy knew he had to tread carefully here. If he did it right, she might lead him to something significant. 'What did he ask you to do?'

'He sold drugs. He'd do the deal with some regulars, he said they were all posh people, nothing dangerous. They'd telephone him or get a message to him, tell him where they were going to be. All I had to do was hand over the package he gave me. It were only small, no one'd ever notice. That's what he said. And he were right for a while.'

'I see,' said Guy. A clever scheme, and perfect for an innocent maid. 'What went wrong?'

'I told him I didn't want to do it any more. I got seen by a footman once and he threatened to grass on me if I didn't give him some of the money. But when I told Ronan he got nasty.'

Ronan. Guy repeated the name to himself so as not to forget it.

'And then, there was that party. I saw Dot collapse, that's why she fell, it were horrible. I panicked. I was frightened of what I'd seen, that I'd get the blame. It seemed easier to leave. I'd been paid for that night's work, I had enough to get to Paris and Muriel had told me about Mr Molyneux. We'd planned to go away together so I had a passport too.' There was a sob, the sound of someone finally telling the truth. 'I knew it were wrong, I knew my family'd worry but I thought if they knew what I'd been doing they'd cut me off. Somehow, once I was in Paris I felt far away from it all, safe. As if it weren't real. Then, the longer I were away, the harder it became to get in touch.'

'Why now? Why have you come back, why are you telling me this?'

'I missed me mam. Truth be told, I was engaged to be married and he broke it off. I couldn't stand another minute in Paris then. It was Dad who said I was to let you know I wasn't missing any more. Dad told me you were good to him, always telling him if you'd made any progress trying to find me. It were only fair.' She wrote something on her notebook and put it back in her pocket. 'That's it. I'd better go now.'

'Wait,' said Guy. 'Who took the drugs from you at the parties? Did you know their names?'

'I can't remember.'

Guy took a deep breath. 'Please, Rose. This could be important. You won't get into any trouble for it but it might help with something else I'm working on. Anything you can remember about them at all? What they looked like even?'

She hesitated but then she told him. 'The most regular was an American woman, pretty, I think she said she was an actress. There were two or three men I always seemed to see but I can't remember much about them. And there was a married couple, posh. He had blue eyes and she had black hair. I think their name was Milliney, or Mollony or something like that.'

'Mulloney? Kate and Shaun Mulloney?'

'Yes,' said Rose. 'That was it.'

'And Clara Fischer, was that the actress?'

'Aye, it was.'

Guy thought quickly.

'Rose, did you come back to London from Paris at any point since you left in 1928?'

'No, sir.'

'Listen carefully, I don't want to alarm you with these questions. I only need to eliminate you from another inquiry. But can you prove you stayed in Paris for all that time?'

'Yes,' said Rose. 'I shared an apartment there with several other girls, and I worked at Les Chats. Besides, I didn't want to come back then. I was safer in Paris.'

'Did you meet Mrs Mulloney in Paris or London after 1928?'

'No, sir.'

'Did you ever go to Venice?'

'No, sir. Sorry. I've got to go now. Thank you for coming here to meet me. Thank you for what you've done for me and my mam and dad.'

She walked off through the doors to the kitchen and Guy picked his hat up and left too.

CHAPTER FORTY-SIX

After that meeting, Guy was in a state of bewildered excitement. He dug out the file he had kept on Rose, and pulled out her photograph again, putting it in his pocket. Then he stamped the buff folder 'Case Closed' and put it away. DI Stiles was still out for the afternoon and the case they were officially working on was quiet until a new lead came in. He knew he should be making further investigations but he needed – wanted – to talk to Louisa first. It only took a quick telephone call to the Guinness house and he was in the kitchen at Buckingham Street, with her sitting opposite him at the table. She looked pleased to see him, he thought; he hoped he wasn't imagining it. Even so, he made sure he got down to business quickly.

'I met Rose Morgan,' he said.

'The missing maid?'

'Good memory. I know you saw this before but I wondered if you might look at her photograph again. Do you think you saw her at any time other than in Paris, at the Molyneux salon? She told me that she earned money on the side by getting extra work at balls and dances as a maid—'

'I did that, too.' She had blushed slightly. 'I needed the money, same as she did. I didn't like to tell you before. I know it was silly of me.'

Guy said nothing but gave her smile. 'She told me that the real money she earned, however, came from a drug dealer. He would pass her packages to deliver inside a party.'

'I didn't do that!'

'No, I know you wouldn't have. But I wondered if you might have seen her because she mentioned that three of her regular clients were Mr and Mrs Mulloney and Clara Fischer.'

'Let me look.' Louisa held it in her hands and stared at it for a while. 'Yes, she's the one I saw.' She closed her eyes as if reliving the moment. 'I didn't think about it again. What with the maid's death that night, I must have forgotten it. But it explains why she recognized me when I saw her at Molyneux – she left the room as soon as she came in and I couldn't think why.' She looked at Guy. 'I was working at Grosvenor Place the night the maid died and she was there, too. When I was in the kitchens, I opened the back door to a man and she intercepted, told me that it was for her. I saw him pass her something but I couldn't think what it would be. Then, later, I saw her talking to Miss Fischer and Mr Mulloney.' She put the photograph down and folded her arms on the table. She looked absolutely calm and almost beautiful, thought Guy. 'It's definitely her. Was it opium in the package?'

'I think so.'

'Oh my God. She was in Paris when the Mulloneys were there. Might she have supplied them? Could it have been Rose?

Mrs Mulloney didn't want the autopsy because she said the family would discover that Shaun took opium.'

'I hadn't thought that,' said Guy. 'I feel somehow it's not her. She was a middleman, not the dealer. Without him, she probably didn't know how to get hold of any drugs.'

'That might be what she wants you to think. Could she have been in Venice? There was a maid who delivered Clara her tea. I never saw who it was. The man on the reception desk told me not to say anything, that the maid was worried she'd be blamed. I knew it was the opium withdrawal that had killed Clara, or so I thought at the time, which meant I never did say anything. And – oh!' Her hands flew to her face. 'The "R" in the appointment book – *Rose*.'

Guy thought about this. He was less inclined to hasty solutions, as seductive as they were. He'd been in the police long enough to know you needed more. 'I don't know, Louisa. She says she never left Paris and she can prove it. Besides, there's no motivation. And if she was guilty, she'd hardly have telephoned me to let me know she was back in England.'

Louisa had to admit there was something in that.

'But I am concerned about the man she was involved with. He's a dealer, and he supplied all three. And she says she's frightened of him.'

'I know how that feels.'

'I know you do.' Guy longed to reach out and take her hand but he didn't dare. Not yet. 'His name was Ronan.'

'You mean, "R" for Ronan?'

Guy shrugged, trying to downplay it but he felt, at last, that they were getting somewhere. 'Now all we need to do is find him.'

*

Louisa saw Guy out to the back door and they said goodbye, but just as she was about to close the door he blurted out: 'I'm not married, you know.'

Louisa stopped. 'What did you say?'

'I never married Sinéad. She's gone back to Ireland. I just thought you should know. I'm not saying that it's anything that would bother you. Or not. I don't know why I said it really.' He felt miserable suddenly. 'I had to tell you.'

Only, when he looked at her, she was smiling at him. She didn't say anything but her eyes were wet. 'Thank you, Guy,' she whispered.

If things had changed between them, he couldn't be certain yet. He only knew for sure that if he could love anyone wholly and completely, it could only be Louisa Cannon.

CHAPTER FORTY-SEVEN

It took two days of leaving messages at the restaurant where Rose was working before she finally telephoned him back.

'What is it, sir?' she said, sounding afraid.

'I need to know how to get hold of Ronan—' began Guy before she interrupted him, close to hysterical.

'I can't have him know I'm back, he'll come after me, I know he will—'

Guy was forceful this time. 'He's not going to know anything about you. Miss Morgan, there's a murder investigation and I need to eliminate Ronan from my inquiries.'

In the distance, Guy could hear two men talking in the café behind her.

'When I needed to get hold of him I would leave a message for him at a tailor's in Jermyn Street. There was a Mr Wilkins, he'd let Ronan know the address of where I'd be working that night, and what time. Then he'd come and meet me if he had any clients who were going to be at the same dance.'

'What was the name of the tailor's?' Rose gave it to him and

Guy thanked her. He hoped he wouldn't have to bring her into court as a witness but he knew he couldn't promise it, so he didn't.

Mary Moon was only too pleased to assist Guy in the next stage of the inquiry. 'I'll ask Harry's sister to lend me a hat,' she said. 'She'll have something stylish, I'm not sure I've got anything quite right.'

'Please, Mary,' said Guy, doing his best to keep his patience in check. 'It doesn't matter all that much.'

'Yes, it does. All these posh people ask Mr Wilkins to pass a message along to Ronan, for their drugs. It won't do for him to suspect I'm not quite the right sort.'

'Fine, do what you need to do,' muttered Guy. 'Just be there, 121 Jermyn Street, at four o'clock. I'll wait further along down the road.'

'I won't let you down,' said Mary, practically running out of the door to get home and change.

Later that afternoon, Guy waited on Jermyn Street for Mary, who came out of the shop after a mercifully short ten minutes to let him know how it went. 'I had to wait until there was no one else in there, but I asked for Mr Wilkins and at first I pretended to enquire after some buttons for a shirt.'

'Good. Then what?'

'I said, "Could you be so kind as to let Ronan know that the dance tonight is at eight o'clock, at the Aurora restaurant on Dover Street," and I added that I would be able to meet him outside. Mr Wilkins noted it all down and didn't seem in the least concerned.'

'Did you leave a name?'

'Miss Margoyles.'

'Well done, Mary. Let's hope it works.'

Rather to Guy's surprise, it all went very smoothly. At eight o'clock that evening, he stood with Mary outside the Aurora restaurant on Dover Street. The nerves he felt in the pit of his stomach were due to the fact he hadn't disclosed anything of this investigation to DI Stiles. He wanted to prove he could do it alone; this would turn out to be either foolish or a stroke of genius and right now he couldn't say which it was.

Only a few minutes after eight, a scruffy man in a pork pie hat approached them. 'Miss Margoyles?' he enquired.

'You must be divine Ronan,' said Mary in a voice Guy hadn't heard from her before; she sounded as if she had been born in Buckingham Palace.

'That's me,' he said throatily and nodded at Guy. 'Who's this?'

Before Guy could say anything, Mary had continued with the charade. 'This is divine Paul, my friend.'

Ronan eyed him shiftily. 'Right, well, I haven't done business with you before, so let me lay out the terms. I assume you're after the Midnight Oil?'

Mary nodded. Guy could detect a faint nervous look around her smile but otherwise he was impressed.

'That's five pounds, upfront but not here. We'll go for a little walk around the corner, shall we?'

'How perfectly divine,' said Mary and Guy gave her a look. Any more *divine* and he'd expire in an ungodly puff of smoke.

As soon as they were around the corner, Guy stepped

276

close to Ronan and quickly slapped handcuffs on him. 'What the f—'

'My name is DS Sullivan,' said Guy, showing his police badge. 'Come with me quietly, if you don't mind.' Ronan didn't struggle but continued to swear copiously, pausing only to ask who had grassed him up.

'It wasn't one of your clients. The best thing you can do is walk along and answer some questions about an investigation I'm working on. I'd like to do this discreetly. If you help me, I'm prepared to overlook your proposed misdemeanour with Miss Margoyles.' No need to say yet that if he booked Ronan for murder, the drug deal would be a minor charge. On the other hand, he had no right to take him into a station for questioning. This was going to have to be carefully managed.

'At least let me have a fag.'

They stopped while Ronan pulled out a cigarette with his free hand, then a lighter.

'Go on, then,' he said after he'd exhaled the first puff. He had all the insouciance of a man who was accustomed to being stopped by the police, and just as familiar with being let go. 'What is it you're after?'

'Do you know Clara Fischer?'

Ronan pushed his hat back off his forehead and jammed the cigarette in the corner of his mouth. 'Thought you was going to ask for some of my goods. That's how it usually goes with you lot.' He gave a sigh. 'Been a while since I heard that name. American, I think. She was a bit of a naughty one, you could tell. What she gone and done, then?'

'She's dead.'

Ronan didn't look too moved by this piece of news. 'Oh,

blimey. Well, like I said, it's been some time. You got what you wanted now? I've got places to be.' He jiggled his arm, attached to the cuff that Guy had secured on them both.

'Not yet. Do you know Shaun and Kate Mulloney?'

Ronan shuffled his feet at this and threw his cigarette on to the pavement. 'Yes, I knew them. They were trouble. Always calling me up in the middle of the night, wanting more stuff.'

'Did you see them in Paris?'

Ronan gave a loud guffaw. 'What? Nah. I ain't even ever left London. Born and bred here, no interest in going anywhere else.'

'Nor Venice?' Guy had a feeling this was slipping away from him.

'No, told yer. Never gone foreign. I don't have one of those passport things. My dad went to France in the war and it did him in. Why would I want to go there?'

'Where were you on the ninth of February, 1929?'

'Now, look. If you're going to ask me these sort of things, I think you're supposed to take me down the station and I can call my solicitor.'

'Have you got a solicitor, Ronan?'

He stuck his chin out. 'Might do.'

Mary spoke up, in her normal voice now. 'Quite likely you don't, though, isn't it? I think you should help DS Sullivan here.'

'Tell me that date again.'

Guy repeated it.

'Amazingly enough, I do know where I was,' said Ronan. 'I'd had a nasty accident, nothing I need to go into with you now, but the consequence was that I was in hospital, laid up with a broken leg and a few smashed-up ribs. I was in for three weeks.

Cost a small fortune it did. Anyway, you can check with them, the Queen Mary's in Lewisham.'

Guy's heart fell all the way to his boots. He'd check but it looked as if Ronan had an ironclad alibi. He wasn't a pleasant character but he wasn't a murderer either. Still, there was one thing Guy could still do.

'I'm arresting you on suspicion of possession of drugs with intent to supply.'

This time, Ronan's choice of expletive was enough for Mary to blush.

CHAPTER FORTY-EIGHT

A s Diana and Bryan had been busy with various engage-
ments for a few days, it had taken longer than planned to
arrange for Guy to come to Buckingham Street to interview
them. He had met Louisa beforehand briefly, and brought her
up to the date on the most recent developments – or rather, he'd
said grimly, non-developments. It had been a disappointing time.

Inside, Diana was at her desk and Bryan was, unusually, also
in the morning room, reading a book of poetry on the sofa.
Louisa heard him reading a few lines of Blake out loud, something about a foe outstretched beneath a tree, to which Diana
was saying, 'Bryan, darling, that's lovely but I really *am* trying
to write this letter,' just as Louisa came in.

'Good morning, Mr Guinness,' she said. 'Ma'am. I do apologize but DS Sullivan is here. On police business. Is it possible
he could have a few minutes of your time?'

Diana slammed her pen down. 'Oh, really! What is it now?'

Bryan was calmer. 'If he needs to ask us something, I think
we had better let him. Yes, Louisa, show him in.'

Guy entered, looking too tall for the delicate furniture of the room, the wrinkles of his suit showing too clearly. Diana and Bryan, both so slender, seemed like china dolls beside him. 'Good morning, Mr and Mrs Guinness. I'm sorry for this, I'll keep it brief.'

'Good,' said Diana, though she wasn't completely unfriendly.

'It's a simple question I need to ask, though it's about something that happened a while ago. When Mr Mulloney died in Paris, I believe he came to your house after dinner hours before he passed away. Did he eat anything there? Anything that nobody else ate?'

'What on earth are you asking about that for?' said Diana.

Bryan, who had stood up to greet Guy, put both his hands in his trousers pockets and closed his eyes, as if to call up the images of that night. 'I have to admit we'd all had quite a bit to drink. It's not completely clear in one's mind.' He opened his eyes again. 'But why are you asking this? I thought it was established quite quickly that he died of his ghastly sesame allergy.'

'Yes, sir, I know that was what the doctor's certificate stated. I just can't help thinking that it's rather strange. He surely wouldn't have ordered anything that had sesame in it at the restaurant you dined in.'

Bryan screwed his eyes up again and rocked on his heels. 'No, he didn't. We all ate steak and *frites*, except for Mrs Mulloney who had some sort of fish thing, I think. And no pudding, I remember, because we had gone rather overboard on the cocktails. It takes away one's appetite.'

'Kate's dish contained sesame,' said Diana. 'That's what everyone thought at the time.'

'I see. Even so, was there anything back at the house that he

281

could have eaten that might have caused the reaction?' Guy had taken out his notebook.

'I went to bed,' said Diana. 'I don't know what you all got up to after that.'

'We had some more drinks, listened to some music,' said Bryan.

'Please, sir. I'm sorry to press the question. But could you think carefully. Was there anything else eaten?'

'Oh, I don't think so. The cook would have gone home.'

'The cook *had* gone home,' confirmed Louisa. 'I was in the kitchen after Mrs Guinness had gone to bed, and I was alone.'

'So, no . . . ' said Bryan. He looked into the fire briefly. 'Oh – yes, I do remember something. I mean to say, we really were rather tipsy. But I think Mr Mulloney was complaining at some point about being hungry, how he hadn't eaten enough of the *frites* and Mrs Mulloney was chiding him, saying he was always on the prowl for food. Then he spotted a box of chocolates, I don't know where they came from. I hadn't had any of them. I think he more or less scoffed the lot. Perhaps Kate had one too. It can't have been those, can it?'

'I believe Mr Meyer brought them,' said Diana. 'Anyway, they don't contain sesame, do they? I'm sorry to disappoint you, Mr Sullivan. It seems we can't help.' She gestured towards the door. 'We mustn't keep you from what I am sure is pressing police business. Good day.'

'Thank you, Mr Guinness, Mrs Guinness,' said Guy bowing his head slightly as he left.

As Louisa said goodbye to Guy moments later, she abruptly recalled that Diana was right: Luke had brought the chocolates.

Not only that, she had sampled one of them when she'd gone to retrieve Diana's book while they were out at La Coupole. She remembered hoping the sweetness would settle her stomach after the horrid fishpaste sandwiches. Knowing that Diana wouldn't eat them, she was fairly sure no one would notice one missing from the box. In short, she and Shaun had eaten the same thing, and she had been sick all night, too.

Later on, a kitchen maid knocked on Louisa's door to say that Mrs Guinness wished to see her. She hastened down the corridors but she was given something of a dressing-down. 'Where have you been? It's almost seven o'clock, I've had an exhausting day and we have a dinner here tonight. There's so much to *do*.'

Louisa apologized and prayed that the dress Diana wanted to wear was one that was already clean and ironed. Thankfully, it was. A long, emerald-green chiffon number that floated in diaphanous layers, worn with a diamond necklace that almost shone light on to Diana's lily-white neck. By the time she went downstairs to greet her guests, she was in a better mood and Louisa tried not to wonder too much quite what the long list of things to do could have consisted of other than checking Nanny Higgs had put the boys to bed, Mrs Dudley (a new cook, as Mrs Mack was installed in Biddesden) had cooked everything, the maid had set out the drinks and Louisa had helped her dress and do her hair. Having cleared up the bedroom and readied it for Diana's return later, Louisa went down the stairs quietly. She would normally avoid going past the drawing room but she was hoping Luke was one of the guests this evening, and that she might just catch his eye.

The house was warm and the noise of the guests chatting

could be heard before Louisa reached the ground floor. There was no music on the gramophone player tonight, Diana having instructed that the atmosphere was to be more sombre than usual, given the recent funeral. Louisa hovered at the edge of the doorway and saw that the room was full, with people both sitting and standing, almost all with a drink in one hand and a cigarette in the other. Most of the women were dressed in black or dark colours, the men in evening dress though some had dandyish touches – a colourful handkerchief in the top pocket or purple socks. There were familiar faces, the usual set who prayed at the altar of Diana, recognisable as much to anyone who read the diary columns as to Louisa. Dora Carrington was there, too, with her heavy fringe, no make-up, looking utterly bereft, not talking to anyone, not drinking her drink. Then Luke stood up from somewhere in the middle of the room – he had probably been sitting on the footstool – and saw Louisa. He came over and she tried to arrange her face to look normal and wasn't at all sure she'd succeeded.

'Hi,' he said. He swayed very slightly. 'How are you?'

Louisa decided to bite the bullet. 'Can you escape for a minute?'

Luke swigged his martini. 'I say, how mysterious. Of course, old thing.' He was only just on the right side of not slurring.

Louisa led them both into the morning room, which was always empty when Diana wasn't in there writing her letters after breakfast. Luke sat down but Louisa did not. She fiddled awkwardly with the *objets* on Diana's desk, as if she had gone in there to straighten things out. She couldn't think how to start.

'Come on then, what have you brought me in here for? Be quick about it. I'm not far off finishing my drink.'

'Are you really friends with them?' Louisa said, nodding her head in the direction of the drawing room.

Luke looked confused. 'What sort of question is that?'

'I mean – do you like them?'

He stopped and also looked in the same direction, as if he'd be able to see through the walls and remember who was there and what he thought of them. 'Haven't we discussed this before? You know it's complicated. I'm not one of them, am I? But yes, I enjoy being in their company. I like it when I get asked to dinner. It's more than I ever thought was possible when I was a hack, writing them up for my sordid little column.' He gave a laugh as if he'd made a joke, but Louisa knew it was a hollow one.

'And Mr and Mrs Mulloney. What did you think of them?'

Luke's head jerked back. 'I barely knew them. They seemed glamorous and attractive. It's ghastly, everything that's happened.'

'That night, in Paris, when Mr Mulloney died. Do you think it was the sesame allergy?' Louisa was pretty certain she wouldn't win any prizes for her interview technique but impatience was getting the better of her.

'That was the conclusion, wasn't it? Louisa, this is a strange time to have this conversation. It happened such a long time ago and now we're here for poor Mr Strachey . . . '

'I know,' said Louisa. 'I'm sorry, I should have thought about the funeral. It's only because I met up with Guy today and he told me that he is looking into it. Mr Mulloney's death, I mean.'

'Why?'

Louisa had to tread carefully here. She couldn't let Luke know everything they were thinking. Not yet.

'I think because it turned out Clara was given an overdose,

it's making him look at everything again. It's nothing more than a policeman's mind at work.' She tried to give a lighthearted chuckle. 'We were trying to think if there was anything that Mr Mulloney might have eaten that could have caused his death.'

'Such as *sesame*, at the *restaurant*?' Luke's tone was distinctly sarcastic.

'But it seems unlikely, given his serious allergy, that Mr Mulloney would have ordered anything with sesame in it. What about the drinks once you were back at the house? Can you remember if he ate anything that was in the drawing room that night? Something that nobody else had? Mr Guinness mentioned a box of chocolates but he didn't know where they came from.'

Louisa held her breath. Would he admit to bringing the chocolates?

Luke gulped down the last of his drink. 'Of course it's not the bloody chocolates, I brought them. I don't know what the hell is going on here, Louisa. But I think you're on dangerous ground. Kate confessed, didn't she? I don't see what good can come of raking this all up again. I even wrote it up for the paper – it got me my promotion, if you remember. The last thing I want is to have to tell my editor that the story was something else altogether. Better to leave this alone, don't you think?'

Louisa said nothing. She couldn't. In that moment she realized she had got it wrong: those chocolates had never been intended for Shaun Mulloney. When Luke had arrived at the house, he said the chocolates were a present for Diana. He wasn't to know she was going to put them to one side and not eat them. If Shaun Mulloney ate them, it had been by mistake. If the chocolates killed him they had to have been poisoned, as no box of chocolates contained sesame. What if he had died but he hadn't been the target? And she knew what Luke thought of Diana Guinness. He didn't like her. Could it be that he *hated* her?

And Luke had stolen Kate's diary.

'Yes, of course,' she said. 'Sorry, forget I said anything.' She left the room before Luke could see the fear on her face.

CHAPTER FORTY-NINE

The following day, Louisa offered to run some errands for Diana and so was able, in between the post office and the dressmakers, to dash to the Knightsbridge police station and ask for DS Sullivan. Guy came out quite quickly and Louisa explained that she didn't have much time, there was one thing she wanted to talk to him about.

'What is it?' He looked rather sweetly dishevelled. His clothes were clean but she suspected his jacket had been rather hastily put on in order to come out meet her. His glasses needed a decent polish.

'I spoke to Luke Meyer last night.'

'Yes.' He looked neither pleased nor displeased at this news.

'He was at the house, you see. It seemed like a good moment.' She waited for him to say something but he didn't. Nervously, she carried on. 'The thing is, I remembered that I had taken one of the chocolates while everyone was out at the dinner and then I was sick all night. What if it wasn't the fishpaste sandwiches but the chocolate? I only had one and was sick, Shaun ate the rest of them and was dead.'

Guy rubbed his nose. 'Poisoned chocolates, is that what you mean?'

'Maybe.'

'Where did the chocolates come from?'

This was the question she didn't want to answer but she had to. 'Luke Meyer. He brought them, remember.'

Guy couldn't hide the surprise. 'Your friend, the journalist? But why would he want to kill Shaun Mulloney?'

'That's just it,' said Louisa. 'I also realized we are looking at it the wrong way. If it was the chocolates, they were meant for Mrs Guinness, not Mr Mulloney.'

'In other words, we're not looking for motivation to kill Mr Mulloney but Mrs Guinness,' said Guy. 'Golly, Louisa. I think you've done something here. That removes Mrs Mulloney's motivation to kill her husband at the very least.'

Louisa wanted to jump with the high drama of it. She hardly dared speak in case it came out as a mouse's squeak. 'What do we do now?'

Guy glanced back at the office. 'I'm not busy now. I think I should come back to the house with you. I assume Mrs Guinness is at home?'

'Yes, she is. So is Mr Guinness.' This bit, Louisa didn't like. She knew they would not enjoy the discussion but having got started, she didn't feel that either of them could stop.

Louisa followed Guy out of the room and into the hallway. 'I know how it looks but I can't believe that Luke would have deliberately poisoned those chocolates,' she said.

'Why? Because he's your friend?'

'No. Well, yes. I don't know, Guy.'

'Did he have a reason to want to kill Mrs Guinness?'

Louisa sighed. 'I don't know, I don't think so. Why would he have tried then and not again?'

'Supposing he did try again, and failed, and we don't know about it.'

Louisa walked towards the front door, where she would let Guy out. 'There was a weekend, about a year ago I think, which Diana spent with Lytton Strachey where she was very sick and everyone thought Dora Carrington had tried to poison her. Perhaps Luke was there then?'

'Would he have tried to kill Clara Fischer too? *And* Kate Mulloney?'

'It seems too ridiculous.'

'Unless it's not one person doing all this.'

'What? Two people in tandem? By coincidence or together?'

Guy gave a shrug. 'It's worth considering.' He looked down at Louisa and smiled. 'Two people in tandem is not always a bad thing, you know.'

'Go on,' said Louisa but she was smiling too. 'Be off with you.'

CHAPTER FIFTY

～

There weren't many facts at her disposal but this Louisa knew so far: Luke had brought the chocolates to Paris; she had eaten one and been sick all night; Shaun had eaten, at the least, 'most' of them and died the following morning. If the chocolates didn't contain sesame – and it would be strange if they did – then they were poisoned. Also, the chocolates were not intended for Shaun Mulloney, Luke having said they were a present for Diana; a fatal mistake had been made. Luke presumably did not see Shaun eat the chocolates, it must have happened while he was down in the kitchen talking to her. Was he not watching them at all? If he meant Diana to eat them, why did he not press them on her more assiduously? He may have been too drunk.

Was Diana the intended target? Luke didn't like Diana, she knew that. It was one of the things that had bonded them together: the uncomfortable awareness that they both needed her yet found her cold and selfish. But however much Louisa felt unsympathetic to her mistress, she had never had the slightest desire to kill her. Was Luke really made of such horrible stuff?

It didn't square with the man she had got to know and like so much – but then, she had always been wary around him, too. She had told herself it was because she wasn't sure if he was talking to her because he enjoyed her company or because he thought he would get gossip he could use for his column. Unless she had sensed something more sinister at hand.

These thoughts went round and round in Louisa's mind as she got on with her day's work, which continued to be as uneventful and easy as usual. Diana was a little more demanding than when Louisa had first joined the household, having a greater sense of herself as she grew in maturity as a mother and wife. But she was distracted these days. Books were picked up and put down again minutes later, a page hardly having been turned. Even when she played with her boys when they were brought down for an hour at teatime – usually her favourite time of day – her thoughts seemed to wander. And she was snappier than usual with Bryan, who was rarely able to put a foot right in spite of what appeared always to be the very best of intentions.

A few days after the interview with Diana and Bryan, and now that the immediate aftermath of Lytton Strachey's funeral was over, the family went down to Biddesden. Bryan was always happier there and Diana was generally content to return, though not this time. She chafed at leaving London and the parties and opening nights she would be missing, whining that she could easily stay behind on her own, but Bryan pointed out that Dora Carrington was coming to stay and in light of what had happened they could hardly cancel. 'Yes,' agreed Diana reluctantly. 'She so kindly wrote and said she would give me one of Lytton's waistcoats, to remember him by. I could get it altered and wear it.'

Having arrived back and settled Diana in, Louisa went to her room, a pleasant space that was not in the attic but one floor below, a little closer to Diana's bedroom. It had been decorated very simply but it was all her own – no children or other servants to share with – containing little more than a single bed, a chest of drawers, a long mirror and a framed Constable print. The best feature was a large sash window that overlooked the gardens, and Louisa threw it open now to breathe in the clean air that she believed she could taste as well as any seasoned dish. The trees were still bare but there had been an unseasonable few days of warmth which had tricked some of the blackthorn into coming out early. It looked as if snow had settled on their branches. On the outskirts of the land, Louisa saw three horses out with riders. Bryan had bought them from a riding school, so that guests might take them out and enjoy the grounds at a pleasant trot. It was quite likely that Dora Carrington had arrived just before them, with her husband Ralph; Pam had probably taken them out. As a young girl she had been the keenest rider of all the Mitford sisters. Louisa thought she could make out who was who on each horse: the man certainly; then Pamela, who was not stout exactly but not as narrow-waisted as Diana; while the smallest, slightest figure, like an ant, had to be Dora. To Louisa's horror, as she watched, the horse with Dora on it suddenly reared up and bolted towards the road. The tiny figure seemed to be holding on but was violently bumped up and down, and as the horse turned the corner on to the road, the rider was thrown off completely.

Louisa ran downstairs and sounded the alarm, and quickly Bryan went out in his car to the road, perhaps hoping to stop the horse before it ran off or caused any damage. Thankfully, it wasn't long before Dora was brought back to the house and propped on the library sofa with a rug over her legs. Diana had asked Louisa to fetch Dora some hot chocolate, a bowl of cold water and a flannel. 'I'm perfectly all right,' Louisa heard Dora say. 'It was a shock, that's all.'

'You must be careful,' said Diana, who was bent beside the artist, dipping the flannel into the water, wringing it out and laying it on her friend's forehead. 'I couldn't bear it if something happened to you after Lytton.'

Perhaps Dora hadn't realized Louisa was still there because she said to Diana quietly: 'I only wish it had killed me. I long to meet him again and nothing else.'

As softly as she could, Louisa left the room. She did not know if love like that was something one could wish for but she knew that she was starting to find her life very lonely without it.

The following morning, however, all of these things were put to one side when Louisa received a summons that changed everything. Called in by the butler, a jovial man called Ellis, who was nice to all the servants so long as they covered up the fact that he drank rather more of Mr Guinness's wine collection than a mere 'tasting' would normally allow, Louisa took the telephone in his office. Louisa almost never got rung up and when she did, it was rarely good news, so it was with some trepidation that she spoke into the mouthpiece. 'Hello, it's Louisa Cannon here.'

'Louisa! Thank God you're there.' It was Luke, sounding out of breath.

'Luke? Where are you?'

'I'm at the station, in Andover. I know I should telephone

Diana but I don't want to see her. Just you. Do you think you could hide me in your room for a bit?'

'What? No, Luke, I can't. Why on earth do you need me to do that?'

'Please, I'll explain but I can't do it here, in a public phone box. Can you send Turner to come and pick me up?'

'Not without telling Mr and Mrs Guinness, no.'

There was a grunt of frustration from Luke. 'Please, Louisa, I wouldn't ask if there was anything else I could do.'

'Take a taxi. I've got some money, I'll pay it when you get here. Ask them to come by the farm entrance. Miss Pamela might see you but Mrs Guinness won't. I'll meet you there in half an hour.'

Luke Meyer was running away from something and she had just agreed to be his accomplice. She only hoped she wouldn't regret it.

CHAPTER FIFTY-ONE

Louisa was standing by the blue farm gates, shivering in her cloth coat, though the sun was shining. Fortunately, it wasn't long before she saw a taxi coming along the road. He'd been lucky then – there was only one taxi that served the station in the mornings and you took your chances if it was out on another job. There was no sign of Pamela but it was not yet eleven o'clock, when she usually came in for elevenses (Pam not needing much excuse for a cup of tea and a ginger biscuit). She was likely out in the barns checking they had been properly cleaned after the milking of the cows.

The taxi drew up beside her, Luke got out and Louisa paid the driver. She had to hope Mr Suggs wouldn't say anything to anyone in the village about the lady's maid up at the big house having a fancy man coming to see her on the sly. For that was how the gossip would go. Luke looked as if he hadn't slept all night – his hat was crumpled, his suit had a stain on one side, the top three buttons of his shirt were undone and there was no tie to be seen. He wasn't even wearing a coat.

'I need a drink,' he said.

'Thank you, Louisa, for the taxi, you mean?'

'God, yes. Sorry. Thank you for the taxi.' He paused. 'I need a drink.'

'I don't know that that's a good idea. A bath and a change of clothes is what you need. But you haven't got anything with you.'

'No. Let's get inside and I'll explain.'

'Will you see Diana yet?'

'Looking like this? Not a chance.' The circles under Luke's eyes were dark enough to black a grate.

Louisa felt her best chance was to put Luke in Pamela's kitchen. She might not be best pleased when she returned, but she and Louisa were friends and it would be easier to explain Luke there than in the house. Knocking first, to check Pam wasn't in, they pushed the door open and went inside. Luke sank into a tatty but comfortable armchair by the kitchen fire – Pam liked to sit there with a dog at her feet, while she read a book in the evening – while Louisa made him a cup of tea and some toast. He ate it like a man denied food for forty days and nights.

'Now will you tell me what's happened?'

Wiping the crumbs away and before he'd quite finished his last mouthful, Luke started to explain. 'I was arrested last night, well, in the early hours of this morning, actually.'

'Arrested? What for?' Louisa felt a ball of panic in her chest. Had someone else been on his trail, all the while she and Guy had been trying to work out what had happened?

No.

He sighed and spoke without looking at her. 'I was in the public lavatory at Covent Garden.'

Louisa looked at him blankly.

'At one o'clock in the morning. Rather the worse for wear.'
He turned towards her now and raised his eyebrows. She could
see she was supposed to read his meaning as he didn't want to
have to say it out loud.

'Were you arrested for being drunk?'

'No, Lou! Come on, *think*. I wasn't alone . . .'

The light switched on. 'Oh, yes, I see.' Louisa poured them
both a second cup of tea. 'What happened? Not in the lavatory.
With the police.'

'It was hideous, Louisa. I was in the bogs alone and a man
came in and he propositioned me. We . . . you know. I'm not
going to spell it out.'

'*He* propositioned *you*?'

'Yes! It's happened before. But this time, afterwards, he
arrested me. I didn't understand what was going on at first, I was
laughing, thinking it was part of some game. But then I realized
he was a policeman. The bastard meant it and took me down
to the station.'

'Why didn't you threaten to say what he had done?'

'Because the balance of power does not exactly lie with me in
that situation, does it? And he said if I said anything, he'd make
sure I went down for three months with hard labour. In the end,
he kept me in a cell for a few hours. I was finally allowed out
this morning on bail.'

'Who paid for it?'

'I didn't have to pay, I had to sign something to say I wouldn't
abscond. But I've got to go to court in two weeks' time.'

Louisa looked at him sympathetically. 'I know it must seem
horrible, Luke. But it's not as if everyone doesn't know this about
you. It's not going to be a shock to anyone.'

'It would be to my aunt. She'll cut me off if she finds out, and she's all I've got.' He burst into tears then, awful racking sobs, just as Pamela pushed open the back door. It creaked louder than a haunted castle and at least gave them fair warning.

Louisa stood up and rushed over to Pam, dressed in riding breeches as she invariably was. 'I'm sorry, Miss Pamela,' she said. 'Luke Meyer is here. He's a friend and he needed somewhere to recover from a rather difficult time he's just had. I couldn't take him into the house.'

'I see,' said Pamela. She walked over to Luke, who had stood up, if rather shakily, wiping the tears away with the backs of his hands. He'd never pass a parade inspection. 'Have I met you before? You look familiar.'

'I was at your sister's wedding,' said Luke. 'But we might have met at a party in London? I seem to be at most of them.' He grimaced; it was probably meant to be a smile.

'I doubt it, I prefer *not* to be at most of them,' said Pamela. She walked briskly to the stove and, having checked there was enough water in it, put the kettle on. 'Are you going to tell me what happened?'

Louisa and Luke looked at each other and though his face pleaded 'no', Louisa answered with a mouthed 'yes'. Pamela was nothing if not cool in her ability to face facts plainly.

'It's a delicate matter,' she began. 'Mr Meyer was arrested last night on a public order offence. He's been released on bail but faces trial.' Luke, who had sat back down in the chair, was studiously avoiding Pamela's gaze as Louisa recounted the details. 'He can't quite face returning home just yet, because he lives with his aunt, Lady Boyd, and she may—'

'Die from the shock?' interrupted Pamela.

Luke's head snapped round. 'Yes,' he said. 'How do you know?'

'I know what a public order offence means and I know your aunt,' said Pamela. 'She designs spectacularly clever menus. She did a dinner for the Harlesdens in Mayfair last June that I went to. The *hors d'oeuvres* were quails' eggs with celery salt, the first course was a clear broth with caramelized onion rings floating on the top, the second course was duck *à l'orange*, the third course was mint sorbet, the fourth course was a chocolate bombe with white chocolate ice cream in the middle.'

Luke was agape. 'Yes, probably,' he said at last.

Louisa, almost as an aside, said, 'Miss Pamela's recall of menus has legendary status in the family.' Which made Pam smile.

'The point is,' she picked up. 'You are quite right. She will not understand this *débâcle*. The question is: does she have to know about it?'

'I don't see how she can't find out,' he said in small voice. 'She can be difficult but she's all I've got really. Mother and I don't speak much, and my father and I don't speak at all. I've no brothers or sisters, nor even cousins I know well. She took me in and has looked after me for years. This is going to go on my record and I can't promise that it won't make it into the papers, let alone the grisly prospect of prison. Oh God! I wonder if I shouldn't admit the whole thing before she finds out elsewhere.'

'You are in a pickle, aren't you?' The kettle was whistling and Pamela took it off and replenished the teapot. Louisa admired Pam's calm, she had always been the bulwark of the family but even more so now she ran her own show and could indulge in the things she enjoyed; all things that the others teased her were the occupations of a common housewife: cooking, gardening and even cleaning her own house. But she was bright and she understood people, understood perhaps better than all of the sisters the need for a private, inner life that was not necessarily explained to anyone else. She would comprehend Luke's need to protect himself. 'When is the trial?'

'In a fortnight.'

'Then I suggest you stay down here for a bit until you decide what to do. There is a spare room above the stables, where the groom used to sleep. We don't have one there any more as the gardener's boy likes horses, so he's been taking care of them and he lives in the gardener's cottage.'

'What about Mr and Mrs Guinness?' said Louisa. 'What will they think if they see Luke here?'

'Neither of them ever go down to the stables but I think if we cobble together a groom's outfit – an old pair of trousers and a cap, that sort of thing – they won't see you. It's extraordinary how people so often don't see what is right in front of their own eyes.'

Luke shivered with relief. 'Thank you so much, Miss Mitford. I can't say that I understand why you are being so kind to me but I'm very grateful for it. How can I repay you?'

Pamela sipped her tea and regarded him coolly. 'I shouldn't worry about that too much. I'm bound to think of something.'

CHAPTER FIFTY-TWO

Dear Guy,

    *What I have to write is shocking, please know that I
write it down only because I must stick as closely to the
facts as I possibly can. LM is down here at Biddesden.
He was arrested in the early hours of this morning, on the
charge of committing a public order offence in a public
lavatory in Covent Garden. He is on bail and there will be
a trial in a fortnight. If found guilty, I suppose he will be
imprisoned for three months or more.*

    *The poor man. I know what we have suspected of him
but I can feel only terrible pity. LM cannot bear the idea
of his aunt discovering the charge as she may throw him
out. LM lives with her and she is the only family he can
depend upon. He telephoned me from the station down
here and I had no option but to bring him to the house,
though he has seen no one else but Miss Pamela, who
kindly suggested he stay in the former groom's empty room
above the stables, more or less in disguise so that Mr and
Mrs Guinness do not see him. Just for a few days. He*

cannot face any company; of course, his friends are aware
of his preferences but he is afraid the arrest is shaming. So
long as he is here and I can keep a (very) close eye on him,
I am sure he is unable to cause any danger.

That said, I am unsure about our theory now. If
you could only see him, you would realize he has been
destroyed by what happened to him. He doesn't have the
manner of a cold-blooded killer.

Tell me if there's anything I should do while he is here.
What I'm saying is: write to me.

Yours,
Louisa

Before she had time to regret her last line, Louisa licked
the envelope and sealed it, then left the letter in the house's
post box, addressed to Guy at the Knightsbridge police station.
She would do as she had promised, and keep a watch on Luke.
Having failed to get anything out of him before, except for a
defensive reaction, she was hopeful that now he was in a more
vulnerable state he would be truthful.

However, with Diana's distracted condition, where tasks
were being taken up and dropped erratically, Louisa found it
difficult to find the time to escape the main house and go up
to find Luke. When at last she did, the following afternoon,
Pamela found her first, dashing out of her brick-and-flint cottage and along the path Louisa was walking on.

'Miss Pamela. Is everything all right? I'm so sorry again
about imposing Mr Meyer. I wasn't expecting you to
put him up.'

Pamela waved her off. 'One must always do what one can for

a fellow. The only thing is, Dora Carrington has been up here and talking to him.'

'Do you think she realizes who he is?'

'No. She's in a pretty desperate way. It probably doesn't matter but what with both of them being like that, I can't think it's good for either of them.'

'Will she mention him to Mr and Mrs Guinness?' This was enough to panic Louisa.

'Who can say? But you might tell him to be more careful.'

Louisa had to bear the brunt of the responsibility, in other words. 'Yes, Miss Pamela, I will.'

Louisa went round to the stables, cursing her lack of proper gumboots – she'd have to polish her own shoes as soon as she got back to the house – and walked up to the room above. An outside flight of wooden steps led up to the door, behind which was a single, large room, whitewashed with a bed and some empty shelves. She knocked and heard Luke's voice call out, 'Who's that?'

'It's me,' said Louisa, her head through the door. She saw him sitting on the edge of his bed, looking still rather pale and nervous, though less tremulous than before. True to her word, Pamela had dug out some old trousers and a workman's linen shirt, both big and loose on him. 'Did you manage to sleep last night?'

'Hardly. This bed is lumpy, the room is cold and I'm sure the hay is making me sneeze.' He rubbed at his face as if to wake himself up. 'But I know beggars can't be choosers.'

'Have you spoken to your aunt?'

'I sent a note to let her know I was staying down here for a few days, on an unexpected invitation.'

'Good. Have you seen anyone?' This was a test.

'Only Pamela, briefly. She brought me up some soup and bread.'

He'd failed. Damn.

'Miss Pam told me she saw you talking to Dora Carrington earlier.'

'Oh yes,' Luke feigned suddenly remembering. At least, that's what it looked like. 'Not for long. She came up to look at the horses. She said she wanted to let the one that bolted know that she forgave it. She's very sweet, if awfully sad. Like a daisy that's closed up its petals and not realized the morning has come.'

'Did she know who you were?'

'No, I kept the cap on and my face bent down, told her I was a groom. I played the part rather well, if I say so myself. Spun a tale about a badger caught in a trap and how I'd shot it to put it out of its misery. Rather an authentic invention on the spot, don't you think?'

Louisa wasn't at all sure this was the sort of story Dora Carrington would have appreciated. It seemed very insensitive of Luke.

'Yes, well, I have to get back soon but I wanted to know if you had thought about what you're going to do.'

'What can I do? I have to go to court, I have to take whatever sentence they give me.' He flopped backwards and lay on the bed, eyes wide and staring at the ceiling.

'You're a grown man, Luke. You have a job, you'll have to get your own place like many others do. Perhaps you should start over in a new city.'

He propped himself up on his elbows and turned to face her then. 'You're cold,' he said. 'If you want to get rid of me, you'll have to try harder than that.'

'Just – be careful, Luke.' Louisa had to get out of there before she panicked.

She walked back to the house quickly and let herself in through the boot room, where she heard voices just off to the side: Bryan and Dora Carrington. She could hear them though they couldn't see her and something about the way they were talking made her press herself to the wall, so as not to disturb them.

'Thank you so much, Bryan,' Dora was saying. 'Ralph's old gun has completely disappeared and we have such trouble with the rabbits at Ham Spray House.'

'It's a Belgian 12-bore,' said Bryan. 'Shouldn't be too difficult for you to handle.'

Louisa heard the sound of him locking the gun cupboard again and they walked off.

CHAPTER FIFTY-THREE

꩜

Three days later, after Luke had left, Diana and Bryan were telephoned by Dora's husband. He had gone to London for the day and when he returned his wife was dead. Wearing Lytton Strachey's yellow dressing gown she had gone to their bedroom and balanced the gun that Bryan had lent her on the floor, its muzzle at her side, before she pressed the trigger with her toe. She had been discovered by Virginia and Leonard Woolf, dropping by to see how she was, and it had taken her six hours to die.

The house was shaken by this news. Dora had been a frequent and pleasant guest to the house and all the servants had liked her. Bryan was distraught that he had lent Dora the gun, though Diana told him over and over not to blame himself. She was desperately unhappy, she would have done it somehow.

Louisa was less sure. She, herself, was racked with the guilt that she had known the conversation Dora had had with Luke, and that soon after Dora had borrowed the gun. Had Louisa become an accomplice to Luke's casual, horrifying attitude to life? Having written to Guy to tell him that she felt pity for Luke, she wondered if she had done the right thing, after all. Guy had sent her a brief note in return, telling her he would abide by her instinct but asking her to be careful nonetheless. He also said he had finally heard from the French police with regard to Shaun Mulloney but there had been little to relay: Mrs Mulloney had denied an autopsy in France and the body had been repatriated quickly to Ireland. Guy had been in touch with the relevant authorities in Dublin but it appeared that as there had been a death certificate already signed by a doctor in Paris, there had been no further investigation by Shaun's family and he had been buried. However, the French police still had not released the statements they had taken down at the time and he was going to push for these. He had to be circumspect, however, because he had not had his superior sign off this review of the case.

Together with the news about Dora, Louisa wanted no more of this introspection into the darkness. She decided she was no longer going to delay on the things that had become important to her. Nor, it seemed, was Diana.

After the news of Dora's death had been received, Diana had announced that she was leaving for London as quickly as possible. She arranged for the boys to stay behind with Nanny Higgs before she, Bryan and Louisa were driven up by Turner. The journey was done in just under three hours but felt considerably longer with the oppressive silence in the back seat, the young couple not talking at all. Louisa felt no less heavy-hearted but she was comforted by the thought of her plans.

Arriving at Buckingham Street, Diana disappeared into the

morning room and was quickly on the telephone, talking in a low voice, making one call after another as if she felt the need to be connected to as many people as possible. Bryan went out to his club, which probably meant he would be gone for the rest of the day. Eventually Diana rang the bell for Louisa.

'There are three different parties I'm going to this evening,' she announced. 'I'll leave here at six o'clock and I don't know what time I'll be back. There's no need for you to wait up. Please prepare my black silk, the one with the three-quarter length sleeves. I'll wear it with the Molyneux evening coat, and you'll need to get the Guinness necklace from the safe. The one Lady Evelyn gave me.'

'Yes, ma'am,' said Louisa. A whole evening to herself. She knew what she was going to do.

As soon as Diana had left the house – dressed in funereal black and rubies, unaccompanied by Bryan yet not looking sad, looking young and excited – Louisa followed soon after. She was in the best dress she had, a hand-me-down from Nancy of navy silk with huge white flowers printed all over it, and with a flattering nip in the waist. Walking fast to Hyde Park Corner, she hopped on the bus for a quick ride to the stop by the Natural History Museum, and then walked to South Kensington, which took her less than ten minutes. It was cold and the sky was low and dark, a metallic tang to the air as if a storm might break, but she was feeling light on her feet. As she turned into Pelham Street, she saw the red awning of the restaurant she had chosen and standing underneath it, his hands in his coat pockets and looking nervously about without seeing her yet, was Guy.

Louisa practically ran over to him. The sight of him, now that she had made her decision, made her feel as if she had burst herself open like a paper bag filled with confetti.

'Guy.' She touched his arm and he looked slightly startled as though he couldn't quite believe that she had turned up as she had said she would.

'This is all rather mysterious. Why wouldn't you tell me what this is about?'

'I'll tell you inside,' she said. Now, they had all the time in the world.

'We're going in there?'

'Yes! We're going in there, and we're going to sit down and have supper together, and we're going to talk.'

He looked uncertain then.

'About good things, we're going to talk about good things, I promise you.'

Relief bloomed on his face, and he pushed open the door to let her in first.

Sitting opposite each other in the restaurant, there were a few minutes of awkwardness while the waiter fussed over their napkins and brought over the wine and menus, before finally leaving them alone. Guy started to read his menu but he looked at Louisa over the top of it. 'I can't eat until I know what this is about, Louisa,' he said.

'I know,' she said, feeling an intoxicating blend of certainty of what she was about to do with nervous bubbles in her throat all at once. She took a sip of wine and worried she wouldn't be able to swallow it but the warmth of the alcohol relaxed her. She put the menu down and looked at Guy. 'It's about us.'

'Us?' She could see him still afraid that this might not go the way he would like it to go.

'Yes. I don't know how you feel about Sinéad, and I know that was all very recent. No, please.' Guy looked as if he was about to say something. 'I need to get this all out. I mean to say, I understand if you need some time. But I've realized that, well …' Her prepared speech suddenly turned to ashes in her mind. It seemed both too trite and too serious. What if he didn't feel the same? She had to keep going now she'd started. 'Everything that's happened recently, these terrible deaths, these unhappy people, and the things in the news – the world is such an unhappy place. And I don't want to be unhappy, too. I don't want to feel that life has passed me by and I haven't taken the chance to do the things I really want. That's not to say I know exactly what I want, but there is one thing.' She was running out of oxygen and she didn't think she'd made any sense, Guy was looking at her with kind bemusement, his eyes creasing at the corners with those dear lines. 'I want to be with you, Guy. I don't think we should be alone and apart any more, but it's not fear that's making me say this. It's happiness.' She blinked, afraid she might cry.

Guy reached over the table and beckoned. She placed her hand in his, warm and strong, and felt safety wash over her as his fingers closed over hers. 'You don't know how long I've wanted to hear that from you,' he said, quietly.

'I think I do,' she said, half gulping the words.

Guy leaned further over the table. 'If we weren't sitting in here, I'd kiss you now.'

Louisa laughed, the tension she'd felt in her stomach gone completely. She looked around the room. There was one other couple in the window, and the waiter was busy pouring wine for another table, his back to them. 'I'd say we could risk it anyway.'

Guy raised an eyebrow. 'I say, Miss Cannon. Will you always surprise me like this?'

'I hope so.'

And briefly, but for long enough to feel the softness of each other's lips and the tremors pass through them, behind the menus held up as a screen, they kissed.

For the next two hours, Guy and Louisa talked as they had never been able to talk before. There was so much of each other's past they knew already but all at once they had a future that was both unknown and certain, stretching ahead of them, to be shared. They talked about holidays by the sea they wanted to take, that they would both like to stay in London but perhaps find a house with a small garden that Guy fancied he'd like to have a go at. They hedged around the idea of children – it seemed too soon to wish for everything to fall into their laps – but playfully teased the picture of them both as an old married couple in a cottage by the sea with heaps of grandchildren. When they left the restaurant, Louisa's hand in Guy's, they walked with the easy certainty of a couple that have loved each other for years and always would.

CHAPTER FIFTY-FOUR

G uy and Louisa walked through South Kensington, not yet wanting the night – this fateful night – to come to an end. The rain had been and gone while they were inside the restaurant, leaving only faint traces behind with wet cars and slick reflections on the pavements of the street lamps. It still wasn't late, there was yet the sense of London being alive, changing shifts from day workers to night workers and party people.

Unable to say out loud anything of what they were feeling, the two of them continued silently, trying to calm their whirling thoughts into submission and failing, as they turned into Old Church Street. Just up ahead of them on the right was the Chelsea Arts Club and it looked as if a party of some sort had come to an end, as the men and women flowed out on to the pavement. They were of another time and place, Guy thought. Never would he see any one of their kind on the streets where he lived. The women wore long coats of rich textures and many colours, worn loose and open, showing flashes of the reds, yellows and oranges beneath as if their bodies were aflame. Their heels were high, their faces made up and they were shouting as if they hadn't realized there was no longer any music above which they needed to make themselves heard. The men were perhaps more soberly dressed in dark coats and top hats, though there were enough flourishes for the occasional artist to make himself known. Were they afraid that without a paintbrush in their hand or an easel before them that they might be mistaken for a City pen-pusher? They announced their integrity instead with cravats, winding scarves and pipes. Guy was enjoying watching this strange species as they grouped and broke off, like peacocks in a mating dance, when he felt Louisa grab his arm to make him stop walking. She nudged him to the side of the pavement, into the shadows by the wall.

'What is it?' he asked, half hoping and half shocked that she might be trying to kiss him in the street.

'Shhh,' she said. 'Look. That couple there, on the right.'

Guy looked but it took him a while to make his eyes focus. They weren't too far away, in fact, only a few more steps and he and Louisa would have walked right past them. But it was unlikely that the couple would have even noticed. They were standing a way apart from the crowd outside the club and he saw that the small, slim, blonde woman was Diana Guinness. But the man she was standing with was not Bryan. He was tall, and he was holding his hat in his hand, showing his thick mass of slicked-back dark hair, a large face with high cheekbones and a strong nose that sheltered a black moustache. He looked vaguely familiar but Guy couldn't quite place him. Diana was looking up at him intently, hanging on to his every word as the man was talking in what looked to be a serious, quiet way, meant only for her ears. Their heads were angled so near to each other that you could almost see the magnetic force between them and it looked as if they might kiss at any moment, like bath bubbles on your fingertips put too closely together.

'That's Sir Oswald Mosley,' whispered Louisa. 'I recognize him from the papers.'

'The politician?'

Louisa nodded. 'Diana met him a few weeks ago. I knew there was something different about it and she's been in a strange mood lately. Apart from everything else, I mean.'

'Ah.' Guy wasn't entirely sure what Louisa meant but even he, with his terrible eyesight, could see that whatever was going on between Diana and Sir Oswald was not something her husband would have approved of.

'I hope she isn't going to be an idiot,' sighed Louisa. Then she looked up at Guy and he thought – we're in the shadows, aren't we? And he pulled her into him, and they kissed again.

Back at work the next day, Guy marvelled how a change in his happiness could have such an effect on even the most prosaic of minutiae. The tea at work tasted better, the people around him seemed gayer and kinder, and if they weren't he cared not a jot. Even so, there was a task he had to complete. It was the very last thing he wanted to do but he knew that he had to, not only because it was right but because Louisa had asked it of him last night.

Excusing himself from the station on an errand, he grabbed his hat and coat and headed over to Covent Garden station, taking the Piccadilly underground from Knightsbridge. A busker was playing saxophone at the entrance to the platform and Guy was feeling so jolly he dropped a half-crown in his hat.

Out the other end on to Long Acre, packed with market stalls, Guy threaded his way to the police station, where he asked for PC Marshall at the front desk. 'He's on the beat today,' said the constable. 'But he's only just started, you might catch him if you head out quick enough. He usually starts with a cup of tea at Joe's caff. Out the door, second street on the left.'

Guy walked fast to Joe's and as he pushed open the door, a uniform was on his way out. In spite of his lowly rank, he was older than Guy, with jowls and eyes the colour of shrapnel. 'PC Marshall?' asked Guy.

'Who's asking?'

'DS Sullivan, Knightsbridge. Might we have a little chat?'

'You'll have to walk with me, I'm on duty.'

'Lead the way,' said Guy, with an insouciance he didn't feel. For all his pleasure in apprehending criminals, Guy was not a man who enjoyed confrontation.

They walked along the narrow pavement, jostling against each other and having to separate crocodile fashion as others pushed past, people hurrying to work or appointments. By the time Guy was able to speak properly, his breath was short, undermining what he had hoped would be his gravitas as the senior policeman.

'I understand you arrested a Mr Luke Meyer recently.'

PC Marshall didn't break his stride. 'Yes. What of it?'

Whatever had happened, this was a man on the back foot. Guy knew he had to tread carefully. He couldn't incriminate himself by interfering in criminal justice before he had forced PC Marshall to retreat.

'He's a personal friend of Mr Bryan Guinness.'

'Thinks that puts him above the law, does he?'

'No,' said Guy. 'But it does buy him a good lawyer.'

'Best of luck to him, then.' Not once had PC Marshall looked at Guy but kept his eyes straight ahead.

'Mr Meyer has given a second statement of the events that night, to us at CID.'

There was a momentary break in his rhythm then.

'Right. And this concerns me because?'

'PC Marshall. I suggest you think carefully before you repeat that question. I think you know what Mr Meyer will have said. Now, we can take this to court and have it all heard there, or you can realize that you made an error in your arrest, and have the charges dropped immediately.'

PC Marshall still didn't look at Guy but he stopped walking. 'You and I know this is how policing works. All I'm doing is upholding the law.' He pushed his face closer to Guy's. 'Are you doing the same, DS Sullivan?'

Guy didn't flinch. 'Magistrates don't see it quite like that. I don't think you want to be another Reginald Handford, do you?'

PC Marshall sneered. 'I can see it's my word against his and you've decided to believe the rich man. Money always talks, doesn't it?'

'What's more, PC Marshall, I'll be keeping an eye on your arrest record. I'd stick to the petty thieves if I was you.'

PC Marshall made no reply to this but walked away and disappeared around the corner.

CHAPTER FIFTY-FIVE

~~~~~

In April, the Guinnesses moved out of 10 Buckingham Street to 96 Cheyne Walk. Diana made this house her own, painting over the old walls and panelling in white, and washing rooms in pale blues, pinks and golds. It was ineffably pretty, particularly with the first-floor drawing room that overlooked the River Thames; but instead of enjoying this suffusion of light and water, Louisa was beginning to feel oppressed by the secret life that her mistress was now leading. This was due, in part, Louisa knew, to the fact that she was hiding her own affairs of the heart. However much she condemned Diana's treatment of Bryan, Louisa understood – to a degree – the compulsion she felt.

Louisa had met Mosley only briefly and watched him at a distance once or twice, waiting discreetly for Diana as she talked to him after they had bumped into each other somewhere. Rarely, of course, had the encounter not been orchestrated in advance. The new house in Cheyne Walk also happened to be quite close to the headquarters of Mosley's New Party's Youth Movement in the King's Road, where he organised fencing and gymnastics for the young members. Though the New Party had been dissolved, the Youth Movement remained, and Diana always referred to him as 'the Leader'. It wasn't hard for Diana to find a reason to go shopping nearby and for Mosley to appear in the street, apparently by accident. More than once, Louisa had been compelled by her mistress to admire his fitness and the strength of his figure; he was fourteen years older than Diana and yet her husband's youthfulness never favourably compared.

Louisa and Guy, meanwhile, were doing their own sneaking out to meet. She wasn't quite ready yet to admit the idea of marriage and was grateful that Guy hadn't brought it up. She thought he might have been sensitive to Sinéad receiving any news of an engagement less than two months after he had broken with her. At least, she hoped it was no more than that. Louisa knew now that she was in love with Guy and she knew, too, that it was different to whatever it was that Diana had with Mosley. Where Louisa felt comforted by the idea of Guy and revelled in the safety and strength he could provide, Diana seemed to be distracted by a kind of madness, thinking of little else other than where Mosley was and how she could meet him. She was increasingly careless of discovery by Bryan, though Louisa was confident that Diana had not discussed her burgeoning feelings with either Nancy or Pamela. Nor did she think Diana and Mosley had become lovers. Diana was a prize, publicly on view and constantly watched by admirers and the press. It was dangerous for her to do anything that broke the code of what was expected of her, and she was still devoted to her boys. All the same, there was no doubt that it was merely a question of *when*, not *if*, they would cross that line.

*

However, there were advantages for Louisa, with more time spent in London at the new house, particularly as Diana chose to leave the boys with Nanny Higgs at Biddesden and was losing hours to her 'distraction', whether on the telephone trying to find out which social engagement both she and the Leader were invited to or actually at the events themselves. This meant Louisa had fewer demands on her day and was able to do things for herself in a way that had never been possible before. There were lunches with Guy, in themselves an indulgence, even if they were mostly little more than egg sandwiches on a park bench. They talked freely, of their past, of the books they were reading (Louisa was more of a reader than Guy but he had started to take up some of her suggestions), there was a trip to the cinema to see A *Farewell to Arms*, and walks around Hyde Park, admiring the blossom. There was also talk of murder.

Guy had pursued the police in France for details of their investigation into the death of Shaun Mulloney, but when they came finally through, they were brief. The chef at the restaurant where the Guinnesses and their friends had eaten that fateful night had been questioned and he had been adamant that there was no sesame in anything that Mr Mulloney had ordered. But he had conceded that as there was sesame in other dishes made in the kitchens, there was the possibility of cross-contamination. The waiter who had taken the order said that no one had mentioned the danger of sesame to any of the diners. Given the symptoms of Mr Mulloney's death – vomiting, stomach pains and cardiac arrest – the doctor stood by his decision to rule the death as accidental and caused by an allergy. All in all, there wasn't much to go on.

Except for the chocolates.

Guy and Louisa were strolling through the park on a bright and breezy day, when spring was definitely near if not yet quite arrived, taking advantage of a long-ish lunch hour, in itself a novelty for them both. 'Have you spoken to Luke recently?' Guy asked.

'No, he's been lying low since the arrest. I know he went back to his aunt's, safe in the knowledge that she hadn't discovered anything about it and the charges have been dropped. But I get the impression it rather knocked him off his perch. Diana hasn't mentioned him lately but then, she doesn't mention much except the Leader.'

Guy raised an eyebrow at this. She loved him for his feelings on the subject: it was not so much that he was moral, though he was, as that he disliked unkindness. And Diana's treatment of her husband, as she pursued another man, was unkind.

'I think you should drop in on him,' said Guy. 'I can't. It would be too official.'

'All I got was a defensive reaction last time.'

'Perhaps you should be more direct. Ask him where those chocolates came from, where he bought them. Even if he realizes that you suspect him, I think it's a risk worth taking.'

'Fine,' said Louisa. 'For you, I'll do it.'

'You don't know how glad that makes me feel,' said Guy.

'So show me.' And he did.

CHAPTER FIFTY-SIX

Louisa telephoned Luke the very next day, arranging for them to meet. They met at his suggestion in Lyons' Corner House on the Strand, and when she walked in he was already sitting at a table for two at the furthest end from the entrance.

Under the electric lights of the café, Louisa was shocked by Luke's appearance. He was gaunt, with hollows in his cheekbones and his eyes slightly bulging out of their sockets. His skin was grey and even his hair looked thinner.

'What's happened to you?' she said as she pulled her chair out.

'Hello and how lovely to see you too.'

'I'm sorry but you look awful.'

Luke grimaced. 'Is it really that bad? I was wondering why no one had asked me over to the Lily Pond.'

'The what?'

'It's the name the waitresses have in here for that area in the corner.' Louisa looked and noticed that there were only men sitting across from each other at the tables where Luke had indicated. Some of them wore rather less than conventional clothing and she was fairly sure one of them had pressed powder on his skin.

'Oh,' said Louisa, wondering how she hadn't noticed before. She needed to get to the point. 'Wasn't it sad about poor Dora Carrington?'

'Yes, that was wretched, wasn't it? I suppose it wasn't really surprising though, everyone expected it of her after Lytton died.'

'You spoke to her, didn't you? Down at Biddesden.'

Luke was startled by this. 'A little, yes.'

'You told her you shot a badger, to put it out of its misery.'

'What of it?'

'That's quite a dangerous suggestion to someone like Miss Carrington, isn't it? Knowing how unhappy she was at the time, after Mr Strachey died.'

'Are you suggesting she shot herself because of something I said to her?'

Louisa glanced away. 'I don't know.'

'Well, you *should* know,' said Luke. 'That's a pretty awful thing to say to me.' He started coughing and it led to a minor fit. Louisa waited it out.

He sighed then and was about to speak when a waitress came up and asked for their order. Luke ordered Earl Grey tea with no milk, only a slice of lemon and nothing to eat. Louisa asked for tea too, and a scone. 'I can't eat,' said Luke. 'Everything makes my stomach turn. The police wrote to say they were dropping all the charges but I suppose I'm still feeling the after-effects of that ghastly time.'

The waitress had returned to set their tea things down but mercifully left swiftly. Luke was pouting, either because he was cross or for the benefit of the Lily Pond, or both.

Louisa thought she had better pull back for now. She still wanted to know how he had obtained Kate Mulloney's diary, in which she had spelled out her anger against Clara and Shaun, but decided that would be better left for another day.

'Could you pour my tea? Thank you. Now, tell me what's happening with Mrs Guinness and the Leader.' He had moved smoothly on.

Louisa interrupted the flow of milk. 'Is this for your newspaper?'

'No, darling. I can hardly lift a pen these days, let alone clack on the typewriter.'

She looked up at him, as if she could check how truthful he was being. 'There's nothing to report. What have you heard?'

'What haven't I heard, more like. London is awash with filthy rumours. There's always plenty to say about him as it is. I don't think anyone has ever mentioned Mosley's wife without the adjective "long-suffering".' The breathless gossip put a little colour back into his cheeks.

'I don't think they're lovers, if that's what you're asking. But I do think she's enamoured. She believes he's a brilliant political mind.'

'Hmm. Rumour also has it that his New Party dissolved because some of his co-founders think he has fascist ambitions to be an autocratic ruler. He went on a trip to visit Mussolini earlier this year. That tells you something.'

'I didn't know,' said Louisa, genuinely surprised. Beyond the brief articles the Italian correspondent wrote in *The Times* about Mussolini she was quite ignorant about him but she had read about the fears that surrounded his ideas. Fascism built roads, seemed to be the nub of it, but anyone who disagreed with his ideology was disappeared from public life, either literally or fig-uratively. It didn't seem to be the freedom everyone had fought for in the war.

Luke took another sip of his tea then but it prompted another coughing fit, at the end of which he looked quite green.

'Do you think Diana knows about his ambitions?'

'I hardly think she couldn't. Pillow talk, dear. The trouble is, girls like Diana were brought up to fall in love and get married. They don't understand the dangerous power of sexual attraction and get carried away when it hits. I spend my life repressing sex. She needs a lesson from me.' He allowed his eyes to fall briefly on a good-looking waiter as he walked past.

Louisa understood something of what he was saying but she also felt terribly sad, if not for Diana then for Bryan and their two boys. If only she could rush back to the house and scoop the boys up, protecting them from the heartbreak that was coming their way as certainly as a wave crashing on the rocks. Of course, she could not.

CHAPTER FIFTY-SEVEN

For the next three days, Louisa was at Biddesden, accompanying Diana as she returned to see her boys and Bryan. It was a quiet time, with Diana spending all her waking hours with Bryan, going for long walks along the river and reading their books together in the evening. When Louisa brought Diana her tray in the mornings, she was more muted than she had been in London, less full of lively chatter and gossip and plans for her day. She was always delighted to receive letters from her sisters, childish and enthusiastic missives from Decca and Debo. 'Decca's Running Away fund is building up nicely, she says,' Diana reported on the second morning as Louisa tidied up the bedside table. 'And Debo says eight new chicks have hatched and she's in a fury because Muv won't let her keep them in the Hons Cupboard.' Diana snickered. 'No, I'm sure she won't.'

'What's the Hons Cupboard?'

'It's that little room on the top floor where the linen is kept.

The girls have taken to spending hours in there because it's so filthy cold in the rest of the house. Not like lovely Asthall.'

Diana opened another letter. 'Lady Evelyn,' she muttered, scanning the pages. 'Oh, she says they're thinking of selling Grosvenor Place.' She put the letter down and stared into the distance. 'Probably because of that awful evening. You know, when the maids ...'

Louisa nodded. She remembered. She had been working in the kitchens that night.

'That was just before Bryan proposed. He said that dreadful accident made him realize how short and precious life is.' She looked at Louisa then, her eyes as blue as the Antarctic Ocean. 'It *is* short, one mustn't waste a second, must one? One should live life to the absolute fullest, not doing anything dreary but surrounding oneself with love and beauty.'

Louisa, folding items in Diana's underclothes drawer as this was said, could not help but smile, though she thought the statement did not bode well for Bryan somehow.

In any case, it was something else Diana said that set that dog off again, jumping up in Louisa's mind, refusing to be ignored.

On the third day, Diana wanted to return to London. Louisa was packing her mistress's case as she and Bryan argued over her returning alone.

'You would be bored stiff,' Diana pleaded. 'It's wall-to-wall cocktail parties and luncheons with Nancy and Tom. He's over from Berlin only for a short time and we will be doing all that family rot. I think Nanny Blor might even be bringing down the little ones to see them.'

'I like seeing your family,' said Bryan. 'You know Tom and I get on well.'

'Yes, but darling, don't be difficult. You'll have a much nicer time here getting on with your writing. And it's so much better for the boys if you're here.'

As she always did, Diana got her way.

CHAPTER FIFTY-EIGHT

~~~~~

As promised, on their return to London, Diana was out almost constantly. Louisa was required to be there for the mornings when her mistress woke, and the late afternoons when she rested before preparing for the evening's rounds. But she was told she did not need to wait up for when Diana returned at the end of the night. Louisa knew this was because Diana always hoped to 'bump into' the Leader and did not want to run the risk of leaving a party too early.

Of course, this suited Louisa perfectly. Guy had received a telephone call from Rose Morgan wanting to meet him. He had let her know that Ronan was safely locked up in prison and she had decided it was safe now to see Muriel Delaney, the little girl she had felt guilty about leaving behind. Guy had suggested to Louisa that she come with him to meet Rose, to which she readily agreed. Partly because she was curious and partly because they were spending every free moment they had together.

She was waiting for them in a tea room in Knightsbridge, not far from Guy's police station. As soon as they walked in, Louisa wondered how she could have forgotten her before, though it was clear her years in Paris had given her a style that wouldn't have been there when she was working as a maid. Rose greeted them with a nervous smile and they sat down opposite her at the small table. 'This is Louisa Cannon,' said Guy but Rose stopped him.

'Yes, I remember. That is, I don't think I knew your name but I saw you twice, didn't I?'

Louisa agreed and shook her hand. 'It's funny how it all comes back, isn't it?' They ordered tea and Rose began to talk, everything tumbling out in a rush in her Yorkshire accent, unchanged by her years abroad. Louisa had the feeling that Rose hadn't been able to talk about any of what had happened to her family and that she and Guy were providing her with the shoulders she needed. First of all she checked that Ronan had definitely gone to prison, which Guy was able to confirm. 'It'll be some months before he's out.'

'And he doesn't know it was me that told you how to find him?' she frowned.

'No. There's bound to be somebody seeking revenge on him for being short-changed and he'll think it's them. You're in the clear,' Guy reassured her.

Louisa poured them each a cup of tea while Rose talked. 'I saw you at that party when Dot had that accident, didn't I? At Grosvenor Place,' said Rose.

'I'd opened the door to a man who said he was a friend of Ronan's – and you came running over.' Louisa saw the images replaying in her mind. 'I noticed him give you a package but I couldn't think what it would be.'

'I worried about that,' said Rose. 'That's why I panicked when I saw you again in Paris.'

'Did you ever supply someone called Luke Meyer?' Louisa wanted to know. It wasn't her business, strictly speaking, but it felt important.

Rose thought for a second or two. 'I don't think so, but I might have done. I can't remember all their names.'

'No, of course not.' This didn't quite reassure Louisa. 'Did you tell Mr Sullivan that you saw Dot fall?'

Rose put her cup down. 'I did, it were shocking. They – that is, Elizabeth and Dot – had gone through the gate, and were leaning on the glass, but they had their hands holding on to the railing behind them. They looked fine but Dot she . . . ' Her eyes blinked as she remembered the terrible details. 'She sort of passed out. I saw it. Her eyes rolled backwards, and her hand let go and that's why she collapsed through the glass.'

She looked at Guy then. 'That's what frightened me. I thought if I was near, and I had some of the drugs on me, not to mention I'd been seen talking to Ronan, I had to get out.'

While Guy reassured her, Louisa thought back to that night in the kitchens and the last time she had seen Elizabeth and Dot. She remembered something she'd not thought about and now she bitterly regretted the failure of her memory. It was Dot, stealing some devils-on-horseback off a plate, and the assistant cook shouting out that they were meant for young Mr Guinness, 'special for him'. Someone in that kitchen had tried to poison Bryan Guinness but killed Dot instead. Could it be the same person that had killed Shaun Mulloney by accident, with the chocolates intended for Diana?

CHAPTER FIFTY-NINE

After they had said goodbye to Rose, Louisa walked with Guy to the station and outlined her plan to him and arranged for them to meet again, with Mary Moon, at Grosvenor Place the following day at eleven o'clock.

Louisa busied herself in tasks for the rest of the day and tried not to think about what might happen, but come the morning, she woke with goosepimples on her arms and legs though she was perfectly warm in her room at Cheyne Walk. It was early but the sun had come up and she took the opportunity to go down to the kitchen and have breakfast before anyone else had stirred. The household was small when it was only Diana there, just the live-in cook, Mrs Dudley, with a kitchen maid and a tweeny who came in daily. A gardener came by for an hour or two each day, largely because Diana had plants throughout the house that needed watering; a larger team oversaw the long garden at the back that seemed to run practically to the river's edge. It was a quiet and civilised corner of the world, with a wide range of books on the shelves that both Mr and Mrs Guinness read, a growing collection of records for the gramophone player and a radio in the morning room. In only the few years since her marriage, Diana had the acquired the confidence to make Cheyne Walk entirely her own.

Having carried out her work as necessary and seen Diana off to meet Lady Halifax at Peter Jones before a luncheon in Mayfair, Louisa set off to Grosvenor Place, hurrying a little. She wasn't late but she was enthused and the fresh breeze seemed almost to chase her down the street.

Guy and Mary were approaching the house just as Louisa turned the corner but she almost stopped when she saw there was another man with them. He looked tall and elegantly dressed from the back but when he turned around, looking up and down the street, she realized who it was: the detective who had interviewed her after Mrs Mulloney's body had been discovered. She hadn't enjoyed that experience much and he had shown much suspicion of her. She hoped he wouldn't upset her plans. Mary saw her first and waved, then broke away from Guy and the other man, to catch Louisa before she reached them. Mary started to say thank you to Louisa for suggesting to Guy that he request Mary be the assistant uniform but Louisa interrupted her.

'Is that DI Stiles?'

'Yes, how did you know?'

'He interviewed me for . . . It doesn't matter. Why is here now?'

Mary looked apologetic. 'The inquiry into the death of the maid was his, Guy couldn't open it up again without his permission. He insisted on being here. But I'm sure it will be fine.'

'I don't know,' said Louisa, feeling her stomach sink. 'I don't think he trusts me.'

'He'll probably have to question you. You're a new witness, you see.'

Louisa knew there was nothing to be done so the two of them walked up to Guy and Stiles, where there was a polite exchange of handshakes and introductions. Stiles looked at Louisa without giving anything away about what he was thinking. 'We've met before, of course. I'm interested to hear what you've got to say but I can't help thinking this is going to be a waste of time.'

Guy stepped in then. 'Sir, until we ask the necessary questions we won't know for sure, but it's very possible that Miss Cannon has pulled together various pieces of a much larger puzzle that none of us have seen.'

'But why couldn't we have done the interviews at the station?'

'Because that might alert the chief suspect, sir. This way, we can make a discreet inquiry without setting off any alarms.'

'Fine, Sullivan. I'll let you lead the way on this but it's going to be on my head if any of this backfires. I'd like you to keep that in mind.' He turned to Louisa. 'Miss Cannon, you and I will be having a chat of our own.'

'Yes, sir,' she said.

As agreed, Louisa took them round to the back entrance, where she knocked on the door. It was opened by a maid who recognized Louisa but was taken aback to see her surrounded by two men and a policewoman. 'What's going on?'

'It's nothing to worry about,' said Louisa. 'I know we look like quite a crowd but I rang yesterday and made an appointment to see Mrs Norris, she's expecting us. Well, me.'

'I see. You'd better come in then. She'll be in her sitting room, I expect.'

They were left waiting in the hall while Mrs Norris was

fetched, and she arrived quickly, walking with the brisk steps of every efficient housekeeper. 'Miss Cannon,' she acknowledged and waited for Louisa to introduce her to the assembled group.

'May I ask what this is about? There's rather a lot of you here.'

'Sorry, ma'am,' said Stiles respectfully. 'We won't take up any more of your time than we need to, I promise. It's just a few quick questions. As you will remember, I led this inquiry shortly after the event, but something new has come up for our consideration and we need to take another look at what happened that night. Would you mind if you took us through the events of the evening?'

'You'd better come through to the kitchen. Follow me.'

Feeling as if they were on a guided tour, they all walked along the narrow corridor to the kitchen, a large basement room with narrow windows along the top of the walls, just enough to let out the steam and heat on a busy night. Today, it was quiet, with the family away and only the servants to feed. Two kitchen maids stood at the wooden table that dominated the room, while a third stirred a pot on the stove. Off the kitchen were three anterooms: a still room for the pastries, a scullery for the washing up and the cook's office. This last was practically a cupboard, with cookbooks and a desk with sheaves of old menus piled up haphazardly. A man of prodigious stature balanced on a narrow wooden chair in front of it.

'Mr McCaffrey,' called out the housekeeper, and he got up as quickly as his figure would allow, absent-mindedly wiping his hands on his apron.

'What can I do you for?' he said jovially, then took the smile off his face when he saw Mary's police uniform.

'The police are here,' said Mrs Norris. 'I'm sure they're very

335

sorry to interrupt your work but they have some questions about the night the maid died.'

'I wasn't here that night,' said Mr McCaffrey, holding up his hands in innocence. 'I've been taken on since but I've heard all about it. They talked of little else in here for months after.'

'Which girls were working here the night of Elizabeth and Dot's accident?' asked Mrs Norris. Louisa saw the back of the girl stirring the pot stiffen, while the two chopping carrots and potatoes dared only to glance quickly up at them.

'Meg,' said the cook. 'Meg, get over here.'

The girl at the stove slowly put down her wooden spoon and came over to them. She seemed to be the same age as Louisa and rather surly-looking.

'Before we continue,' said Guy, 'I wonder if someone might show PC Conlon here the upstairs landing where Elizabeth and Dot stepped on to the skylight?'

Mrs Norris nodded. 'I'll take her myself.'

'Take notes,' whispered Guy to Mary. 'It's always possible I missed something before, like a loose latch on the railing's gate.' Mary nodded and followed the housekeeper out.

Stiles turned to Louisa. 'I'd like you to wait for us. Mr McCaffrey, would you be so kind as to allow Miss Cannon to take a seat in your office while we interview Meg?'

The cook was agreeable and Louisa was sent to sit by the desk, feeling like nothing so much as a dunce sent to the back of the classroom. But she took heart that Guy was close by and would give her the details she needed to hear. She needed to know if she was right.

CHAPTER SIXTY

~~~~~~

G uy and Stiles had agreed in advance to conduct this informal stage of the inquiry together. This meant Stiles could be absolved of having investigated formally if it turned out to be nugatory. Equally, if further developments did ensue, Stiles needed to have been present. Guy was conscious of being closely observed by his superior and wanted to make sure he showed the promise of being a good detective inspector. This kind of opportunity did not often present itself.

The three of them positioned themselves at the other end of the kitchen table, away from the gawping vegetable choppers, and waited for Mr McCaffrey to busy himself with another task. Meg stood sullenly before them, her hair tied back neatly under a mob cap, her apron a plain linen smock. She looked like something out of a Shakespeare play, thought Guy.

'Could you tell us your full name, please?'

'Margaret Hawkins, but everyone calls me Meg. What is this all about?'

Guy knew this attitude. It was the one where the police were nothing more than interfering busybodies at best, ignorant accusers at worst.

'Miss Hawkins, we have reason to believe that the death of your friend Miss Martin may not have been entirely accidental. We need to review the events of the evening of the fifteenth of June, 1928.'

Meg shrugged, the best he was going to get as permission to continue. Stiles raised an eyebrow and looked at his watch.

'Mr McCaffrey wasn't here but you were, we interviewed you at the time.'

'Exactly,' said Meg. 'I don't see why we have to go over it all again.'

'It's only procedure.' Guy tried to sound reassuring. 'In case there was something you didn't think of then that might have occurred to you later. Can you tell us again who was the cook that night?'

'Some posh woman was brought in to oversee it all, Lady Boyle? Something like that. She told us all what to do.' Guy couldn't be sure but it seemed that her inability to recall the name properly was forced.

Guy noted the name down. It might be important even if he could not see the connection.

'I know this is asking you to remember something that happened quite a long time ago but can you recall who cooked what that evening?'

'It was all the usual duties. Each maid has their own job to do, the vegetables or the pastry. I'm assistant cook so I did the main dishes for the dinner earlier, and oversaw the breakfast for the whole party.' She allowed a note of pride to creep in.

'To be clear, you and the other maids did all the cooking, Lady Boyle did no actual cooking herself?'

'No, she just stirred and tasted, told us what to do.'

There was a cough at the other end of the table. The girl chopping the carrots, who, Guy noticed, actually had carrot-coloured hair frizzing out beneath her cap, had put her knife down and was staring at them.

'Yes?' Stiles asked.

'Sorry, sir, I don't mean to interrupt, it's just I couldn't help hearing what you was saying.'

Meg turned her back on the girl and looked at Guy. 'Don't listen to her, sir. She's simple.'

'I'm not simple!'

Meg spread her hands out as if to say, '*See?*'

Guy walked along the table and gently spoke to her. 'What was it you wanted to say?'

'That Lady Boyle sir, she did cook something. She made devils-on-horseback, special like for young Mr Guinness, sir.'

The hairs on the back of Guy's neck prickled. He trusted that sensation: he knew when something was up.

'You were working here that night, were you?'

'Yessir, but I was in the scullery then, washing the pots. No one ever noticed me in there, sir, but I was here. I've been here ever since, and I've worked my way up to vegetable maid, sir.'

'Well done,' said Guy. 'And you saw Lady Boyle cook something?'

'Well, sir, yes. There were other trays of devils-on-horseback but she had some that she did separate, they were for Mr Guinness.'

'Did Mr Guinness eat them?'

'I don't know, but Dot did.'

'Dot Martin, the maid that died?'

'Yessir. I was in the scullery and I took a break for a minute, and I saw that posh cook put the plate down and then Dot took some off the plate when they walked past. You can pop 'em in your mouth quick, sir, they're only little things.'

'Bacon wrapped around prunes, aren't they?'

The redhead nodded. 'Meg shouted at them, sir. I remember, it give me a shock too and I got back to work.'

'Thank you,' said Guy. 'You've been very helpful.'

CHAPTER SIXTY-ONE

⌒

Back outside, Stiles made his excuses – one of his usual long luncheons – and left Guy, Mary and Louisa to review what had happened. As it was a clear day, they decided to walk back to the station together, talking as they went. Mary confirmed that she had found nothing to contradict Guy's notes or the inquest. The skylight through which the maids had fallen had been adequately cordoned off by railings and a secure gate. Access was required only to clean the opaque glass and this was done, Mrs Norris informed her, by someone leaning over with a long-handled mop. No more than one person at a time ever went on it and it was assumed the weight of both the girls at the same time had caused the glass to break.

'But it was because their hands slipped on the railing that they fell through, that's what the other maid said, the one who was watching.' Mary had read the notes through too.

'Yes, and that corroborates what Rose told us, though she thought it was more that Dot passed out. The question is: did she eat something that made her dizzy? Something that caused her

341

to lose her grip on the handrail?' Guy was asking the question but he had decided the answer.

'Those devils-on-horseback, you mean,' said Louisa. 'I saw her take them but I thought nothing of it until we saw Rose.'

'Yes, it looks as if you were right. Meg and that red-haired maid have corroborated your story of seeing Dot eat some.'

'What's more,' Guy carried on, 'we know that particular plate was intended solely for Mr Guinness. But who is this cook Lady Boyle and why would she want to poison Mr Guinness?'

Louisa gave a start. 'It's not Lady Boyle, it's Lady *Boyd*,' she said. 'Luke Meyer's aunt. They live on Wilton Crescent, the same road that Rose worked on. She must have hired Rose whenever she was taken on as a caterer for the bigger parties.'

Guy looked at her in shock. 'Are you sure?'

'Yes, pretty sure. I met her briefly in Venice and thought she looked familiar then but couldn't remember why. It must have been because I'd seen her in the Grosvenor Place kitchens. She wasn't there the whole time, you see. The assistant cook was left to prepare the breakfast.' She paused. 'There was a footman, sent upstairs with the plate, presumably to find Mr Guinness. Lady Boyd must have instructed him, only the housekeeper spotted it and I was told to fetch him back because it was too early to serve them.'

'But why would she want to poison Bryan Guinness?'

'Perhaps it wasn't personal,' said Mary.

'But the plate was destined *for* him.' Louisa felt the pieces were not fitting together properly just yet. 'I think I need to talk to Luke, ask him if his aunt has ever voiced dislike for Mr Guinness.'

'Agreed,' said Guy. 'I want to talk to Meg Hawkins again, too. I think she knew more than she was telling us. It's possible that

Lady Boyd talked to her after the accident, perhaps to prevent her saying anything about that plate.' Guy pushed his hat back slightly and looked up to the sky. 'We have to do this right. If Lady Boyd is guilty, we need hard evidence or a confession. We can't risk her finding out yet that we're on her case. And we still don't know her motivation. Without that, we can't be certain.'

'What if she sent those chocolates to Paris? That could have been Lady Boyd targeting Bryan again. We thought those chocolates were from Luke but what if they were bought by her to give to the Guinnesses – she could have tampered with them.'

'What with?' said Mary. 'Didn't you say Shaun Mulloney died of an allergic reaction to sesame? There can't have been sesame in the chocolates.'

'Perhaps he died from poison, not his allergy. We don't know because there was no autopsy. His wife was afraid his family would discover that he took opium, so she blocked it,' Louisa explained. At once she stopped walking and grabbed Guy's arm. 'Oh my God. Luke.'

'What?'

'Rachel – that's her name. R for Rachel. She must have been the one that Kate Mulloney met.'

'Did they know each other?'

Louisa thought hard, calling as much as she knew to the surface, trying to piece it all together. 'They might have had Rose in common. Rose and Lady Boyd both lived on Wilton Crescent. Rose said she was employed by a cook who worked at smart parties: Lady Boyd. And Rose supplied Kate with her opium.' She stopped and closed her eyes. 'Luke. I thought it was him, and it wasn't. Last time I saw him he looked terribly ill, thin and grey. I thought he looked like Clara Fischer did, and wondered if drugs had got hold of him. But what if I was wrong? What if his aunt is poisoning him?'

Guy grimaced. 'I suppose it's possible.'

Louisa felt beads of sweat break out under her hatband. 'Then I must hurry. I've got to go back to Cheyne Walk quickly in case Diana has left any sort of message for me there about when she'll be home later to change for the evening. I can go straight over to his house then.'

'I'll stay at the station,' said Guy. 'If you need me, you can reach me there.'

They parted, and Louisa hurried back to Cheyne Walk. But the message she found there was not from Diana, it was from Luke. And it meant she was too late.

Dear Diana,

Forgive me writing to you like this but I did not want to go without saying goodbye. I hope you can find it in your heart to understand why I have done this. You have been a good friend to me and I loathe the thought that I will cause you sadness and trouble. But I have been left with no choice. My aunt has discovered the truth about me and who I really am. You know what this means for me. If I cannot live as I truly am, I do not want to live at all. Where I have been trapped, I wish only for you to do as you must with the Leader. I have filed a final article for the newspaper about your affair: if the world knows, you will be free!

With love,
Luke

CHAPTER SIXTY-TWO

—————

The note had not been put in an envelope but folded in half. It could only mean that Luke meant for others to read it. She certainly wasn't going to show it to Diana. Was the threat about the article real or empty? Kate Mulloney had written a suicide note, too: could it be more than a coincidence? Trembling, Louisa read the note over and again then realized she was wasting precious time. Stuffing the paper into her coat pocket she ran out of the house and had a moment's blind panic while she couldn't think how to get to Luke's house. Wilton Crescent. It wasn't far but what was the quickest way to get there? Taxi, surely. Cursing, she ran back to the house, in through the side entrance and up the stairs to her room to fetch some money. Every month, after she was paid, she drew cash from the bank, in order to send some to her mother as well as to have five pounds to keep in her room, for no more reason than she liked the feeling of riches it gave her to know it was there and could be spent at any time. In fact, her habits of frugality and her childhood poverty meant she rarely splashed out on any kind of extravagance beyond rose-scented soap, so she knew there would be enough at the bottom of the vase that she never put flowers in. Grabbing the money, the adrenalin coursing through her, she felt as if the blood had rushed too quickly to her head and a wave of nausea passed over. Quick, she had to be quick.

In the kitchen, on her way out, she saw the tweeny. 'Tess, did you take this note for me?'

Tess, only seventeen and nervy, said yes, she had.

'Who delivered it? It's got no stamp.'

'A boy on a bicycle. He knocked and said he'd been told to be sure the mistress got it quick.'

'When was this?'

'Not quite half an hour, miss.'

Louisa had to think on her feet. If Luke had messengered the note over, there was just a chance that he wouldn't have succeeded yet. She gave the note back to Tess. 'I need you to walk as fast as you can to the police station in Pavilion Road, and ask for DS Sullivan.'

'I'm supposed to be here, miss.' Tess looked worried. 'Supposing Mrs Dudley comes and asks for me?'

'Don't worry about that, this is much more important. I'll explain to Mrs Dudley later if I have to. Please, Tess. Give this to DS Sullivan and tell him to go to 31 Wilton Crescent and I'll be there.'

'DS Sullivan, 31 Wilton Crescent,' repeated Tess.

'Get your coat and go, soon as you can. There's no time to lose,' said Louisa as she ran out of the door.

Just beyond the Embankment, the River Thames flowed cold and grey. She couldn't look at the Albert Bridge, one man walking slowly over it, another peering over the side, without wondering how Luke had chosen to do it. There was a flash when she wondered if she'd jumped to the wrong conclusion – perhaps he was just on a train somewhere! But she only needed to touch the paper in her pocket to know she'd guessed correctly first time. With relief, she saw a hackney carriage drive by and waved frantically to hail it. 'Where too, miss?' asked the driver.

'Thirty-one Wilton Crescent.'

She got in the taxi but he didn't drive off. 'Why aren't you moving?' She had to stop herself from shouting.

The driver looked startled. 'Sorry, miss. I assumed you were holding me until your guv'nor came out.'

Now was not the time to be furious about being seen as a servant, incapable of so much as hiring her own cab. 'No, it's for me and I'm in a hurry.'

The drive seemed to take as long as an expedition by Captain Scott, but what was in reality only thirty minutes later, the taxi pulled up outside Lady Boyd's house. The church next door stood as large and placid as before, its eyes and ears closed to the street. Thrusting the money into the driver's hand, not waiting for change, Louisa ran up the steps of number 31 and pushed at the front door. It was locked. She did not want to knock and alert Luke: either he would not yet have succeeded and be hurried along, or he'd deliberately ignore her anyway. Then she noticed there was a window below pavement level that had a small gap at the top. She ran down the short iron staircase that led to the basement entrance and pushed on the window: it gave immediately and, checking that no one was watching from the street, she dived in.

Inside there was a musty smell, the common problem of damp, though the room itself was tidy. It was presumably once the servants' domain and would have been filled with the tools of their trades, but now it housed only a butler's sink with a box of soap flakes standing beside it. Some dark clothing soaked in the sink, and a shirt of Luke's, bone dry but unironed, hung from a drying rack on the ceiling. There was a plain wooden table and two chairs that didn't match in height or colour, and the floor was brick tiles, smooth from a century of shoes and washing. On the shelves were uneaten tins of cat food and a packet of rat poison amongst the various bottles of household bleach and scrubbing brushes. Louisa removed her boots and felt the coolness of the floor through her woollen stockings. The door was shut but she pushed it open easily, quietly, and walked up the dark, narrow staircase, fear pushing at her throat like a damp hand. The door at the top of the stairs was backed in worn green baize and before she turned the handle she pressed her ear to it briefly but the silence was as thick as fog.

Slowly, she inched it open and looked into the hall. It was dark, a shaft of light coming only from the arched glass above the front door. The rooms that led off it were closed, stifling sound and light still further. With one hand on the banister, she moved step by step, not too slowly, not too quick, dreading what waited for her, hoping she'd got it terribly wrong.

CHAPTER SIXTY-THREE

hoeless, Louisa moved silently but not slowly up the stairs.
With each step she remembered things she had seen as if
turning the pages of a photograph album, each image taunting
her: how could she not have seen what was right before her eyes?
The maid eating the devils-on-horseback meant only for Bryan
Guinness, cooked by Lady Boyd. Dot falling to her death. The
chocolates brought to Paris by Luke. The sudden death of Shaun
Mulloney. Her own night of sickness. Lady Boyd's watchful
expression in Venice.

The frail, pale, dead body of Clara Fischer.

The blood that trickled from the heart of Kate Mulloney.

Step by step, the censure did not relent.

Louisa passed the dark stillness of the drawing room with its
vast portrait of the unsmiling Sir William. Running now, Louisa
went up another flight of stairs and saw a door firmly closed.
She turned the handle and pushed it open, not even knowing if
this was Luke's bedroom, making the best guess she could. This
room, too, was dark, the curtains had been drawn but hurriedly

perhaps, for they didn't meet completely in the middle and the shaft of sunshine that came through was enough for Louisa to take in the unhappy scene. A single bed was pushed up against the wall furthest from the window, a table beside it had books piled high and a lamp that was switched off. On the bed lay Luke, fully clothed and on top of the sheets. His shirt collar was undone, one arm lay on his chest, the other hung limply by his side, dangling over the side of the bed. In this glance, Louisa took in the scene but could not see yet if he was breathing. He made no sound. On the bed, strewn around his body, were a number of assorted medicine bottles. Several of them had their lids off.

In the furthest corner from the door, her face hidden by shadow, her hands calmly in her lap, sat Lady Boyd. As Louisa came in, she looked up but otherwise did not stir.

'Luke!' cried out Louisa and ran over to him, catching only a shocking glimpse of his ashen pallor. But before she could reach the bed she felt a strong hand on her arm, pulling her back.

'There is nothing to be done,' said his aunt. 'Leave him be.'

Louisa tried to wrestle herself free but Lady Boyd's grip was tight. She could feel the tips of the fingers that would leave bruises tomorrow.

'He's at peace now,' she intoned flatly, the phrase sounding like a rosary bead prayer that has been repeated forty times.

'What have you done?' gasped Louisa, feeling as if she would suffocate from this monstrous, heartless presence.

'I?' said Lady Boyd. 'I have done nothing.'

'Those pills—'

Lady Boyd released her hold on Louisa and smoothed out her skirt. 'Luke found them in the medicine cupboard. They are from when I was a nurse. It is unfortunate that he put them to this use.'

Louisa looked at her and realized she was talking to a madwoman. She had to be, none of this made any sense.

'We have to call an ambulance. He needs help. We might be able to save him.'

'There is no saving him.' Ice edged her words, like the first frost of the year. 'My nephew is beyond redemption.'

'Why?' Perhaps she could rationalise this insane situation, make his aunt see reason, if there was any reason to be had.

'To take one's own life is the ultimate crime against God.'

'But he hasn't taken his own life, has he?' said Louisa. She couldn't risk accusing her just yet. She had to get out first and call an ambulance, pray it wasn't too late. If Guy got here soon he could help.

Her breath ragged but her will determined, Louisa left the room and started to run down the stairs, holding the banister firmly, afraid her stockinged feet would slip easily on the stairs. Her boots were still in the basement but she could not go and get them. She ran down as she heard Lady Boyd coming behind her, a light but firm tread, step by step by step. At the bottom stair, Louisa jumped and ran to the front door, almost throwing herself against it as she turned the handle but it rattled uselessly in her hand. She pulled at it but there was no give. The door was bolted at the top and the bottom, Louisa reached up and undid the top but as she reached down, almost choking from the lack of oxygen she had failed to breathe in, Lady Boyd was standing behind her.

Her stance was calm, too calm.

Louisa's skin prickled. If she were a cat her hair and tail

would be standing on end. She thought of the rat poison in the basement.

Guy, he had to be here soon. Where was he?

'It was all you, wasn't it?' said Louisa. If she couldn't turn around to undo the bolt, she would keep her talking, stall her until Guy arrived.

'All what, dear?' Lady Boyd stood in the shadows, her face unreadable.

'You tried to poison Bryan Guinness at the ball but failed, so you tried again with the chocolates sent to Paris with Luke that killed Shaun Mulloney by mistake. You gave Clara the opium. And Kate Mulloney was sacrificed to stop the police from looking for you.' She tried again for a confession. 'What have you done to Luke?' Louisa reached behind her and gripped the door handle. It centred her, gave her reassurance that Guy would be here, that it would open. She would be safe soon. But she had to do this first.

'What have you done?' she accused again.

That was before she saw the hypodermic needle that Lady Boyd held in her right hand.

CHAPTER SIXTY-FOUR

Louisa kept holding the door handle. Please come, Guy, please come soon. Had he even been at the station when Tess delivered the note? She couldn't be certain, she could only hope. It was all she had.

Lady Boyd looked almost restful as she held the needle at her side, filled with a dark liquid. There was a small smile on her lips, though her eyes told Louisa nothing.

'They were all godless people. Heathens, sinning against Him, time and again with their bodies, their drugs.' She spat the words. 'I had to carry out His will.'

'Even Luke?'

'Luke broke my heart. He betrayed me when he revealed himself to be—' She stopped and revulsion covered her face. 'I saw that letter from the police. Luke tried to hide from me but nobody can hide from Him.'

'What did you do to Luke?' Keep her talking, thought Louisa, don't let her have time to act. 'Have you been giving him poison?'

For a split-second Lady Boyd looked stricken but it passed. 'Slowly but surely. If he had shown remorse, if he had given himself up to God, I could have stopped. But he wouldn't.'

'You mean *you* couldn't stop. You sent the note, I see it. Why did you bring Mrs Guinness into it?'

Lady Boyd stood completely still. 'That hag. Spoiled and rotten. She has everything but it's not enough for her, is it? No, she has to dishonour the vows she took before God by committing the deadly sin of adultery. It should have been her here, not you. But you will do instead. God tells me what to do, you see.' Louisa was pressed against the door as Lady Boyd stepped forward. 'He is telling me now, dear.'

Louisa stiffened her whole body, as if she could create a physical resistance to the needle, prevent it somehow from piercing her by hardening her skin. Her grip on the door handle tightened and then, as if she had willed it, she felt the knob resist her slightly. It was being held on the other side. Guy. In that tiny moment as Louisa was distracted, Lady Boyd saw her chance and took her final step but as she did so there was the sound of movement on the stairs. In her confusion Louisa thought she saw Luke and tried to shout out for him – could it really be him? – but a sudden pain stopped her, she gasped and her hands moved down to her stomach, quickly pulling the needle out.

'I did it for Him,' cried out Lady Boyd and then fell back, pulled by her nephew, who was shouting, telling her to stop, telling her this was all over now.

There was so much noise, thought Louisa, her mind clouding, feeling weaker, the sounds both more insistent and distant. She almost sensed more than heard the pummelling on the door and muffled shouts calling her name, calling Luke. Staggering, she turned around and undid the final bolt, opened the door. She let him in. Guy, here at last to save her.

CHAPTER SIXTY-FIVE

After that, everything had happened quickly, if hazily. Guy had not come alone but with Mary in a police car, followed by an ambulance. Both Louisa and Luke were taken to hospital, accompanied by a constable. After Luke had been given emetics, he had almost recovered and once awake, begged to be allowed to see Louisa. He found her lying in bed, in discomfort but no great pain. Lady Boyd had not managed to plunge the needle far and it had not caused any serious internal damage; so long as she rested, she would recover well. For the moment, she was grateful to lie in a clean bed, attended to by a nurse, and to look out of the window at the blue sky of spring. It made everything seem lighter and more hopeful once more.

Luke had approached her bed cautiously but she was pleased to see him. They embraced and Luke had sobbed with the relief: it was over. At least, this part of it had ended for him but there was much to explain.

'How did you know to come and find me?' he asked.

'Your aunt sent a note to Diana, as if it was from you, saying you were going to take your own life.' She squeezed his hand. 'I'm so sorry, Luke.'

He shook his head. 'Don't be, I'm so grateful you came. I should have seen it coming. I knew she wasn't well in some way but I chose not to see it. She was all I had.'

'We don't see the things we don't want to see. I do understand.'

Luke blinked away the tears. 'Perhaps. But I think I knew more than I could ever admit to myself.'

'Do you mean to say you knew what she had done?'

'I didn't know about the devils-on-horseback for Bryan, and certainly not that the maid had eaten them by mistake. But I did wonder about those chocolates. When it was realized that someone had to have given Clara the opium I did strongly suspect, because I had noticed Aunt go missing when we were all in the church. She must have followed Clara out and been the one who took her bag. Only, when Kate was dead, it seemed to fit that perhaps Kate had done it after all. She stole Kate's diary, too. But I'm afraid when I saw it I was too overcome by nosiness and the thought that I might be able to sell a story or two from it.' He looked shamefaced and Louisa didn't have the heart to remonstrate with him over this; his own guilt and the knowledge of who his aunt really was, was punishment enough.

'Do you think she made you sick?'

'There could be no explanation for it other than she was slowly poisoning me.'

'She told me she saw a letter from the police. It must have been the one dropping the charges.'

'Yes, she steamed it open and read it before she gave it to me. I thought I'd kept it from her but I was a fool to think that. She wanted to control every element of my life. It had always been like that but it got worse in recent months. But you see, I couldn't think what I'd do without her and, I know it will sound ridiculous to you, no one else had ever cared for me. Aunt, in her twisted way, seemed to mind what happened to me.'

Louisa took Luke's hand in hers. 'Anyone would find that hard, you mustn't blame yourself.'

'Only I was completely wrong about her, wasn't I?'

'But not about us,' said Louisa. 'Nor Guy, or Mary. We all came, as quickly as we could.'

Luke smiled at that. 'So do you think there's a chance for me?'

'Everyone deserves a chance,' said Louisa. 'Even us.'

A few hours later, Guy came to the hospital with a brown paper bag of grapes, an exotic delight. He looked exhausted but it was tinged with exhilaration at the work he had done that day. 'She confessed everything,' he said. 'It was a moral crusade. She believed Bryan Guinness was caught up in evil practice against God's works because the family money was made from alcohol.'

'And he was in the way of Luke, who might otherwise marry Diana,' interjected Louisa.

'I think Luke had the lucky escape there,' said Guy. 'She said she had been sorry about the maid's death, though she hadn't known it was because they'd eaten the devils-on-horseback. The chocolates had been intended for Bryan and Diana, but when Shaun was killed instead she had reasoned that God had changed the target and that He had his reasons. Discovering that Shaun had committed adultery had only confirmed that belief.'

Louisa could only shake her head in wonder.

'Clara she saw as helping her move more swiftly to an end that was already coming, and that she deserved to go straight to hell as a drug addict. She had seen her leave the church and take the opium. Back at the hotel, she intercepted the maid who was taking Clara the tea you'd asked for, and put the opium in it.'

'Which must have been why the maid didn't want to talk to the police,' interrupted Louisa. 'What about Kate Mulloney?'

'Lady Boyd knew that the police were investigating Clara's death, so she had to throw them off the scent. She was especially concerned when Luke was called in that he would be arrested. She poisoned Kate first, then used Kate's own gun to make it look like suicide. She was the "R" in Kate's appointment book. They had met for luncheon that day, and then arranged that Lady Boyd would go to her house later. It had been easy for Lady Boyd to contact Mrs Mulloney and offer her Christian help and sympathy, given that they had briefly met in Venice. That was also where Lady Boyd stole the diary, after Mrs Mulloney left it on a desk where she had been writing letters. That connection between Clara and Shaun made her an easy victim.'

'And then Luke,' said Louisa. 'She was poisoning him, too. Bit by bit, but still.'

'That seems to have been the hardest one for her, which perhaps explains why she didn't give him one fatal dose. I think even in her own deranged way, she did love him but she loves God more. She tried to see it as the ultimate sacrifice, like Abraham and his son.'

'What will happen to her, do you think?'

'Hard to say but I think she'll be committed to Broadmoor. It's unlikely she'll ever see the outside world again.'

Louisa was quiet at this. 'We must help Luke to get on his feet.'

'I'm sure he'll be fine. He has a future ahead of him now. His aunt was never going to give him that. He can live as he truly is, with no fear.'

'Yes, that's true.'

Guy looked at Louisa then, and she felt a pleasant sensation in the lower part of her stomach that was quite separate from any of the earlier pain.

'Perhaps we, too, have a future ahead of us now?' he said gently.

'Yes,' said Louisa, turning her face towards his. 'We do.'

CHAPTER SIXTY-SIX

❦

After Louisa had been discharged from hospital, she returned to work, with the agreement that she would attend to Diana when she was in London but would no longer travel down to Biddesden. The excuse given was Louisa's need to recover but the truth was they both knew that Louisa would not work for her for much longer. This seemed a gentler way to end things while Louisa tried to work out what she would do next. (And there was an increasing realisation that Diana was also thinking about what *she* would do next.) Louisa still wanted to work, and Guy supported this, the difficulty being that while she did not want to be a servant or shop girl, she had no school qualifications to speak of. As it was, jobs of any kind were hard to come by but it looked as if the worst of the depression in America and its consequent effects in Europe, might be coming to an end; there was hope that opportunities would improve soon. In this respect, of course, they were wrong.

Louisa, still basking in her romance with Guy, was increasingly disturbed by Diana's involvement with Mosley. She had come to recognize the daily letter that arrived from him, eagerly opened by Diana when she received her breakfast tray and which was replied to by the second post. Newspapers were scoured daily front to back – 'I must understand *everything* that is going on' – and Louisa overheard Diana tell several friends that the Leader was a prime minister-in-waiting: 'They all say it in the House.' Bryan, who preferred to discuss the novel he was reading or a play he had seen the night before, was sidelined by his wife's political discussions on how the National Government was failing the country. They both shared a love of their children but if Diana was at home, her mind was constantly restless unless she knew when she would next see Mosley. It did not make for a very relaxing atmosphere for anyone. Yet, Diana's social whirlwind did not ease up – she became more ravishingly beautiful by the day, it seemed, and had been painted by several leading portrait artists. She was even rather unexpectedly asked to play the part of Perdita in a production of *The Winter's Tale* but turned it down.

In this feverish state of romantic angst and social dervish, it was predictable that Diana should decide that she and Bryan would hold a huge party at Cheyne Walk for her twenty-second birthday in June. Louisa's instinct for the disruption that felt imminent was heightened when she saw that Mosley and his wife were on the three-hundred-strong guest list. Louisa was not invited to the party but Diana had asked if she might attend in the capacity of chaperone to Decca, now fourteen years old. 'Strictly speaking she can't officially be there but it would be such a shame for her to miss out,' said Diana. 'I thought perhaps if you were with her, you could take her off to bed at a reasonable hour and then she will be perfectly happy, and so will Muv.'

Louisa agreed, and so on the night she was there as the sisters and Tom gathered at the start of the party to wish Diana a happy birthday before the evening officially began. Lined up together they were an exceptional collection of beauty and personality. Nancy with her dark hair and green eyes, confident now with her growing reputation as a witty writer, if troubled that Hamish and she had still yet to marry; Pamela, with healthy colour in her cheeks and happy with her farm life; Unity, now in her own debutante season, with large hooded eyes and red lips; Tom, tall and attractive; Decca, who looked most like Nancy with high forehead and short chin, but a kinder, more inquisitive soul. And the birthday girl herself, who drew gasps of delight from even her own siblings.

'I'm wearing as many diamonds as I could get my hands on,' she had teased, dressed in pale grey chiffon and tulle that fell to the floor as softly as whipped egg whites.

'It's not just that,' said Nancy suspiciously. 'You look as if you've eaten lightbulbs. You're radiating happiness. It's positively sick-making. What's going on?'

Diana had waved this off. 'Absolutely nothing. I'm happy to see you all here. We're going to have a wonderful night.'

Decca, feeling shy, had sat with Louisa in the long garden, scented by the full bloom of the roses and with a Russian orchestra playing outside for those who preferred to dance in the open air, rather than the panelled drawing room inside. They watched as the waves of beautiful people arrived, each one more expensively, divinely dressed than the one before – Louisa knew some of them and Decca pointed others out: Winston Churchill, Augustus John, Robert Byron, Evelyn Waugh. The maids were dressed in green and white flowered dresses instead of a uniform, and there seemed to be enough champagne to fill the Thames over again. It was an intoxicating sensation, teasing all her senses, but it felt somehow unreal. As if it were a perfect painting of how life should be but could not be, a screen that hid the grotesque figures and darkening skies behind.

At eleven o'clock, Louisa took Decca inside and saw she went to bed. They could still hear the strains of music coming through the upstairs window. Decca was not in the least bit tired and asked a thousand questions about who the people were and what did they do, and why were there poor people in the world and could they not share some of the food that was left uneaten at the end of the party, none of which Louisa felt she could answer. They were both unsettled by it all, so when Decca asked Louisa if she could find Unity, just to come up and say good night to her, she agreed.

Through the house Louisa wandered, trying to find Unity but there was no sign of her. She saw Nancy, attempting to pull Hamish into the dancing, him resisting but not crossly. Tom was endlessly, smoothly moving in circles with various beauties in blue feathered boas and silver lamé dresses. Pamela was sitting on a bench talking intently to a man who looked swarthy and serious. The air inside was heavy with cigarette smoke, cigar smoke and scent; Louisa went into the garden, to look for Unity there but saw Luke instead. He had recovered from the poisoning – confirmed to have been arsenic – and looked his handsome, curly-haired self again.

'Hello, you,' he said. He had been holding court in a group of three or four people but broke away to greet his friend.

Louisa smiled at him. 'I'm trying to find Unity. Decca wants her to go and say good night.'

Luke grimaced. 'I saw her, talking to Diana and that awful man. I thought Diana admired him the most but Unity knocks her into a cocked hat. She was practically gaping.'

'You can never resist a gossipy remark, can you?' But she was only gently teasing. Luke had recently been appointed London correspondent for a newspaper in Berlin. 'Where were they?'

'At the bottom of the garden, I think. Hiding in the trees.'

Louisa padded softly on the grass, in between the people talking and drinking. No one noticed her. There was no sign of Unity, so she kept on until she had almost reached the tree that marked the end and there was no further to go. Underneath it stood two figures, close together. Without meaning to and yet without stopping herself, Louisa slipped behind a rose bush in the dark, and listened to what they were saying. She knew no good ever came of eavesdropping but she felt as if so much hung in the balance of what was said on this evening with its charged atmosphere that she could not afford to miss it.

Diana and the Leader were declaring their love for each other.

'Darling, you know I shall leave Bryan. I can no longer be married to him, not now I feel this way and you do, too.'

Mosley kissed her. 'I think you should. So long as you understand that I cannot ever leave Cimmie.'

'I do understand,' Diana said softly. 'But somehow, the idea of being quite alone for the rest of my life does not frighten me. Not if I know you love me. I will put you first in everything I do.'

'Everything, my darling?'

Diana nodded and Louisa turned away, unable to bear it any longer. She walked up the garden, through the house and out of the front gate, on to the street where men and women impatiently pushed past to wherever they were headed. In amongst all those thousands in London, Louisa only needed one person. She was going to find him and this time she wasn't going to let go.

HISTORICAL NOTE

❧

This novel is based on a number of real people and events but it should be noted that the murder plots and all conversations – bar a few lines when Bryan proposes to Diana and when Diana and Tom talk in Venice about the Nazis (with the kind permission of Anne de Courcy) – are entirely imagined by me, the author.

The death of Dorothy Martin at the Guinness dance at 10 Grosvenor Place in June 1928 was a real, tragic event. Dorothy and her friend Elizabeth Tipping were housemaids, sent to bed at midnight by the housekeeper. On the servants' landing, they had tried to view the party by going on to the glass skylight, which broke. Dorothy fell thirty feet and died almost instantly, Elizabeth was badly injured. The inquest recorded an accidental death.

Dora Carrington was an artist who was known to be in love with the writer Lytton Strachey; she was married to Ralph Partridge, who had also had an affair with Lytton. The three of them lived at Ham Spray House, close to Biddesden. After

Lytton's death, Dora asked Bryan for the loan of a gun to shoot the rabbits but instead turned the gun on herself. He was much distressed at what he felt had been his own hand in the incident. It had also happened that Diana had been very sick the first weekend she went to stay at Ham Spray House, and rumours had begun that Dora had poisoned her food out of jealous spite (Lytton liked Diana very much) but Diana never agreed that this had been the case.

Evelyn Waugh, initially a good friend of Nancy's, had become very close to Diana in the wake of his divorce. He dedicated his novel *Vile Bodies* to her and Bryan. Sadly, after her son Jonathan was born, she and Evelyn seemed to fall out and were never friends again in quite the same way.

The incident of Luke's arrest was based on events surrounding PC Reginald Handford, a plain-clothes policeman suspected of manipulative practices in arresting homosexuals in public urinals in 1927. After a court trial, he was ultimately found not at fault but there was 'tacit condemnation' of police operations in urinals and the agent provocateur method. Before the trial, Handford made fifteen arrests in eighteen months; in the following five months he made none, claiming that he was concentrating his efforts on suspected persons and pickpockets instead (from *Queer London*).

The story of Rose Morgan planning to run away with the little girl Muriel was based on Rose O'Grady and eleven-year-old Muriel Dunsmuir, who went missing in 1929 from Lytton Hall in Putney. Muriel's father had died three weeks previously and she and the maid planned to run away to start a dance act. Muriel's aunt had been married to the *couturier* Molyneux, though the two were found after three days in Ireland.

The character of Lady Boyd emerged from an understanding of the divide between the generations in the aftermath of the First World War. Those who had been brought up in the Victorian and Edwardian eras were bewildered if not angry at what they saw as the fast-paced, loose morals of the men and women who embraced the changes that the 1920s brought. The clashes – whether expressed theoretically or violently – between the class, gender and political divides were not easily resolved against a background of increasing global economic pressure. Quick developments in technology, culture and fashion all had an impact on each other as well as on politics, which became increasingly extreme at each end of the spectrum. We all know how that ended . . .

In June 1932, Diana and Mosley declared their love for each other at Diana's birthday party, though Mosley told her he would never leave his wife. In October 1932, Mosley launched the British Union of Fascists, with himself as leader. The following month, Diana told Bryan she would be leaving him, and in January 1933 she moved into a flat with her boys. Mosley remained married to his wife Cimmie until she died in May 1933, shortly before Diana's divorce came through. Mosley and Diana married in Goering's drawing room with Hitler present, in October 1936.

BIBLIOGRAPHY

I read a lot of books in the course of researching this novel but am especially grateful to:

Diana Mosley, Anne de Courcy (Vintage, 2004)

Queer London, Matt Houlbrook (University of Chicago Press, 2005)

To Hell and Back: Europe, 1914–1949, Ian Kershaw (Penguin, 2015)

Hons and Rebels, Jessica Mitford (Phoenix, 2007)

A Life of Contrasts, Diana Mosley (Gibson Square Books, 2002)

The Mitfords: Letters Between the Six Sisters, edited by Charlotte Mosley (Fourth Estate, 2007)

We Danced All Night: A Social History of Britain Between the Wars, Martin Pugh (The Bodley Head, 2008)

Lady Killers: Deadly Women Throughout History, Tori Telfer (John Blake, 2017)

Life in a Cold Climate: Nancy Mitford, the Biography, Laura Thompson (Review, 2003)

ACKNOWLEDGEMENTS

My deepest gratitude to Anne de Courcy and her biography *Diana Mosley*, which was written only after she had conducted long interviews with Lady Mosley and been given unprecedented access to her diaries. There are details and a sense of Diana's personality from de Courcy's book that she has very generously allowed me to use here. For those who are interested in reading further on Lady Mosley, I wholeheartedly recommend this biography.

I cannot write these books without the expertise and generous advice of Sue Collins, Celestria Noel and David Strang. All mistakes that remain are, of course, entirely my own. I am also very grateful to Mindy Stubbs and Lucie Dutton for personal insights into the life of Diana.

As ever, I am always, daily, grateful for the warm support of the brilliant Sphere team at Little, Brown. Thank you, Ed Wood for your guidance and inspiration. To Steph Melrose, Gemma Shelley and Laura Vile for getting this series noticed, to Andy Hine and Kate Hibbert for their amazing work selling the series all around the world. And to Catherine Burke and Charlie King for steering the huge ship that sees our books reach land – and readers – safely through the publishing storms!

A huge, Flat Iron-sized thank you to Catherine Richardson and the wonderful Minotaur team at St Martin's Press, as well as Hope Dellon, whose influence never leaves me, and Sally Richards for all her warm encouragement across the pond.

Thank you to my glorious agent, Caroline Michel of PFD, and her tireless assistant Laurie Robertson.

Finally, for my family. I do it for you but I couldn't do it without you and your loving support, your creativity and, most of all, your terrific sense of the absurd. Thank you, my darling Simon, Beatrix, Louis, George and Zola.

Help us make the next generation of readers

We – both author and publisher – hope you enjoyed this book. We believe that you can become a reader at any time in your life, but we'd love your help to give the next generation a head start.

Did you know that 9% of children don't have a book of their own in their home, rising to 12% in disadvantaged families*? We'd like to try to change that by asking you to consider the role you could play in helping to build readers of the future.

We'd love you to think of sharing, borrowing, reading, buying or talking about a book with a child in your life and spreading the love of reading. We want to make sure the next generation continue to have access to books, wherever they come from.

And if you would like to consider donating to charities that help fund literacy projects, find out more at www.literacytrust.org.uk and www.booktrust.org.uk.

Thank you.

hachette
CHILDREN'S GROUP

little, brown
BOOK GROUP

*As reported by the National Literacy Trust

Publishing in September 2020

The Mitford Trial

A timeless whodunnit with the fascinating Mitford sisters at its heart, *The Mitford Trial* is inspired by a real-life murder in a story full of intrigue, affairs and betrayal.

It's lady's maid Louisa Cannon's wedding day, but the fantasy is shattered shortly after when she is approached by a secretive man asking her to spy on Diana Mitford – who is having an affair with the infamous Oswald Mosley – and her similarly fascist sister Unity.

Thus as summer 1933 dawns, Louisa finds herself accompanying the Mitfords on a glitzy cruise, full of the starriest members of Society. But the waters run red when a man is found attacked, with suspects everywhere.

Back in London, the case is taken by lawyer Tom Mitford, and Louisa finds herself caught between worlds: of a love lost to blood, a family divided, and a country caught in conflict.

Praise for The Mitford Murders

'Keeps the reader guessing to the very end' *Evening Standard*

'A lively, well-written, entertaining whodunit' *The Times*